Messiah

Messiah

a novel

TONI SORENSON

Covenant Communications, Inc.

Published by Covenant Communications, Inc.
American Fork, Utah

Printed in the United States of America
First Printing: April 2011

17 16 15 14 13 12 11   10 9 8 7 6 5 4 3 2 1

ISBN-13: 978-1-60861-216-1

For Dave and Mary Ward
Para un millon de razones

There is no way I can adequately thank Margaret McConkie Pope, the teacher who instilled in me a love for the scriptures and taught me that the most important message of the Book of Mormon is simply that *Jesus is the Christ!*

Charlene Price sustained us through her love and service; without her, this book would not exist. Thanks so much to JJ for always being there. Sylvia, Sherry, and Krissy took me to the lands where this story really took place. Lisa, I could not have finished without your support. Always, thanks to the committee for faith and inspiration, pointedly to Kathy and Robby who never relented; and thanks to the evaluators who gave me guidance for rewrites, especially Barry. I am deeply grateful to the thousands of readers who realized *Master* is so much more than a fictionalized account of our Savior's life. I hope that same spirit permeates the pages of *Messiah.*

Thanks to my children, who put up with more than a year of hearing me say, "Okay, as soon as I finish the book." They are my world. To my littlest guy, Elder Gomez: "You inspired this story."

I am well aware of the DNA arguments surrounding the setting of the Book of Mormon. I have traveled them in my research. I chose to set this story in a certain location because that is where I felt most inspired. What matters to me is not so much *where* the people of the Book of Mormon lived, but that they *did* indeed live. I testify that they did. The Book of Mormon is a true account. My hope is that *this* story will motivate you to find greater meaning in the pages of *that* book.

Most people say I don't exist.

I hear them suppose that I'm merely a rumor, a symbol, an idea, but that I was never born of flesh and blood. I smile and sometimes I weep as I mingle among the touting unbelievers, and even among those filled with flailing faith. I hear what they say. I see how they live. I minister among them and they know it not.

No matter. I have a story to tell. To this cause I have given my life. My story is not worth telling because *I* amount to anything but because the *message* I bear is paramount.

Believe my tale or not, it asserts from the pages of holy writ. Learn from past mistakes, or find yourselves left to yourselves.

History is drawing to its conclusion. Pride has built a final faulty throne for the masses. Sin soils until it suffocates. My message now is the same message I've cried my entire mission. It lifts. It cleanses. It lights all that is dark. It will bring you peace in turbulence; it will bend your knees in gratitude.

It saves. It liberates.

One word.

A single word begins and ends my story.

That word?

Messiah!

—Kiah

One

The wild cat looks at me with vexed yellow eyes. A fat tongue, the pink of a morning sunrise, flicks out to wet her pointed whiskers. For a second my empty stomach tightens; sweat trickles down my forehead and stings my eyes. Her belly might be as vacant and deprived as mine. I battle my fears and climb higher, toward where she is crouched on the edge like a black shadow. For a terrifying moment it's impossible to tell which of us is doing the stalking. Then her long, sleek tail flips in one perfect curve and she vanishes.

My name is Kiah, and on the morning this story begins, my greatest desire is to prove that I am a worthy warrior. I want my mother to see me as a son she can depend on, who will one day ease the burdens of her difficult life. I want my grandfather to know that his stories and faith live in my heart. I want my only brother to recognize me as his equal. And I want my God to know me as His own.

I tell my pounding heart to calm. I tell my worried mind to trust my instincts. I am on the threshold of my fourteenth year, a time our people deem that childhood is left behind for the braveries of manhood. I should be a son of the commandment by now, but my mind fails me when I try to read or memorize from the holy books. I'm better at reading the tracks of wild animals, shooting an arrow straight, or skinning a *keeh* than I am at writing letters or reciting scriptures, especially in front of a congregation.

Those in my village call me a loner. I suppose their judgment is not far from accurate.

It's hard to catch my breath as I scale upward, over rocks and through jungle. All my life the hills above our village have been dense with growth, green and lush, alive. But now that we are forced into a famine, what *looks* green does not *feel* green. I put my hand on a bed of moss and feel it crunch beneath the palm of my hand. The leaves on the branches look green, but they are brittle and crumble like dust between my fingers.

I've spent my life hunting these rises, yet the trail I'm on now is unfamiliar, and an uneasiness lodges in my mind that won't go away. I force myself forward, winding through the thick of the tangle, leading to the steepest side of the mountain where the rocks are black and sharp as a blade's edge. My sandaled feet slip from time to time, sending rocks and dirt cascading below me. A single error on my part and I will be the one tumbling downward.

It dawns on me that after days of trailing this beast, she has led me to a place so out of the way that if I did plummet, no one would be able to rescue me . . . or recover my body. Not even my only brother, Calev, who is older and already one of our village's most noble warriors. No. If I die today, my body will be left to wild beasts, and my mother will be left with yet another sorrow to bear on her thin, already burdened shoulders.

Where did the cat go? She's a female—smaller and more wiry, much more unpredictable than a male. Doesn't she sense that I have no intention of killing her? I only want to track her, observe her, learn from her. I want her for my teacher because a cat like her is a warrior that can teach me much. We are both solitary hunters. We are both strong, yet patient. We do not hunt for pleasure, but that does not mean we don't enjoy our hunts. We do not kill unless there is a reason to kill.

A branch breaks somewhere above me, and I stop to listen. The sound leads me to veer to the south, where the rocks are not so unstable and there are more trees and vines. The cat suddenly screeches as if bidding me to follow. I do, and the tangle thickens. In places I am forced to use my blade to cut a path. I tell myself that I am fearless, even though my blood stops in my veins when I put my hand out to grab a vine and my skin brushes the rippling body of a snake.

I fear little, but of snakes I am terrified.

I do my best to keep my hand from trembling; I don't want to give the snake reason to strike. There are many ways to die here, and I would prefer to plummet to the bottom of the gorge rather than die from the fangs of a serpent.

It is what my grandfather calls a *divided* snake—its body is divided into exact rings of black and red, with a narrower band of white dividing each. Grandfather says it is cursed because it is divided in its thinking . . . something I *cannot* be. As a warrior, I cannot be brave one day and a coward the next. If I am to be a warrior for our coming Messiah, He says I must be all or nothing.

My grandfather is a wise man, a priest, and though his body is now weak, he still possesses the spirit of a warrior. He is brave like a hunter and faithful like a believer. I have never seen him divided in his commitment. I want to be like him when I am a completely grown man.

I cannot allow the snake to sense my fear. Fear has an odor to it, Grandfather says—an odor that tells a predator when prey is weak and vulnerable. I wonder . . . can the snake smell the tiny beads of sweat that have gathered on the back of my hand?

I remain completely still until the snake flicks its forked tongue and slithers away. I look up through a dappled canopy of vines and branches; another snake could fall down on me from any one of them. One misstep and a serpent could strike my bare leg. Despite that threat, I move on, rehearsing traditions that give me courage.

Not only do I picture my grandfather lifting his sword, I imagine Father Moses' staff as it becomes a writhing serpent, a display of God's power. I see Father Nephi journeying through the deadliest parts of the wilderness, fleeing from his angry brothers; surely his band of believers encountered ringed snakes and screeching cats. I think of King David and Father Abraham and the prophet Elijah. I think of Enos and how his prayers were answered in the deepest parts of the forest where only God could hear his pleas.

Since I was young, stories of these men—these warriors—have stoked my imagination and my ambition. Now thoughts of such men fuel my courage. I lift my blade against the choking vines and become victorious like Captain Moroni.

The inner leaves on the barge tree glisten with dew, and I realize it is still early morning, though my aching legs convince me the day is well worn. I lick the dew from as many leaves as I can reach. It's not enough moisture to cure my thirst, but my parched tongue is still grateful. I gaze at the rise of the tree. Barges are carved from thick-trunked trees like this one—barges used to travel the waters of the lower lands. I am not completely familiar with those territories; my village is nestled in the higher lands. Yet from this vantage point I can see a far-distant shimmer of water. In this time of famine, even the shorelines appear to be relenting.

Perhaps I can venture all the way to the water's edge and find a better way to help sustain my mother and my grandfather. I imagine my brother returning from his military training, his dark eyes shining with pride at what I've managed. There will be wealth sufficient for him to pursue Eliana, the girl who has stolen his heart. He will not stand before her wealthy father as poverty's child but as a man with ample means to support a wife accustomed to a roof that does not leak rain and clothes so fine and colorful they compete with the most brilliant birds and flowers: red, yellow, indigo.

Calev, being the elder son in our small family, is privileged to have official military training. He has been gone with our village commander for a long time now, but before he departed I saw the looks he exchanged with Eliana. Their feelings were clear and mutual. My brother may not be wealthy, but he is strong and able. He would make a worthy husband to Eliana.

When he returns it will be his responsibility to train me, his younger brother, in warfare. I wonder what new skills he will teach me. I hope Calev will be surprised by how much independence has taught me. I will bring him here, to this unfamiliar place, and he will shake his head, astonished by my warrior skills. Mother says that ever since I was able to crawl, every stick I held became a sword, every rock I hoisted became a weapon. I have been a warrior, she says, from birth.

Not Calev. He prefers to craft weapons rather than use them. He is never completely pleased with the design of a sword or the strength of a shield; he's always attempting a different model, crafted from a harder wood or thicker bark. His skills are recognized but not appreciated. But because he is four years older than I am, he had no choice: he had to become a warrior.

The cat screeches again, and the hairs on my arms rise; a small stream of sweat drips down my face and stings my eyes. Today I will prove that I am the true warrior of the family. I will obtain food. Wherever there is a cat, there is prey for that cat. Maybe the Lord will bless me with a *keeh*, perhaps two, that I can carry triumphantly across my shoulders. Our entire village will feast. Honor will be brought to my family.

Eliana's father, Hem, is not the village chief, but there is no man more important to our village; he is a merchant of means, the man who directs our main marketplace. When he sees that I have brought meat for the hungry mouths of Elam, he will say, "Are you not the younger brother of Calev, the boy who favors my daughter?"

My face reddens at the fantasy, at the pride I imagine as I pave the path for my brother to pursue the girl he loves. Hem has no respect for Calev . . . yet. One day he will. For now, Hem cannot see beyond our family's poverty and shame—but soon he, along with everyone else, will see the truth: Calev is a gifted craftsman, I am a warrior, Mother is an angel, and Grandfather is a man of God, as sure as the prophet Nephi is a man of God.

Nephi is kin to our family. He and his brother Lehi are named after our ancient forefathers Lehi and Nephi, the first prophets to inhabit this land nearly six hundred years ago. I can't help wondering what things were like then, before the land was dotted with inhabitants; before mounds were formed, like giant ant beds; before the great pyramidal temples were constructed, one sunbaked brick laid upon another; before the trees were felled and the air made sooty from so many cooking fires. What would those early inhabitants think of the promised land now?

Brittle leaves crunch beneath my weight as the sun climbs the sky and I climb the mountainside. Everywhere I look I see the ravages of famine. The ground, once moist and green, is now parched—parched by the lips of our prophet, Nephi, who prayed that famine, not war, would humble us and bring us to repentance. It seems we are always being called to repent.

Grandfather knows the ways of goodness and truth and tries to teach them to me. My mother also knows these ways and also tries to teach me. I *want* to be good. I want to believe all that they believe. A part of me is ashamed because my faith is not as strong as it should be. I keep that fact hidden in my heart. I try to memorize the scriptures, I observe the many commandments, but I have never heard a voice from heaven like Enos . . . have never witnessed a miracle like Grandfather, who was with the prophet Nephi and his prophet-brother Lehi in the Lamanite prison when mighty miracles occurred. Perhaps I will never be known for my faith, but I will be known for my courage.

I come across a small indentation where the cat has stepped, leaving a clear paw print. It's very large, and I sniff the air for urine just to be absolutely sure that I am not tracking a male cat. Males mark their territory to defy other males from entering. But there is no hint of urine and I scramble upward, wondering at the possibility that I might be tracking a *pair* of mountain cats. That would not be good for me. But then I catch sight of her again. She is solo, arching her back on the brim of a porous rock above me. She's small, and the obscured rosettes in her black coat glint in the sun, shining like jewels. She looks right at me and then flares away, taunting me to chase her.

When I can't go on without stopping to catch my breath, I look up and see a city of caves carved into the black rock high above. I mark the spot in my mind, for it is where I can obtain the prized shiny black stone that makes the sharpest blades. But if the cat has gone there I know my chances of spying her again are small, for she is the same color as the precious rock. I look around and see no sign of other beasts. No *keeh* trails. No droppings. Only a few birds fluttering among the rustling branches. I ease myself down and my head lulls back against a round stone; my eyes barely close when I hear a branch snap. Every muscle in my body stiffens.

The cat has to be near. Very near. If it lurks above me it can pounce.

My eyes scanning the ridge above, I leap to my feet and thunder through the brush, hoping to frighten the cat—but as I approach a small clearing below, a new kind of fear surges through me.

What I see is far deadlier than a wild beast. A clutch of men break through the opposite side of the clearing—a band of men united in purpose, cloaked in secrecy, dedicated to destruction.

I see a band my people call *Gadianton*.

Two

Murderers.

I hit the ground knowing that if they find me—a boy they'll assume to be a Nephite spy—my fate will be bleaker than it would be at the claws of the hungry cat. These men are masters of torture and evil. I try to not stir at all, to not even breathe. *Lord, protect me,* I silently pray, a prayer that ascends with as much sincerity as my young, terrified soul can gather.

At first I'm sure they've heard me, but the men laugh carelessly and I ease forward so I can get a clearer view. I expect them to be dressed like savages because the deeds they do are savage—but they're not cloaked in loincloths, their faces are not stained with fresh blood. They look as ordinary as any of the men walking through Elam; they might have been farmers, artisans, merchants, or soldiers. Some carry themselves with the same ramrod pride as most judges. Their skin is the same shade as mine. They greet each other like brothers, laughing, joking, and talking about their families—their *families!*—and their spoils, how they have plundered a village on the far side of the mountain.

I wait, my stomach souring at one man's horrific account of what he did when he came upon an innocent maiden. I listen, trying to keep my mind focused so that I can take back any bit of information that might help keep our small village from being their next target. I know I will have to be accurate in retelling this account to my grandfather, who believes that the Gadianton robbers will be the downfall of our entire Nephite people.

"They are the sons of Satan," he has told me. "It is his devilish design they follow."

He has taught me that there is a distinction between a *robber* and a *thief.* A thief steals from within a family or a village. A robber attacks a family or a village that is not his own.

I know the story of the robbers, and I try to remember it now. Grandfather was only a boy himself when a man named Paanchi wanted the people to elect him chief judge. But his brother Pahoran was elected to the judgment seat instead, and Paanchi was executed for treason. In retaliation, Kishkumen—one of Paanchi's supporters—assassinated Pahoran. At that very moment Satan united Kishkumen and his associates into a secret pact to protect each other's identities.

Now I'm looking from my hiding place at the results of that pact. Gadianton became the leader of Kishkumen's group and promised that if he became chief judge he would appoint his fellow robbers to positions of authority. When Kishkumen killed the new chief judge, Gadianton took his followers and fled into the mountains.

Father, I pray, *protect Elam, protect my family, spare my life.*

One of the men coughs and spits off the edge of a rock, then looks up abruptly; for a second I think he's spotted me. But he spits again, then turns and joins his friends. I see for myself that Grandfather is right: they are men who delight in the vilest acts of mankind. I hear them speak out against Nephi for the famine. I hear them threaten Nephi's life, and I can't wait to report to Grandfather so he can get word to the prophet and his family. My best friend—really my *only* friend—is the prophet's grandson Jonas. Though they live on the outskirts of Zarahemla, more than a day's journey from our village, my fondest memories are of playing with Jonas, laughing, pretending to be warriors. I wonder what he would think if he could see me now.

The robbers hate Nephi because he is bold in speaking against them, in rallying our people to seek them out and destroy them. Nephi prophesies that if the robbers do not repent, they will pay—we will *all* pay. I will pay with my life if they discover me.

The sun sits high in the sky and beats down with a powerful fist; beads of perspiration dance on the backs of my hands, but a shiver shoots through my body as I look upon true evil. If it were possible, I would lunge at all of them, bring each one of them death with my blade. I count; there are twelve robbers, all of them grown men—all of them capable, I'm sure, of skill with the sword, cimeter, clubs, bows and arrows, and every manner of weapon known since the days of Father Adam. They are warriors—warriors for evil.

Listening to their boasting, I realize that no village is safe from their corruption. No son of God is safe from being harassed and even murdered for standing for truth. No daughter of God is protected in her virtue because their dark, murderous minds believe that to rob a girl of her virtue is an act of valor.

I shiver continuously and struggle to *not* shut my eyes against the scene. I silently pray again for strength and a spirit of calm. I turn my face carefully to the side and use my tongue to prod a fallen twig into my mouth; my teeth clamp down on it to keep my jaw from shaking. There is a scripture that Grandfather quotes . . . something about being still and trusting God. I wish I could remember it, and I beg forgiveness for neglecting my synagogue studies in favor of hunting and exploring.

As faith follows the words of my prayer, my stomach stops churning. My body stops quivering. My teeth stop chattering. I creep closer and realize that the men have taken to chanting a common code, a secret oath. It's not familiar to me, but they seem seasoned in their common words, in the act of sharing the same handshake. I hate the way they chant so routinely. I hate the way they laugh so raucously. I hate the way they boast of evil and their own courage.

I do not know what it is to take the life of a man, but I know that I would destroy them all if I could.

Clearly, one man stands out as their leader. His back is turned to me, but his hand is in the air, and in his grip is a blade that glints in the sunlight. Even from my somewhat distant vantage I see that it is a fancy blade with a jeweled handle. He slices it through the air as he talks. I see that he is a stout man with broad shoulders, draped in a cloak the same hue as the purple flowers that grow in the highlands. Obviously, he is a man of means and power.

I watch as two others unload the burdens from their backs, burdens of stolen goods: jewelry, pottery, and weapons. The amount of wealth makes me blink. This is why these men are called *robbers* and not *thieves*; they work in skilled bands, coming from the outside and robbing strangers. The punishment of thieves, who work alone and steal from their own neighbors, is exacted by the wronged village people. If this band is caught, their punishment will be military—they might even be executed. But if Grandfather is right, even the highest government seats are stained with blood and sin.

I know now with certainty that he is right: Gadianton robbers are evil to the centers of their hearts. If this is the wickedness we are allowing to penetrate our people, surely we will face total destruction.

My own heart leaps in my chest at the fantasy that I might be the warrior to somehow thwart them. But the men are large in stature, loud in boasting, and they clearly have no reservations about killing. I count again. Yes, twelve. Have I stumbled on the full quorum of their leadership?

My blood runs chill as water from a high mountain trickle, for in the full light of day, the leader turns his face toward me, beckoning his followers to bow to his supremacy.

I gulp. My eyes go wide.

There is no doubt. The man I am looking at is the very man whose respect I'd intended to earn. He is Hem. He is the father of the girl Calev loves.

Three

Grandfather releases a long breath. "Secrets are heavy things, Kiah. I suppose your heart is weighed down with the knowledge of what you've learned."

My hands and feet won't stay still. I'm so anxious I want nothing more than to shout to everyone what I've learned. I want Hem to pay for being such a traitor. Grandfather bids me to be silent, but I'm feeling as though ants are crawling over my body and taking refuge in my hair. "We have to do something. We have to tell."

"We have to be wise and judge with caution."

"No. We have to judge with haste! Hem has deceived all of Elam. Why won't you take me to the judges' chambers so I can report what I have learned?"

"It has been discussed and decided. Your word against that of a man like Hem's is nothing more than a lonely boy's fantasies."

Every muscle in my body tenses. "But all they've heard is *your* report. Perhaps if I told them myself, I can make the judges believe me."

"The judges are Hem's friends. One is his brother-in-law. They did not believe me, Kiah. They will not believe you."

I want to argue, but the hard stare Grandfather directs at me tells me not to challenge the matter further.

Grandfather leans on his walking stick as we begin to walk. He is not yet old—his hair still has the black shine of obsidian—but he is no longer the young warrior he once was, wielding a sword in defense of freedom, a skill he'd learned from noble men like Helaman. Though he walks with a limp from a wound inflicted during our latest battle with our Lamanite brethren, Grandfather is still my hero and my confidant. His sword, the one he used to defend our current prophet-brothers, Nephi and Lehi, is now in the hands of *my* brother. I hope it will protect Calev. And I hope he will believe me, his younger brother. Calev will think of me as valiant when he learns that I am the one who spotted the robbers. I am the one who survived the encounter without being caught.

Grandfather and I have just passed the bend behind Elam—the vantage point where the entire village is laid out. Small wood and stone houses are nestled in spots where the tangle has been cut back and small garden walls erected. Cooking fires are sparse now because there is little food to cook. There are footpaths where people walk, and there is a great highway outside the village that leads to the city. Our most visible landmark is our marketplace, constructed of the same gray and brown sunbaked bricks as the great temples in Zarahemla and Bountiful. My fists clench as I think how Hem rules everything and everyone inside those marketplace walls.

Grandfather and I walk side by side into the thicker part of the wilderness. I can see anyone approaching from both directions. I make a futile attempt to try to speak more slowly. "Grandfather, you believe me, don't you?"

"Of course, son."

"How could Hem betray his own people like this?"

"Deceit is nothing new."

"But it's new to me. He's a man respected by everyone—even *you* have trusted him."

"Yes, that's true. I took Hem to be a righteous brother. He has sat in many councils with me."

"I keep thinking of Eliana. He's deceiving *her*, Grandfather. Imagine how she will feel when she discovers her own father is a robber."

Grandfather's smile is quick and kind. He knows of Calev's feelings toward Eliana. All of Elam knows. Grandfather's grip on the cane tightens ,and he gets a watery, faraway look in his eyes. "I was not much older than you when your grandmother won my heart. And even though she is dead now, I have never been able to give my heart to another woman."

My memories of my grandmother are as wispy as the morning mist that blankets Elam, but I feel like I know her from the stories Grandfather tells and the way his voice cracks whenever he mentions her. "You loved her very much."

"I *still* love her."

I can tell Grandfather is in deep thought, and I try to keep quiet as we walk at his slow pace. My heart pounds in my chest at the memory of how close I came to being discovered by the Gadianton robbers. I laid still as stone all the time they were meeting; even after I was confident they were gone and I heard their final fading footfalls, I did not move. Only when red ants bit into my bare leg did I get up and, keeping a safe distance, follow the robbers' narrow trail that eventually led to the main highway. There, in the distance and the shadows of dusk, I saw the men separate. Some walked toward my village; others headed in the opposite direction, blending into the crowds of people as subtly as smoke.

Grandfather taps his cane, kicking up parched earth. "Keep walking, Kiah. Movement is what my body needs to restore itself." A tinge of guilt strikes me. The night Grandfather was injured I was away from home hunting with my friend Jonas. A small band of renegade Lamanites came to plunder our village. Grandfather and Calev protected our home and people, and news of their bravery tore through Elam and beyond. For days afterward I heard stories of their tandem courage. I wonder—if I had been there, could I have protected Grandfather from being wounded? He doesn't blame Calev. Instead, he talks of how my brother swung his blade as sure as Ammon at the Waters of Sebus.

We've come to a knot of tangled roots; some of them reach up from the ground like gnarled, desperate fingers, ready to trip an aged man. We've taken this journey a thousand times, maybe more. I usually recite the names of the trees and the flowers, and I can identify every bright-colored bird by only its call. But today my mind is elsewhere. "Who can we trust, Grandfather? If Hem is a traitor, who else betrays us?"

"That is a question only God can answer, child, for only He sees through our disguises and into our hearts."

I take Grandfather's elbow to steady him. When I was a baby toddling along this path, he had been absolutely sure of his step. When I stumbled he lifted me, wiped the blood from my scraped knees or elbows, put me straight again. Back then Calev walked with us, but that time has passed—and now *I* am the one steadying *Grandfather.*

"All the way down the mountain after seeing the robbers, I was asking who is trustworthy. How do we know who else is part of the secret band?"

"You recognized only Hem?"

"Only Hem."

"Then we have no proof of anyone else, no evidence. Judgment requires evidence. Without it, the matter is reduced to your truth against Hem's lies."

"I'm not absolutely sure I could find the place again, but if I could, I'd show you where they met. Let me explore and I'll bring back some of their stolen treasures for proof."

"No! You will *not* do that, son. Do you understand?"

"Why not?"

"Because if you have plunder in your hands, those robbers will claim *you* are the one who stole. Do you understand now how complicated this matter is?"

I think about what he is saying. "I'm beginning to."

Grandfather takes a deep breath and asks, "What do you think causes a person, a *good* person, to turn away from righteousness and toward sin?"

"The devil."

"It's good, son, that you recognize the reality of the devil, but it's more than just prodding from the devil. It's *pride* in our own hearts." The word comes out like it's bitter in his mouth. "Pride can lead an entire people away from God. This is a season when we've turned away from His commandments while our brethren, the Lamanites, are anxious to obey."

"No, Grandfather. Lamanites are still wicked. They're the ones whose clubs broke your leg and weakened your back."

"That's true—but only in part." Grandfather switches his walking stick to his other hand. "You know that I despise the distinction between Lamanites and Nephites. Pride caused our fathers that first division, and today pride continues to divide us. Pride is what has divided my own house, my family. Pride is what sent your father sneaking away on a moonless night and what has kept him away all of these years." He pauses, clasps his hand over my shoulder. I realize he wants to be sure that his words about my father—his son—have not caused me undue pain. The truth is, any mention of my father stabs at my heart. But I was an unsteady toddler when my father slunk away. I have not seen him since, though word of his doings does reach us from time to time. Now he lives with another wife, another set of children in a village on the far side of the last mountain ridge. I am grown enough to know that pride is not the *only* reason my father left us.

Grandfather dabs at his misty eyes and wipes his nose with the back of his hand. He always goes moist at the mention of the son he lost. It seems to me he is sadder about the loss than my own mother—a wife shamed and abandoned and left to care for and provide for not only Calev and me, but for her faltering father-in-law as well. The thought of my mother swells my heart.

"Kiah, mark my words: *pride* will prove the downfall of our people if we do not repent."

I can't hold back an unexpected smile. "Grandfather, you include yourself with the sinners. You're the most righteous man I know." Grandfather treasures commandments like they're precious gems. Not only did he stand with the prophet-brothers Nephi and Lehi he has stood alone many times to defend his faith and the honor of our tattered family.

We go silent and step aside as a group of women pass, carrying on their heads baskets of the day's harvest of fruit. Normally the fruit is succulent this season of the year, but their baskets are only partially filled with shriveled citrus.

Always devoted to showing women proper respect, Grandfather greets them and asks after their families. They return his greeting with smiles and shyness—all but Oshra, the one woman in the village who is never hesitant to step forward and speak. She asks grandfather boldly, "How is your leg?"

"It's healing fine. Thank you."

Oshra swivels her head toward me. It's a gourd-shaped head wound in tightly braided black hair. Her cheeks sink in as though she's always sucking on a sour lemon. As it always is when she addresses me, her tone is high and drawn out. "And your mother, Kiah—how is she?"

It's the same question Oshra asks every time we encounter each other. "My mother is well, thank you."

Oshra glances at the other women. "Anat's suffering is a strength to us all."

The others nod like soldiers in training.

I have no patience with this woman. She does not care about my mother; she only wants to *appear* to care. If she cared, she would invite my mother to join her and the other women as they go about their village chores. If Oshra *really* cared, she would not avoid my mother, expel her, or manage to unearth painful history whenever they happen upon each other.

Mother tries not to care, but she cares. Slump shouldered, with a broom in her grip, she hums while she tends to our little hut, never venturing further away than she absolutely has to. She sings me the songs of our ancestors. The way she describes Jerusalem in detail—it's as if she was born there. She teaches me of Fathers Abraham, Isaac, Jacob, and Lehi. Because of her, I love the teachings of Nephi, Mosiah, and Alma. My grandfather is a great warrior, but my mother is a warrior of a different kind.

Oshra smirks. "How is your schooling, Kiah? I hear you struggle with memorization."

My face goes hot. Grandfather puts his walking stick out and comes to my defense. "Kiah is an excellent student. I'm surprised you hear anything about his progress, but then your husband, Gomer, is privy to that information, isn't he?"

It's Oshra's turn to blush. Her husband is a slow-witted man who cannot read or write and makes his pittance by cleaning the synagogue school. Gomer would be dismissed if it were known that he gossips with his wife about what happens in the school.

She can't wait to make her leave, and I can't wait to change the subject from my lack of performance in school. It might be gossip, but Oshra is right; I have great difficulty memorizing.

When I'm sure Oshra and her friends are out of earshot, I ask, "If Hem stands as the leader of the robbers, who else has deceived us? I'm sure the money changers have; they're always suspicious. Maybe the coppersmith, maybe the weavers. Maybe everyone who works and sells in the marketplace belongs to the secret sect."

"Slow down, son." Grandfather runs a thumb beneath his headband. His forehead is slick with sweat. "Dividing good from evil is not always as easy as dividing the wheat from the tares. If we Nephites had been wiser, we would have hunted the band, converted them by the word of God—or the sword. Instead, we embraced them, partook of their spoils, and now we pay the price."

His words drive through me as sure as a nail.

"You're aging into a serious boy, Kiah. Soon you will be a man, so I expect you can bear the burdens of this knowledge."

I cherish the times he talks to me as one man to another. "So how are we going to bring Hem to justice?"

Grandfather doesn't answer, and the path before us narrows as we climb. The rocks are sharper and more difficult to navigate. The air grows thin, and he is forced to stop from time to time to fill his lungs. "We are not going to bring Hem to justice. We are going to wait on the Lord."

"But why?"

"The Messiah is the answer to all of your questions."

My eyes focus on a *chak*, a red-winged bird fluttering on a high branch. "Sometimes I don't understand all you want me to. I thought my information about the robbers would upset you, scare you. I imagined you'd throw your hands into the air, perhaps snap your walking stick in half. Instead, you act as calm as if I had informed you that Oshra is the village mouth."

His smile comes and goes. I tug at the cloak I'm wearing. It is woven from the soft plant that grows in the plain below our village. Other boys my age wear cloaks dyed from the red blossoms of the highlands. My cloak is the hue of dirt, ordinary and plain like me—but it is new, something my mother fashioned, and though she worked hard to make it fit, it is too tight in some places and too loose in others. I tug at it in frustration.

Grandfather forces a smile. "I will talk the matter over with the prophet."

"Good. You will tell him everything?"

He nods.

Nephi and Grandfather are of the same generation. They have fought side by side, have served and preached together. Nephi's wife and my dead grandmother were cousins, so the families have spent long hours together—sometimes in my grandfather's small, wilting garden, other times behind the tall wall of the prophet's garden—always talking of the coming Messiah.

Grandfather sighs. "Nephi has much on his mind. The very destruction of our people is his worry."

"Exactly! That's why he must be told."

"What makes you suppose that Nephi has not already discerned the truth about Hem? Nephi is a prophet."

I frown. "If he *does* know, then why hasn't he revealed it? Why hasn't he stopped Hem and his band of robbers?"

"You can be assured, child, that a true prophet always has his reasons."

"But—"

He holds a straight hand to my face. "This famine that our prophet has prayed for . . . these rainless clouds that hang overhead . . . do you know why they will not let down their moisture?"

"Why?"

His eyes narrow and he waits for me to answer my own question. "Pride."

I do not want to hear a sermon on pride. I do not want to hear that the coming of the Messiah will resolve all of our problems. I want to hear how we are going to oust Hem from power, how we are going to dismantle the band of robbers.

I tune back into Grandfather's sermon in time to hear him say, "Once again, pride has brought our people to the brink of destruction."

I shrug my shoulders, imagining that I could take the red-winged bird down if I had my slingshot. I tell Grandfather, "The rainy season is due shortly. Then the fruit will grow again, the corn will sprout up—and our bellies will be full."

Grandfather bows his head and begins a prayer, a prayer that begs God to bless our family, our village, and Hem and his robbers—that their hearts will be turned away from evil. I bow my head but do not close my eyes. What use is there in praying for Hem? If I had my small bow and a straight arrow, that red-winged bird would be falling feathers.

"Kiah, as sure as Nephi is a living prophet, no rain will fall until this people humble themselves and kneel in repentance."

I think of my own father and the pride that drove him from our family. I think of Hem and how he stood proud before his robbers while they divided their plunder. I think of my own life and how pride swells up inside of me—how I want Calev and everyone else to recognize me as a warrior.

I look into my grandfather's eyes and realize that if pride has to go before the rains can come, surely we will all shrivel and die first.

Four

Nature is determined. In spite of the fact that the rains do not come, tender green blades push up from the dry, hard ground. Our village pulses with hope. Even Mother sings with a new vigor while she sweeps and tidies our small garden and moves our two water vessels from one side of our hut to the other.

In spite of the fact that there is little to eat, my body grows. It used to take fifteen steps to make it from the east side of our wall to the west side. Now I make the journey in eleven. It takes only six steps for me to cross from one side of our hut to the other. And our garden wall, woven of dried vines, once loomed above my head but now reaches only to my shoulders. Maybe by the time Calev returns I will stand as tall as he does and he will look me straight in the eyes, seeing a man where there was once a boy.

One morning after a windstorm I gather the strewn branches and help Grandfather repair the broken hinge on our garden gate.

"I don't know why you're going to so much trouble," I say. "No one bothers to enter our yard."

He hands me a mallet, a tool carved by Calev, its head just right for pounding a nail in place. Grandfather frowns. "It's true we seldom have visitors. Are you lonely, Kiah? Why don't you invite boys from the synagogue to go hunting with you?"

I stare at him and want to shake my head. Elam has a population of more than two thousand people, most of them young, but I have never had friends who stop by or invite me to join them in their games or expeditions. The boys my age at synagogue are tolerant of me, but even flat-nosed Benjamin, who played with me when we were younger, now feigns excuses to avoid me.

Perhaps Grandfather does not realize what he is suggesting. He *does* realize what he is doing when he calls me and Mother to the shade of our only garden tree, where he leads us in a prayer of thanksgiving. *For what?* I nearly ask as our hungry bellies growl in anticipation of relief.

Relief does not come.

Neither does justice.

Hem goes about his market business unchanged, loud and demanding of every vendor. When he passes us he greets Grandfather with a shout and a fast embrace. He ignores me completely, and I wonder if he is aware of the charges I tried to have brought against him. If he is, he hides his awareness well, smiling and showing Grandfather enthusiastic respect.

"Yarden, you're still walking with a crutch? I expected a man of your faith to be able to heal himself." Hem laughs, spit shooting between the gap in his front teeth.

Grandfather doesn't flinch. "Only the Messiah has power to heal, Hem, but I am getting stronger every day. How is your family?"

Hem shakes his head and the fringes on his dress sway. His cloak is dyed green to match his headband. The leather sandals on his feet reach halfway up his leg, while Grandfather and I are both barefooted. "What's a man to do who lives in a household of girls?" He laughs so loud people turn their heads to stare. "It is the reason I spend so much of my time in the marketplace. What brings you here today?"

Grandfather holds out a bag of feathers that I have helped him gather from tree nests and the jungle floor. "I hope to trade these for a laying hen."

Hem scoffs. "Hens are not laying eggs, Yarden. Not in this famine. If you want that to change, you should counsel Nephi to alter his judgment against us." There's a sudden edge to his tone.

Grandfather taps his walking stick on the rock pathway so hard and so many times that Hem moves his sandaled feet backwards. The sound rises and ricochets around the stone wall of the marketplace. A gray-haired woman grinding corn cranks her head to look in our direction. I breathe in the aroma of wood smoke and grilling meat. Not everyone in Elam is without food.

Grandfather lifts his stick and aims it at Hem's chest. "The *prophet's* judgment is not against us. The Lord has seen the shadowy places of our hearts. He knows our secrets, Hem. Until we repent, I suppose only your fingers will be greasy."

I look down to see that Hem's fingers indeed shine with grease. He's probably been pulling meat from the bone of a goat. I look closer and see that the rim around his mouth shines from grease. The man's eyes narrow and focus on me.

He knows. *He knows.* In spite of my warrior stance, my bare feet scoot back and I brace myself for a confrontation. I will stand for truth. I will tell the judges and the people of Elam that the leader who directs the marketplace is a robber.

But it doesn't come to that. A group of men approach Hem and he looks away from me, dismissing us as if we were his servants. He greets the men with open arms and laughter, and I look, hoping that I will recognize them as robbers too. I don't.

"Why is Hem so arrogant?" I ask.

Grandfather shoots me a warning frown and waits until we have traded our feathers for a hen so lethargic that she doesn't even cluck as I tuck her beneath the crook of my arm.

We are back out on the main road before Grandfather answers my question. "Hem was once a boy much like you, Kiah. He was born to a mother who was a harlot in the neighboring village of Calno. I don't know that Hem ever knew his father."

My mouth hangs open in shock.

"He struggled as a boy. An uncle took pity on him and put him to work as a errand runner in the marketplace. It was there he met his wife, Sherrizah. Her father was the chief of the marketplace both here and in Calno."

My brain gets hinged on a thought like our garden gate in the wind, swinging back and forth: *Hem was once a humble boy who knew poverty and shame.* "How did such a boy end up marrying a woman whose father was so important?"

"I am not Oshra and will not spread gossip, but there was only *one* way Hem knew to assure his marriage."

The look on Grandfather's face puzzles me, but then I realize what he is not saying. I realize, too, how devious Hem can be when he sets his sights on something. I've made an enemy of the man. There is no telling how he will exact his revenge. I pray I—and not Grandfather or Mother—will be his target.

"Have you sent word to Nephi about Hem?"

"I have."

"And?"

"Kiah, it is time for you to move forward and put these thoughts of Hem behind you."

"How can I? You saw the way he glared at me. He knows that I tried to bring him before the judgment seat."

"Yes, he knows."

• • •

Hope rises. Hope fades. Starving fowls and wild animals chomp the grass to its roots; the sun bakes the stubble, and within days of budding hope we are

back living in the land of death. Grandfather prays. Mother retreats to the shade
of our walls, where she disappears as sure as a shadow. They both encourage
me to practice making letters and to learn scripture. I try, but even flat-nosed
Benjamin laughs at my efforts. I feel frustrated and take refuge in the highlands,
swinging my sword, aiming my sling at the tiniest creatures because game is
almost impossible to find.

Even the faithful in Elam say that our suffering is Nephi's fault. When
the climate within the church grows volatile, Grandfather sends an epistle to
the prophet. I'm curious about its content, but he does not tell me of their
exchange, and I have no right to ask.

The famine continues.

I see Eliana and her younger sister from across the courtyard of the
church. She smiles faintly at me, but we do not speak. I wonder if she still
favors Calev. When I see one of the other village boys—a soldier already
returned from duty—smile at Eliana, I feel anger smolder inside of me.

When I am called on to pray, words sometimes come out of my mouth in
the wrong order, and Grandfather is patient with me as I struggle to set them
right. Morning, noon, and night we recite our set prayers. We pray over any
morsel of food that we might be fortunate enough to set before us. We pray
with fervor and faith, but nothing changes.

My mind will not release its thoughts of Hem. My teacher tries to encourage
me in my synagogue studies, telling me I have a keen mind, but my mind is
mostly on how it feels to wield a sword, how I will have to straighten my legs
to bear the weight of true armor. While my lips move in unison with the other
students reciting scriptures, my thoughts imagine what it would be like to press
the tip of my blade into Hem's throat, making him confess the ugly truth.

Those secret thoughts ignite me with guilt.

Afternoons and evenings are my solace; I wander the hills in hopes of
finding peace and strength. I do not have sufficient food to fuel my body's
growth; my arms and legs are thin, my muscles weak. There are times when I
barely have the strength to pull back my sling.

"Be patient," Grandfather tells me. "Concentrate your aim on the coming
Messiah. He will bring salvation to us all."

My impatience is as sharp as my appetite. "Tell that to Kahana's family."

Yesterday Kahana—a cousin and friend to Eliana—was buried, her tiny
body shriveled by the famine. I saw it myself: her cheeks were shrunken like a
withered piece of fruit; her eyes were dark caves.

My remark is harsh, and it immediately saddens Grandfather. But my
anger is stronger than his sadness. "Why didn't Hem take care of Kahana? He
was her uncle. *He's* the one the famine should kill."

"Kiah! Be cautious of your tone. We do not know all the ways of the Lord." Grandfather's eyes are hard. "We must trust and remain faithful. God will reward and God will punish."

"Then why isn't Hem punished?"

Grandfather looks at me with unblinking eyes. "God's justice is not our justice."

"I don't understand. So much of what you say is a mystery to me."

"Son, you have proven yourself. Have faith that the demands of justice will be met."

"But I *don't* have faith, Grandfather," I blurt out, not at all like the confession I had imagined. "You have great faith. Mother lives by faith. I don't."

"You underestimate yourself, Kiah. Your faith is as a seed. Look at that mighty mango tree in the garden. In the beginning it looked to us like a weak twig, but beneath the ground roots were taking hold. Now when the wind whips and the storms come, that tree does not topple because its roots are strong and secure. That is as your faith."

I crane my neck and look up. The tree is huge; its branches shoot out like an entire city—a home for birds and squirrels and monkeys. Is my faith really like that? I get lost in thought for a moment, and when I turn back Grandfather is pointing a finger toward the blue sky of heaven. "Thou shalt not avenge, nor bear any grudge against the children of thy people, but thou shalt love thy neighbour as thyself. . . ."

What is he saying—that I'm supposed to *love* Hem? No. That can't be. "What are you telling me?"

"I'm telling you that we must go on as we have. We must keep the commandments and wait with patience and faith."

I don't want to wait. I want Hem brought to justice *now*. "I've never been this anxious, Grandfather. It feels as though I've been brought to the edge of the sea and am instructed to stand ready but not to plunge into the water."

Mother comes from where she has been boiling roots, pounding them into an edible paste. She offers a heap to Grandfather and one to me. "You miss Calev, Kiah. We all do."

Respectfully, I refuse the food she offers. "What about you, Mother? You must eat. You're like a skeleton hung with skin."

"Oh, Kiah. I will eat as I clean the pot. It does my heart good to feed you for you're a growing boy. Your brother will hardly recognize you when he returns."

"When will that be?" I ask, knowing she does not have an answer.

She holds the root paste out to me again, and this time I thank her and dip my fingers into it. As I swallow it, my stomach screeches like the mountain cat that I quit trailing when I came upon Hem and his band. "I am sorry that I do not provide better for my family."

"You brought a *t'uul* home last week, and the roots we eat now came from your own digging."

The *t'uul* I brought home was not much more than soft fur and bones; it should have hopped away when I chased it. Instead it made little effort to escape. I look down at my hands and see the dirt that rims my nails. Mother is right—I do provide, but not enough. How can I tell them of the storm that is churning inside of me? I want to provide meat in abundance *now*. I want the rains to pour from heaven *now*. I want to be able to quote scripture and understand the law the way Grandfather does *now*. But my tongue is heavy and dry—worthless. Under the law we have hundreds of commandments. I should know them all; I should *keep* them all, but ever since I saw Hem all I can think of is *an eye for an eye*.

Grandfather's expression is sober. "God's law is set higher than we can imagine. When the Messiah comes the law of Moses will be fulfilled, and then you will understand, Kiah, that God's laws are balanced between justice and mercy."

"But what about now? I've heard you say that our laws are just but our lawyers are not. How can there be justice and mercy *now*?"

A tear seeps from the corner of Grandfather's eye. He wipes it away with the back of his hand. "One day, Kiah, you will not be so eager for justice to weigh heavy. One day when you are the one being judged, you will beg for mercy to outweigh justice."

I ignore his prediction. "Grandfather, Hem has to be stopped. Have you heard the rumors that he aspires to the judgment seat?"

"I have heard. The story is more than rumor; it is true."

I'm livid. My fists tighten. My jaw clenches. "How can he?"

"Hem is a well-known, powerful leader. If the voice of the people elect him, then—"

"Then he will destroy Elam!"

"Kiah, do you see why it is so very important that you get a complete and proper education?"

"This has nothing to do with me or my education."

"It does. There are many judgment seats but only one chief judgment seat. If that seat belongs to a righteous man, our government is fair. If a wicked man sits in that seat, our government is corrupt."

I'm frustrated and speak with a harshness that borders disrespect. "I do not have the mind or the desire to be a judge. I want to be a warrior."

A small gasp comes from Mother's direction.

Grandfather wipes moisture from his lip and raises his voice in a rare rage. "A warrior, Kiah, who is only skilled with a weapon is a warrior that can do only limited good in defeating men like Hem. If you really want to be a warrior, you will learn to control your temper, and you will wield knowledge and faith along with your sword."

We are both so stirred that we do not pay the attention we should. When the hinge on the gate squeaks, we both look up.

"Greetings, Yarden."

We rarely have visitors, but now we have three. Two of them wear the cloaks of judges. The third man, the one in the middle, is the man Grandfather lifts his chin to. "Greetings, Hem."

Five

The men are smug. Have they overheard our conversation? Has Hem come to seek vengeance for the accusations I made, the ones Grandfather presented to the judges? I am afraid, but not so afraid that I don't look directly at Hem's large, doughy face. His beard is sparse and uneven and carries a red cast in the waning light.

Grandfather extends his condolences for the death of Kahana.

Hem nods. "The family has begun the mourning period."

"I will pay my respects."

Hem steps forward, and I instinctively step in front of Grandfather; my trembling hand reaches to finger my own concealed dagger. I will use it. I swear to myself—if the men threaten him in any way, they will pay with their lives. But the exchange seems harmless, and in a moment the men proceed up the narrow pathway, seemingly uninterested in our presence. Grandfather waits until they are gone and then leans down to whisper, "We cannot be too careful. There are ears all around."

I wonder what business the three of them have together. "Why are they together? Should I follow them? I can track them and find out."

"No! Kiah, you must stay away from Hem. Do you understand?"

"The other judges could be robbers too."

"You cannot go through life suspecting everyone."

"I can't help it."

Grandfather closes the gate and latches it with a twist of vine. "In these days of evil it is difficult to tell who wears a mask of deceit and who does not."

I still have my fingers wrapped around the handle of my dagger. "Kiah, if you focus on Hem, then your heart is not set on the Messiah. He alone should be your focus."

My grip on the dagger only tightens when I see Hem pause, turn around, glare back at us, and smile.

• • •

One day follows the next, and our lives do not change. The marketplace does not change. The school does not change. The weather does not change.

"Cheer yourself, son," Mother says. "The Lord does not measure time by the rise and fall of the sun like we do." She is lying in a small rectangle of shade within the mud walls of our home. It is one of the few places where relief from the heat can be found. "For weeks you have been so restless. I think it is the monotony. Every day brings the same relentless sun and suffering."

"I wish Calev was here."

"My heart misses him every day too."

"I should trade places with him. I should be the soldier. Calev should be here with you."

Mother sits up, and a patch of sunlight strikes her cheek; her skin is so thin I can see a mesh of thin blue veins. Her eyes are dull and her voice low. "It seems that way, doesn't it? My sons are very different, and yet you are both warriors in your own way. When our Messiah comes, Kiah, you will see yourself as you are, good and faithful, brave and kind."

"When . . . when will the Messiah come?"

She attempts a smile. "Are you prepared for His coming?"

"No. I don't know. I want to have faith like you and Grandfather, but if having faith means I have to stay confined in the walls of the synagogue or the pages of the scriptures, then I'd rather be in the highlands stalking a wild cat or a band of robbers."

Her hand covers her mouth, and her head turns from side to side. I can see that my words scare her.

"I'm sorry, Mother. It's just that I want to do something exciting, but I live in this village where the people are starving, waiting for either rain or death. Waiting for a Messiah that I do not know."

"He knows you, Kiah."

How can I tell her that I doubt that? How can I tell her that the Messiah does not seem real to me? What seems real is the angst I feel, the emptiness in my stomach, the weakness in her smile. I want to be in the hills hunting, but the last three treks I made saw me come home empty-handed and weaker than before.

"You are restless, Kiah. Go to the marketplace. See if there is any work you can do to earn a bit of bread or an offering of meat. You need nourishment. Go now."

My feet are out the open door before she has finished speaking. I pass homes that are larger than ours, put together with bricks or mud instead of thatch. I smell smoke and see faces. Though I lift my hand in greeting, few people raise their chins to recognize me. My feet kick up dust from the dry ground. I pick up my pace and pretend to be in a hurry. I can see the synagogue where it sits on a rise, but I turn and move to the flat of the village where the marketplace is laid out in a giant square. In thriving times there might be a hundred or more vendors sitting on the ground, their wares laid out before them. Now there are only about thirty. All of them stare wide-eyed and disappointed when they see me enter the main gate.

Surrounding the marketplace is a waist-high wall made of piled stones and growing vines. If it were not for the famine the wall would be green, red, and yellow with the blossoms of the vines. Now it is nothing but unpromising brown.

Right away I spot Hem. His back is turned to me, but I recognize his indigo cloak, his broad shoulders, and the curve of his full belly. Why does his presence turn my blood cold, like the blood of a reptile? Why do I care that he seems content, even jovial?

I skid to a halt and watch him as he greets people with a smile and a laugh so boisterous it rings in my head until I feel an ache that makes my empty stomach lurch. When there are no more people to greet, he moves from vendor to vendor, his palm open, ready to collect his fees. I notice that when he is upset with someone his voice deepens and he tugs at the bottom of his thin beard. I'm imagining how he would yank at it if I found a way to corner him and confront him, just him and me and my blade. Suddenly his head turns, and his squinty eyes bore right into me.

I go still as a cement god. But then I breathe: Hem is not eyeing me; he has his sights on whoever is behind me. I wheel around to see Eliana and her sister Tamar walking toward their father. I look at her, but she doesn't see me.

"What are you doing here?" he asks, his words spitting between gritted teeth.

I get out of the way, moving off the main path and behind a stack of empty woven baskets.

"Father!" Tamar says, lifting her arms out to Hem.

His cheeks puff red. His eyes look around, and his voice is low and rumbling. "I've told you girls not to come here."

"We're hungry, Father," Tamar says. I suppose that she is about eight years old, only half the age of Eliana, and seems slight—perhaps sickly. "We don't want to starve to death like Kahana."

From my hiding place I see Tamar's tears. I also see the basket weaver staring at me, pretending not to be aware of Hem or his daughters.

Hem takes hold of Tamar's elbow. "Go back to your mother and tell her that I will bring food tonight."

Eliana's hands sit on her hips. "That's what you told her last night and the night before."

Hem's jaw clenches. "I will not be spoken to in that tone. It's the tone of your mother, Eliana. I will not stand it!" I see his fat fingers tighten into a fist.

My spine goes straight. If the man lifts his hand to her, I will lunge. I swear to myself that he will not harm her while I am close enough to stop him.

"Father, I mean no disrespect," she says, easing toward him, her head bowed, "and I know how important appearances are to you, but we are in need of sustenance. While you eat from the market, we go hungry. Mother and Tamar are not well. You must keep your promise to bring home food."

He jerks his head. I squat, ready to spring like a wild animal. But then Hem's demeanor shifts. I look to see a band of women, baskets atop their heads, enter the pathway. Hem releases Tamar's elbow. He smiles and greets the women, and I recognize Oshra's shrill voice.

"Good day," Hem says. "A fine day for a bargain."

"I suspect so," Oshra says. "It's unfortunate that we have nothing with which to bargain. Look, sisters; see for yourselves—the marketplace sells goods, but no produce. What good are pots and baskets and spices?"

"There is still grain to be had—for a price."

"Exactly!" Oshra snaps. "A price so outrageous none of us can afford it."

"Perhaps not on Gomer's pittance from the synagogue," he says to Oshra. Then, looking at her sister, he coos, "But your husband is a wealthy money changer at the temple. I am certain you do not suffer."

"My husband might well be a man of means, Brother Hem, but when there is a famine, even the rich suffer."

Oshra and her band hum and nod in agreement.

"This famine is Nephi's fault," Hem shouts. "What kind of prophet curses the land he claims to love?"

One of the women smiles at Tamar, who still has tears on her cheeks.

"What kind of prophet prays for the destruction and suffering of his own people?" Oshra asks.

Her sister frowns. "Nephi has prayed for famine to humble us, to rid us of the evil and the robbers that plague our people and way of life."

Hem's nostrils flare. "The robbers abide in the high hills. They are no threat to us. As for my own household, we do not suffer." He snorts, thrusting his round stomach forward, glaring at his daughters who have backed toward me, so close I could reach through the stand of baskets and touch Tamar's hand. "We have plenty." He looks to Eliana for support, but her eyes glance downward.

Oshra scoffs. "Your wife weighs little more than Anat, the miserable woman who has no husband to support her."

I am outraged at her insult toward my mother, but it is Hem who explodes. "How dare you! How dare *you* talk to *me* in that manner!"

Oshra's sisters and friends pull her back and try to silence her. Hem's fist goes tight again, and I think he will strike the woman. I would not lunge to her rescue if he did. A woman has no right to speak to a man—especially one of Hem's standing—with such forwardness. I don't disagree with what she says, but the arrogant way in which she says it is punishable.

Eliana and Tamar continue edging toward the baskets. Toward me.

"Let's go to the sparkling stream," Tamar whispers. "I don't want to be here."

"Maybe we should wait until they are gone. Father might come up with some morsel for us to take home to Mother."

"No, he won't. Let's go before his anger turns on us. I can't stand to be hit again. I can't."

"Shhh," Eliana says, taking her young sister by the hand. "Let's go. Maybe we can find spears growing by the streamside."

Tamar pauses and looks up at her sister with a half smile. "Remember how good those used to taste when Mother put them over the fire?"

Eliana frowns. "The skinny green stalks? I hated those, but right now I would eat a hundred if they were set before me."

The basket weaver looks at me silently. She raises a finger and I fear she might point me out, give away my presence, but instead she puts her finger to her lips and sucks at the blood where the hardness of the reed has cut. I look at her with sympathy and gratitude.

Hem is still bickering with the women. Eliana and Tamar step away from the baskets, but before they make their retreat, I am on my feet, hurdling over a pile of reeds, hurrying through the maze of the marketplace, rushing toward the narrow gate at the opposite end of the square, the exit that leads in the direction of the sparkling stream.

Six

The sight startles me. I don't know what else I expected, but the once-sparkling stream is hardly a trickle. The mud around it has dried into gray layers, like rings inside a tree. The source of the water is a small underground spring above Elam. Even that is surely running dry.

The stream got its name because in times of plenty, the afternoon sun breaks through the canopy above and makes the water sparkle. Now it is dark and dull. I look for tracks of the hard-shelled *aak*, but there are none. Any fish that might have thrived are long gone.

Today the place is deserted, and I tuck myself out of sight. I don't know why I am hiding to spy on Eliana and Tamar. I suppose I am lonely and bored. The sisters take longer than I anticipated, and from the water vessels balanced atop their heads, it's clear that they made a stop at home.

They're talking to each other, but I'm too far away to hear; I creep closer. It feels wrong to hide, but I don't want to scare them. It would be dishonorable for a boy my age to be alone in the presence of a girl Eliana's age. I think of Calev. He would swat the back of my head for hiding like this, watching the girl he cares about. But that is exactly why I am here—because Calev cares about Eliana. I want to be sure she still cares about him.

"I'm hungry," Tamar says in a whiny voice.

"I know you are, sister. Look along the bank. Surely something is growing that we can eat."

"Everything is all dried up." Tamar walks along the bank where I walked. She stops and kneels down. "Someone else is here! There are tracks."

I go still and hold my breath. They can't find me lurking like this. It is wrong, and I'm sorry I am here.

Eliana kneels beside her sister, looking at the fresh footprints. Then she looks around. "No one is here now. Keep looking for mud crawlers or roots. There has to be something that others left behind."

Tamar looks for a time but then calls across the way to her sister. "Why do you think Father eats at the marketplace, but brings us hardly anything?"

"He brings us food."

"Not enough. I'm always hungry. Mother is too."

Eliana stands up and flips her long black hair over her shoulder. She is not the most beautiful girl in the village, but she is caring and her eyes are kind.

Tamar sets her pot by the edge of the stream and rushes into the water, kicking mud. Eliana bursts after her, and the sisters laugh like little children, carefree and unaware that they are being watched.

I don't wish to disturb them, but I do want to find food for them. In addition to the small blade that I always carry, I have my slingshot. Staying as quiet and concealed as I can, I move back into the murkiest part of the foliage and follow the water's edge upstream, where I dig for water roots. They are white bulbs, hard to find; they grow deep in the soil and are bitter in taste. I wish I could offer more, but I dig until my fingers plunge through mud to wrap around a fat root that takes a great deal of effort to retrieve. When I do, I think how my mother's eyes would light seeing I have finally managed something that can be turned into a meal.

When the murky water clears, I see my own face in a small, dark puddle of water. The sight startles me. My features have changed in the seasons since I've studied my own image. There are dark rings beneath my eyes; my black hair is so long it falls in curls around my face. My features seem broader, but my cheeks seem hollow. I don't look much like Calev, whose features are more chiseled. I can't quit looking at the boy-man who looks back, but then there is another splash and my eyes follow the trickle downstream. Eliana is trying to teach Tamar how to balance a water vessel atop her head. I suppose that while I was digging for bulbs, the girls filled the pot with water. I hope they knew to fill it from the deepest point where the mud is not so thick.

Tamar is reluctant. Eliana is patient, and her encouraging words make me realize what my brother favors about her.

The sisters struggle. The little girl does not want to bear the weight of the full pot. Eliana's patience seems infinite.

"You must keep your shoulders back—like this." Eliana takes the pot and lifts it to her own head. She sways for a moment and I think she might topple, but then she stands as straight as a stalk and the pot does not splash a drop as she demonstrates walking back and forth. "It can be done. It must be done."

"Why? Because Father expects it?"

"Don't use that tone when talking about Father."

"He eats while he lets us go hungry."

"We've had this discussion. The vendors and the shoppers would lose faith in the entire marketplace if they saw Father hungry and ill like so many others."

"You're angry with him too. You used a tone with him today."

The momentary happiness vanishes from Eliana's face. "I only wish Father showed greater kindness to Mother."

"Mother cries a lot."

"I know."

"My stomach aches," Tamar whimpers.

"I'm hungry, too," Eliana says.

I finger the fat white root that is in my grip. I am painfully aware that my mother and grandfather need the nourishment, but they are not here. Eliana and Tamar are. Unable to quell my enthusiasm, I step out from the shadows and shout, "I have food!"

Eliana gasps and lunges back. There is a splash, then a terrible clatter. The little girl screams. In the chaos I rush forward and realize that my muddy offering and sudden appearance have caused the water vessel to fall and break. By the time I run toward them, splashing and shouting, the girls are terrified. *I'm* terrified because their shouts might bring swift punishment for me.

"Don't be afraid! It's me—Kiah!"

"Kiah! Were you hiding, watching us?" Eliana's long hair is wet and muddy. Her dress is soggy. Her sister is crying. Eliana's tone is accusing and reveals genuine fright.

I understand her fright. Not only did I startle her, but it's not proper for a young man of my age to be in the presence of a budding girl, not unless we are accompanied by an elder. I know this, and yet I could not help myself, so I stammer, "No. No. I mean yes. I was watching you, but only for a moment. I didn't mean to frighten you."

She kneels to calm her sobbing sister. "You didn't mean to frighten us? You jumped out of the jungle, Kiah. You could have been a wild beast or a . . . a . . . a robber. You know they steal girls."

"I'm so sorry. I only wanted to give you this." I stretch out my hand to offer the fat root, but my clutch holds nothing but my mud-covered blade. I look back and realize that somewhere between there and here I dropped the root in the muddy water.

Eliana backs away, protecting her sister like I am a renegade or worse—a robber. Little beams of sunlight break through the leaves above us and the shadows that fall on the sisters' faces are sharp and dark. If those same shadows break down on me, my face must look terrifying to them. "I'm sorry," I repeat. I want to go back and find the dropped root. I want to wash the mud from my hands. I want to pick up the broken pieces of their water pot and—

"You're a strange boy," Eliana says. "A very strange boy."

"I am a man."

"You are a *boy*," she repeats. "A strange boy who wanders alone."

My spine goes straight. "I am a warrior."

She doesn't come right out and laugh, but her lips curve upward in a smile that reduces me to a boy. My face goes hot; my fingers tighten around the blade in my hand. There's a lump in my throat that threatens to choke me.

"I'm telling Father," Tamar announces.

We both look at her. She's the picture of distress, all mud and water and tears.

"I'm telling my father that you jumped out and scared us and broke our water pot. He'll punish you. Our father is *mean*!"

The idea of Hem coming after me—or worse, after my grandfather—to demand the price of the pot is a thought that sets fire to my chest. "Please," I stammer, "please, I will restore your broken pot. I only meant to share my food with you."

"What food?" Eliana asks, her eyes narrow and accusing.

"I had a root. Let me go back and I will find it. I heard you say you are hungry, and I only wanted to give you what I had."

Eliana looks at me. There's a streak of mud across her chin.

"What's wrong with you?" Tamar asks, peeking out from behind Eliana. "You look scared. You're scared of us—we're girls." She giggles.

I brush my hair out of my eyes with my hand—my *muddy* hand. I try to blink the mud out of my eyes but only end up smearing more.

Eliana laughs. Her sister laughs. Soon I am laughing too, and the three of us pick up the shards of the broken pot. I hear myself make a promise to replace their pot with a larger, better one, though I have no means to do so.

"Don't concern yourself over a broken pot. We can obtain another water pot. If you really want to help us," Eliana says, her tone turning serious, "you will ask your grandfather to approach the prophet. Your grandfather is his kin, Kiah; the prophet will listen to him. My mother says that only Nephi can unstop the heavens."

Tamar pipes in, "Father says the famine is Nephi's fault."

If I tell the truth that I know, the truth about Hem, these girls will know broken hearts. Eliana might even resent me for being the one to divulge the truth. I can't tell what I know, so I try to sound wise and kind like Grandfather. "There are certain things that must happen before the famine can end."

"Like what?" Eliana snaps the question.

"Before the rains can come, we must repent of pride, and the robbers must go. They must be destroyed." The words are out of my mouth before I realize that in essence I have told her that her father must be destroyed before grain can grow again.

Eliana does not even flinch, and I know then for certain that she knows nothing of her father's role as a Gadianton robber.

"People are starving to death," Eliana says. "What kind of prophet does that? My cousin Kahana died because her family has no food."

"Couldn't your father supply them?"

Eliana's dark eyes pool with tears. I regret my words and wish that I could take them back. "Father is very frugal with food. He says it is more valuable now than money."

"I . . . I . . . I know this is hard on all of us, but the Lord will not let down the rain until we have repented and until the robbers are cleared out of our land."

"Hush, Tamar," Eliana says when her little sister bursts into another frenzy of tears.

"The robbers steal little girls," Tamar says, speaking straight to me. "I heard my mother and my aunties talking about it. They didn't know I was listening, but I was. The robbers took a little girl from another village. They never brought her back."

Eliana kneels to embrace her sister. "You don't need to be afraid, Tamar. Our father will never allow any harm to come to us; he will protect us from the robbers."

My mouth opens, but I cannot tell what I know. I move slowly back until I find the dropped root. I wipe it the best I can and hand it to Eliana, who accepts it with a bow of gratitude.

"Kiah, has your family received any word from Calev?"

"No. Not recently."

Eliana looks down, and I sense there's something she is hesitant to say.

"What is it?" I ask.

"I had a nightmare. I dreamt of Calev."

I smile. "He would be pleased to know that you dreamt of him."

"No. You don't understand." She lowers her voice and bites down on her bottom lip. "Kiah, I dreamed that our soldiers came back to Elam . . . all except Calev. I dreamed that he died."

Seven

The only word we receive of Calev is that he has volunteered to join a military force to hunt out and purge the Gadianton robbers. I say nothing of Eliana's dream. My mother looks away, toward our mud wall, her eyes teary at the news. Grandfather raises his walking stick and shouts, "Finally!" I sulk off into the hills and manage to bring back two small ground fowls that we savor, supplication for the safe return of my "warrior" brother.

Most mornings I reluctantly but obediently walk the worn path beyond our home and past the other poor huts of Elam, beyond the rows of larger houses with bigger courtyards, to the rise where the synagogue sits as the jewel of the village. In the afternoon its mudded walls shimmer when the sun hits it, but in the morning the edifice looks as tan as the underbelly of an *aayin*, one of the fierce reptiles that thrive near the great river Sidon. I haven't seen the river that runs near the temple in Zarahemla in many seasons, and I wonder how much of it has evaporated during the famine.

Gomer, Oshra's thin-framed husband, is stooped over, pulling moss from between the cracks in the cobbled entry. He looks up and gives me a toothless smirk. Behind him is a trio of boys, older than me, richer than me, smarter than me. Andrew, their leader, elbows the other boys, and they give me their own smirks. I wait by Gomer until the boys have entered and found their seats.

"Recitations today," Gomer says.

I nod, knowing that he will stand at the back of the room and hear me stammer. Knowing that he will go home and tell his wife, who will find a way to bring my failure up to Mother. After all these years, I cannot see why my lack of performance still interests people.

"You work hard," I tell Gomer, biting back what I'd really like to say. "I want to thank you for the labor you put into keeping the synagogue so clean and proper."

Gomer looks at me with eyes yellow where they should be white. He begins to cough, and I step around him and walk under the main arch. The vine-walled synagogue courtyard is large enough to hold a thousand people, but the thatched and mudded structure itself barely accommodates a hundred worshipers. It's just as well because the only benefit of being inside is to keep the sun from shining down and the wind from blowing like it tends to do on the rise.

Most of my studies are done in a little schoolroom at the side of the main building. Every village in the land of Nephi—even the smallest—has a synagogue because all that is required to maintain the Divine Presence is a *minyan*, a quorum. There is also an ark where the sacred scrolls are kept and a table from which they are read.

Elam's table was built by Grandfather's father's father. It is made of hard jungle wood that worms and insects do not eat. I like to look at the ornate carvings that edge its sides and think that my brother inherited his artistic abilities from our talented ancestor. It helps me to shadow the shame that our father brought to our family.

The table is situated where a slat of light falls from the east in the morning and the west in the afternoon, always lighting the table—in part to remind us of God's light. The *amud*, the main post, is also made from the hardest wood of the jungle, a felled tree that that leaves me curious. How was it ever brought from the jungle to the rise in the first place? It might have taken hundreds of men to carry it.

I once saw a giant snake that was as long as the post is tall. It took nearly a hundred men to lift it and carry it away from Elam. If we were not a band of believers, obedient to the commandments of Moses, the snake would have been killed and eaten. But the law of Moses tells us that snake meat is not clean meat, so the monster serpent was carted off and set free in the highlands.

The memory still makes the hairs on my arms stand firm.

I pause at the entryway into the main worship area and look in the opposite direction. When I stand in this spot facing this way, Grandfather says I am facing Jerusalem, land of our first fathers. I am told that Jerusalem is a white city made of stone. I am told the temple there is made of stone with walls so high arrows cannot rise high enough to penetrate the city. I'd like to see Jerusalem, but it is so foreign to me—so far away that the sun, something I can witness for myself, seems more real.

For a single doubting second, I wonder at the God Messiah. I have never seen Him. I've only heard stories. I have never felt His presence. I've only heard stories. I have never known His power. I've only heard stories of how it is by His power that my doubt, my fears, my sins will be atoned for. I don't understand and I don't dare divulge my doubts for fear I will disappoint Grandfather and Mother, who believe in a God they've never seen with every breath they draw.

The day drags on as Benjamin, my instructor, teaches us. I listen to the heroics of Alma and Mosiah. I fall asleep when Benjamin reads from the pen of Isaiah. When it comes my turn to read I stand—and, as always, I stumble over the words. My face flushes hot; I hear Gomer sigh and Andrew snicker.

What does it matter?

When prayers are recited my lips move. I know the words but do not feel their import. I want to be in the high hills. I want to be with Calev—creeping into the camps of robbers, surprising them, fighting them, killing them if necessary.

Mother greets me at our garden gate. She watches as I wash myself clean and while I kneel in prayer. She feeds me a pitiful portion of corn gruel. I eat it knowing that she has not eaten this day. It gives me strength to go back to the stream and dig for roots. I find two, not as large as the one I gave to Eliana and Tamar, but better than nothing. That night my mother turns those roots into a paste she grills over a flame.

While Grandfather meets with his fellow priests, Mother makes faint letters in the dirt of our small courtyard with the tip of her finger. "Trace these," she says. "Practice here and it will not be so difficult for you when you are required to write in front of your teachers and other students."

The fact that my mother knows how to read and write is uncommon. It is to her father's credit that he had his daughters educated. I wish I had known my mother's family. They lived in a village near Bountiful that was plundered when I was only a baby. Mother will not speak of the deaths of her family, but I know she despises war and violence.

Kneeling on the ground next to her I let her hand guide mine. Her marks, though faint, are smooth and precise while mine are clumsy and blunt. They do not appear to be the same letters.

After much practice I win her approval and she nods, allowing me to make the best of the fainting hours of the day. I rush to the hills and try to find any game that might provide meat for my family. That night when I return empty-handed, Grandfather rises from his hammock. "Son, do not be discouraged. It is not your responsibility to provide for this family. It is mine."

"With all respect, Grandfather, your leg will not permit you to hunt like you once did. If I didn't have to go to school every morning, I would have better luck hunting."

"There will be no school for you tomorrow morning," he says, grinning. "Tomorrow I've arranged for you to join the village hunt."

My heart beats faster. "Really?"

"Yes. I'm only sorry that I won't be accompanying you."

Whenever a village hunt occurs, anything acquired is shared with the entire village, including the widows and orphans. I have always been considered too young, so this announcement swells my chest with pride.

The chief hunter is a man named Merari. He is strong and sullen. He wears a necklace that jingles with the teeth of the wild cats he has killed. The teeth are small and curved and yellowish-brown; some of them are chipped. I have always loved staring at his necklace.

I'm so excited that sleep won't come. As soon as our morning prayers are over I am ready at the gate when Merari appears.

"You will stay behind me," he tells me, putting both hands on my shoulders, peering into my eyes. The man has a scent about him as pungent and ripe as a wild animal. "I will be responsible for you, Kiah, so you must obey every command I give you."

I nod, so excited I can feel my heart beat in my throat. Usually, fathers and sons hunt together. Since I have no father, Merari will serve as my mentor. I could not ask for a better one. Because he approves of me, the others in the band, mostly men, pay me no mind.

Instead of going into the high hills that I know so well, our small band heads back through our village and off onto the main road that leads to Zarahemla. I know not to question anything, only to follow. Our weapons are humble, mostly carved of wood and stones, the blades made of obsidian, and I think about the caves I discovered and how so much of the black rock lies ready to be picked up and brought back. The few small pieces I managed to return with have already been set into wood handles to make the blades that I carry now.

Long before we reach the city, Merari turns down a narrow, overgrown vein that leads to the lowlands. I think we must be headed toward one of the many bodies of water in that direction. I grow excited.

"Why are the West Sea and East Sea named so?" I ask Merari. "The West Sea does not lie to the west nor the East Sea to the east."

He smiles, showing a mouthful of teeth, clean and straight. "They are only names," he replies, "probably given by the first of our fathers to land here. You're right, Kiah, they don't designate direction."

I tuck my chin to keep from looking as pleased as I feel. Besides Grandfather, no other man in Elam has ever shown me such concern or attention. Before

I posed my question we walked in relative silence, but now Merari talks like a professional teller of tales found in the marketplace.

"When our first fathers arrived in this, the Promised Land," Merari says to anyone who will hear, "Lehi and his family discovered many animals they had never seen."

I'm not sure what he means. He asks me, "A *keeh* to Lehi in the land of Jerusalem . . . did it look like a *keeh* here in the Promised Land?"

The thought is new to me. For the first time Jerusalem seems real to me, and suddenly our first fathers—Lehi, Nephi, Laman, and Lemuel—do too. If Mother's stories are right, our forefathers came from a land of sand and barren waste. Here there are stretches of desert, but when there is no famine, our land is thick and lush. It makes sense that wildlife would be different.

"What if the animals in Jerusalem *were* different?" I ask.

"What if they were?"

My mind starts spinning. In hearty growing times our hills crawl with many different animals, many different types of *keeh*. Some are small with spindly legs; others are squat with short legs. They all have their own names. There are many types of wildlife, and Elam even has names for animals that are different from the names used in distant villages.

Merari smiles again. "It is just something I've wondered about. The genealogy of my family tells me that Jerusalem was a land of sand and heat. Our stones are mostly grey and mossy; theirs were white and smooth. When I ponder the stories of our fathers, I wonder how our worlds were different."

I wonder too. When Merari speaks, the scriptures seem like the tales and teachings of real people—real men and women of God. A hedge inside me begins to break apart. If only Benjamin could make the holy scriptures so vivid.

Merari hoists his bow high into the air. "Do you know the story of Nephi and his broken bow?"

I nod.

He laughs. "Even Father Lehi murmured for want of food. Imagine how Elam will greet us if we return with nothing to fill their hungry bellies."

"*Our* hungry bellies!" one of the other hunters laughs, but there is an edge to their laughter; our bellies *are* empty. Our backs ache, our feet are hot, and our sweaty bodies are cloaked in dust.

We trek during the days and camp at night. We find food sufficient for our needs but far from our wants: mostly juiceless fruit and roots. Merari finally stops when the ground beneath our feet feels sodden. A forest of dry reeds surrounds us, and I realize I am in territory my eyes have never seen. It is flat and endless, a blend of grays and browns; the air smells loamy and rich.

Merari's face is hard. "In better times the shoreline would be here."

I squint and shade my eyes; the shoreline is far in the distance. When I kneel to adjust my sandal, I'm surprised by a paw print in the dried mud. It is far from fresh, but there is no doubt that it belonged to a cat.

"Did Jerusalem have wild cats?" I ask as we continue on.

"Did a young David kill a lion before he killed Goliath?"

"What does it mean . . . the word *lion*?"

"I understand it means cat or *chakmool,* perhaps like the spotted leopard that you are so fond of tracking, Kiah. But whether it was a cat like those that infest our lands, I do not know." Merari smiles. "I see it in your eyes, son. Your head is filling with questions. That is good. We *should* think on these things. We must never forget our first fathers or the sacrifices they made for us."

To think of Lehi and Nephi as real people makes me want to read the scriptures more deeply. To think of David wrestling a wild *chakmool* makes me want to immerse myself in his teachings.

That night we camp and eat boiled stalks and mud fish, tiny little creatures that crawl deep in the damp black soil. They taste different than anything I've ever eaten, and even though I'm very hungry, it's difficult for me to swallow them.

The next morning our hunt begins before sunrise. Merari teaches me how to stalk and kill waterfowl. It requires patience and the ability to lay flat in the sour-smelling mud with its biting bugs, but the game is fat and meaty and I cannot wait for my mother to obtain our family's portion.

I didn't pay too much attention before, but a small group of women have followed behind us. They are quick to pluck the feathers and clean the birds. They say nothing, only work, and the thought crosses my mind that these women are Lamanite slaves. Slaves are not uncommon among us; they are the ones often compelled to smooth our roads, to clear bush for farms, to construct our walls and buildings. I have never given much thought to slaves, but these women look so sad and beaten that I feel pity for them.

We eat that evening. The smell of roasting fowl makes me so hungry my head feels dizzy. I sit on my haunches near the fire, watching the meat sweat fat that sizzles in the flames. My mouth waters. My stomach screams. I want to grab an entire bird and devour it. But I soon learn that there is an order to one of Merari's hunts. First, he eats. Then his seasoned hunters eat. Then those like me are given what is left. If we leave anything—bones or skin or gristle—the slave women can eat.

Merari gives me a wing; its ridge of meat is dripping with fat. I look over and see one of the slave girls trying not to stare at me. I want to share my food with her, but my own hunger overtakes me and I'm ashamed at the mournful portion I offer her and the others.

I feel guilty, but I know if I ask Merari for more food he will only deny me and look upon me with disapproval. Instead I say a prayer for the slaves and realize halfway through my prayer that words alone will never feed them.

The hunting experience teaches me much. I see that a large group like ours is able to hunt more successfully than I could by myself. It takes a certain number of people to flush out the birds, more people to lead them, and yet others to bring them down with slings and arrows. Then the slaves run to find them and bring them back.

Though I could not hunt here successfully by myself, I am pleased with my aim with a sling. I take down three birds fewer than Merari himself. He rewards me the final night with an entire breast of meat and I eat—but I offer the best and biggest portion to the slaves.

Merari sees me do it and does not look displeased.

By the time we return home we are tired and happy and laden with meat the slave women have smoked so it would not spoil during our travels.

Grandfather gnaws the meat and sucks whatever marrow he can manage from even the smallest bones. I can tell from the look on his face that he is pleased with me, though he does not say it. Mother makes a broth, and I see her sip it with her eyes closed in prayer. Afterward, I ask her, "Will you please trace more letters? I am eager to learn now. I *want* to learn."

She smiles but her eyes go wide. "What has brought about this change?"

"Merari made the scriptures seem alive. He asked me many questions, and at night around the fire he told stories of unfamiliar beasts and prophets so real I could imagine their faces."

Grandfather chuckles. "I thought that's what your Mother and I have been doing all the years of your life."

He's right. They've both told me stories from the scriptures many times, yet only now has a yearning to know them and to believe them been lit inside me.

"I'm grateful," Mother says as she kneels beside me, smoothing the dirt in our small courtyard to make my writing pallet. She draws a set of letters and then hands the stick to me.

It is dark before I finally give up tracing letters and crawl into my hammock.

Eight

Time melts.

The sun is fierce.

The hard ground grows harder.

Jacob, the beloved high priest in our village, perishes from want of food. It comes as a surprise to us because the cloaks he wore were loose and full. He and Grandfather were close, and Grandfather rends his inner garment as a symbol of the tearing pain he feels at the loss of his friend. Since the priest's only sons have all died in battles, I am called along with Grandfather to aid his widow in the burial preparations. She too looks ready for death; she's a walking shadow, and the sight of her frailty makes me fear for the life of Mother.

"It is not fair."

"No, it's not fair," Grandfather agrees, "but there is no covenant that promises life will be fair. We are only promised that God will be with us."

As much as the scriptures are coming to mean to me, as hard as I am working to learn to read and write so that I can better understand, it is impossible for me to understand why covenant-keeping people suffer while men like Hem go on about their business, getting fatter and laughing louder.

"Grandfather, why would Nephi do such a thing to us?"

Grandfather's hand clasps over mine. "Son, do not believe what you hear. I know the rumors that tear through Elam, but Nephi is not to blame for this famine. He sealed the heavens because he did not want us to die in battle."

"What *did* he want, Grandfather?"

"Nephi is a prophet of God, Kiah. Do not doubt that. A prophet loves God first, and he loves the people of God. Nephi sealed the heavens that we might humble ourselves and turn from sin and return to God."

"But innocent people suffer. Jacob. Kahana. You. Mother. It's not fair that men like Hem—"

"Stop, Kiah. Not another word about Hem. Your focus must be on *your* life, not *his*."

"I'm sorry. You're right."

After scarce and precious water is contributed to purify Jacob's body for burial, the task is given me to weigh the priest's body so we can determine how many spices we need for the burial. Once uncovered, the old priest is nothing but withered skin and brittle bones. He weighs so little it is no strain for me to lift his body; in spite of my best efforts, an angry pain smolders within me. How can this good man's suffering be God's will?

Even Grandfather shakes his head. Beneath his beard, I see his lip quiver.

After a while I ask, "Do you fear for the prophet's life? People are so angry at him."

"I have lived a long life, son, long enough to know that a man cannot walk in faith if he allows fear to be his companion. No, I do not fear for the prophet. God is Nephi's protector."

"How can you have faith that never wavers?"

Grandfather adjusts Jacob's hands, molding his long, thin fingers as if the man was praying. "My faith is in the Messiah."

How can I tell my grandfather that to me the Messiah does not seem real? What *does* seem real to me is the dried-up mud of the sparkling spring, the disappointment of Merari's latest hunting expeditions. What seems real to me is Jacob's withered corpse.

I want the Messiah to bring me the same hope that He brings Grandfather. I want to speak of Him with the reverence Mother does. I want to believe, but my heart struggles and weighs heavy with guilt.

We help the widow tear strips of cloth to wrap the high priest's body. Her hands shake while her tears fall down and stain the cloth like sullen raindrops. I wish Grandfather would offer her words of comfort, but the only thing he offers is to sit with the dead priest's body for the required three days.

I've never seen Grandfather look so discouraged. The wrinkles and scars of his life crease his skin.

"Pray," the widow says, casting her eyes on Grandfather.

He nods, and I hand him the box we have brought. There is a slight tremble in his hands as he unfolds his prayer shawl in commencement of the burial.

"When will the Messiah come?" the widow asks.

Grandfather gives her a drawn-out answer about how every prophet since Adam has foretold the coming of the Messiah, but all I can do is look at Jacob's dead body and wonder if any of us will live long enough to witness the coming for ourselves.

I keep my doubts to myself. I pray that fear will leave me, but it stays. There are days when the scriptures seem real to me, and there are other days when they are only words. There are times my prayers are more meaningful and times when they, too, are mere words.

Benjamin, my synagogue teacher, falls ill, so most of my days are lost in hunting. Animals are easy to find—all I have to do is watch for circling vultures. Death is everywhere.

Mother is more placid than ever; she is little more than a shadow in the corner of our hut. She rarely ventures out, hardly ever speaks anymore. I haven't heard her sing in so long. Grandfather's leg has mended but he is weak; when he is not with his fellow judges, he sleeps in his sling tied between two bowing trees in our humble courtyard.

I miss Calev. If my brother was home we could hunt in tandem. I could talk to him of the unrest that is growing in Elam. I heard Andrew and the other boys at the synagogue talk openly of a plot to murder the prophet. God might protect Nephi, but what of his family? My best friend is his grandson Jonas. What will happen to Jonas if Nephi's home is attacked?

I want to go to Zarahemla to warn Jonas, but Grandfather says the prophet and his family are well aware of the threats and that I am needed in Elam. The only thing that changes during the coming days is a deeper withering. Others starve and perish, mostly the very old and the very young. We measure more spices, we tear more burial cloth. Every day I beg God to strengthen my family—to protect my brother, whose face and voice I can no longer remember clearly. My own strength, even my desire to scale the high hills, is gone. The men hang their heads and send mournful prayers heavenward. Instead of linens and jewels, the women wear sackcloth and ashes.

Our only joy comes when we hear occasional word of Calev's bravery and success as a warrior. His captain is a noble man called Uriel. He sends word to Mother that Calev is safe and doing much good in the cause of freedom. I ache to be fighting at his side, to make Mother and Grandfather proud of me too.

We also hear that the robbers are more desperate and brutal than ever, burning part of a not-distant village after they plundered it. We hear that they destroyed the village synagogue, tormenting the innocent and murdering at will.

One night beneath a full, unblinking moon, Grandfather says, "Kiah, bring the spade. I want you to help me bury my treasure box."

Grandfather's treasure is sparse: a few skins engraved with scriptures, a necklace worn by my grandmother, a comb from her hair, a few trading coins that cannot buy food because there is no food to buy.

I dig a hole deep enough to satisfy Grandfather, and we bury his treasure box directly below the sling in which he sleeps. I know that it is not a safe place, but it makes him feel better, and that is what matters most. We place a layer of stones and dried leaves over it as protection. I am certain the rest of Elam is doing the same thing, trying to protect what little they have left from the greedy, bloody hands of robbers.

I try not to think about Hem, but my thoughts always come back to him. For all I know, he will lead his band of robbers into Elam and destroy our entire village. If it happens, the people will deserve it because they would not listen to me—so Hem goes about his business with his stomach out and his chin in the air.

The courts do hold some trials. A few men are found to be robbers, caught red-handed and brought before the courts. There are enough witnesses to find the men guilty. They are sentenced to jail; one man is even executed, stoned in a field by the old ball court.

On the afternoon of the execution I stand back, watching as Hem too stands back. His face is as blank as a cloudless sky.

"Yarden," he greets Grandfather, "it's a pity to see this old ball court lay in ruins."

As much as I despise Hem, he's right. The ancient ball court was built many years before, and the stories of its pride still resound, but now it is a pile of stones chewed and broken by the jungle brush. When I was a little boy, Calev and I used to try to run the entire length of the court, all the time holding our breath. We never quite made it.

Grandfather says, "The court was a blessing to Elam as long as it was used for sport, but when it became a pit for brutality, the elders deemed it dead."

Hem scoffs. "I know the history, Yarden. I know the blood that was spilled on these stones, but it's a pity to see it lay waste like this when the villages around us have kept their courts intact."

"It seems a proper place for a stoning."

Hem's eyelids go heavy as if he's in thought. When they lift, he glares right at me. *Glares.* I'm so startled I tumble against Grandfather, nearly knocking him over. He reaches to steady me, and Hem chuckles. The grip on my arm tightens as Grandfather shakes his head, warning me to keep my composure. And so I watch as Hem moves from one man to the next. When he stops to speak with Abner, Elam's coppersmith, I think right away that Abner must also be a secret robber, plotting to rob and kill and destroy our village. I hate the way I suspect everyone who encounters Hem; after all, Grandfather often talks to him, and Grandfather is no robber.

The crowd grows thicker. I hear whispers of people being anxious to see blood spilled. I hear shouts of anger. A group of men and boys pass by; they are the appointed executioners. Andrew and two of his friends are among them. They seem excited, their pockets bulging with rocks, their fists clenching more.

The robber brought to the center of the ball court is a small man with a shorn head. His eyes protrude from his face as if they are swollen. He says nothing, but even from where I stand I can see that his jaw rattles.

I stare at Hem to see if the men exchange looks. Hem doesn't seem concerned with the purpose of our gathering; instead, he is still talking loudly and enthusiastically about the possibility of restoring the ball court and once again training a team to compete with those of other villages. I know it is a sin, but I hate the man. He leads a band of robbers. Hem should be the one in the center of the ball court.

The chief judge steps forward to announce the robber's crimes. The people go still.

I look again at the man who is about to die. He deserves to die. There is no doubt in anyone's mind that this man is one of Gadianton's—Hem's—cohorts. He is Calev's enemy. Yet my heart goes soft. Instead of a plunderer, a vicious soul who would murder my own family, I see a man whose ribs and scars show through the tatters in his cloak. I see a man who shakes like a cornered beast. I see a man that I pity. I turn and walk away before the first stone is thrown.

• • •

Benjamin recovers, but he is not the same as before he took ill. The teacher who tried for so many seasons to instruct me in the commandments had dark wavy hair; now his straight white hair falls to his shoulders. The transformation is disturbing.

"He looks like a ghost," Andrew whispers to me as we weave new banana leaves onto the roof to keep the sun from beating down on us while we study.

They are the first words Andrew has spoken to me that were not meant to make me doubt myself.

I feel sorrow for Benjamin's suffering. "He was very sick," I remind Andrew. "His wife and baby died while he was ill."

Andrew spits on the ground. "And yet listen to Benjamin preach. He reveres Nephi, the man who brought this famine on and caused the deaths of his wife and child—the man whose curse caused his own hair to change. No prophet of God would pronounce such misery on us. We are righteous people." Andrew twists a leaf in his hands. Normally the leaf would be soft and pliable, but it looks scorched around the edges, and it crinkles when he twists it. He stares at me and spits again. "Nephi and every other fool whose prayers keep this famine going will pay. Mark my words."

I mark his words. That night I warn Grandfather again of the rising threat, not only against Nephi, but against every faithful leader who prays for the people to change their hard hearts. "If this rage continues to swelter, someone could take revenge on you, Grandfather. Perhaps you should not be so vocal in your support of the prophet."

"Kiah, you know me better than that. Do not fear what man can do; fear what God can do."

I say nothing, but I think of what Andrew's anger can do. It stems from his home, where his father and brothers see their wheat and barley crops fail season after famine-plagued season. I fear what Hem can do with his whispers to one man after another, stirring up anger and contention. I fear what will become of us if I do not prove myself a more skilled hunter. Twice more I've accompanied Merari, but even our organized hunts bring in game that is starved to little more than breathing skeletons.

It makes no sense to me why Grandfather continues to insist that I attend school, hunched over, learning to read and write in the language of our fathers. In spite of all my practice and help at home, the letters that come from my efforts will forever be awkward and indecipherable. Benjamin's patience seems to have waned with his suffering. At least twice a day he strikes me with his punishing stick, leaving red welts on my fingers and hands. At least twice a day the other students, most of them younger and brighter than me, snicker.

"Your brother did not have such trouble learning," Gomer says to me when I am the sole student left out in the courtyard. "Calev's fingers could draw the letters—the numbers, too. His tongue could recite the scriptures. I used to enjoy listening to holy words come off his tongue."

I say nothing. I hate the way Gomer's dark, snakelike eyes look at me. I hate how he grins his toothless grin. Why do I care what Gomer thinks of me? He is an unlearned man, relegated to cleanup around the synagogue.

Though my hunting skills have slackened, I am a warrior in the making. Why can't anyone recognize that and value me for the skills I *do* have instead of diminishing me for what I *lack*?

An angry, unsettled feeling rises in me as sure as any fever.

All I want to do is show my bravery for the Lord by fighting with the weapons I've crafted myself. They are not as fine as those Calev crafted, for sure, but they are fine enough. While my tongue stumbles to recite commandments, my imagination takes me to the battlefields, where I slay wicked Lamanites and vile robbers. I imagine I am in combat with Hem. I always come out the victor, and the entire village honors me with a celebration—but in the midst of the celebration, I imagine Eliana standing back, her face twisted in pain at the loss of her father. That is always where my vision halts.

• • •

Finally, *finally* another rainy season arrives, and with it come ripe, promising clouds that blot out the unrelenting sun. Hope rises in the hearts of our people. Even Grandfather's dull eyes brighten. A wind stirs through our village, carrying the salty scent of the distant sea and dusting my mother's table with the bleak powder that was once our moist, rich soil. The barren dirt coats everything: my hands, my face. When I bite down, I feel grit in my teeth.

I miss Calev, and I imagine the echo of his laugher swelling in the small space of our hut, bouncing off the walls, spilling out the door because it cannot be contained. I picture the way it lifts Mother, and how Calev's laugh always makes Grandfather laugh too. I cannot make them laugh, no matter how I try.

Some nights my dreams turn to nightmares, and I imagine that war has silenced my only brother's laugh.

I hunt the foothills but lack the stamina to venture high into the climes I love most. I think about the black cats that prowl the jungle. It has been a very, very long time since I've heard their nighttime screeching. I think about the robbers and wonder how they are surviving in their high hiding places. I imagine myself fighting alongside my brother, hand-to-hand, blade against blade. I imagine our duo victorious in every battle. It's sad that the only strength I have left is for imagining—for in the morning when I wake from my warrior dreams, my limbs are weak, my head aches, and I want to continue lying in my sling next to Grandfather.

In spite of the constant rumblings against the prophet and his followers, an epistle for fasting and prayer comes from Nephi. The epistle winds its way throughout the dusty land until every village has received the same instruction. Most people are eager to heed the prophet's counsel, but not everyone. I have not seen Hem in a long time, and do not know how he and his household are receiving the instruction.

Fasting is not a challenge for our small village, for we are used to going without food and water. Now the majority of us rise early and begin our supplication before dawn. Those who no longer believe Nephi is a prophet of God mock us, but throw only words our way as we climb toward the synagogue. Even in a faithful village like Elam, there are unbelievers—men who worship idols made by their own hands, men who burn sacrifices to the gods of rain and wind and thunder. These are men who do not work, but sell their wives and children—men who make wine from the fruit of the vine and are drunken even as early in the morning as this.

Most of the unbelievers live on the outskirts of Elam, in the lowlands where they eat the forbidden flesh of snakes and land-crawling reptiles. Their children do not attend synagogue; their wives do not sell in the marketplace. At the beginning of the rainy season, the pound of their drums sounds like endless thunder throughout the village.

Mother fears the unbelievers; I see it in her eyes. Grandfather has spent countless hours preaching to them. Once, when one of their children fell from a high tree, Grandfather laid hands on the child to restore his health. After that, the unbelievers have never molested our family. The more brutal ones—their faces painted with bright reds and yellows, their foreheads and cheeks pricked with needles until scars dot their faces—relish in frightening the women and children and in harassing the elders of the synagogue.

Today they follow behind us, curious about our gathering. Mother wraps her arms around herself the way she does when she is frightened. I am afraid too because I sense a rising spirit of contention. Grandfather seems oblivious, anxious to do what the prophet has called us to do: gather in fasting so that we can pray as one body, with one purpose.

Father, I pray silently, *please let this be sufficient to end the famine.*

Villagers flock to Elam's small synagogue courtyard. I wish the prophet could see them. He would know for certain that the famine has served its purpose. We are purged from pride, from sin. There is no strength left to sin. It is time to release the rain.

My mouth hangs open when I see Hem and his family come into the courtyard. He is hardly recognizable. The man drags one foot behind the other, shuffling with sagging shoulders and eyes that do not seem focused. Sherrizah holds his elbow, and I can't decide if she is strengthening him or if he is helping keep her balanced. They both appear aged and ravaged.

Grandfather limps over to greet Hem with respect and peace. I can see from his face that he too is surprised at the demise of Hem.

Tamar grins when she sees me, and I smile back. Eliana allows her eyes to meet mine, but when I look toward her father, she dips her head as if in shame. Eliana is thin—too thin—and her once-shiny hair is so dull and barren that the pink of her scalp shows through in places. How? How could such a change have occurred in such a short amount of time?

Both sisters wear ashes in their hair to signify humility. Eliana grips her sister's hand in protection, and I wish Calev was here to see that it is her kindness that makes her beautiful.

"Are you all right, son?"

My mother has slipped beside me. She too is dressed in sackcloth; none of her clothes are made of fine, soft linen though, so I don't suppose she suffers too much from the coarseness of the animal-hair weave.

I smile. It's impossible not to smile at my mother's gentle kindness. I suppose when she was Eliana's age, she was beautiful. To me, she still is.

"Son, I do not wish to be alone."

I understand. I've never seen so many unbelievers, and I fear they've come not only from Elam, but from the wilderness and other villages. I hear them murmur, and I see them mingle with some of Elam's own.

I grip my blade and ache for a chance to use it. It's this anger—this hatred—this overpowering resentment that burns within me. I feel so helpless, so worthless standing here, doing nothing more than listening to prayers and preaching.

"I wish I was on the battlefront," I whisper to Mother. "I wish I was with Calev instead of standing here."

"You *want* to be in battle?"

"I do."

Mother's eyes flare until I see gold flecks shine through the deep brown. Her tone is suddenly harsh. "Everything in life is not a battle, Kiah."

"How can you say that? Everything we do requires a fight: finding food, finding water, making fire. Keeping the serpents and insects out of our home is a battle. I saw you earlier today, Mother; it was a battle for you to face Oshra and to hear her pretend to be concerned about our family. I saw how your lips pressed into a straight line; you were battling back the words you wanted to say to her. I know it. Every act of life is surely a battle."

I did not mean for my words to be so sharp. Mother hangs her head in defeat, and I realize I've won this small battle. I've managed to steal her smile, but the victory tastes bitter.

Now Elam's high priest, Lem—the man who took Jacob's place—stands on the front steps of the synagogue where we can all see him. He is missing his right eye, a battle wound, and wears a patch of leather across that side of his face. Lem asks Grandfather to lead our wasted people in desperate prayer.

Nine

After Grandfather's prayer, we move from the synagogue steps to the shady side of Elam's largest worship pyramid. It is only a gray mound compared to the giant pyramids of the temple grounds in Zarahemla, but it is all we have. It is the favorite meeting place for the judges and the priests.

I bite my tongue and wipe sweat from my face as the gathering continues into the heat of the day. A few birds sing in the high trees. I hear children laugh, and I hear parents warn them to show reverence. We have come to pray for the famine to end. The land around is flat and brown until it meets with the green jungle horizon line. The stone of the pyramid is dappled gray, like the river rocks in Zarahemla. How they were moved here is a mystery no one can explain—a mystery that Grandfather calls a miracle, though the pyramids were here long before he was born. In their shelter I feel small but safe.

We pray.

We listen to preaching.

We sing.

We pray again.

The sky remains cloudless. The sun remains strong.

We continue praying, and then Grandfather, using his walking stick, climbs to the high step. I bow my head and silently thank God for healing him.

"And if the time comes that the voice of the people doth choose iniquity," Grandfather shouts, "then is the time that the judgments of God will come upon you; yea, then is the time he will visit you with great destruction!"

I know he's quoting a prophet, but I can't remember which one. A loneliness grips me, and I miss my brother. I miss Jonas, my only real friend. It's been so long since I've seen him that I wonder how he's changed.

A crackling bolt shoots through me as Grandfather testifies, "My brothers and sisters, Nephi is a prophet of God. If, and only if, we heed his words will the curse upon this land be lifted."

A burly man, his face dotted with scars and his feathered headdress red and lopsided, hurls curses at Grandfather. Others, even believers, murmur. Hem seems agitated; he tugs at his beard, and I think he is going to shout out some type of protest. His mouth opens and closes like a fish caught in a net. His wife pulls at his sleeve, and he says nothing. I walk around to the side so I can get a clearer view of Hem. It's then I realize that he has been stricken with palsy. The right side of his face sags, and spittle threads from the corner of his mouth. One eye droops. He says nothing because he *can't* speak. I know that it's wrong, but a swell of satisfaction rises up in me. Grandfather was right: sometimes it is best to wait patiently and to allow God to deliver justice.

"Our Lord sees our penitent state," Grandfather continues. "He knows our hearts. There is no thought we think that He does not know. No deed we do of which He is unaware. Pray that our afflictions might humble us to the point of repentance."

I watch Hem. His sandals shift uneasily, back and forth on the smooth stone surface where he has stationed himself. He seems unsteady, and Eliana rushes to his side so he can use her shoulder for a crutch. The only discouraging part of seeing him so weak is seeing her so wounded. She may have been upset with her father's refusal to provide ample food for their family, but there is something in the tenderness with which she treats Hem. It makes me wonder about my own father. Is he suffering too? Does he ever think of the wife and sons he abandoned? Does he feel concern for his own aging father? Any feeling I have for my father is sharp and hard, without a shred of the tenderness that defines Eliana.

I wonder when and how this mishap came upon Hem. Did he feel pain? Did he wake up one morning unable to control his own face? I can't help but smile when I see villagers approach him with their pity. He tries to wave them off, but his words are slurred and his hand will not rise with either height or speed.

As my grandfather speaks, I wonder if his sermon condemns Hem. Has God convicted Hem of his crimes? He looks penitent in his sackcloth, his hair sooted with ashes. What is concealed in his heart? Does his band of robbers still see him as their leader, or do they see him as less now that he is so broken? I see him look up and search the crowd until his eyes meet those of the coppersmith. Abner's fiery red head stands above most in the crowd, and I see him quickly look away when he realizes Hem is staring at him. Is Abner also one of Hem's robbers? Who else? I scan the crowd; it's large because our need is large. People from the outlying areas have come also, hoping to be part of a movement that ends this famine. I can't help but be suspicious of nearly everyone.

Mother has retreated to the outskirts on the side with the other women, though she does not mingle with them. My heart aches for the endless days she spends as an outcast. It's not fair. When I was younger I used to imagine that my father would return to our village, to our family—that he would beg my mother's forgiveness and restore her good standing and that of our family. I used to imagine that he would fashion a bow for me, that we would sharpen arrows together and hunt, the four of us—Grandfather, Father, Calev, and me. Time has pinched those dreams from me.

Now that I am older, sometimes when I see my mother so ostracized and lonely, I have a flash of hope that a righteous man will take note—not only of my mother's beauty, but also of her good heart and gentle tongue. If she married again, I would not have to worry about caring for her like I do now. But other than Grandfather, is there a truly righteous man in our entire village? His sermon now pounds at our pride, telling us that our colorful cloaks and shiny adornments are symbols of pride and division. He reminds us that we can outwardly hide our sins but that God looks deeper—into the very centers of our hearts.

Tension in the crowd is building. Nephi's name is either revered or resented. Twice I hear people mention Grandfather's name in the same short breath as Nephi's.

"Why have we this day substituted our colorful clothes for sackcloth?" Grandfather shouts, trying to drum up enthusiasm from a group that has no energy for enthusiasm.

A few voices in the crowd reply, "To demonstrate humility."

"And why do we put ashes on our heads?"

"To demonstrate repentance."

I feel eyes staring at me, and I turn to see both Hem and Eliana gazing in my direction. From a distance across the great flat of the pyramid I cannot tell whether it is me they are seeing. Regardless, the fear I felt is gone. What can a man so weak and afflicted do to punish me?

Grandfather finishes with his stirring testimony of the coming Messiah. I wait to see if he requires help climbing back down the steps. He manages slowly but with dignity. A priest takes his place. Baruwk is one of the younger judges, a stout man with a deep voice that carries easily on the breeze.

"Ye are sinners! This famine has been brought upon the innocent by the sins of the guilty!"

A few voices around me mutter. Hem's cheeks bulge and turn an angry red when the man mentions Gadianton's name. Again I see the exchange between Hem and Abner. I also think I see Abner look at Noah, the grieving father of Kahana. What is going on between all of them? "You are sinners!" the judge cries out. "Sinners and nothing more! If you do not repent we will all face destruction!"

"Who does he think he is?" Noah calls out. "He's not a prophet; he's only a priest."

I hear the word *believers* spit out of several mouths, like it is foul to be among those who believe. It's then I realize that the people are in the process of physically dividing themselves—not only the men from the women, but those who do not believe in Nephi from those who do.

My throat tightens, and the backs of my hands bead with sweat, exactly as they do when I sense a snake is nearby. Something is about to happen. Something deadly.

Again, Hem's eyes meet Abner's. Is it a signal?

In that instant a rock flies past my face, nearly pelting me. I duck, and the stone lands directly in the chest of the young priest. He cries out just as another rock slaps the side of his head. Blood spurts, and he takes cover behind one of the two giant stone pillars. Chaos erupts. The crowd flees in every direction. People scream. A rock hits me in the back, and I feel the pain all the way into my head.

Everywhere I look I see panic and fear. People shout and rush in all directions. It is as though we are all dry wood set ablaze by the flame of red-hot anger. I look first for my mother and see that she is being pushed and shoved. As I rush to her, I spot Grandfather's crumpled form, lying on the ground, people pounding over him like he is already dead.

Ten

The warrior in me fights like it has never fought before. I've never battled for a greater cause. With Grandfather's own walking stick, I beat away anyone who would step on him or bring him further harm. His face is bloody and already swollen. His right arm is twisted and angled to the side like it has been broken.

"Grandfather?"

His eyes are closed, and he does not stir.

"Grandfather! It's Kiah! Are you all right?" I take his hand and lean down to speak into his ear. "I'm here. No one else will hurt you."

It takes a while for Mother to reach us. I've never seen her so horrified. Her already-rent dress is ripped further; her braid has come undone, and her hair falls around her shoulders in tangled black strands. Her eyes look like those of a wounded doe.

"You are believers!" A woman I don't recognize shouts at Mother, then throws her head back and spits in Mother's face. I want to fling myself at the woman, but Grandfather gives my hand a squeeze.

"We cannot allow their anger to ignite ours," Mother shouts over the chaos of the crowd, wiping her face and kneeling beside me. "Kiah, we've got to move him."

"I'll carry Grandfather. Tell me where to take him."

The crazed courtyard is flat and barren except for the gray steps of the pyramid. Some people have climbed above us and are pelting rocks down on the crowd. From the corner of my eye I see Andrew and his friends having some sort of confrontation with our synagogue teacher, Benjamin.

A few others are on the ground, being trampled, but for the most part there is only a wild stampede of anger and fear. People are taking out their suffering on one another, blaming those who believe in Nephi for the famine.

Grandfather moans when I lift him, and I'm surprised at the weakness in my own body. It's difficult for me to hold him; my back spasms and my knees quake.

"Are you all right, Kiah?"

"I'm fine, Mother. I can do whatever is required of me."

"Then move quickly. We've got to get out of the way."

I ask her to stand in front of me, and I bend my knees slightly so that I can heft Grandfather into a better position. A sudden pain sears through my shoulder, and I look up to see that Andrew has thrown a rock, nearly hitting Grandfather's head. Andrew calls me a name that means "fatherless son." Then he calls my mother something even worse.

I can't chase after him—but if I could, I would push him from the highest steps of the pyramid. As it is, Grandfather is so limp and heavy that I stumble. My own body shakes. I have never felt such emotion; it's as though there is a blaze inside of me burning to get out. I want to fight, yet I cannot— instead, I must tend to Grandfather.

"Concentrate," Mother orders. I've never heard her shout like this, and her voice seems unfamiliar to me. Everything is unfamiliar. We are a divided people: believers against unbelievers. Neighbor against neighbor. Even brother against brother. It's impossible to comprehend how we could turn on our own so quickly and so viciously.

Whenever any enemy has come against us, we have banded together, but now we are fighting among ourselves. The one word I hear shouted over and over is *Messiah*. Those who believe in Him are fewer than those who do not; that is clear to me now. I know the side my family occupies . . . I know the side I am on.

"Let me take him."

I look over and see Abner, the coppersmith. He is tall and able and has Grandfather in his arms before I can protest. He carries Grandfather off to the side where we are partly concealed by the column opposite of the one where the priest took refuge. I do not trust Abner, but he is strong and quick in helping.

"I saw you and Hem," I shout.

Abner's only response is to take his outer cloak off so he can make a pillow for Grandfather's bleeding head.

"Thank you," Mother says. Her trembling fingers are pulling Grandfather's hair back so she can inspect the gashes in his scalp. Some of them are deep and gushing, and rage overtakes my fear.

"You are most welcome," Abner tells her.

There is no way I can miss the exchange between my mother and the coppersmith. It lasts no longer than a flash of lightning, but it is real. I see the way he looks at her, even if it only for an instant. She barely raises her eyes to meet his, but I see it. There is a charge between the two. I can't consider it now. I can't. There is no time to worry about Abner's intentions toward my mother. All I can focus on is making sure that Grandfather is all right.

Abner shares the last drops of water from his waterskin to wash away Grandfather's blood, and I am relieved to see that the wounds are not as deep as I thought. "Look around," Abner says "Our people have gone mad."

I stare at him suspiciously. Why is he helping us if he is conspiring with Hem? He is large in stature—so large he would have stood out if he'd been among Hem's band of robbers that day. I would have seen him, recognized him. He is well-known throughout our village, for he is a man of tragedy. His wife died giving birth some time back—as did the baby. Since then he has been a sad shadow around Elam.

Watching Abner move, I cannot help but be impressed with the fluid way he moves, fast and sure, wielding away anyone who might bring Grandfather further harm. He is like a self-appointed guardian . . . but is Abner attending Grandfather or my mother? For so long I've wished a man would pay proper attention to her, but now I feel strange and resentful.

"What happened?"

We all look to see that Grandfather is blinking. He looks dazed, but he is aware. Mother is quick to wipe the blood from his eyes and drizzle the final drops of water onto his lips.

"Kiah and I are with you," she says. "A mob broke out. You've been knocked to the ground. Is your arm broken?"

He struggles to sit upright and winces when he tries to straighten his arm. "Where am I?"

"We've sheltered you as best we can, Yarden. You will be all right."

"Abner?"

"Yes, my friend. I will let no more harm come to you or to your family."

Grandfather's chest rises and falls. His eyes roll back and I hold my breath in dread, but finally he asks, "What of the others? The judges? The priests?"

"I've never seen Elam in such chaos. It's horrific."

I peer around the pillar; from our vantage I see that much of the chaos has settled, but it is far from over. There is still shouting and screaming. A few others are taking refuge where we are. Two women nearby are crying over the beaten body of a man that lies in a heap. I should go help, but I do not want to leave.

"Kiah?"

I bend and kiss Grandfather's cheek. A tear falls from my face to his, and I feel foolish—boyish—for crying.

Abner asks, "Yarden, what can we do? This division is strong."

Grandfather leans against his shoulder. "A divided snake is the most dangerous."

Abner and Mother think Grandfather is speaking nonsense, but I understand him completely.

"Grandfather, do not fear. We are not divided. We stand with the believers who await the Messiah." I'm surprised at my own words, at the strength of the conviction that burns within me. It is finally faith? Anger? Hatred? Fear? So many emotions.

"This is only the beginning," Grandfather mumbles.

Abner looks over and sees the two women endeavoring to move the fallen man. He rushes to their aid and brings the man over to us; the women follow. The man is dead. I look at his body long enough to see it is that of the young priest Baruwk.

There is a sad exchange between Grandfather and the women, and Mother tries to comfort them.

Abner stands on a step higher than the rest of us. Loud enough for everyone to hear, he announces, "This is Hem's doing. Hem is responsible for this good man's death."

I'm shocked at the declaration.

Cradling Grandfather's head in her lap, Mother looks up at Abner. "I saw Hem. He has palsy now."

"I saw him too," Abner tell us. "I saw him give a signal to Noah. I'm sure Noah's pockets were filled with stones. So were the pockets of others."

Mother seems confused. I am confused, too.

"Why didn't *you* stop Hem if you saw what he was doing?" I ask.

Abner looks at me like he's only just now aware that I am there, but when he speaks to me there is no condescension. "I didn't know exactly what he was planning. I only kept my eye on him because the man is never up to good. Even in his sickly state, Hem is still a dangerous man."

Does Abner know? I want to question him, to press him for the truth, but it is rude for someone of my age to pressure an elder, even under these circumstances.

"Hem is a bitter man. He's angry with God for punishing him with palsy. He should be humble and penitent; he's not."

"What should we do?" Mother asks Abner. "Where can we go that will be safe?"

Abner's hand reaches out and grips my shoulder. His fingers are almost twice as long as mine, but he squeezes just hard enough to let me feel his strength. He looks to Mother. "Anat, your son and I both understand that as long as Hem is still around, no place is safe."

Eleven

So Abner knows. He knows the accusation I made against Hem, and he knows that it is true. Though I want to be the man of the family—to take charge and make decisions—I do what Mother does: I look to Abner for guidance. He calls over a group of men who help move the body of the young priest. Mother gives her wrap to the widow so she can conceal her sorrow.

"Should we go back home?" I ask, not knowing if it is safe for us to walk through Elam, not at all certain we'll be protected in our own small yard and hut.

"Do you want me to go find Pazel the healer?" Abner asks Grandfather.

"No. No. I want to go home."

"I can carry you back to your home," Abner says to Grandfather.

"You will have to take me further than that if I am to be safe. It's no longer safe for me here—or for any of us." The gash on his forehead oozes fresh red blood, and every time he moves his arm he winces with pain.

"I'm thirsty."

"Let me fetch you water, Grandfather. I'll go to the well."

"You won't be safe."

"I *will* be safe.

Abner thrusts his empty waterskin at me. "Take this. Fill it at the well. I'll carry your grandfather back to your home. Your mother will be safe. Go. I'll meet you shortly."

I hesitate. "Grandfather says we won't be safe at our home."

"If Abner is there we will be fine," Grandfather struggles to tell me.

Abner is a man that I do not know, cannot yet trust.

"Go!" Grandfather says, his head falling back into the folds of Mother's lap.

My feet fly as I wind my way through a scene of confusion and destruction. There is no longer an angry mob. Those men have dispersed, gone back to their holes like snakes into the ground. Families are left divided. Women weep.

Children look frightened. Men look stunned. I am uncertain of exactly what has happened, but I am also unafraid. A fiery surge, primal and fierce, courses through my veins. My blade is sheathed against my thigh, and I know I will use it without hesitation. I've never fought another human being, but I will to protect my family. I am not only willing for battle; I am eager.

There are others at the well—wounded people, waiting to draw water from a hole that yields only dregs. The water that comes up is clouded but precious. A trio of village elders stands around, relegating the precious commodity request by request.

"My grandfather was trampled," I tell them. "I do not wish to fill an entire vessel, only this waterskin."

"Your grandfather is Yarden, a priest?"

"Yes."

"You too are a believer in the coming Messiah?"

There is no hesitancy, though for the first time fear clutches my throat and threatens to choke my words. "I am a believer."

Immediately, I feel stronger.

The men exchange looks. One draws his wooden sword, and fear tells me that he is going to slit my throat, but he points with his chipped blade. "Fill your pouch and tell your grandfather to pray harder. Elam needs his faith."

I draw enough to fill the pouch, and a slave girl appointed to the task offers me a cup. I look to the men for permission before drinking. They indicate that it is all right for me to take the cup, and I do so gratefully. As I gulp the water down I realize how long it has been since I've savored such an indulgence. For so long now I have had to sip carefully the allotment that Mother fetches. I do not recognize the girl who offers the cup, but I cannot help but look at her. Her eyes are green, the color of spring leaves, and her skin is fairer than my own. Where is she from? I would like to know her name, but there is no time and no opportunity. My pouch is full, my cup is empty, and I am ushered off with a swipe of the monitor's blade.

I look back, but the girl is handing another cup to another thirsty person. She makes me think of Eliana. Has she gone back to her stone home with its high walls? Does she know that her father raised his feeble hand to cause all the trouble? Does she know that he is evil?

I return with the waterskin, and Grandfather gulps gratefully. Mother drinks. Then Abner holds it out to me.

"I had a cup at the well."

Only then does he take a drink. I lean over and whisper so that only he can hear. "I'm going to go make sure that it's safe for us to leave here. I'll go check the back way, the old trail that runs in front of the ball court."

Abner doesn't deny me or treat me like a child. "Be safe and return quickly." He nods and I slip away before Mother can protest.

Most of the people have returned to their homes and I hurry, taking a shortcut behind the synagogue courtyard, beyond the ball court where the robber was stoned. I run, holding my breath to see if I can make it the length of the court. I imagine a time when trickball players kept a rubber ball in the air, never allowing it to touch the ground. I run down the centerline and then curve over and jump high to try to touch the stone hoop that the ball must pass through.

Though I have never attended such a game, Grandfather says that there was a time when the winning team was forced to sacrifice their lives in honor of the false gods they worshipped. There are still tribes who sacrifice their players. The idea frightens me, and I let my imagination run along with my feet, slapping over the stones, jumping high, trying to keep an imaginary ball from hitting the ground. I twist and turn, using my elbows, my knees, my head, and even my shoulders to keep the ball in the air. If it falls to the ground I will be flogged.

I breathe before I reach the end. When I finally stop I see him. He sits alone on a stone bench, his head buried in his hands.

Hem.

The warrior in me rises tall and strong. Hatred for this man and his deceit rage larger than my stature. I look around and realize that no one is around but the two of us.

"Where is Eliana?"

He does not raise his head.

"Where is your daughter, Eliana? Is she safe?"

I can't be sure of his words because he mutters, but I think he says, "She abandoned me here."

"Good."

Now Hem lifts his head. Half of his face is the face of a man, the other half belongs to a creature. One eye is swollen, and his beard is thick with dirt and what I take to be a mix of vomit and blood. It looks like he has taken a foot to the face. "Good," I say again, though for a different reason.

I glance around just to be sure. Yes, we are alone. The nearest people are off in the distance, occupied with their own troubles. "I know who you really are," I say. The blade is out of its sheath, in my grip, and I am aware that I want nothing more than to plunge it into his chest. I could do it and walk away. Better yet, my eye catches a glint, and I see that Hem too has a blade. It is small and one of the few blades I've ever seen made mostly of metal. It rests at his feet, and I know that I could grab it and stab him with his own blade.

That would be justice. There would be no witnesses, and Hem would never again give an order to hurt anyone else.

His black eyes—pig's eyes—look at me as a river of red spit runs out of the side of his mouth.

"You've caused all of this. You and your secret band of robbers. I know all about you."

He makes a strangled sound, and I see a mix of confusion and fear in his twisted expression. I have never felt so brave, so angry, so overtaken with hatred. What did the ancient prophet Nephi say . . . it was better for Laban to die than for an entire nation to perish because of unbelief?

My fingers tighten around my blade and I look around again, just to be sure that we are alone. Killing Hem in his weakened state will be as easy as Nephi slaying Laban in his drunken condition. But would it be the *right* thing?

A vile, evil side of me turns a face to Hem.

I want Hem to feel fear. I want him to experience what he and his band have caused women and children and even brave men to experience. In one fast move I snatch his blade. He gurgles and tries to slide away but falls over and struggles to right himself.

"Do you know me?" I ask.

A fresh strand of saliva pours from his mouth.

"I am Kiah, grandson of Yarden."

He keeps making strange choking noises as I recount the day I came upon him and his band of robbers. "I know you are aware of my accusations. You thought you had gotten away with murder and plunder and sin of every kind." I smile and wet my lips like a beast ready for first blood. "But you, mighty Hem, have gotten away with nothing."

The blade slashes through the air, this way and that, demonstrating to him what I am about to do to his throat. His nostrils flare. Spit runs. His body convulses and he begs, mumbling, "Do not harm me—I beg you."

"I will not *harm* you," I say, growling. "I will *kill* you so that you can never harm another." I lift my hand but my arm feels heavy.

"Father, what am I to do?"

Usually my prayers are uttered in silence, but this one comes out loud and pleading. I slam my eyes shut and feel lost in the darkness. The hatred within me drains out, like sweat from pores. I feel weak and ill. The knife is still lifted, but I am not the warrior I thought myself to be.

"Kiah! Kiah! Kiah, please, I beg—no!"

I look and see Eliana charging toward me. On her face is the same mask of terror that her father wears.

Twelve

The trip to Zarahemla should take only one full day, but with Grandfather so weak and disabled—limping, with his arm in a sling—and our unrelenting caution for our safety, it is three full days before we reach the highway outside of the great walled city. All along the way I wonder how Grandfather and Mother can be so content. People are divided, malicious and bloodthirsty. Our lives are in jeopardy, and yet Grandfather and Mother plod along in complete peace.

I can tell Grandfather is in great pain, but his testimony is strong. "Kiah, one day you too will have the personal revelation that Jesus is the Christ. We belong to His church and His cause. The world can crumble around us. Horrific things can happen. Let them come, for we know whom we serve and for what cause we continue."

I doubt that I will ever feel the peace Grandfather does. I almost *killed* a man. I wanted Hem to die, even to suffer. I wanted to rid Elam of his deceit and danger. Eliana's expression was powerful enough to drive me back. Now she believes I am capable of cold-blooded murder. I'm not. I know that, but she does not. What will she tell Calev? How can our families ever unite in marriage now?

"Are you feeling tired, son?" Mother asks. "We can stop and rest in the shade."

"I'm not tired; I'm just thinking." I can't stop thinking. I haven't told Mother or even Grandfather what happened. How can I? But when Grandfather announced that we were leaving Elam to spend time with Nephi, Jonas, and their entire family, I was eager to leave.

"What of Calev?" Mother asked. "He'll return home from battle and think we have abandoned him."

"I will send an epistle to Uriel," Grandfather said. "Calev can join us in Zarahemla."

We walk on, mostly in silence. Abner follows behind, our small family's rearguard. He says he is protecting Grandfather from the angry mobs that still prowl, ready to attack anyone they feel is responsible for the famine. Believers are their targets—and no one believes in Jesus Christ with more fervor than Grandfather. At every turn in the road he lifts his voice to testify of the Messiah's love and power to restore the sinner. Abner has to hold back the crowd, has to threaten those who threaten Grandfather.

I realize that Abner is dedicating his time and risking his own safety for more than Grandfather. He is making the sacrifice so that he can be near my mother. The two barely acknowledge each other, but their feelings are obvious.

Mother has expressed a desire to go into the city to make a sacrifice at the temple, one that she prays will heal the wounds of our people and bring Calev home safely. Since we have no money for a dove, Mother has brought an embryonic ear of corn, the most tender she could find, wrapped carefully in cloth.

I know little of the temple and the worship that goes on behind its high walls. When I was an infant I was presented there; when I was older I accompanied Grandfather to one of the festivals.

A group of people walks past us, and a girl my age turns to look at me. I think of Eliana and how I tried to explain why I had raised a blade to her father.

"Your father is a robber, a Gadianton robber," I told her then.

She stood in front of me, her mouth open so that I could see the pink of her tongue.

"He leads the robbers. I saw him meet with them."

"You lie!" she said.

"No. I speak the truth. I realize he is your father, but Hem is an evil man. You must believe me."

"Believe *you*? Kiah, you hide in the bush and scare us. You are *nothing* like your brother—you're just a crazy boy with a knife."

I think of the fear in her eyes, and I think of the victory in Hem's. His final look toward me was one of vengeance. He will extract from me a price one day, a price I do not want to try to imagine.

• • •

When we reach the walls of the prophet's home they seem higher than I remember, made of the same gray-dappled stone as the pyramid in Elam. The wooden gate is heavy, and two servants stand beside it as guards. Grandfather announces who we are and why we have come. I feel anxious—ready to see Jonas, ready to forget my life in Elam.

The gates swing wide open, and Nephi, the son of Nephi, hurries to greet Grandfather. They embrace as brothers; Nephi, a burly man with dark hair and sunbaked skin, is careful of Grandfather's injured arm. I hear a shout and look to see Jonas running toward us. He is the son of Nephi, grandson to the prophet Nephi.

Jonas's bare feet slap the carefully laid stone of their courtyard. He tilts a head of curly light brown hair. "You've changed. You look like a man, Kiah."

My shoulders go back, and I can't help smiling. "I was just thinking the same thing about you, Jonas."

Their home is nothing like our dried-mud-and-grass hut. It's more like a fortress with its stone walls and floors of packed red earth—its rock tower and gardens that still bloom red, yellow, and purple. The collection of water for purification is ornate and large, though there is little water for washing. The famine has not spared the family of the prophet.

When I was younger I never noticed, but now I see the skill that went into constructing this compound, due mostly to the talent of Jonas's father, Nephi, who has mastered the art of cement and how to layer it over wooden structures to make everything smooth and uniform. I can't help staring and feeling like I've somehow walked into another world. There are others around: servants, kin, and cousins that watch us from a distance. I've forgotten what it feels like to be around a large family. We greet each other as kinsmen. Up close I see that Jonas's eyes are ringed with dark shadows and his arms are thin where muscles used to bulge.

"How long can you stay?" he asks. "I can't wait to go hunting with you." A glint from his belt reveals that Jonas has a new knife.

"Kiah and his family will reside here for a while," Nephi tells his son. "I know I can count on you to make Kiah feel welcome."

Jonas grins and I feel a weight lifting from my shoulders. Here I can be young and carefree. Here I can forget the ugliness we left behind in Elam.

Already the servants are helping Grandfather and Mother into the courtyard shade. Others are bringing a washing cup that we might properly cleanse our hands. All I can feel is relief and hope that we are safe and in a better place.

I see that Mother's cheeks are damp with gratitude as she is greeted by the women of the family. Bosma, the prophet's wife, kisses the tears from Mother's cheeks. Jonas's mother, Devora, is named after the buzzing insect that makes such sweet nectar. It's a good name for her because she is sweet and buzzes about, always humming. I love her for the way she unburdens Mother, taking the basket of our few goods from atop Mother's head. This greeting is so very different from the treatment Mother receives in Elam from women like Oshra. I can only imagine what she feels, and I suddenly want to hug my mother, to kiss her cheeks myself. But that is an act a boy would perform, and I am no longer a boy.

A flash of Hem's twisted and frightened face flashes in my mind; I blink hard to erase it. Another servant brings water, and we all drink gratefully.

"Come!" Jonas calls as he darts off.

I look to Grandfather for permission to follow after my friend. He nods and smiles, and I soon find that Jonas's legs are longer than mine; I have to make a real effort to follow him down the grooved pathway, out a back gate, right toward the thick of the tangle. *Chuwens* are thick in the high trees, screeching, hanging by their long, black tails. I hear Mother call after me and I'm tempted to stop and bid her a proper good-bye, but Jonas is running fast and I must sprint to catch up to him.

I might consider myself a man, but the heart of a boy returns to me and I run carefree for the first time in as long as I can remember. We run and run. As soon as there is a break through which I can see the valley it's obvious that the famine's death grip is strong here too—maybe even stronger than in our highlands. Here in the flat fields the famine's destruction is undeniable. Green has faded to a mix of yellows and browns. Plants have withered. Trees droop and produce leaves so brittle they crunch in my palm.

Jonas scales high into the sanctuary of an ancient mango tree. There is no fruit on the limbs—only tiny shriveled things, aborted by the famine. A bird's nest has a trio of speckled eggs, all of them hollow and worthless. We each stretch out on barren but sturdy branches. Jonas lays his head back and closes his eyes.

I have missed my friend. We used to play together often when I was much younger. Back then I would accompany Grandfather and Calev as we walked the highway into the city. Jonas would call to us from the prayer tower in his grandfather's garden. Then we'd spend hours exploring the very places where we are now. This is not the first time I've been high in this fruit tree. I also have memories of times when Jonas accompanied his father into our village whenever they would pass through doing cement work.

"It's terrible, isn't it?" Jonas points to the withering land stretched before us.

"How long do you think this famine will last?"

Jonas flicks an ant from his hand. "I don't know. I wish I knew."

"What does your grandfather say? He's the prophet. He knows."

Jonas shakes his head like he is trying to get rid of a bad thought. "Tell me about your life, Kiah. What has happened with you since I last saw you?"

Words tumble out of my mouth, stories of my adventures in the highlands tracking the black *chakmool*, never coming closer than the day I stumbled upon the robbers. Even though no one else is around, I lower my voice when I tell Jonas of Hem and his band.

Jonas's finger points to a dark, distant field. "See that large portion of black farmland?"

"It looks like a grain crop that was set aflame by lightning."

"By robbers. It's what they did the last time they came down from their hiding places. They stole our floundering wheat, then set the field on fire so we couldn't even glean the remnants."

"I hate the robbers. I especially hate Hem. I almost killed him."

Jonas squints. "You did what?"

I tell him everything. Jonas does not judge me or preach about my faults. He only listens, cutting and sharpening a branch with his blade while I talk.

Jonas slips his blade back into the leather sheath that hangs from his belt. "Maybe you have feelings for Hem's daughter. Perhaps that's why you're so upset that she caught you nearly killing her father."

"No," I say sincerely. "Eliana is the girl Calev favors. I have no feelings for her or any other girl. I'm upset because I nearly took a life, Jonas. The rage that rises up inside me is terrifying."

He smiles. "You don't scare me—and I don't think you would have killed Hem, not when he was so weak and unable to defend himself. It's not like you."

"I hope not. I pray that God will forgive me."

"I suspect He already has."

Then I listen as Jonas talks of his own life. He tells me of apprenticing alongside his father, learning the arts of working with cement. The twinge that strikes my heart is so sudden and sharp it catches me off guard. Why does it hurt so much when other sons work alongside their fathers?

Jonas's face lights up when he mentions Lysa, a girl from Zarahelma who has captured his heart. "She's pretty," he says, grinning, "but she laughs like a donkey." He brays to demonstrate and I laugh, grateful to be away from the sad place my home has become.

"Your father is not choosing your wife?" I ask.

Jonas wipes his forehead with the back of his hand. "No, thankfully. Father makes suggestions but doesn't favor arranged marriages."

I think it's odd that we are talking about marriage. It's not that I don't think about girls—I do, but they don't interest me like adventure. We climb yet higher, and I can see the winding wall of Zarahemla. It's taller than a tall man stands and made of the same gray stone that has built most of the city. I can see the layout of the temple with its own wall. The city is larger and busier than I remember; every road is dotted with crowds going about their business. Most roads are paved with stones, but some are constructed of dirt—and when people walk, little red clouds fill the air. From our high vantage life does not seem crippled like it does from the ground. I can see that the land is scarred, but at least the city is alive with movement.

"Timber is scarce," Jonas says. "Trees are cut when they're still young. It won't be long until even this tree will be hewn down and made into someone's business or home."

The idea alarms me. I know that there is no stopping those who make their living selling timber, but the idea that a tree that offers such refuge will be soon be cut makes me sad. We watch for a long time as people wind their way around.

I see one tall, lone figure walking, and I remember Abner. We simply left him behind us when we entered the prophet's gate. I hope he is not offended.

Jonas and I are still up in the tree when a string of men makes its way down the pathway. The men are carrying weapons and their voices rise angrily.

Jonas goes stiff. He motions for me to stay still while he leans toward me, whispering, "The man in the lead is a judge."

The man in the lead is carrying a club. "What do they want?"

"They want my father."

I sense the fear in his voice. "Why *your* father?"

"They want him to convince my grandfather to stop the famine."

Only God can stop the famine, I realize, wondering who will stop the angry men.

Thirteen

My first worry is for Mother and Grandfather, but by the time we rush back to the prophet's home, Jonas's father is out by the gate facing the angry men. He's not alone; his servants are with him. So is another man who resembles Nephi.

"That's my uncle, Timothy."

"Your father doesn't have a weapon to defend himself." I reach for my blade.

"He has God on his side."

I look at Jonas's father—Nephi, son of Nephi. He is a man built of hard labor and warfare. His back is broad and his muscles strong. In one hand he clutches a holy book, something rare to see outside a synagogue.

Jonas creeps closer, ready to defend his father if necessary. I creep closer, ready to defend Jonas if necessary. It's only been days since a scene like this played out in Elam. It ended in chaos and at least one man's death. The men here seem every bit as angry, and they are demanding to see the prophet Nephi.

"My father is not well." There is a spirit about Nephi, son of Nephi, larger than even his stature. He is both strong and kind.

The judge lifts his club. "Your father has brought this famine upon our land."

Nephi raises the book of scripture. "The Lord alone can do such miracles."

"Miracles! What *miracle*? We are burying our dying people every day. How long will your father permit this famine to continue?"

I lean over and whisper into Jonas's ear. "Is your grandfather inside the house?"

"Yes."

"Is he safe?"

"Timothy just walked back into the house. He will protect my grandfather—and yours."

My body goes tense with eagerness. "We should do something to help."

"Let's wait and see what happens."

Jonas has the same spirit as his father. It is more than strength and kindness: it is peace. Am I the only one agitated and uncertain?

"Is your grandfather really sick?" I ask.

Jonas nods. "He'll be all right, though. The Lord protects those who serve Him."

"My grandfather is a faithful believer, yet he got trampled by a crazed mob."

Jonas whispers, "But he didn't die. When we keep the commandments we have protection."

"What about Abinadi? He kept the Lord's commandments, and he got burned to death."

I feel scolded by the look Jonas gives me. In the voice of a preacher he tells me, "Sometimes I think even my grandfather, the prophet, doesn't understand everything, but I know that the Lord protects us when we honor Him. I've seen it. Think of Abraham, whose own father was asked to sacrifice him to idols. How many times was Moses sheltered from the harm others wanted to inflict on him? And Father Lehi would have been killed in Jerusalem if the Lord hadn't protected him."

I have to quell Jonas's enthusiasm so our presence is not discovered. I marvel at my friend's faith. It comes so easily to him. For an instant jealousy ripples through me because while my grandfather might not be a prophet, he is a man of God. Faith should flow through my heart too, but it doesn't; it gets clogged by feelings of resentment and pride.

I am lost in my thoughts until I look up and realize the angry voices have calmed. Nephi is speaking to the men about the Messiah and all that we as a people must to do prepare for His coming.

"Follow me," Jonas whispers; he takes off down the path. I follow. After a while he veers into the hedge and into a concealed tunnel; I have to practically fold myself in half to fit through the opening, and I wriggle like a serpent to follow Jonas. Plants have grown up inside of it; branches slice at my bare legs and arms and a thorn scratches my face, but Jonas ducks and bobs with skill. It's not long before the two of us are behind the safety of his courtyard wall.

"Come inside," Jonas says, waving me to enter a side door.

Their home is a palace compared to our hut. It's dark inside because there are no cracks that let the sun shine through the ceiling or the cement walls—

it only filters in through covered windows. It is cooler than standing in the shade. The floors are not all packed dirt; footpaths of cut stones are smooth and against my feet. There are carvings on the wall and growing plants that bloom bright in spite of the low light and scarcity of water. I am tempted to stand still and enjoy being here just as I would stand beneath a refreshing waterfall, but Jonas beckons me to follow him.

Timothy, Jonas's uncle, greets me with the respect due a man. "Your grandfather is resting. Your mother, if you are looking for her, is in the kitchen with my wife and some of the other women."

"Thank you." I feel very grateful that my grandfather can rest in shade and safety. I feel especially grateful that my mother can spend time with other women.

Jonas and I move down a hallway where I see a door that opens to a small room. I look in, and when I do I almost topple over Jonas. There on a bed in the small room is the body of a withered old man. His head is bowed in prayer and his face is partly obscured by his covering, but still I know him. He is the great prophet, Nephi.

I don't know what to say. My mind cannot fathom what my eyes see. The last time I saw our prophet he was nearly as strong as Jonas's father—a man used to hard labor, a man whose body was sinewy and powerful. This man is old and worn to nothing but skin and bones.

Jonas touches my shoulder. "People think that the famine is hurting only *them.* They think the righteous are spared, but I think my grandfather suffers far more than most."

It's difficult for me to comprehend that this is the son of the mighty prophet Helaman. The blood of Alma runs through his veins. This is a man who served as chief judge over all of our land. This is a man who has given his life to missionary work.

I keep my voice low. "You said the Lord protects those who serve Him."

"He does—but He still allows them to suffer."

"Why?" I ask. "Why would God allow your grandfather to suffer like *this?*"

Jonas frowns. "Earlier you brought up Abinadi. Sometimes I wonder if the Lord does not give the most difficult trials to those who claim to love Him most."

I shake the heavy thoughts from my head. "You sound like a prophet in training." I am unable to take my eyes from the man whose faith has sealed the very heavens. What will happen to us if Nephi dies? Will the famine kill everyone?

"Is that you, Jonas?" The prophet lifts his head and hoarsely whispers, "Come in, son. Sit with me for a time."

Like an anxious child, Jonas bounds into the small room. He greets his grandfather and sits on the narrow slab. "Is there something I can bring you, Grandfather? A pillow? A sip of water? I saw Mother broiling some bones this morning. I can bring you broth."

"Your good mother has already brought me broth; thank you." The man's cloudy eyes focus on me. I can tell it's hard for him to breathe, but he forces a smile and says, "You cannot be Kiah."

"I am."

"You have grown, son. Come, sit with us."

There is no room on the bed, so I fold myself and sit on the floor at the side of the prophet.

"How is Yarden?"

It takes a moment for me to realize he is asking about my grandfather; I seldom hear him called by his given name. "He's here, resting in another room. He'll be in to see you later."

"And your mother, is she also here?"

"She is."

"How is your mother, Kiah?"

What can I say about Mother—that she is rapidly starving to death? That she is an outcast? That she is so lonely she accepts attention from Abner? "My mother has much faith."

"Your mother is a virtuous woman. God is mindful of her." The old man smiles, and the skin of his face folds back in layers. His hand reaches out to cover mine. I swear the truth swims in the depths of his dark eyes. They look at me, and I feel as though I have no secrets. The prophet sees into my heart. Does he know that I lifted a blade to take the life of a man incapable of defending himself? Does he know *why* I did it?

We sit in silence for a time, and Jonas seems completely comfortable. I'm not. I have the prophet's warm, trembling hand on mine. What is he discerning about me? He is no longer the strong man he once was. Is this why Grandfather did not press him to take action against Hem and his band of robbers?

We sit. The room is small, and with three people breathing, there is little fresh air. Finally, Nephi clears his rattling throat and says, "There is trouble at the gate."

I listen but hear nothing. No shouting. No voices at all.

"Yes, Grandfather," Jonas says. "Some men are angry about the famine. Father is speaking to them."

The prophet's hand slips away from mine, leaving a layer of sweat on my skin. He bows his head and his eyes close. The room is completely quiet, and I know that the prophet Nephi is saying a silent prayer. When his eyes open he smiles and he seems immediately stronger. "How quickly we forget the Lord God of Israel and His goodness to us." He sounds sad, ready to weep for the wickedness of others. In so many ways this prophet reminds me of Grandfather. I want to ask him when this famine will end. I want to beg him to make it stop, to unseal the heavens and let the rain fall again.

He seems to read my thoughts and says, "When we have repented in our hearts and in our lives, then the famine will cease."

My mouth opens to tell him that we *have* repented. Sackcloth and ashes are worn by even the most arrogant.

"Kiah, you have the heart of a true warrior."

I almost leap from my position on the floor. How does he know what lies within my heart?

"You are a brave young man. There will be days when your courage will be tested beyond anything you can imagine." His words come out slowly, as if he can see an image unfolding in his mind. "In the end, you will prove worthy of the Lord's choicest blessings."

Is the prophet seeing into my future? I've never felt so hopeful, and I find myself kneeling before him, scooting closer. I want to hear more. Nephi smiles and then begins to cough. He coughs so hard Jonas and I both try to bring him comfort. Jonas runs to fetch a cup of water. I try to help Nephi stand, but his legs are so thin and weak that he has to cling to me. I can feel his bones through his scant cloak, and I know that he understands the people's suffering.

When the coughing spell has passed we sit together on the bed.

"You are a true friend to my grandson."

"Jonas is my best friend."

"You two remind me of David and Jonathan. Do you know the story?"

"My mother loves to sing me the stories from the scriptures."

"Your mother has the voice to make every story ring true."

I wonder when he has heard my mother sing.

"What are your ambitions, Kiah?"

"More than anything, I want to be what you said I am: a warrior."

He smiles again. "What's the bravest act you have performed?"

Immediately my mind recalls the black mountain cat, the *chakmool* I trailed. I think of all of the animals I have hunted and killed. My heart pumps at the memory of hiding from the band of robbers. Then I remember Hem's face, twisted in both fear and rage. I wonder . . . can Nephi see it too?

I say nothing.

"Kiah, living without a father requires great bravery. The Lord is mindful of you and your trials. He is also very aware of your desires, and He wants your happiness, perhaps more than you want your own happiness. Do you understand?"

"I'm not certain."

"This famine, has it caused you great suffering?"

"I don't suffer as much as some."

"You are not one to complain."

Jonas walks in and helps wash Nephi's hands before he puts the cup to the prophet's lips—lips so parched they are cracked and lined with blood. Those dark, telling eyes of his look hard at me. "You will be a warrior, Kiah, but not the type of warrior you expect."

Jonas looks at me and shrugs. Neither of us knows what Nephi means, and neither of us asks. Instead, Jonas asks, "Grandfather, do you feel well enough to recount the story to us?"

"Which story?"

"The story of how you were imprisoned in the same prison where Ammon was cast by Limhi?"

The prophet motions for another sip of water and then smiles. "I never tire of telling of the Lord's goodness and mercy and of the power He has to deliver His children."

Jonas looks and me and grins. "*I* never tire of hearing this story."

"Oh, it's more than a story, son. It was a time not unlike the days we have recently lived. I'd grown weary of the iniquity in all our land. My brother Lehi and I decided to devote our lives to preaching the word of God, so I gave up the judgment seat and we went forth in search of those most in need."

"My grandfather was a missionary with you, wasn't he?"

"Yes, he was. Yarden is a mighty man of God and has proven a valiant friend for many years."

"What message did you preach?" I ask.

"We preached the very words our father, Helaman, had taught us: 'Remember that there is no other way nor means whereby man can be saved, only through the atoning blood of Jesus Christ, who shall come; yea, remember that he cometh to redeem the world.'

"Jonas and Kiah, my father taught us just as you have been taught. I say the same words to you that he said to me: 'And now, my sons, remember, remember that it is upon the rock of our Redeemer, who is Christ, the Son of God, that ye must build your foundation; that when the devil shall send forth his mighty winds, yea, his shafts in the whirlwind, yea, when all his hail and his mighty storm shall beat upon you, it shall have no power over you to drag you down to the gulf of misery and endless wo, because of the rock upon which ye are built, which is a sure foundation, a foundation whereon if men build they cannot fall.'"

I look over and see that Jonas's lips are moving with his grandfather's words. He has heard them so many times he has them memorized.

"We preached in Gidd, Bountiful, and Mulek and then in the land of the Lamanites."

Jonas makes a little gasp like he's been caught off guard by this revelation.

"Our Lamanite brethren weren't the only ones who gave us cause for concern. Dissenters from our own people had caused much damage to the church, but they humbled themselves, repented, were baptized, and returned to our land."

"What of the Lamanites?" I ask, thinking how I want to battle them, not preach to them.

Nephi seems to understand this. "The power that was given us from God was an authority greater than the sword, Kiah. Because of the words the Lord put into our mouths and because of the authority with which we spoke those words, eight thousand Lamanites repented and were baptized."

I tried to imagine what it would be like to battle eight thousand Lamanites.

"After our success we went to the land of Nephi. There the Lamanites cast us into the very prison where Limhi had cast Ammon and his brethren."

Jonas scooted forward. "They did not feed Grandfather or his brother Lehi for many, many days."

"I was weak like I am now when our captors came to slay us," Nephi says with a faraway look in his eyes. "But the Lord was with us and we were encircled about as if by fire. The Lamanites saw that and did not dare to come too near us. They were afraid of getting burned, though we were in the midst of those flames and were not so much as singed by the heat—which of course gave our hearts courage. I don't know that I have ever preached with more power from on high. I'm sure your grandfather has told you of this account."

I nod, thinking what it might be like to command fire. I would be the greatest warrior ever. The way he tells the story makes me feel like I have left that room and gone to the very prison with him; I feel the stones around me heating up, I smell the smoke, I sense a power unlike any kind of courage I had ever imagined. I believe every word.

"I told the Lamanites not to fear for it was God that had shown them such a marvelous thing. Then the earth beneath our feet began to shake, and the prison walls shook as if they were about to crumble, but they did not fall. Then came a cloud of darkness unlike any cloud I can describe. I'm telling you, an awful fear came upon the Lamanites and Nephite dissenters who were in the prison with us."

Nephi pauses; tears come to his eyes as he recounts, "A voice came as if it were above the cloud of darkness, saying, 'Repent ye, repent ye, and seek no more to destroy my servants whom I have sent unto you to declare good tidings.'"

"Was it the voice of the Messiah?" I ask.

Nephi's smile widens. "It was not a voice of thunder, neither was it a voice of a great tumultuous noise, but behold, it was a still voice of perfect mildness, as if it had been a whisper, and it did pierce even to the very soul—And notwithstanding the mildness of the voice, behold the earth shook exceedingly, and the walls of the prison trembled again, as if it were about to tumble to the earth; and behold the cloud of darkness, which had overshadowed them, did not disperse—the Lamanites could not flee because of the cloud of darkness which did overshadow them; yea, and also they were immovable because of the fear which did come upon them."

As Nephi talks of such sacred things there seems to be sunlight on his face. He talks of angels and of faith and of the Messiah.

"Three hundred souls saw and heard the things of that day," he continues in a voice that grows stronger by the telling. "They did minister, declaring the word, and convinced the Lamanites until many laid down their weapons of war. They also laid down their hatred and the traditions of their fathers."

He talks of that experience like it was lasting. But it did not last. Pride came. War followed. Now we are in the grips of a deadly famine because people forget God's goodness and mercy. Something is happening to me. I can feel it on the inside. A power is rising up inside of me, setting my heart on fire. I can't explain it, but I can sense it. I know I am in the presence of someone who knows the Messiah. That surety instills in me a desire to know Him too.

Nephi coughs again, and we try to help him find a comfortable position on the bed so he can rest. I fear for him because his breathing is labored and unsteady. I fear for him because he does not weigh as much as I do. I fear for him because most people in the land of Nephi blame him for the famine and the suffering it has caused.

I bow my own head and say a silent prayer. I beg God to heal Nephi—to help him regain his strength. Jonas also has his head bowed, and I think he is offering a prayer very much like mine.

After a while the prophet stirs. "Pray with me, sons. Pray with me that this people might do more than put on sackcloth and ashes—that they might put on true humility so that this famine will finally end."

Fourteen

Even in the midst of suffering, we are restored. Grandfather and the prophet spend many hours talking. Eventually they both seem stronger, and occasionally I even hear laughter coming from behind the garden wall where they walk in the sunshine. Mother moves faster than I have seen her move in so long. She hums while she helps Devora do the daily chores around the house. It makes me happy to hear them making music together. Jonas has sisters; some of them are married, and their small children love to follow Mother and are always tugging on her skirts, begging her to sing to them. Her music, like water to thirsty plants, restores me.

Most of my time is spent exploring with Jonas. Lumber hunters infiltrate the forests, chopping trees and leaving behind a graveyard of mangled trunks and trails where the trees were dragged. Jonas and I are forced to venture deeper into the thick to find game. Twice we bring back meat sufficient to feed the entire household, if only for a few meals. I'm grateful for the strength it seems to provide for Grandfather and the prophet. Grilled meat is something I have not tasted in so long that I let it sit in my mouth for a long time before I chew and swallow. My stomach growls in gratitude.

"Be wise, Kiah," Grandfather tells me when we are alone. "This is a dangerous time for the prophet and his family. As you and Jonas venture outside of these walls, be cautious."

"Do you think someone might hurt Jonas?"

"I know that there are those who would kidnap him if they could. They would ask a ransom—rain—for his return. Do you understand what I'm telling you?"

"You're telling me that no place is safe and no one is safe."

"That is what it comes down to. I've been watching you, Kiah. You are growing into a man who will one day be great."

I do feel different here. "How long are we going to stay with the prophet's family?"

"Until the Spirit reveals to me that it is time to return."

Sometimes I wish my grandfather wasn't so in tune with the Lord's direction. I don't want to return to Elam yet—maybe ever. I think of Calev, but we have not heard from Uriel, which Grandfather says is a good sign.

When the prophet starts to feel stronger he has Jonas and me assist him up the steps to his garden tower. The tower is a work of art, shaped very much like a massive tree trunk with steps carved up one side and a flat landing balanced at the top. The way it rises into the lower canopy makes whoever sits at the top feel like part of the jungle.

Jonas and I can both fit up there—and we have, during morning prayers.

"I made this tower with my own hands," the prophet says when he is safely at the top. "I carried the stones myself from down by the river. I crushed limestone to make cement to hold the stones in place."

"It's very impressive," I tell the prophet.

"I wasn't much older than you and Jonas when I moved here and built the house and tower."

Just being in his presence makes me want to do more, to master skills, to do better at everything I attempt. He seems stronger here atop his tower, and soon the prophet's voice is strong. It reaches out through the branches and leaves, echoes up and down the main highway, and catches the attention of everyone going into or coming out of Zarahemla.

"How could you have forgotten your God?" he shouts.

A crowd gathers. Some are eager to hear his preaching, but most are eager to threaten him.

A man standing near Jonas sneers. "If your grandfather would not pray so loud, would not preach repentance to a people who think they are already penitent, maybe there wouldn't be so much danger."

Jonas smiles. "Grandfather is going to do what the Lord tells him to do no matter how dangerous it is."

One morning Jonas and I venture into the heart of Zarahemla. We avoid the main highway, where someone might recognize Jonas as the prophet's grandson.

"I'm not afraid," he assures me. "It's just that my father has asked me to be careful."

"I know. My grandfather told me that you might get kidnapped."

"I might," he says, grinning, "except for the fact that I can outrun any kidnapper."

Jonas takes off; my lungs are bursting by the time I catch up to him outside the city wall. The crowds are thicker now that we are at the city entrance. There are musicians and dancers, singers and fortune tellers. There are farmers with withered crops to sell and women selling jewelry and linen. My eyes are not used to the contrasts of color and movement. My ears are not used to the sound of so many voices.

We pass the south gate; the smell is rancid because it is the gate where the city waste is removed. Beggars are digging through piles of refuse while swarms of flies hover in dark clouds.

"Keep moving," Jonas says, holding a hand over his mouth and nose to fight away the stink.

I'm not paying attention and almost run into a cart laden with fresh dung. The driver glares at me then looks to Jonas; for a second, I fear the man has recognized Jonas as a member of Nephi's family, but I dismiss my fear and race to catch up to my friend.

We enter through Benjamin's Gate, named after the great king who gave his famous sermon here. So many people came to hear him that he had to have a tower built; even from the tower his voice would not carry far enough, so he had his message written. Grandfather is always quoting to me from that sermon—usually something about service to our fellow men.

Zarahemla is a fortress made of mostly timber, which explains why trees are so scarce. It looks gray from afar because the outside of the walls are coated with gray cement and stones, but the walls are clearly made of wood. Zarahemla is massive and loud. The sound of so many voices speaking all at once makes me dizzy. Men carry lumber; beasts carry burdens. Women walk in groups and congregate around wells. Food is still sold in the marketplaces, only it is very expensive—and every offering seems small and withered.

My nose fills with so many aromas that I cannot separate one from another. There is the smell of charred corn and boiled onions. Women are grinding grain and turning over in their hands the breads I know taste delicious. We cannot afford to purchase them but stare with hungry eyes as they are laid above hot coals to grill.

A few wheeled carts are either pulled by beasts or pushed by men. I wonder how their wheels do not fall apart on the hard, uneven roads—roads rolled flat by huge round stones that require the strength of many men to move them. Roads are always under construction. Slaves and the poorest of the poor do the work, supervised by men with whips in their hands.

Watching them fascinates me. Jonas has to pull me away from staring.

The smell of smoke and incense comes from the great temple, a walled city within a walled city. My heart quickens as we approach the sacred site.

A blind man sits with his back toward the wall, his hand outstretched in desperation. I wish I had something to offer him. I have nothing. Jonas does not have anything either, but that does not stop my friend from kneeling next to the man and speaking kindly to him.

I smell animals and the pungent scent of many people packed together. I also smell the scent of the distant river, musty and shrinking. The air around the temple is usually moist from the nearby waterfall, but it has dried to a trickle. The stones of the walls and pathways are dry, some coated in dust.

Mother told me I was brought here as an infant to be presented. She came to be purified. I try to imagine her then, joyous with motherhood, a rambunctious Calev clinging to her skirts and me cradled in her arms. She does not say it aloud, but I know that my father was with us. He had to be, and yet the idea that I once belonged to a complete family seems impossible. Did Father ever hold me in his arms? Did he ever teach me of the temple? Did he ever love me?

Since that time, I've been back to the temple with Calev and Grandfather, but it's been many seasons since I walked around the wall—since I noted all thirteen gates and learned their specific purposes.

"Why did you stop?" Jonas asks.

"I was just thinking."

"Hurry! Let's go into the main courtyard. I want to see the butchering."

I follow his flying feet down a narrow passage. We run along the east side near the women's gate, and I am surprised at the number of women of all ages that flow like water through the entrance. I wish the prophet could see them in their sackcloth with bowed heads. He'd know then that at least the women are sincere in their repentance.

Jonas keeps running, meriting a few disapproving stares from elders. I'm tired, and the mist of smoke is chokingly thick, but with effort I manage to keep up with my friend. On the south side we slip through the kindling gate where men carry in the wood for sacrifices. Immediately I'm stopped by the scene before me. Smoke is as thick as morning fog. Men are packed as tight as kernels. Sellers have doves in cages, hawking them to the highest bidders. The scent of blood, both fresh and old, almost gags me.

Jonas stops too. He turns to me and frowns. "Does this feel like 'the sanctified house' to you?"

"No. I don't remember it being like this."

He eases forward through the throng. As we approach the butchering area the ground is slick with blood, which runs in rivulets between where stones are laid. It touches my bare toes, and I hate the feeling. A man in front of us slips and stumbles. Jonas rushes to aid him; I wish that I was more like my friend, always quick to serve. One day I will be. One day I will have great faith, like Nephi predicted. One day I will be a true warrior for God.

"Come, Kiah! Come out of your dream and follow me!"

We make our way past the gate of the offerings where priests carry in the sacrifices—mostly fowls, but a few larger animals, too. One vendor is trying to sell long-tailed *chuwens*, but they are not clean animals, so he has a cage crowded with screaming, fighting animals.

I look away, feeling pity for the creatures.

Jonas takes my elbow and speaks into my ear. "The people are desperate and they are wrong. They ignore what my grandfather and other prophets have taught."

I cock my head, uncertain of his point.

"Animals sacrifices are required *only* for unintentional sins. *Repentance* is what the Lord requires for all other sins. Yet look around. These people think they can make a sacrifice and be forgiven; they fail to repent." Jonas lifts his voice and cries over and over, "Repent! Repent! Repent!"

People stare. I wish Jonas would be silent, but he is sincere, and a few men nod their approval. Mostly, though, we both become targets for a wave of rising anger. One man even shakes his fist in my face until I feel my ears go hot and my fists clench.

"Do you want to fight?" I ask.

He shoves my shoulder and calls me a name I don't understand.

My hand goes instinctively to the dagger strapped to my thigh; my face is so close to the man's that I can feel the heat of his breath. The man is much older and taller, but there is fear on his face. I see it, and it makes me want to knock him to the ground.

"What are you doing?" Jonas cries, jerking me away. "This is a house of love. You can't bring your anger here, Kiah. No!"

He's right. I back away, but I do not allow myself to blink. I stare at the man with the fierceness of a wild cat. I stare until he looks away and hurries back into the crowd.

"What is wrong?" Jonas asks. "Why did you do that?"

"That man shook his fist in my face."

"He's angry too—angry and hungry and desperate. Look around. Everyone suffers. Come over to the libation gate. I'll get water for you, my friend."

Through the push of the crowd I see the man again. He is talking to another man, and I think it's the fellow with the dung cart—the one who seemed to recognize Jonas. Has he followed us all this way?

I am ready to stand and fight. I'll fight them all, but Jonas seems unconcerned—only upset that a place so holy could be turned into a marketplace of filth and irreverence.

Water is precious, and while we wait our turn, Jonas says, "I wish I could prophesy like my Grandfather. I wish I could bring people to Jesus Christ with the love and power he has."

"You will. One day you will *be* a prophet, Jonas."

"I could predict the same for you, Kiah."

I laugh. "I want to be a warrior."

"I know, but what is a prophet . . . is he not the greatest of all warriors? Can you imagine a man more courageous than my grandfather—or yours?"

"No."

"Then you have to stand up for Jesus Christ no matter the cost. Think again of Abinadi. King Noah had him burned because he spoke the truth—nothing more. He was a warrior if ever there *was* a warrior."

My heart races; my head spins like a wobbly wheel. When I'm offered a cup of water I realize my fists are still clenched.

"Why are you so angry, Kiah?"

My shoulders lift and fall. What can I say? I have no answer. No reason for the sudden violence that rises within me. What's wrong with me? I have a righteous grandfather. I have a heart for serving God. Yet I feel like fighting.

Jonas slips away toward the outer altar where portions of most offerings are burned, where blood is dashed. I hate the smell. I hate the stickiness beneath my feet.

"When I was younger this was all very exciting to me," Jonas says. "Now it makes me ill. Do people not understand repentance—don't they realize that the person making the offering has to sincerely repent or the sacrifice means nothing?"

"What is *repentance*?" I ask, surprising myself by my own question.

Jonas doesn't condemn my question but answers with wisdom and kindness. "It is to feel true sorrow for what we do wrong. It is to pray, to go to the person we've wronged, to repay him if we can, to know that God will repay him if we can't."

"What if I did not harm Hem, but in my heart I wanted to?"

"You carry guilt?"

"I think I feel guilt, but I shouldn't. You wouldn't. Not if you knew Hem like I know him. Wasn't my situation like Nephi's with Laban?"

His smile is broad enough to show his chipped front tooth. "Was it?"

"What do you mean?"

"I mean the Spirit told Nephi to kill Laban. Did the Spirit of God tell you to kill Hem?"

"No."

Jonas's hand slaps my shoulder. "Kiah, you are a good friend. You are a good person. You must believe that. Pray, and you will know the truth about yourself."

"I pray."

He smiles. "Pray harder."

Just then a group of men approach, and now I am sure that one of them is the man with the dung cart. I also see the man I almost struck. He is pointing again, this time right at Jonas.

"Run!" I tell him. "They've recognized you."

Fifteen

The men chase us out of the temple gate and into the depths of the city. Jonas is faster than I am and he knows Zarahemla—which side alleys to dart down. When I can no longer see him I pause at a corner, trying to decide which direction to take. That is when I feel the blow to my shoulder.

The man I almost struck before now has a club in his hand. He raises it to bring it down on me again, but my hand shoots out and I face him with a blade. His eyes go wide with surprise. The men with him step back.

The man laughs. "You're a lanky, awkward boy. You think you can frighten me with a knife so small?"

My heart is pounding so hard I think it might burst, but I do my best to make sure my face does not give away my fear. I step closer; he steps back. My eyes take in the details about this man: he is shorter than I am, stouter, filthy from carting dung. He reeks, and the few teeth he has left are brown with rot. His eyes are round, and his nose has been broken and set to the left.

"There are five of us together and only one of you. Your brother seems to have abandoned you." The man laughs and pushes out his chest.

It's true. Jonas is gone and I am alone. This is not a fight I asked for, but it is not one I will back away from either. Already I can sense our melee has garnered an audience, but I do not allow myself to become distracted by spectators, even ones who are shouting foul things. I say nothing, only stand my ground. My shoulder hurts from where he clubbed me, and I realize the blade in my hand is shaking.

Like a bull charging, the man comes at me. I think I am going to stab him, aim for his heart, but my feet jump to the side. When the man swings his club and finds no target, he loses his balance and I am able to shove him. Hard. He hits the ground and bangs the top of his head into the stone wall. His friends laugh.

Turning around on his hands and knees, his hand sweeps out to grab his club, but I kick it away. My urge to fight this man is suddenly gone. I do not want to fight at all. I'm not exactly afraid; I just don't want to fight. *Help me, Father,* I pray, *help me.*

That's when strong hands grab me from behind and take the blade out of my grip. Like braided ropes those hands hold me; no matter how I struggle and kick, I am held fast in the arms of a stranger.

"Are you the grandson of the prophet Nephi?" a voice in my ear asks.

The man is holding me too tight for me to turn around and see his face. "No."

He holds me tighter. "This is not the grandson of the prophet."

The man on the ground rises. "He might not be the grandson, but he was with the other boy who *is* Nephi's grandson. I saw him with my own eyes."

"You will not harm this boy."

I jerk and kick and flail. "I am not a boy."

His grip nearly crushes my ribs. "Be still."

"If we hold on to him, we can convince the prophet to call a cease to this famine," one of the men says in a flat tone.

Others immediately agree. "This boy will be our ransom."

"Stop fighting me," the man says, leaning into my ear. "I want to protect you."

I trust him. I don't know why I do, but I do, and I stop fighting.

"We will not listen to you!" someone shouts. "You're a filthy Lamanite."

"I am a Lamanite. I am also your brother. My family suffers from this famine just as yours do. Kidnapping this child is not the answer."

He partly releases me, and my head flops back. That's when I see Jonas. He has managed to climb up to the roof of one of the buildings and is looking down at me with horror etched on his face.

The man who clubbed me steps forward. Both of his hands are clenched, and I fear we are about to engage in battle, but the man jabs the fists into his own eye sockets and cries loud enough for even Jonas to hear him. "My infant daughter died from this famine. My mother-in-law died. My cattle have died. Now I haul dung out of the city. Nephi is no prophet; he is a murderer!"

A cry goes up—a divided cry, for some agree and others defend the prophet. The man behind me tries to speak peace, but no one listens. Another hand reaches to pick up the club, and it comes straight for my face. The man lets go of me in time for me to duck; the blow meant for me strikes him in the chest. But he's tall and strong and takes the blow without toppling. In an instant the entire street is engaged in a shower of fists and shouts and combat.

"Run!" the man tells me, giving me a shove toward an open street.

I don't want to run. I don't want to be a coward, but more than that I don't want to be used to harm the prophet or his family in any way—so I do what I'm told. I turn and race through the forest of flailing arms and legs and make my way to another street where people shop and animals plod, none of them aware of the chaos happening just a few steps away.

Sixteen

Every day that we stay with the prophet and his family is a day that we all grow stronger in body and spirit. Listening to Nephi pray from atop his garden tower, I learn that prayer is more than words. I can feel his faith. I can feel his love as he prays for the very people who want to slay him. In so many ways, he reminds me of Grandfather.

Nephi, father to Jonas, allows me to accompany him so that I can learn about cement. We travel in a large group led by Timothy. Even some of the smaller children are permitted to join us. It's a very long walk into the wilderness before we stop at the base of a hill abundant with the stone used to make cement. Though the stone itself is gray and green and tan, the ground around the massive rippled tones is almost white; the dust clings to my feet and sticks between my bare toes.

Nephi holds up a piece of the rock. "Look carefully at the layers that have built up over time."

I've never studied the layers in a rock before; I'm surprised at how thin and distinct they are.

He talks about how he thinks the stones were formed and how easily they break apart under the crush of harder stones. He smashes the softer rock into a sort of crude powder that he grinds like corn kernels into a clay that he mixes with sand and water to make cement.

Jonas explains, "Sometimes Father heats the mixture over flame. It seems to make it stronger."

I'm not the only one interested in seeing this process. Other workers come to learn from Nephi, who says he is still a student of the process. He seems more like an expert as I watch him mix and pour a bucket of cement into a form made from four equal cuts of timber.

"In the heat of this sun the cement will be dry before we finish eating the bread for our afternoon meal."

We cleanse our hands with what little precious water we brought for such a purpose. We pray. We eat. Nephi is right; by the time we are finished, the mixture has dried and hardened.

I am intrigued and want to learn more, but the next morning Grandfather makes an unexpected announcement. "We are going back to Elam."

My heart sinks. I do not want to return. "But your arm is not healed, Grandfather. And you still limp."

"I'm much stronger."

"I thought we would stay until the famine ended."

"The Lord has revealed to me that it is time for us to return to Elam."

I know that when Grandfather has received revelation there is no room for negotiation.

Mother seems as reluctant as I am to leave. Devora does not want to let her go; the women shed tears at the thought of being parted. I feel like crying, too, but I don't. The morning that we take our leave I hold my shoulders back and make my face straight. "Thank you, Jonas, for many things. Mostly I am grateful for your faith. You taught me much."

"I wish we could have hunted more."

"I wish you two could have hunted more *successfully*," my grandfather jokes.

Just before we leave, the prophet prays for our family. He blesses Grandfather and Mother and even prays for Calev's safe return. It is a mighty prayer, and he specifically mentions me: "And may this young man, Kiah, grow strong in physical and moral strength so that when he enters battle he will not only be ready, but he will be victorious."

When we turn to wave good-bye I know that I am not the same person I was when I arrived.

• • •

Elam does not greet us with warmth, though Abner—running like a madman—meets us halfway, and I cannot miss the smile that shines on Mother's face when she sees his dusty red head.

"I would have met you sooner, Yarden, but your epistle only arrived late yesterday."

"And you've run this whole way already?"

"Yes. Gladly."

Grandfather looks quickly at Mother, who turns her face away, but I'm sure he knows there is a bond between her and Abner. I suspect Grandfather approves. My feelings are undecided, but I am grateful to Abner for showing nothing but kindness and aid.

He bows his head. "I fear to tell you that the tension in Elam has not withered. Others have died. The entire family of Moses, the herdsman, was found dead."

Grandfather appears confused for a moment but then asks, "Moses—the goat herder who dwells out in the desolate land?"

Abner nods. "His herd died also. So much time had passed before they were discovered that it was impossible to tell if they died of thirst or disease."

"Let us pray that it was not disease."

We are not yet in Elam, and already Grandfather's shoulders sag and his countenance dims.

"The elders are anxious to hear if you were able to persuade the prophet."

I shake my head, but Abner pays me no mind.

"Only God can persuade the prophet," Grandfather says, and I see disappointment, or maybe fear, dance in Abner's eyes.

I have my own fear. Returning to Elam I will have to face Hem—and Eliana. I will have to pay for the sin I *almost* committed.

"Do you like him?"

I do not realize Grandfather is addressing me.

"Kiah, do you like him—Abner?"

I look up from my thoughts to see that Abner has gone ahead of us to make sure no one lies in wait to attack Grandfather. The two of us are walking alone.

"I don't know," I say quietly. "Mother seems to care for him."

"Your mother has been lonely for many years."

"How do you feel toward Abner, Grandfather?"

"I am in debt to him. He may have saved my life the afternoon of the uproar at the synagogue."

I wanted to be the one to save Grandfather; a twinge of resentment rises in me because it was Abner, not me, who did the most that day to help. I watch and note that he keeps a proper distance and respect with my mother. For that, I'm grateful.

Abner leads us a different way back to Elam. We pass by a small village that I've heard about but have never seen. The few people there are selected engineers who are testing a new form of building. It's not really *new*; Grandfather says it's how homes used to be constructed, but then timber homes like ours—slabbed in leaves and mud—became the standard. Now a group of engineers have been challenged to go back to the old way—to mound up the earth and make dwellings so safe even fire cannot harm those nestled deep within. They look like giant rodent mounds to me, some as big as small hills, and I want to stop to investigate.

"Your eyes are being opened, Kiah."

"What do you mean?"

"When we first left Elam you were interested only in weapons. Now you talk with excitement of how cement is made, and you want to learn about the mound dwellers. The Lamanites are experts. Perhaps one day you will explore their lands and learn that this world is much larger than the road between Elam and Zarahemla."

He's right. There is a growing desire in me to learn many different things.

When we arrive home I'm grateful to see that our humble home is still intact. I worried that it would be destroyed during our absence, but Abner kept it safe. He has provided us with a supply of dried fish and a few tubers— more food than this household has kept in a very long time.

I am stringing Grandfather's hammock back up when Abner comes around the corner of the hut.

"How is Hem? Has his health improved?" What I *really* want to know is whether Hem told people that I nearly killed him.

Abner doesn't say as much. "Hem still goes to the market every day, but he is unable to communicate. His eldest daughter—I believe you know her, Kiah—" Abner smiles at me when he speaks, "attends her father. She seems very loyal to him."

I say nothing, only nod.

Within a day's time we settle back into life. Grandfather feels well enough to go to the synagogue; Abner accompanies him like a personal guard. Mother flits about boiling fish and mashing tubers. There is no corner to sweep that she hasn't already swept, yet her feet seem to dance and she hums while she moves. Even when Oshra and her brood of gossips walk past, Mother seems unruffled. I know then that she's given her heart to Abner.

I feel confused and lonely. There is no niche for me in Elam, and I feel out of place in my own household. I want to go hunting in the high hills, but I am put on night watch with some of the other young men my age. It's our duty to protect the village from without. I think it should be protected from within but say nothing because there is no one here that I trust with my friendship as I do Jonas.

Mathoni and Mathonihah are twin brothers who used to live in Nephihah but have come to dwell with relatives in Elam because their parents died from the famine. They are friendly enough and very good ballplayers. Mathoni can keep the ball in the air, even the heavy rubber ball, longer than I have ever seen anyone keep the ball off the ground. He uses his elbows, his knees, his ankles, even his head. His brother is good too but not as adept as Mathoni.

It is a moonless night when the three of us are divided along Elam's borders. My thoughts are of Calev. I think back to hunts we shared, how he would roll me out of my hammock at night to show me a weapon or tool he had fashioned. I think of Eliana and wonder how my brother could ever join the family of Hem.

My thoughts are far away when I feel something hit my shoulder. At first I think it's a flying night bug, but then I feel another pelt—this one on my arm—and another on my face. It's been so long I hardly recognize what is happening. Rain is falling from above. The scent in the air quickly changes. The charge in the air changes, too—from battered despair to elation.

My head tilts back, and I see the moon has been overshadowed by a web of dark gray clouds. I want to hold my breath until I am sure, but within a few heartbeats I can see that the clouds are gathering to create a giant storm that will weep great tears to replenish our land and our people.

My feet want to dance. I want to shout praises. The breeze picks up, and I detect the unique scent of rain. That smell fills my nostrils and makes my heart swell in gratitude. My knees bend, and I join those around me in unplanned but mighty prayer. Our faces turn upward, damp with rain and tears. I remember one prayer I heard the prophet Nephi utter: *And now, O Lord, wilt thou turn away thine anger, and try again if they will serve thee?*

Even amid the jubilation I focus on the word *IF*.

If we will serve our God . . . the heavens will not dry up again.

If we will serve our God . . . Hem and those like him will be wiped out.

If we will serve our God . . . battles will cease.

If battles cease . . . what need will there be for a warrior like me?

Seventeen

While I am grateful for the rain, I'm also fearful. Grandfather told me that before the rains could come, the robbers had to leave. Have they? Or are they hidden in homes, within villages like Elam, rejoicing at the rain? Are they lurking like animals in the caves of the high hills, waiting to attack as soon as their strength returns?

It does not take long before most of our village has congregated in the main courtyard to celebrate. Last time we gathered here we turned on each other like wild beasts. I search the crowd. We carry lit torches, but it's raining and the night is dark. I barely make out Mother standing with Grandfather. As sure as mist in the air, Abner looms behind them.

"Kiah!"

Grandfather appears through the rain. His hair is soaked and clings to his drenched face. His smile lights the night as sure as any torch. "Our prayers are answered!"

"Yes, Grandfather!"

I'm worried he'll slip; I take hold of his arm. A streak of jagged blue lightning illuminates and sky, and as it docs I look behind him and see another smile. Eliana and Tamar, along with other village girls, are here laughing and splashing in the downpour.

I can't see well enough to make out Eliana's expression; I don't know if she's seen me or not. I don't even know if Hem is nearby. All I can tell for sure is that Eliana is overjoyed, and her happiness makes me happy.

I hold up my torch and step toward her. When she looks at me there is no doubt—Eliana has not forgiven me. I want to apologize, though I am not certain for what reason. In the end, I did not harm her father, and every word I spoke about him was true.

I'm surprised that instead of turning away, Eliana steps *toward* me. "So the rumors are true . . . you've returned from Zarahemla."

"Yes. We've only been back a few days."

"Is your grandfather healed?" she asks.

"He is much better; thank you."

"You look well."

"I am." The conversation is stiff and difficult. It's not the exchange between celebrating friends. The polite and proper act on my part would be to ask about the welfare of her father, but I do not care about Hem, and I already know he is not well.

She calls through the noise, "This rain—does it mean that we are a penitent people?"

I can only shrug. There is no sign of Hem anywhere near her. She steps closer, and in the flicker of my torchlight I see her hatred up close. I see it flicker in her eyes, giving her the face of someone I don't know.

"That must mean that *you've* repented," she says.

I stand tall and ask, "What do I have to repent of?"

"You believe in an all-seeing God, don't you?"

"Yes."

"Then He saw what you tried to do to an innocent man. You're not a boy, Kiah; you're a diseased animal. Father knows it. I know it. God knows it."

"What you *should* know," I say, spitting the words out between my clenched teeth, "is that your father is far from innocent. He has deceived you, but he cannot deceive God. I saw with my own eyes—he is a Gadianton robber."

She looks ready to strike me. "Then why has God blessed my father? He is healing, getting stronger every day. You're fortunate that he has not demanded your punishment—at least not yet."

The news of Hem's condition surprises me and I'm not sure I believe it, but there is a twinge of fear in me that Hem will indeed seek my punishment. I should tell Grandfather and Mother what happened so they don't hear Hem's version of the story before they hear mine.

Eliana is still talking, and I have to turn my attention away from my own thoughts and back to her. "If my father was a robber like you say, then God would smite him. The robbers are gone, Kiah. The famine is over. And my father is still here."

• • •

As time passes the earth grows green again. It's now easy for my arrows or stones to target young animals for meat. All I have to do is wait by the grassy meadows and take my pick. Soon our wrinkled skin does not hang loose; our bellies do not rumble like tumbling rocks. Grandfather's arm refuses to rise or to hold a weapon, but it doesn't take long before he can walk without having to lean on a stick.

The people of Elam voted Grandfather to be a judge, so now he spends more time with his fellow priests at the synagogue. There is little time for our walks together, and I miss spending time with him. But it's good to see him happy, knowing that the end of the famine has humbled so many people and brought them to the waters of baptism.

Now that the chief judge of all the Nephites is Lachoneus, an acquaintance of Grandfather's and a friend to the prophet Nephi, all of Elam feels a sense of peace. I feel it because in spite of Eliana's claims, I've seen Hem from a distance in the marketplace. He might be stronger, but he is far from recovered.

Mother ventures out from our home more than I have ever known her to. She fills her baskets with plants for making dyes and plants for weaving cloth. She even nurtures new buds in our humble courtyard by our purification pool. It's been difficult to keep it wet, but now water reaches the top; after a rain, it even sloshes over the sides.

Mother sings. She favors the songs of our ancestors, tales like the stories of David and Jonathan, Abraham and Issac, Alma and Amulon. Even though my arms and legs are sprouting like blades of grass, I fold myself to sit at Mother's feet while she sings and skins the animals I kill.

I attend morning synagogue school and rededicate myself to try harder than ever to learn the arts of reading and writing. Elam's calendar-keeper, Raz, senses that I have few friends. He has always been kind to me, but now he takes it upon himself to fellowship me. He is a broomstick of a man with eyes that seem bigger than they should be. He has a reputation in Elam for two reasons: his mind is very keen concerning time, and his wife has given birth to twenty-two children, all of whom survived the famine and other hazards that often claim the lives of children. I feel grateful and honored that he would take an interest in me.

Raz has been designated a special room off the main worship hall. The walls are plastered smooth, and there is a scent to the air that is more musky—different from the rest of the synagogue.

"All things in life are connected," Raz says, moving over so I can sit with him on the carved wooden seat in the corner where he makes his marks and reads the records. A circle in the wall near his seat allows light in but keeps the wind and rain away from the scrolls and plates and other records that he must consult to keep an accurate account of the seasons.

Being in this edifice makes me think of something my mother only recently told me—my father, Gidd, was a scribe. Did he ever enter this building? Did he sit where I am sitting? Did he fill an empty scroll with symbols that tell the times and doings of our people? I wish my thoughts of him would leave, but lately I think often of the man who would be—should be—my father.

"My hand is clumsy," I warn Raz. "My letters are difficult to read."

He smiles and flicks his tongue out between the huge gap in his front teeth.

Raz does not make the letters I am learning. Mine are rudimentary; his are advanced and very intricate, often taking days to perfect. His symbols bring a different sense to each span of time. "Time can be measured by the sun and by the moon, but time is not a straight line," he tells me, whirling his arm around and around in the air. "It is a cycle. Time is measured by God in the rings of a tree; we can know the seasons by reading the rings. Why should we keep time differently than God?"

I soon learn that *keeping time* means understanding the changes of the seasons, the phases of the moon, and the journeys that our earth makes around the fire of the sun. For a man so small, Raz's head is a giant ball of knowledge. Just being in his presence makes me want to learn more.

Raz's knowledge is impressive, but what impresses me most is how he stops everything he is working on whenever one of his sons or daughters happens by. Even if he has been with them that morning, he greets them as if he hasn't seen them for seasons. He smiles and laughs and wraps his arms around them, kisses their cheeks, and listens to whatever they have to say, no matter how trivial. When his wife appears with bread and cheese or a basket of fruit, Raz acts like she has brought him a king's feast.

Watching such a scene stabs at my heart. I ache to be part of such a family. I think of Calev. We have not heard news of my brother for some time. Now, more than before, I miss him.

Raz's teachings sink deep into my mind and heart. I am fascinated by how one circle of time connects with another. How Father Adam's joins with Grandfather's. How the line from Jerusalem to Zarahemla connects. How one season of prosperity always seems to lead to a season of pride and then a season of decline. The cycle appears inevitable.

After many days Raz asks, "What do you think? Would you like to become a skilled timekeeper?"

"I don't know. I've always thought of myself as a warrior."

"You mean a hunter? Because all of Elam knows you are a skilled hunter."

"No," I say, thoughtfully. "All my life I wanted only to belong to a battle, to show the faith of Helaman's young warriors."

"There are many ways to do battle, Kiah; not all of them require wielding a sword or a club."

Looking at the afternoon rays filtering through the little window, I breathe deeply. "I am changing, Raz. If I were to draw the circles of my life, the smallest and most inward would be filled with only one possibility: to become a battling warrior. But over the last few seasons I realize that I could become many things—an expert in cement, an engineer who could design buildings able to stand through a storm, a merchant who could sell wares in Zarahemla . . . or even a timekeeper." I smile broadly.

"You could become a scribe like your father."

There's a catch in my heart. "You knew my father?"

"At one time Gidd and I were friends."

"What was he like?" I wish I didn't sound so desperate.

Raz sets his engraving tool down and rubs his chin. "What was Gidd like? Well, there's a bit of his features in your face, Kiah. Every time I look at you I am reminded of your father's eyes. Mostly, though, you are like your mother. Your father was—*is*—a man of learning. He studied diligently in the synagogue and asked a lot of questions. He was an only son, so he was entitled to military training and took full advantage of that. Yarden was devoted to your father. He taught him the arts of war as well as the arts of peace."

"The arts of *peace*?" I sit on the edge of the bench, leaning into every word.

"The arts of peace are by far the most difficult to master—bridling our tongues, controlling our tempers, filling our minds with good thoughts, and keeping our hands busy building, never destroying. Forgiving might be the most difficult aspect of any war."

I say nothing because my own mind is whirling with an image of a father, a man becoming more real to me as Raz talks.

"Everyone in Elam expected your father to rise perhaps as high as the chief judge's seat. He had that kind of possibility. He was born to lead."

I look down at the floor. It is made of packed red earth. Over time it has been worn smooth, and I wonder if my father's feet ever trod upon the same ground my own feet stand on. "What happened to change my father?"

"Pride."

I look up at the word that I've heard spit so many times from Grandfather's mouth.

"Your father was blessed with many gifts, and the more skilled he became the more prideful he became. He started to boast of his own strength. He tested it out on those weaker. He challenged authority—even that of Yarden. He married your mother, one of the most beautiful women ever brought to Elam, and even she was not enough to satisfy his pride."

Raz stops and rubs his face with his hands. "I've said too much."

"No. Thank you for telling me the things you have. Now I understand why Grandfather thinks pride is such a sin."

"I'm sure you've heard the rumors of how your father felt justified in robbing the synagogue treasury."

I nod. I've heard them all my life.

"Kiah, I see in you many of the same gifts, perhaps more than even your father. As you grow and develop, always give honor where honor is due."

"To God?"

"And none other. A grateful heart can never be a prideful heart."

Raz begins to clean up and organize his tools. I take the broom and sweep the dirt smooth. The thoughts in my head are so heavy I feel a throbbing ache.

"Will I see you again tomorrow?" Raz asks.

I shake my head. "No. I have a journey I must make, and I'm not sure how long it will be before I return to Elam."

Eighteen

Mother is scrubbing our humble courtyard purification pool. Her eyes are wet with worry. "I fear for your safety, son. Such a journey now seems dangerous."

Grandfather seems more sympathetic. "Allow me to go with you."

"I would, but the terrain is steep and dangerous. Your arm is not yet healed; you might injure yourself again."

Grandfather turns his palm up and seems to study the lines in his hand. "There was a time, Kiah, when I was young and strong like you. That time will never return, but one day I will not be so slow and unsteady."

"Must you go now?" Mother asks. "And all alone?"

I nod.

A tear glistens in the corner of her eye. "Surely Calev will be home soon. The two of you can travel together."

Grandfather helps me pour fresh water into the clean well. We pour slowly so that not even a drop is wasted. He smiles at me and turns to Mother. "Allow Kiah this time, Anat. He has made this journey before, and I will bless him before he departs. He will be safe."

"I'll bring back more obsidian than you've ever seen," I tell Grandfather, grinning.

We both know that I am not going high into the hills to search for obsidian. I am going to search for direction. This is my sacred time with the Lord. I have explained my desires to Grandfather. I'm not going to prove to the elders of Elam that I can track and hunt and survive on my own. I'm going to discover for myself the best direction for my life.

"Mother, I'm going to go pray as Enos prayed."

"You don't have to go away to do that."

"I've gone away before."

"This time feels different to me, son."

Grandfather understands my need and desire, but Mother keeps rubbing her temples in frantic circles. "Are you sure Kiah will be safe from robbers?" she asks Grandfather.

"Our own Calev has been hunting the robbers. I have to believe that the famine never would have ended if Gadianton's band was still strong."

"But Kiah, you said you're going to the tops of the back mountains. You don't know when you'll return. This is not a regular hunt, Kiah; this is something more."

"You're right, Anat," Grandfather says, putting his hands on her shoulders, kneading the tension from them. "Kiah is on the threshold of manhood. He needs this time to make that transition." He pauses and his tone is serious. "This is his *deciding* time."

My actual deciding time was seasons before, on the journey when I came across Hem and his band. I cut that trek short and returned without fulfilling my obligation to bring back food for the family and the village. I brought no evidence of my bravery—only accusations that were scoffed at. Mother should understand why I need to go again.

She talks to me like I am a mere child. "What about those new boys in Elam—the twins—they seem nice. Maybe they can go with you so at least you won't have to go alone."

She means Mathoni and Mathonihah, the twins who are so adept at ballplaying. They are kind and friendly enough, but this is a solo venture. "Mother, the point of my journey is that I will be alone."

"Merari! I'm sure Merari would be happy to go hunt in the high hills with you. He's very fond of you."

Grandfather snorts. "Kiah is not a baby anymore. And the hills are always going to hold danger. But the robbers, for the most part, have been hunted out. The last epistle Uriel sent should give you assurance."

Mother sighs. "I know I am outnumbered, Yarden, but Kiah is so precious, so vulnerable." Her chin dips when she looks at me. "You have proven your intelligence. You have talents yet to be developed. Still, all you want is to be a warrior."

"Mother, Moroni was only twenty-five years old when he became chief captain of the Nephite armies."

"That's ten years older than you are, Kiah."

I love the story of Moroni going against the Lamanite captain, Zerahemnah. I've imagined myself on the front lines of that battle so many times. Moroni had prepared his men with breastplates, arm shields, and head shields. He made his band wear thick clothing so the arrows and blades could not penetrate as easily. Zerahemnah's numbers were greater, but his men had only wooden swords and cimeters, bows and arrows, stones and slings. Their naked skin was susceptible to every weapon Moroni's men possessed.

How I would have loved to have fought under the command of Captain Moroni! One day I will arm my own men. I will prepare them and fight alongside them, leading the way. My army will wipe the robbers out once and for all.

"We are living in a rare time of peace," Mother says in a thin voice. "It provides options, Kiah. You could become a priest or a judge or a craftsman."

"Let the boy go," Grandfather says, his tone more firm. "Kiah needs to do this for his own peace. If it will give you peace also, Anat, I will lay my hands on Kiah's head and bless him with a promise of safety."

I don't say so, but every part of me welcomes such a blessing.

Nineteen

I am alone. A pair of eagles soars high above me, and I watch them float against the tranquil blue sky. I think of their strength and design—how they use the wind to their advantage to make them fly high without effort. They use only wisdom and instinct. A feeling of God's majesty soars within me; looking around to be certain I am alone, I kneel.

"Hear, Israel, the Lord is our God, the Lord is One. Blessed be the name of His glorious kingdom forever and ever. And you shall love the Lord your God with all your heart and with all your soul and with all your might. And these words that I command you today shall be in your heart. And you shall teach them diligently to your children, and you shall speak of them when you sit at home, and when you walk along the way, and when you lie down and when you rise up."

It dawns on me then, as I am bowed before my God, that my mother and my grandfather have always taught me diligently. Now their holy, wise words seem to come alive—not only in my mind, but in my heart. My bosom burns. Is this what faith feels like?

Carefully, thoughtfully, I deviate from the prescribed prayer text to write my own. "Father God, I bow before Thee a humble son in need of revelation. I want my life to have direction, passion, meaning. There is a warrior within me, designed by Thy hand. Bless me. Forgive my sins; they are many, and I have no secrets from Thee. Bless my family. Bless my life."

There is a hint of a breeze, and in it I hear a whisper, a voice that speaks not to my ears but to my heart—that one word: *Messiah.* The Anointed One.

I'm not sure what it means to me, and though I wait, I hear nothing more. Slowly a feeling settles inside of me, a sense of strength and peace. When I rise from my knees I have renewed energy to climb.

I make my way high into the back hills. It rains here almost every day now, and the landscape is green and thick. The air smells clean and alive. Animals scurry in the bush, birds fly from branch to branch, and twice the sight of a slithering snake stops me cold. One is a harmless viper, the same green as the grass. It's thick and clumsy, and I am warned of its presence in time to avoid it. The smaller snake that my foot nearly steps on is as thin as my smallest finger. It is black and fast and deadly. I thank God when it slithers away without striking at my bare skin. I would rather face a Gadianton robber than battle a venomous snake.

My thoughts turn to Calev. What sort of terrain has he traveled? What sights has he seen? What kinds of enemies has he fought? Has he been wounded? I wonder how he can tell which Lamanites are penitent and which are still bloodthirsty. I wonder what his training has taught him about flushing out Gadianton robbers when they look so innocent, when they look like a neighbor or a brother—when they wear a mask as convincing as the one Hem wears.

The thought of Hem chases away the peace that had settled in my heart. I think of Eliana being relegated to his side, to speak for him, to be his legs and arms. What a misery for her. I think of how even though he is hindered, he is still harmful.

Hem may have been able to convince others that he is simply a merchant, but I know better. I want him brought to justice. That desire makes me think of Grandfather. One night sitting by our cooking fire I shared my feelings with him, and he told me that there must be a balance between mercy and justice. "It's justice you want for Hem's sins, Kiah, but for your own, it's mercy you beg."

Then Grandfather quoted from the words of the prophet Alma. The passage had such an impact on me I tried to memorize it: "Our Messiah shall bring salvation to all those who shall believe on his name; this being the intent of this last sacrifice, to bring about the bowels of mercy, which overpowereth justice, and bringeth about means unto men that they may have faith unto repentance. And thus mercy can satisfy the demands of justice, and encircles them in the arms of safety."

The words make perfect sense in my head, but if I had to recite them, my tongue would trip and stumble.

A ground bird flutters out from the tangle in front of me. Her feathers are the same shades as dry grass and old branches. I'm caught off guard by her fluttering wings and captivated by the little string of chicks that rush after her. Eight little balls of fluff seem confused and lost, and I watch them scatter, knowing that a hungry snake or a hawk or any other predator might grab them. But the hen clucks and the chicks come running to her, taking shelter beneath her open wings. She gathers seven of them, but one little chick sees her, hears her, and still decides to venture off into the bush.

I think the mother hen will go crazy. "*Bwaaak . . . bwaaak . . . bwaaak!*" Her wings open wide, and she seems to be begging her chick to return.

Once again it looks back, sees her, and continues on its own.

Then there is a scuffle, the rustle of leaves. The chick makes a pathetic sound of death and ultimate defeat. The distraught mother folds in her other chicks and guides them off in a different direction.

I'm saddened by the scene and a little angry with the obstinate chick. What I just witnessed teaches a lesson about justice and mercy, but the death of the chick saddens me.

Over the days I'm not the only hunter in the hills. Groups of men and boys pass me. I try to avoid being seen because being alone makes me a target for robbery or violence.

"Trust no one," Grandfather warned.

So I veer off the beaten roads and climb by forging my own trail through the tangle. Soon I realize how much I savor being utterly alone. As much as I enjoyed my time with Jonas, I'm grateful for these moments when I can pretend to be the fiercest warrior that ever walked the earth. Here, alone, I do not have to feel foolish for dreaming.

I drink from a restored spring where cold water bubbles up like a welcoming fountain. I eat fruit not yet ripe with the season but sufficient to appease my growling appetite. I camp above streams where I can purify myself in fresh running water, and I sleep without fear. I am always looking out for signs of the wild cats, large *chakmools* or smaller cats, but I see no tracks, no markings. I wonder if the famine left them dead.

Keeping a steady pace and getting lost a few times, I find it takes me three days to reach the obsidian caves. The band of black is much thinner than I recalled. The rock is so dark and shiny it seems wet in the rays of sunshine. The caves, too, are much smaller than I remember, and the first one I approach is so tiny I have to squirm to wriggle inside. It burrows back into the earth further than I imagined. I light a torch, but there is not enough good air to keep it burning, so I wriggle back out. It's easy to see why robbers would take refuge in these hills; all around are holes in which to hide.

A tiny lizard pokes its face over the curve of a rock. It seems to stare at me. I stare back, and as I do, the reptile changes from leaf green to obsidian black. If I wasn't already looking at it, my eyes would fail to see the lizard. It's right in front of me, yet because it can shift to fit its environment, I cannot see it. I'm sure there's a lesson in that act, too, but I don't want to think so hard. I want to gather obsidian and plan which weapons I will make from it.

I climb higher. I am careful because the rock is not only sharp, it's hot—baked beneath the day's broiling sun. The ledges are steep, and one wrong move on my part could lead to my death.

There is not much to eat here, and I'm too tired to go back down, so I drink and lay down to sleep, covering myself with skin Mother tanned herself. I wake up several times when I hear sliding rock. Is it man or beast dislodging pieces and sending them plummeting? My throat dries. My heart pounds. My palms sweat. I grip my blade and am ready for a fight that never comes.

In the pinks and oranges of morning I can see what I could not see the night before. Stretched far, far below, clear to the sea, there are signs that the people of Nephi are prospering again, building up waste places, multiplying like buds on a tree.

I find myself wishing that Jonas was with me. I would like to hear his new stories. What do people say now that the famine has ended? Is his family once again safe and esteemed in the eyes of the people? I hope that the prophet's health is completely restored. What was the name of the girl he liked? Elisabeth? Lysa? Yes, Lysa.

Though I don't say so to anyone, since the famine ended I've taken notice of the girls in Elam—no one in particular, but at least I'm noticing now what I had not noticed before.

I spend most of the morning gathering the best stones, small enough to carry yet large enough to be hewn into blades and arrows. With my burden so weighty, it's harder to move and impossible to move quickly. As I turn to leave I find my feet forging a trail toward the camp where I first came upon Hem's band of Gadianton robbers. It would be impossible to find again . . . wouldn't it?

The next day I'm lying on the very ledge where I lay on my stomach watching the evil men spread out their stolen bounty. By the amount of overgrowth I can see that no one has disturbed this place in a very long time. My heart takes flight as an idea spreads through my thoughts and enters my heart.

My instincts fail. I can't tell if I am right or if I am wrong, but I am weak and drenched in sweat by the time I've crawled down to where the men were—by the time I've unearthed the very spot, rolled away the rocks that were meant to conceal the hiding place. I'm disappointed that the pillage is not more, but it is more than our family has ever possessed. There are jewels, a man's ring, a carved stone calendar, a war mask, and an idol in the form of the sacred serpent. My fingers move over the statue. It's meant to symbolize the passage of ancestral spirits. It's meant to symbolize the false gods of this world. Yet it is a god, carved by hours of time and talent—something Terah,

Abraham's idol-worshipping father, might have paid homage to. Is this the idol to which the robbers vow, make their oaths, and dedicate themselves?

It feels heavy and filthy.

We have no image for the Messiah. Will He have the suntanned skin and stature of Nephi the prophet, or will the Messiah have the broad shoulders and strength of Grandfather? It matters not. His image is not in my mind; it burns within my heart. He has blessed me, blessed my family with great bounty.

There is also a musty woven bag into which I stuff the treasures; as I do, I feel something at the bottom. A blade. A blade made not of wood and chiseled obsidian, but of steel—at least the outward part of the blade is coated in metal. The handle is curved to fit neatly into the palm of a hand, and it is inlaid with pieces of jade. I've never seen anything so perfect, and I hold it for a very long time, wondering whose hand held this blade before mine. Has it been used to harm or perhaps kill another person?

I swap the blade for my own crude one, carved of wood and bone and rock. Because its shape is so curved, it feels awkward in my grip, but I tell myself I have never been such a warrior.

My heart thumps in my head and throat. I cannot wait to show Grandfather. I will have proof of the robbers' plunder. I imagine my mother's face. She expects me to bring home meat that she can cook and preserve. I am bringing home abundance that is greater than any amount of wealth our family has ever known. Perhaps we can move away from Elam, closer to Zarahemla. We can live in a solid house with a gate and a real courtyard. Our sacred scroll will be posted to a real door for all the world to see that we worship the Messiah! My mind is wild with dreams.

I hold my blade in the fading rays of light and see that one side is stained—blood has darkened the areas around the inlaid shards of jade. Whose blood is it? Was it used to take the life of a beast or human being? Does it matter? The blade is mine now. But it feels foreign in my hand, and I am wary. I want to hold a blade with which I am familiar. I wrap the bejeweled weapon over and over again in leaves so its edge will not slice through my bag—and perhaps slice into me.

That night the screeches and hoots of the *tunkuruchus* sound around me. I unwrap the blade and sleep with its handle in my fist, my old blade beside me for a backup. Sleep doesn't come. I feel rich, yet I feel somehow wrong. I hold the man's ring and imagine how it would look on Grandfather's finger. I can trade some of the art for combs for my mother's hair, jewels for her arms. I picture Oshra's face when she sees that my mother wears the finest linens, dyed the deep hues of the rich.

We will not need Abner for security. We will have wealth. Oh, how Calev will wonder at the change that has come since I stepped up to protect and provide for our family. I can't stop smiling, thinking how Hem will react when I take this treasure into the marketplace to trade. What will he say to me? It does not matter. I have the treasure. He doesn't. Of course he'll recognize it, but he cannot claim it without revealing the ugly truth about himself.

Or can he? If I present this treasure as my own, can he conspire with others to accuse me of theft? My excitement wanes.

I drift off to sleep but wake moments later to the welcome cry of a *chakmool*. I wait and then return the call. I smile; the famine did not kill them all. I hear bushes break, and I know that wild animals are prowling all around me. I am not afraid, but I am wary—mostly at the possibility that a robber, or maybe a whole band of them, will return to take what I have already taken.

Why they never returned for it in the first place is a mystery. Perhaps it is as Grandfather says: they were hunted and killed.

When sleep refuses me, I slide onto my knees. "Lord, God, my heart is grateful for this newfound bounty. Help me to use it wisely. I am about to become a real man. Bless me with Grandfather's faith, with Raz's devotion to family, with Calev's courage, with Mother's caring, and with Jonas's conviction to do the right thing. Bless me with Merari's hunting skills, and increase my own abilities as a warrior."

I'm still asking for blessings when I finally drift off into a fitful sleep. In my slumber the prophet Nephi's voice fills my head. I feel his hand cover mine. It is warm and stronger than I remember it. His voice is no longer thin but hearty and penetrating. I cannot look away when he looks into my eyes.

"Who are you?" he asks.

"I am Kiah. I am a warrior," I tell him.

Slowly, he shakes his head. "No. You are a robber."

I feel my fingers close around the decorated handle of the blade. "No. I am no robber. I found this bounty. It belongs to me!"

"You are a robber."

The accusation makes my throat swell, my chest feel a sudden cold grip.

"With all respect, I am Kiah, grandson of Yarden, your friend. I am the best friend of Jonas. I am no robber."

"*You* . . . are a robber."

"No."

"Have you not stolen what was already stolen?"

"I did not steal it. It was there for the taking."

"You are no better than Hem's men."

Guilt burns in my veins. My body twists and I hit my head on the side of a log. My eyes open to a layer of morning mist and the first rays of sunlight. It was only a dream and nothing more. Nephi did not appear to me. The voice of God did not convict me. There are no angels around me—just some wild animals and many birds filling the morning with song.

I check to be certain my treasures are safe. And they are *my* treasures. I tell myself that if I do not claim them, they will sit in the earth forever, never any good to anyone.

At daybreak I load my back and shoulders with my bounties. I wish I did not have to forfeit so much of my obsidian, but my knees threaten to buckle. I am not as strong as I thought myself to be, but I am no robber.

This is the message I tell myself over and over as I make my way cautiously down the mountain. I avoid roads where I might encounter other people. When I can no longer avoid hunters, explorers, and lumber cutters, I move off into the very thick of the tangle. It takes an extra day, but on my final morning I find a hiding place high above Elam. It's a terrifying place where serpents dangle from the trees and ground animals scurry about. Careful that no one is watching me, I use a thick branch to budge a boulder free. I hide my treasures, all except for the man's ring and the intricate blade. Then I carefully lay the vines and leaves around and over the boulder so no one can tell the spot has been disturbed.

I feel proud.

I feel victorious.

I have a secret that touts my bravery.

I have a treasure that can lift my family out of poverty.

When a fat *keeh* wanders into a clearing I take him down with two arrows to the neck. It takes me the rest of the day to skin him and carve the antlers from the skull. I use my outer cloak to carry the massive amount of meat.

A breaking in the bushes sounds, and for a moment I go stiff. It could be a *chakmool*, enticed by the scent of fresh blood, or it could be robber or a renegade Lamanite. But it's only another *keeh*—this one a doe, her belly so big I'm sure she's about to drop a fawn. We are living in times of plenty.

The closer I get to my village, the more people I encounter. I know these hills are populated, especially now that the branches bow with fruit. There are terraced spots where farmers failed to produce much during the famine, but now the rows are growing tall and green and I say a silent prayer of gratitude.

Nephi's accusatory voice was only a dream, nothing more.

It's a moist morning; the clouds are hanging low and the leaves around me are drenched with dew. I cannot yet see the details of my village from my high point, but then the quiet of dawn is broken and I hear the pound of music and the rise of voices singing. I wonder what has brought our village together in such festivity. I hurry down . . . down . . . down, scraping and scratching myself because I am not careful as I rush through the tangle to find my answer.

I break into the midst of the village celebration to discover that everyone is rejoicing over the safe return of Elam's warriors.

"Kiah!"

I spin and find myself in the crushing embrace of my brother.

Twenty

No treasure, regardless how shiny or valuable, compares to the joy and value of having Calev home safely. The brother I remember is not the brother who has returned. He hugs me with an enthusiasm that seems forced. I look not into the eyes of a young warrior but those of an old man. There is an angry scar across his cheek where a blade sliced into his flesh. When he smiles now the smile is tilted. One eye does not open as much as the other. Still he smiles, almost as though he is performing. But the joy on Mother's face is genuine when Calev holds her so tight her feet lift off the ground.

Grandfather's cheeks are soaked with happiness. He walks with his shoulders back and his smile wide. He cannot stop slapping Calev on the back, embracing him, kissing his cheeks again and again.

I look around, expecting to see Eliana's face, joyous at my brother's safe return, but she is not among the growing crowd. I do see the face of Tamar, peeking between other people, staring at Calev like he is an idol.

A twinge of cold jealousy poisons me as sure as a serpent's fangs. The venom swims through my veins and burns in my head. I want to run back into the hills and hide—to pray away these hard, bitter feelings. I want to smile and cry and rejoice that my brother and his noble band are home again safe. He is not the only warrior returned. Like Helaman's brave sons, all of Captain Uriel's warriors are back—some more scarred than others but all of them alive.

Grandfather declares our family will fast before we feast. Then we will truly celebrate and give thanks to God for His goodness. Everyone, it seems, wants to join in, and soon the entire village is planning official festivities. Some men come and take the meat from where I've dropped it, but they do not speak to me or acknowledge my hunting contribution. Another surge of resentment courses through me. I want to share. I want to celebrate. I just want to be recognized, too.

But this is Calev's moment. He deserves it . . . and who am I to diminish it? Shame burns the tops of my ears. I tuck my head.

My brother's lips flicker upward in an intentional smile. "You've grown, Kiah." My shoulders go back and I nod, feeling pleased that he noticed.

Grandfather seems to sense my discomfort and walks me away from the crowd. "What is it, Kiah?"

When I fail to respond, Grandfather leans toward me and his tone is serious. "A young, unblemished beast, Kiah—nothing less will do for a proper offering."

"You want me to go back out hunting?"

"For a thanksgiving offering. Nothing but the best."

"Yes, of course."

Calev rests his strong arm across my shoulder. He smells of old sweat. "I'll come hunt with you, brother."

Mother is quickly at his side. "No, you must stay. Kiah just returned from a hunt. Where are your spoils?"

"Some men took them for the celebration feast. I killed a huge *keeh* with only two arrows."

"Good," Grandfather says as if I told him I sneezed. He is too busy slapping Calev on the back to notice what I've done. It's all right. I will go back and return with a proper thanksgiving offering, a flawless dove perhaps.

Grandfather reaches out to grab me. "Where is it?"

"Where is what?"

"The obsidian."

I reach into my inner pocket and retrieve a bag of the precious glasslike rock.

"Is this all you brought?"

Before I can answer, a small crowd gathers and is asking where I found such large pieces of the treasured rock. I do not want to tell them. I do not want to share my secret or lead them anywhere near my hidden pillage.

Grandfather holds out the valued stones. Most are shiny black, but some are specked in white, and a few rounder pieces are swirled with color. "There is enough to share," he announces, taking the attention off me for the moment.

"We'll hunt together," Calev says.

I smile like I am happy. "It's not necessary. You only now returned. I'm sure you want to rest."

Calev sighs. "A hunt in these hills with my brother will be welcome. Come with us, Grandfather."

For a moment I think Grandfather will agree to join us. "I fear I would be a hindrance to you two brothers. My arm still lacks the strength to pull back a bow."

"I want to hunt alone." It's an announcement that comes out louder and harder than I meant, and it startles everyone.

Grandfather looks apologetic. "Kiah has become a seasoned hunter. He's used to hunting alone."

"I'm more than a hunter," I say, feeling a need to defend myself. "I'm a warrior."

Calev almost laughs. *Almost.*

Inside my cloak my fingers wrap around my new blade.

Mother is suddenly at my side. "Make your brother welcome, Kiah. If he wants to hunt with you, allow it." Mother's hands dig into her hip bones, and the look on her face is so hard it make me let go of my grip on the knife.

"It's all right, Mother," Calev says, "if Kiah wants to hunt alone—"

"No! You're only going for an offering. It will be simple and pleasant, I'm sure." She glares at me and my heart races. My lungs refuse to expand. This is nothing at all like the reunion I've imagined.

It's not only our little family who is drawn into the tension; other villagers, including Hem, are staring at us.

"Of course Kiah wants you to hunt with him," Grandfather bellows. "You two are brothers. Why wouldn't Kiah want to spend time with his brother?"

I try to swallow the burning liquid rising in my throat. "Yes. Of course I want *you* to come with me, Calev. I'm sorry. I didn't mean to injure your feelings."

This time he laughs aloud. "Good. It will give me time to hear the story of how my little brother has grown to be almost as tall and strong as I am."

Almost. The word hits me like a thrown rock.

Calev ruffles my hair, laughing. The sound echoes around our little courtyard and vibrates off the ground. It is the laughter of a man.

Twenty-One

We hunt in awkward silence. With Mother and Grandfather no longer there to push us into conversation, Calev and I have few words to share. It's as though I'm with a stranger; my heart feels broken. Why did I say what I said? Why did I try to spoil Calev's return?

"I'm sorry," I finally say.

"Why are you sorry?"

"You deserved honor, and I just wanted to be recognized because I'd brought meat. It was selfish."

He laughs again, and it's a sound I don't recognize—a sound I don't like.

"It was time for the celebration to end. I'm no hero."

"That's not what Uriel says. He couldn't stop boasting about you."

"I did not serve alone. There were fourteen other village warriors."

"But Uriel says you were the fastest—the bravest."

"Uriel is kind."

The awkward silence returns and slams a wedge between us. My brother seems stronger and older. Though he knows these hills as well as I do, I'm younger and faster, and he allows me to lead the way. More than once I look back to see him leaning against a tree trunk or pausing to catch his breath.

"Are you all right?" I ask.

"Go! I'm fine. There's nothing wrong with me."

There *is* something wrong with Calev. I don't know what it is, but something is not right.

"Is it Eliana?"

"Who?" he asks, his eyes narrowing.

"Eliana."

"The village girl?"

"The girl you favor."

He laughs again, a stranger's laugh. "I was a boy then. I'm not a boy now."

"I know, but she is a kind girl. She asks about you often."

Calev only shrugs.

More silence. I think I'd like to trust him with my secrets. I'd like to pour my soul out and tell him about Hem. I'd like to confess my guilt and my quest for greater faith. I'd like to zigzag up through the hills and lead him to the robbers' hiding place. I'd like to tell him every detail and show him the treasure.

I don't. I don't know why.

We move upward along the main road. We pass others, some of them hunters. If they know Calev, he stops to talk with them. I see how they look at him—with respect and honor.

Calev seems jovial when talking with others, but once we are alone and we move into the thick of the tangle, his mood becomes dark and quiet.

Our goal is simple: to find a thanksgiving offering worthy of Calev's safe return.

"You've changed," he tells me.

I look across at the brother I barely recognize. "*I've* changed?"

"Yes, you've grown in more than stature. You seem hardened. Are you angry?"

I feel my face go hot. "Why would you ask that question? Why not ask me how I managed to take care of Grandfather and Mother during the famine?"

"I'm sure it wasn't easy."

"It wasn't! There was no food. No water. I don't know what you were going through, whether you had enough food, but we didn't. People died, Calev. Kahana and Jacob, the high priest. One man's whole family perished. Did you know that Elam was divided?"

He looks as surprised at my anger as I feel. "How was it divided?"

I unload, trying to tell him everything—how absolute bedlam exploded at the peak of the famine, how Grandfather was nearly crushed in the confusion. I have no words to tell him how family fought against family, separating believers in the Messiah from the unbelievers. I try to describe our mother and how she became little more than a breathing skeleton. I try to tell him how I hunted, mostly alone, to provide anything and everything for the family. I try to open my heart to him, but my brother yawns.

As his mouth opens mine closes.

Calev turns his back to me so he can pick leaves from the plant that grows soft like the underbelly of a new lamb. I stop talking, and he does not seem to notice, but goes on making a sort of bed. Still not looking at me, he folds himself down with a sigh.

"Are you weary?" I ask.

"More weary than you can know." With that, Calev eases himself into a curve and closes his eyes. I stare at him. Did he even hear a word of my revelations? Did he care at all? He rolls over, and I'm still staring at him when Calev starts to snore. Without thinking, I check to make sure that no insects crawl on him. I see that his legs are scarred and his back carries the imprint of what looks to be a wound made by the piercing of a javelin.

What has my brother lived through? What has happened to change him from the quiet, confident boy who roamed Elam, mastering school, hunting, whatever challenge was before him? His scars are serious. How did he keep such injuries from festering? Every village has a healer who knows which leaves to mash to draw out the poison that comes with every wound; Elam has Pazel. Who tended to Calev's wounds? Looking at him curled up so tight, like an animal in a nest, I try to imagine all that my brother has been through. I try to feel love for him, and I do. Its intensity fills my chest.

His snoring stops, and Calev sleeps soundly without making any movement or sound. If I did not know he was there, half covered by leaves, I would be caught off guard. He only wakes when I lift my bow at the sight of a perfect dove, fat with wings of white. It has lighted on a branch above Calev.

Before I can draw my bow back he's on his feet. He's behind me, and his hands are tight around my throat.

"What are you doing?"

I can't answer because I can't breathe.

He lets go when my bow drops at his feet.

"I'm sorry, Kiah. You startled me. Never startle a warrior."

I say nothing because there is nothing to say.

A warm sensation of envy floods through my veins. My brother is a true, seasoned warrior. I am a hunter and a dreamer—little more. The bird is gone, the branch empty. We start back down the hill.

"Grandfather said you were part of an army that hunted Gadianton's robbers."

"I was."

"Did you kill them?"

He waits a long time before he replies. "Being a warrior is much more than taking the life of an enemy."

"What's wrong with you?" I demand. "Back in the village you seemed so happy, almost giddy with joy. Here you hold yourself like an old, worn man."

"It's the price of war. I must show the face of victory even if I feel defeated in my heart."

"What? What are you saying, Calev?"

"I'm not saying much. I have no tales to tell."

I push anyway. "Did you hunt Lamanites?"

"Yes."

Now that we are going downhill, I have to slide down the steep sections to keep up with his fast march. "Who else?"

"Anyone who made himself an enemy to the people of Nephi."

"How did you know which Lamanites were believers and which were not?"

He laughs, and it's an ugly laugh. "They make it very clear."

"Calev, there's something else I want to tell you."

"What?"

"I don't know if I should."

"Then don't."

"Calev, what's the matter with you? I've waited this whole time, praying every day for you to come home safely so we can hunt together and talk."

"I don't want to talk," he says.

"Maybe I do."

"Then talk." Calev sits on a moss-covered boulder and leans toward me.

I try to make my story build with excitement until I reveal that the leader of the evil band turned around to show the familiar face of Hem.

Calev drops his jaw. "Hem? From the marketplace?"

"Yes."

"What happened?"

"Nothing! I told Grandfather. Grandfather told the judges. They decided that it was my word against Hem's. They believed Hem. Or maybe they didn't even bother to ask him. All I know is that Hem continues to live free and evil. I hate him, Calev. I promise you Hem is evil."

"He is if he's a robber."

"*If?*" My bare heel digs hard into the earth.

"I don't mean to doubt you, Kiah. It's just hard to imagine Hem as a Gadianton. I remember him as arrogant and rich and rude. That's all."

"Well, now he's afflicted with palsy. You should see his face—one side hangs down, and he cannot speak a clear word."

"You seem pleased about that, brother."

"I am. He deserves it." I want to tell Calev about the time I raised my blade to take the life of the traitor, but I stop myself. Something in me hesitates to trust my own brother completely. "Calev, our leaders know about Hem—even the prophet knows about Hem—and yet they have done nothing to punish him."

"Maybe you just aren't aware of his punishment."

"What do you mean?"

"There are many robbers who have gone before the judges and the elders. They've been called to repent and they've repented. Only those privy to such circumstances know about them."

The idea that Hem might have confessed his grievous sins, that he might have been punished away from watching eyes, that he might stand forgiven— the idea is too much for me.

"Look!" Calev lifts a finger to point at a dove, white with white-tipped wings.

"It looks exactly like the one I almost shot."

"Do you want to shoot this one?"

"No. You take it, Calev."

And he does. My brother lifts a dart, sets it in a small round chamber, and blows. The bird keels over, and I am able to retrieve it as it comes to rest on the bow of a low branch.

"It's almost as if God wanted this bird to be your offering." The dead dove lies flat in my cupped hands.

"Remember Abraham and the ram?" Calev asks.

"I remember."

"You still sound angry, Kiah. Don't be. I'm not your enemy—I'm your brother."

Twenty-Two

The celebration begins after our fast has finished. The whole village appears at the altar to give thanks and make sacrifice for the safe return of Elam's warriors. Grandfather beams that we are able to lay a dove so perfect upon the altar.

My brother stands across the crowds with his fellow warriors. Some of them are drunk with wine, and I see Calev tip the cup to his lips. Then tip it again. I hope Grandfather doesn't see him. It would disappoint him; he's been boasting continuously of Calev's near perfection.

Elam's new chief priest is Buki, a father to a household of girls. His skin is fair and smooth; his words are quick and pleasing to the crowd. I know he and Hem are friends, and in spite of the office he holds, I do not trust Buki.

In a gesture of grandeur that upstages our white dove, Hem donates a lamb from the marketplace. It is flawless, and when it is hooked in the main archway it barely bleats or kicks, almost as if it is waiting to be sacrificed. The blood doesn't even splatter its pure white coat.

I study Hem carefully. He does not look like a penitent man to me, though he does appear stronger and seems more able to make his words understood. Is it possible that he was a robber and is now forgiven? Maybe it reduces to the fact that my word against the reputation of such a man was not enough to bring him before the court. I don't know the facts; I only know that standing in Hem's presence makes me scratch at my arms, my neck, my face. It's like his proximity infests me.

Buki talks with him. So do the twin brothers, Mathoni and Mathonihah. No one seems repelled by Hem like I am. Even Grandfather greets Hem with the usual brotherly kindness. When Hem sees me he lifts one side of his face in a menacing smile, and I suddenly feel like an outsider in my own village. I should be fearful, but my hatred for him outweighs my fear. He stands not only free, but free to boast. While Grandfather and Calev have brought honor to our family, everyone in Elam remembers the shame of my father's sins. Why should they be remembered while Hem's are buried? It is not fair.

It's also not fair the way Eliana has been reduced to wait on her father's needs. She stands at his side ready to wipe drool from his beard. Another man might feel embarrassed and not come out in public. Not Hem. He is as proud as ever, even though Eliana has to interpret for her father when he can't make his words clear. He leans against her strength. Her mother, Sherrizah, is nearby, and Tamar plays with the village girls her age—but Hem relies only on Eliana.

It's impossible to miss the way Eliana looks at Calev. She is smitten, smiling every time he casts his eyes in her direction. I also notice how he looks at her, his eyes heavy with drink. He might have spoken the truth when he told me that he was not interested in Hem's daughter, but now that he has seen her, his face speaks a different truth.

"What's the matter with you, son?" Mother asks me. "Are you ill?"

"Why?"

"You look shaken. Do you have a fever?"

"No. I'm well. Really." Why isn't she looking at Calev as he is openly drinking wine?

Abner is behind Mother—not directly, and far enough to be proper, but always looming near her. She seems to relish it as much as I resent it.

She tells me, "Perhaps you should go lie down. I'll make you broth."

"I'm all right."

"Isn't it wonderful to have your brother home?"

"Wonderful."

More than anything I want to flee Elam. I want to go back to live behind the high walls of the prophet's courtyard. I want to be with Jonas, who is my friend—not my accuser, not my competitor. I want to go where eyes do not stare at me with hatred or pity or where eyes fail to see me at all.

"Don't look so forlorn, brother; Hem's daughter does not interest me."

Calev stands next to Mother, speaking so loudly I'm sure everyone can hear. I want to put my hand over his mouth and make him be silent. My brother reeks of wine. "You are free to pursue Hem's eldest daughter."

My body shakes, and my face burns like it's next to a flame. "Hush, Calev. She can hear. Everyone can hear."

It feels like every eye in the crowd is on me.

Mother looks mortified. She grits her teeth and tries to keep her voice low. "Calev, you've had too much wine. You should not speak of such things."

Calev grins. "Why not, Mother? Eliana is older than Kiah; he's just a boy. But he favors her."

"No, I don't!"

"Shhh!" Mother says in her fiercest tone. "The poor girl can hear every word you boys say about her."

I look over and see Eliana staring at us. Her face is pale with pain. Hem stands beside her. His mouth is open, and the dumb look on his face makes me wonder if he realizes that his daughter is facing absolute humiliation.

Calev's head moves side to side. His voice only grows louder. "I've seen maidens so fair they make Eliana look like an ox."

Mother's hands slap over her own face. She moans with shame and embarrassment.

I want to plow my fist into my brother's slurring mouth to keep him from saying anything else that would hurt Eliana.

Calev pats my cheek. "Don't look so angry, Kiah." He blows the ripe scent of wine into my face. "She's yours if you want her."

With that, my brother turns his back and walks away toward Grandfather, who stands away in the crowd and who offers a broad, oblivious smile to his hero grandson.

Twenty-Three

Time passes.

While the embarrassment of that awful night does not fade, it also does not remain on the surface of our lives. It gets buried along with every outburst or cruel act that comes from Calev, a soldier whose wounds are not all on the surface of his skin.

Calev rests while I grow restless. I want freedom. I want adventure. I want excitement. I want something to happen besides the regular routine of everyday life.

Peace is still not peaceful to me.

Calev's moods teeter from times when he can't stop laughing to times when he hides his face and weeps for no reason. He spends much of his time walking the hills with Grandfather. They invite me to come along, and I do—sometimes. But I feel like an outsider with my own family. They talk of valor and of faith. Grandfather is mesmerized by the stories Calev recounts. I feel envious of the experiences that my brother had fighting for our families and for our freedom and for our faith. He knows what it is to feel the pain of a battle wound. He knows what it is to face an enemy during the final breaths of life. He knows all the things I can only imagine. His body is scarred with the marks of courage. The only scar I have is one where I sliced my own hand with my blade.

Abner makes his intentions clear toward Mother, though he's careful to keep his proper distance. It's just one more bit of gossip for Oshra and her friends to spread about our family.

I still don't know how I feel about Abner. He is kind and quiet and always eager to help. Maybe too eager. Abner's gift is to work with metals. He invites me to his shop, a cavelike workplace on the south road out of Elam. Actually, his is only one in a line of shops where men work with rocks, extracting different metals from them, experimenting with making useful things like tools that do not break, engraving plates that do not tear or crumble. It's fascinating to me how different rocks produce different metals—how Abner knows how to extract them, refine them, mold them into jewelry or sheets so thin they can be engraved with one of his writing tools almost as easily as writing on leather or bark.

"It's not a new practice," Abner explains, "but I learn something new with each experiment."

It's a noisy place, and I understand why it's set on the outskirts of the village. White-hot fires burn, and the smoky air smells strong and unpleasant. Many men are working hard—some carrying large stones, some breaking the stones apart, others grinding the smaller pieces into powder. The water from a stream is gathered in a large *mikvah*-like pool, and Abner has found a way to circulate the water so that it pours back into itself like a circulating fountain. I stare at the running water while he talks.

There is a clear order to their process, but I know I would lose my mind in employment so monotonous. All of the men—even tall ones like Abner—have hunched shoulders and faces creased in soot.

The walls of his shop are made of lumber coated with something that resembles Nephi's cement, though it is darker and has a smoother surface. It makes me think of the coating on my new blade.

"I know that you intend to marry my mother."

"I would be honored to be her husband. Anat is a virtuous woman."

"I've never seen my mother so happy," I admit, and he smiles. "But can you marry her? She's been married before. What does the law say?"

I ask the question because I know that Abner does not know the answer. He is not an unbeliever, but he is not valiant in his belief. I had never seen him at synagogue until he began to favor Mother, and then he went only because Grandfather accompanied him.

"I do not know the law," he admits, his smile gone, "but I know that I will make a way for our marriage. I have been given Calev's and Yarden's approval. I would very much like to have your approval, Kiah."

"I want only what is best for my mother."

And so one day follows the next. I hunt. I study. I practice my numbers and letters, and I hone my timekeeping skills with Raz. Nothing satisfies me. I dream of going to battle, but there are no battles. We are living in a time of peace.

Calev seems unhappy too. He has never mentioned Eliana again. No one has mentioned the unkind incident at the celebration. I wonder if Calev will follow Uriel's path and become an army commander. But war seems to hold no interest for my brother. Some nights Calev does not come home at all. When he does return, his body is pungent with wine.

If Mother or Grandfather notice, they say nothing. Mother dotes. Grandfather wants Calev to study the law and become a judge or maybe aspire to the priesthood.

"Why not both, like you, Grandfather?"

"A man with your skills can be anything he desires."

Calev laughs at the idea.

I shrink back, aching for Grandfather to make such a promise to me. But he doesn't.

Calev sinks into a string of dark days; he sleeps late and hardly talks. Finally, he accepts a position from Abner; he is to be a scout, locating the most valuable veins of ore deep in the earth. I think of my obsidian peak and wonder how long it will be before everyone knows of it. I think of my treasure, buried and safe in the ground, and say nothing of it.

There are a few villagers who still stand against those of us who believe in the coming Messiah. Grandfather calls them *dissidents* and seems relieved when they gather their families and leave to join the Lamanites.

As chief judge of our people, Lachoneus seems honest and harsh on those who break the law, especially anyone suspected of executing the secret oaths of Gadianton—except, of course, for Hem, who seems to be gaining power and popularity in Elam. I try to avoid the marketplace and any encounter I might have with Hem or his faithful daughter. How can I ever look at her again?

When Calev is not working for Abner he is obligated to train me in the battle skills he learned. My favorite days are when we join with other returned warriors and their younger brothers and relatives on a flat field by the old ball court; there we practice with our weapons. Not to boast, but I am quicker and stronger than even most of the seasoned warriors. Calev gives me recognition when I earn it. His praise motivates me to grow stronger and work harder.

I show no one—not even my family—my treasure. Checking on it gives me solace, a strange feeling that I know something others don't, that I possess something greater than others might imagine. Holding the ring in my hand, feeling its soft curve, touching the inlaid jewels one at a time seems to give me a strange feeling of power. Who crafted this ring? Did the metal come from Abner's shop?

One day I will bring it to light. Everyone will see that I am not just a boy so ordinary that no one takes note. One day I will wear it myself, give it to Grandfather, or sell it in the marketplace. For now, I finger the man's ring. It's very intricate and is too large for even my thumb. I wonder who might have worn it before. Who could afford to wear such an extravagance? Where is the owner now, and how did the ring end up in the robbers' treasury? All I have are questions. No answers.

I choose not to use my new blade . . . for now at least. The only time I bring it out is when I am by myself. Then I hold it and use it to ignite my imagination. Some days I am an ancient king—other days I am a chief judge. On a few days I lead an imaginary band of robbers. With the blade in my hand, my imagination knows no borders.

Grandfather helps me fashion small weapons from the obsidian I brought back. Together, we have made some impressive arrowheads and points from the hard, black stone. We tried to entice Calev to help us, but he seems to have lost interest in weapon making.

"You are very skilled at making weapons," Grandfather tells me, smiling with pleasure.

"Thank you, but what good are they in times of peace?"

His eyes brim with sudden sadness. "Our peace will not last. We are a proud people; as we prosper, pride overtakes us. Surely, Kiah, you will have cause to use your newfound battle skills."

I brighten, but Grandfather is harsh with me.

"Have you not learned anything from your brother?"

"What do you mean?"

"Has he not taught you that war is to be avoided, never to be sought? Calev has seen battle. He has seen men fight and die. He is a changed man, and you would be also if you had such experience."

"I *want* to experience war."

"I know you do, and that fact is very sorrowful to me."

"I'm sorry, Grandfather, but it is something that lives within my heart."

He smiles, but there is sorrow in the effort. "It will not be long until unrest returns to our land."

"At the synagogue I hear that the church is growing even more than it did during the famine. Is this true?"

"Yes, son. People are gathering to prepare for the Messiah."

"You sound like He might come tomorrow. Could it be that soon?"

"It won't be long; the signs are plentiful."

"Why aren't you happier, Grandfather?"

"I *am* happy, son. I've lived long enough to know when to savor a season of peace. You have never seen our people truly at war."

"Yes, I have. We've fought the Lamanites and the robbers."

"There will come a time when peace is what you'll seek."

I don't tell him so, but I know that he is wrong.

When Calev first returned home it was clear that he was the stronger and more skilled swordsman. As the season wears on, my skills improve. I practice everything he teaches me. While the morning clouds sit on the ground, I rise and work to improve my aim and my steadiness. What I lack in scripture scholarship I make up for in warrior skills. Even Calev's captain, Uriel, praises my skills.

He brushes a hand over the top of his sunbaked, bald head. "You will make a powerful warrior."

My heart swells.

"Don't tell Kiah that," Calev chuckles. "We won't be able to live with his pride."

The captain smiles at me. "When the time comes I will be happy to have you join my army."

My heart leaps, and I can feel it pulse with the first excitement I've felt in a very long time. I stand tall next to my brother, and it is the first time I realize I am now as tall as he is. My spine is still straight while his already slumps. My feet are fast and sure while his drag.

As soon as Uriel is out of earshot, Calev loses his smile.

A surge of anger rushes through me. "What's the matter, Calev? Are you jealous that your captain praised me?"

"You're a fool, young brother."

"A fool?" I raise my blade and wood strikes wood. "I'll show you what a fool I am!"

Calev uses both hands to swing; my sword clatters out of my grip and lands on the ground. Calev bends down and hands my sword back to me. I'm so humiliated and angry that I hesitate before accepting it. I don't want to feel like this, but I do.

"Kiah, I know you wish to enter battle, but I don't wish that for you. War is not what you imagine."

I hold my sword and whip around to leave. How, I wonder, does my brother know what stirs within my imagination?

Twenty-Four

An entire season passes in peace. Then another. I think I will go crazy with boredom. I train with Uriel, I hunt with Merari, I hunt alone. I study. I pray. Sometimes I think I receive answers; other times all I hear is silence.

I look at the girls in the village, but none of them interests me.

Eliana avoids me, and I don't blame her.

The old ball court is resurrected, the vines cut back, the ground rolled flat by slave labor directed by Hem. He has convinced the government to rebuild the court and to train a new team of ballplayers, lead by Mathoni and Mathonihah.

"One day Hem will require you to join the team," Calev tells me.

I laugh.

Calev doesn't.

Grandfather spends most of his time preaching, not only in our synagogue, but in the outlying villages and even in Zarahemla. His message is always of the coming Messiah. Calev accompanies him on a lengthy journey to Bountiful, and I spend my days with Raz, learning to make my letters and symbols more exact. I engrave on stone, bark, and leather, and when I improve, I engrave on some of Abner's metal plates. Even pounded thin, they are not easy to inscribe.

"You have the skills to become a scribe," Raz tells me. *Like your father.* He doesn't say it, but I hear it anyway.

I don't wish to offend him, but I do not wish to become a scribe. He seems to sense my feelings. He cups his hand over mine and teaches my fingers how to draw the symbols of battle—how to take a blank parchment and tell the tale of war through drawn pictures. I learn to replicate soldiers and officers, I learn to draw enemies and weapons, I learn to depict numbers even into the thousands . . . casualties and victors.

I fall in love with the craft of storytelling through pictures. Using a variety of quills and other writing instruments, I learn to draw whatever I imagine.

I feel inspired by the table in the worship hall, its beauty carved by my own ancestor.

"It was hard to get you started," Raz laughs. "Now it's impossible to stop you. One day you will become a great artisan. You will depict our history through art."

I smile. "I am not even a son of the commandment."

"Yes, you are. You were that long ago when you reached your thirteenth year. At that time you became a man of duty toward God."

"I mean I have not memorized the law like I should have. I cannot read the scriptures without making mistakes. I'm not responsible for the holy scrolls."

"You will prove yourself." He makes a circle in the air with his arm. "Give yourself enough growing seasons, and you will be a great man of duty toward God."

• • •

The prophet and his brother Lehi pay our village a visit. From our humble synagogue they teach of Christ and what we must do to be forgiven of our sins. Everyone seems at peace; Lamanites are welcomed across our borders, and we are allowed to venture into their territory.

Nephi and Lehi baptize many, and the church in Elam swells.

"Do you still desire to be a warrior, Kiah?" Nephi asks me.

He is strong again, his eyes clear and penetrating.

"I *am* a warrior," I say, repeating my declaration for him the way I have so many times for others—mostly for myself.

"There will come a time when you are asked to step to the front of the *real* battleground."

"I hope so." Though I cherish the characters I inscribe from my imagination, it's not the same as lifting my blade against a *real* enemy.

The prophet looks at me with love and I wish he could stay forever, but he and Lehi are traveling with their band of missionaries, moving from village to village, city to city. I wish Jonas was with them, but he is off with his father making structures of cement.

• • •

Hem grows strong again. Though he still slurs his words and uses Eliana as Moses used Aaron, his power in Elam is elevated. His reconstruction of Elam's ball court stirs great interest and enthusiasm and brings him honor and power in the eyes of the judges—even Buki.

"It would do great good to our morale if we returned to the days of entertainment," he announces.

There is a type of election, and the voice of the people choose to make the game of trickball their sport. If Hem declares a young boy has to play, then that boy has no choice but to join the team. Mathoni and Mathonihah are chosen team captains. I am relieved when I am bypassed and do not have to spend my days keeping a rubber ball in the air with my knees, feet, elbows, and head.

"Is it true that in some Lamanite ball courts the losing team is sacrificed?" I ask.

"It's true," Calev answers.

My brother and I are on a rare joint hunt down by the water's edge where Merari took me long ago. Now the water is higher than ever. Fowls are plentiful, and eggs are easy to find in ground nests.

"Have your war journeys been deep inside Lamanite territory?"

He gives me one of his blank stares. All day Calev has been in a jovial mood, but now that we are winding down for the night he sinks. "They not only sacrifice the losing team; sometimes the winning team is sacrificed as well—for honor."

"Then I'm grateful Elam will only be playing for sport."

We walk on, and I want to talk with my brother in the easy, free way that Jonas and I talk. I ask, "What are they like?"

"Who?"

"The Lamanites."

"They are like us."

"No, they can't be. Maybe the ones who have accepted Jesus, who have been baptized, they are more like us, but what of the ones who hunt Nephites like we hunt waterfowl?"

Calev lifts his eyebrows. "For pleasure? For sport? Kiah, I've told you many times, war between our people and the Lamanites is not something you should desire."

But I do desire it. I want a chance to finally prove myself—to live the life that I've always dreamed of living.

We hunt and have no problem bringing down waterfowl that we roast over a smoldering spit. While he pulls meat from a leg bone he says, "You're getting old enough to be thinking of marriage. Do you still favor Hem's daughter?"

"I never favored Hem's daughter. *You* favored her, Calev. You know you did."

"But she holds a place in your heart now."

"I feel sorry for her. Nothing more."

He tosses the bone behind us into the bushes, and a quick flash from the past plays in my mind. I see the Lamanite slave women who followed us when I hunted with Merari. That was a time of want. This is a time of plenty, but there is never a time for waste.

"I feel sorry for how I acted that night. I was drunk."

"You said some shameful things."

He shrugs. "I have no interest in the girl, really. You are free to ask Hem for her hand if you want."

"I don't. I never wanted her. But she's a kind-hearted girl who deserves a life better than the one she has."

He shrugs again. "I love someone else."

I almost choke on the meat in my mouth.

"What? Who?" My mind races through Elam, thinking of every maiden that might have stolen my brother's heart. There are many, but I have seen nothing of Calev's interest in any girl. "Is it someone from Elam, or someone you met while you were working for Abner?"

A spindly legged bird screeches and beats its wings to rise. We watch without lifting our bows. And keep watching until the sun makes us squint.

I wait for an answer. Everything about Calev is serious.

Finally he lets out a long sigh and meets my gaze. "I'm afraid that's a secret I can't tell even you."

Twenty-Five

Elam is growing—adding people and homes, businesses, an expanding marketplace, the burgeoning ball court—but I feel like it is shrinking. It's too small for me. There are days when my lungs refuse to fill because there is not enough air in our small village. I am thinking of approaching Mother and Grandfather, telling them that I have to depart Elam, when Mother approaches me.

She chews her bottom lip and is careful with her words. "I know that the Lord has blessed you with great strength and ability. You provided for this family when you were still a child. Now it is time to sharpen your mind as well as your weapons."

"You want me to obtain *more* schooling?"

"Yes."

The idea of more schooling, higher learning, is something that frightens me more than the growl of a wild animal. I open my mouth to protest, but already I know it's a losing battle. "I have studied with Raz. I know how to write. Put anything before me; I can read it."

Mother wipes little specks of meal from her hands. She's been grinding corn. "I'm proud of your progress, but now we are in a time of peace; you must take advantage and progress."

The thought of more schooling makes my skin sticky with sweat. "At school everyone looks at me. They talk about me. I feel ashamed. You can't imagine—"

"I know what it is to be stared at. I know the feeling of shame."

"Of course you do. I'm sorry."

Lately Mother has been the object of more gossip. After declaring his intentions to us, Abner is taking his time courting Mother. Oshra and her band torment Mother about it.

"What is it you want me to learn in school?" I ask.

"The commandments."

"I know them."

She lifts one eyebrow higher than the other. "All of them?"

"How many commandments are there?" I ask.

She frowns.

"See!" I say, seizing upon the subject. "That's a question even teacher Benjamin and the others don't agree on. How are we expected to keep all of the commandments when we don't even know what they all are?"

"How many do you think there are?" she asks.

"Too many."

"Be careful of your tone, son. When speaking of the commandments, you cannot be light."

"But there are the positive commandments telling us what we should do, and there are negative commandments telling us what is forbidden. There are commandments that don't even apply to us now that we are in the Promised Land instead of in Jerusalem."

Mother's hands go to her hips and her mouth twists.

"Hundreds. Mother, Calev feels the same way. I've heard him tell you so. There are more commandments than there is room in our heads."

I think I see a smile flicker across her lips. "The commandments should be kept not in your head, Kiah, but in your heart. Tell me, son, is there room in your heart for the commandments of God?"

"Yes," I say, quickly. "I just can't remember them all."

Mother laughs, and I know that all she has ever wanted for me is whatever will bring me closer to the Lord. It's what I want for myself too, but sitting listening to endless preaching and teaching, being tested and failing in front of others, is not something I want to do.

I think back on my education. It began when I was seven years old in a small area below the women's gallery. Sitting on the ground in part of a half circle, I tried to learn the truths that the teacher taught. To have no other gods than God. To honor mothers and fathers. That commandment has always confused me. How can I honor my father?

"I wish I could have educated both of my sons."

I realize she is talking about the fact that Calev got the better education because he is the firstborn son. He not only got the military training, he received lessons in the law, mathematics, and astronomy. I could be envious, but I'm not.

I know that I am by age a son of the commandment already. I also realize I lack the education that I should have. But if I went back to school now I would be surrounded by children. "Mother, I want to be obedient, but I can't do this. The scriptures are difficult for me, and I don't even understand my own birthday text."

Mother knows it by heart. "Say it with me," she urges, and my eyes look to her lips for aid. "Be strong and of a good courage, fear not, nor be afraid . . . for the Lord thy God, he it is that doth go with thee; he will not fail thee, nor forsake thee."

"I *am* strong," I tell her. "And no one has more courage than I do. I'm not afraid."

"You fear returning to school."

"I'm not afraid. I just don't want to do it."

"I believe it is best for you, though I cannot force you to do it."

"I can."

We both turn to see Grandfather standing in the open doorway. He looks stern. "We've talked about this before, Kiah. During times of peace there is purpose—and that purpose is to learn. During times of war there is no time for studying. You have this opportunity before you. Choose wisely."

"I have a choice?"

"It's not my desire to force you, but we both know I have the right."

"Will you allow me to think about it?"

"Of course."

"In the high hills?"

Grandfather and Mother laugh.

"That is not only my hunting ground; it's where I go to think, and yes— to pray." A flash of the many times I've knelt in prayer outside by myself enters my mind. "I do pray. I will pray again about school. It's just that in Elam I feel so confined. Everyone knows me and knows—well, our past. They know my ambitions and my shortcomings. At school I've never earned favor. The teachers at the synagogue don't wish for me to return any more than I wish to return to my studies."

"Would it make a difference if you were able to move to Zarahemla and live with Jonas? You would be given new teachers that have no reason to judge you on anything beside your abilities."

My heart jumps. This is my chance to break out of Elam. "Mother, would that be acceptable to you?"

She sucks on her bottom lip. It takes a while for her to answer. "I think everyone in this family is ready for change. Go with my blessing, Kiah."

• • •

I go.

But instead of heading in the familiar direction of Zarahemla, I find my feet turning toward the unknown.

Twenty-Six

On my way to the new territory, I veer off the path and look at the spot where I buried my treasure so long ago. Much time has passed since I've checked on it. The area is dense with vines and overgrowth. I have just decided not to chop into it when I spot a nest of writhing, newly hatched snakes. I know from their flat heads and dappled scales that they are venomous. I back away swiftly, telling myself that I am not afraid when I am *very* much afraid. The sun is at its crest, yet my face is cold and slick with sweat.

If I chopped the snakes and cut the overgrowth, such damage would surely invite the curiosity of any explorers who happened along. It's obvious that no one and nothing has invaded my secret. I'm sure the items I buried are safe beneath the stone and tangle. I try to remember what they look like. I wish I could show Raz the calendar. And the war mask—if I donned it, would Hem recognize where I got it? One day I will retrieve my treasures to sell—if not to help Mother, then to help myself. I will use the money for a dowry when I find the right wife.

My desperation for adventure overpowers me, and I move away from the areas I've traveled before. I hadn't planned to, but my feet move toward the sea. For days I trek territory that is new to me. Exciting. I see faces I don't know, people who do not look on me with judgment. Lamanites and Nephites are not always easy to distinguish, and the closer I get to the water's edge, the more everyone seems to blend into a single people. But so far no one has threatened or even disturbed me.

The cities are laid out in square blocks, not always equal in distance. Their marketplaces are not central like Elam's, but spread out—on one street vendors are selling cooking wares, on another the street is lined with vendors selling earthen pots. The music is different because the language is different. The people here speak the same language I know, but they speak so fast that it's hard for me to understand much of anything.

Atop a stone pyramid I mistake for a temple, I see for myself the horrors of idol worship. A huge stone statue of something that appears to be half man and half creature burns, its hollowed-out belly bright with fire. There must be thousands of people gathered around it, chanting, dancing, calling for a sacrifice. They pray to the statue, beg it for fruitful crops and success in war.

What war?

I turn away from the sacrifice they make: a young girl, her hands and feet bound with tender vines, her mouth gagged. The chief explains in a tongue I can barely understand that the stone god requires human blood and will not grant them next season's crops—will not protect them from their enemies—unless the sacrifice of a human heart is made.

I am dizzy trying to fathom such a god. I want to stop them, but know I cannot. I break through the gathering crowd and lope down the road. I do not stop until I can no longer hear the beat of their drums. I vomit. The God I worship requires the sacrifice of a broken heart, but not a beating heart.

A whisper deep from within me warns me to turn around and go back toward Elam, but the excitement of the unknown, the danger of walking among enemies, is still too enticing.

The scent in the air changes. The sun seems lower in the sky, and my very skin feels different. I come upon a city that is laid out much like a larger version of Elam. The marketplace is massive and busy. It's more colorful than anything I've ever seen, and the food is plentiful. The aroma of fresh fish grilling over flames reminds me that all I've eaten for days are roots and berries.

I stop to listen to a man preach. His headband is brilliant with feathers—orange and green, yellow and blue. His feet are shod with leather that laces almost to his knees. His necklace is a replica of the statue that just consumed an innocent girl's life. I cannot tell whether he is a Lamanite or an Amalekite. This is the land where they all seem the same.

The preacher sees me and lifts his chin. He also lifts his voice: "As a prophet I tell you that whatsoever a man does is no crime. Our creator did not mean for one man to rule over another. We have been bound by foolish traditions for far too long."

His message is one I've heard before in my own village—but there it is preached by men who do not know the Messiah and His message.

I exchange some cacao beans for a piece of fish and a portion of bread. The food is delicious, but my stomach turns at the so-called prophet's message.

"This life is a time for living. When we die there will be no punishment for those who enjoyed the appetites of the flesh. For those who cry that a

Christ will come to separate away the sinners, I say *liar!* No Christ will come. There is no Messiah. Those who wait for His coming are fools."

A feeling stirs within me. It starts in my loins and travels up through my body until my heart feels ready to burst. Though the man is garnering the approval of the crowd, I know the words he speaks are not the teachings of a true prophet. Nephi would never utter such things. Grandfather would pull the man down from his platform.

"There *will* be a Messiah!"

The prophet stops and points into the crowd. His finger is aimed at me.

"I am Kerem, son of Kerem," he introduces himself. His hair and skin are fair. "What are you called?"

"I am Kiah, grandson to Yarden. Our village is Elam."

Kerem lifts a small, carved staff. "You are a Nephite boy."

"I am a Nephite, but I am not a boy."

A few people snicker.

"And you know something I do not know."

"I know that we await the coming Messiah."

Kerem does not snicker. He does not smile. He moves toward me and the crowd follows. "This Messiah that you speak of, tell us about Him. Feel free to step up on the platform. Teach us, Nephite."

My tongue feels swollen. My head feels empty. But my heart is pounding with a desire to defend the Messiah. I do not stand on the platform, but I do raise my voice. "The Messiah is the Son of the living God."

Kerem makes a face. "What more can you tell us?"

How I wish that Grandfather was beside me now. I try to say what he would say, but there is no power behind my declaration. "I know that He will be born of flesh. He will come to redeem us. It is through the ultimate sacrifice of His life that we will find Atonement."

"You use words I do not know. What does *redeem* mean?"

"To buy back."

"So we are sold?"

I'm starting to feel confused. I'm afraid of saying the wrong thing, for I know Kerem is like a predator waiting to pounce on its prey. I am the prey, weak and vulnerable. *Lord, help me.*

"Where are your words, Nephite boy? You confuse me."

The crowd is with him. I feel them closing in on me, and I start to wish that I had kept my mouth closed. "We are in bondage to sin." I've heard Grandfather say the same thing so many times, but the words are weak and pitiful coming from my mouth.

The man slaps his chest with an open palm. "*Me?* I am in bondage to sin?" His arms sweep over the people. "Are you in bondage to sin?"

"No!" they cry as with a single voice.

Kerem's light eyes go dark. "Who are *you* to call *us* sinners? Who are you to tell us of Messiah? Have you seen Him?"

"No."

"Has He talked to you?"

I stumble backwards; a group of men are pushing against me, and I think of the time in Zarahemla when I had to flee. I'm in a strange city with strange people. Why couldn't I have just stayed quiet? "Jesus Christ is the name of the Messiah who will come to redeem us all if we are willing to repent."

Kerem scoffs at the word. "By what authority do you come here to condemn us?"

The crowd breathes as one, and I know I am in serious peril.

Kerem jabs my shoulder with his finger. "You do not know your own Messiah. You have no means to know of His coming or even of His existence. You worship an invisible god."

More laughter.

"I know He will come!" A flicker in my heart ignites into a flame. "I *know* the Messiah will come."

"You know no such thing. You are a foolish boy who has been taught foolish things. Are you not the grandson of a Nephite?"

"I am."

"You have no father?"

"No. I have no father." Immediately, I'm something less than nothing.

"What is your business in Shimnilom?"

"This city is called Shimnilom?"

He laughs and everyone seems to join in, mocking me. "You don't know where you are? Who travels with you, boy?"

"I am alone."

"You are alone. And you have violated our laws, telling us that your invisible god is greater than the god we know, we see, we worship. It is a crime, Nephite boy, for you to preach such blasphemy!"

The crowd closes around me. Hands, many pairs of hands, grab at me, yank me—first in one direction, then another. I fight. I struggle. I reach for my blade.

"Prison!"

In the next instant my neck jerks forward, and I feel a pain at the back of my head. I refuse to faint. I can feel my body being dragged, and I refuse to lose consciousness. Their shouts grow thin and distant. The image of Kerem's face blurs. I only need to close my eyes . . . for a moment.

When that moment is over I force my eyelids open because there is a terrible sensation moving across the bare part of my leg.

"Help me, Lord!" I plead aloud when I realize that I've been thrown—not into prison, but into a pit thick with slithering snakes.

Twenty-Seven

Black and thin. Yellow and fast. Green and sluggish. Tan and red. And at least two pure white snakes are either on me or around me. They are like twisted ropes, great and small, rattling, snapping, hissing, and coiling themselves around each other.

I fear to breathe. I fear to allow my heart to beat.

I've been dumped into a pit of vipers. The walls are made of stone, and the space is so small my legs are not stretched, but bent at the knees. I allow my eyelids to barely flutter. What comes into focus is a ring of faces staring down at me—the object of the people's entertainment. I hear laughter, but mostly I hear blood coursing in my head.

Have I already been bitten? I feel no pain, only the gliding scales against my legs and arms. I see delirious faces smirking at me. People laughing, pointing.

"Where is your Messiah now? Is He coming in time to deliver you?"

Rings and coils of my greatest fear thrash and slither all around me. They are hot, like burning logs; I know it's because they have taken on the temperature of their surroundings, which means the pit will keep getting hotter. What does that matter to me? I won't be alive.

God . . . oh, my Father.

Someone tosses a giant bullfrog into the pit, and the snakes dart and slide in every direction. The creature stands no chance and is quickly struck by a variety of gaping, fanged mouths. One snake is so powerful it rips at the frog's leg, practically pulling the creature in two. If I die now or if I die in a hundred years, I will never forget the tortured sound that frog makes as it is bitten over and over by vipers.

My eyes close, and my heart opens. *Father, protect me.*

It's all I can think to pray. I see an image of Mother's grief-stricken face when the days pass and she realizes I will not be returning. I know that

Grandfather prays for me when I am away; I hope he is praying for me now. Calev—will he miss me at all?

The weight and warmth of a snake moves toward my face and slithers across my forehead. A mouth hisses close to my ear. I want to cry, but even the shedding of a tear might be the cause for a fatal strike.

I pray again, silently, desperately. There are no set words, only a supplication so strong and sure I know heaven has to hear. *Father, I know that I am unworthy of such a request. I know that I lack faith. Protect me. I'm afraid. I'm alone. I'm a fool. But I'm Thy son, and I know that Nephi and Lehi and Grandfather were protected in the prison, I know that Daniel was protected in the lions' den, and I know that I can be protected now.*

The snake ripples across my face. I open my eyelids to a mere slit again.

The crowd is screaming, and it's difficult to make out their words. I see Kerem. He is standing with his arms high in the air. "What do you fear, Nephite boy? If your god lives to deliver you, let Him deliver you now!" His laughter is enough to shake the ground, to agitate the vipers, to end my life.

Two men push past him to make their way to the edge of the pit. They are carrying a vessel with a lid. When they tip it sideways a nest of tiny black vipers, no bigger than ground worms, falls into the den. Again, the rest of the snakes hiss and strike and crawl all over me. Some bite each other; one large brown snake is trying to swallow a yellow snake, headfirst.

The people want me to stir. They want me to scream. They want to me to try to crawl out of the pit so that the snakes will attack me. I lay as still as a corpse and never stop praying. My mind moves away from the snakes and winds back to a time when I was still small enough to hold my mother's hand. A man in Elam was struck by a rattling snake. He lived near us, and I went to his courtyard and watched him lying on the ground. He did not die—not right away—but his leg went red and bloated. The next day that red leg was black. The next day the man was dead.

I've seen others suffer viper bites, and the fear of my fate should be making me quake.

It's not.

I lay still. Even if I wanted to, I don't think I could move. A peace in a place where there is no peace fills me and makes my body heavy, unable to even blink.

The louder the crowd, the more snakes they toss in, the greater my tranquility. I can still feel the snakes. Hear them. I know I am surrounded, and yet the fear that gripped me has left.

Am I already dead?

If I was, Kerem would not be so red faced and furious.

"What is wrong with the vipers? Why are they not striking? We know they favor Nephite flesh!"

He gets a roar from the spectators.

My body and my mind are still. I don't even twitch.

Kerem kneels down and reaches into the pit with his staff. He pokes at the snakes. They coil and hiss and strike only air. "Your Messiah never was," he hisses as sure as a snake. "He never will be."

"My Messiah lives!"

I say the words. My lips move, my tongue moves, and the snakes around me move. If I must die then I will die, but I will not save my own life to deny the truth that has filled my entire being. I know now what I have not been sure of: Jesus Christ is the Son of God. His great plan of redemption includes me. No matter what my fate is, my faith will not be struck down.

Someone suggests that perhaps my God, my Messiah, is protecting me.

I smile because I feel it.

Kerem, eyes bulging, raises his staff and brings it back down, this time to stir the pit until my life is ended.

But one snake's reach is greater than the so-called prophet predicts. It is a divided snake, red and black with bands of white. It is fast and sinks its fangs into the wrist of Kerem. The staff falls and clatters against my legs. The snakes are frenzied. The look on the man's face is complete shock. Slowly, he lifts his arm and stares at the dangling viper that refuses to release itself. Kerem tips his head and stares. His followers back away until he alone is standing above me.

Then the snake drops back into the pit.

Kerem looks down at me. His mouth opens and closes. He appears completely confused.

Everyone had been so loud; now they are quiet and I can hear my heart thunder. I can feel the snakes. One little one, yellow as a mountain flower, has wound itself around my small finger. I don't shake it off; I just let it nestle there. As I look at Kerem, his face seems to change. For a moment I see the face of Hem. Then I see the face of a flat-headed snake with shiny black eyes and a mouthful of fangs.

"Your Messiah," he says, sounding like he is being strangled, "He is your Savior?"

I look at him, knowing my eyes testify to my convictions.

"Why is He a savior?"

Because we all need saving, I think silently.

Kerem backs away until I can no longer see him. I can no longer see any face or hear a single voice.

Father, be with me.

The snakes continue to wriggle and writhe. I lay unmoving.

I wait.

I wait on God.

The sun beats down. I smell a foul odor. I hear a city gone silent. Darkness slowly descends, and I realize that the people have left me to the snakes. Tomorrow when the sun rises they will muster their courage to peer over the edge and see what is left of me.

I wait.

I wait on God.

As darkness fills the night, a melody fills my head. *Be still and know that I am God.*

It's the scripture that Mother likes to sing. It's the melody she has sung to me a thousand nights. It may be what she is singing tonight in Elam. I wonder if she is staring at the same white sliver of a moon that hangs over me.

I wait.

I wait until God tells me to move, and then I bring myself upright. Snakes I can feel but no longer see are restless. Together they make the sound of wind moving through leaves. The little yellow snake is tight around my finger, but I uncoil it and let it drop.

I stand. I slide my sandals between a layer of thrashing snakes, trying not to crush them beneath my weight. I reach high for the edge. It's too far up to grasp. I have to take my sandals off, step over and on snakes with my bare feet. I have to wedge my toes between the stones and writhe like a snake myself to climb free.

"Oh God, I give thanks," I say aloud just as I am about to escape the vipers' den unharmed . . . just as I feel the fangs of a snake sink deep into my bare heel.

Twenty-Eight

The white slice of moon is hiding behind a gauzy cloud. I look up and cannot find the guiding star; it's too dark. Then I look around me. I thought I was alone—thought all the people abandoned me in the pit to suffer an agonizing death. I was wrong. There are still people around, lining the street. I can barely make out their faces in the shadows of night, but I can see their eyes. Their eyes are wide with wonder and horror.

My heel hurts—the same pain I would feel if I'd run my blade across it. My foot drags a bit behind me, over the stone and dirt road. I look but do not see Kerem. A snake bite, even the most venomous, does not kill right away. I know that the purpose of a snake bite is not to kill but to immobilize the victim. If I were in Elam I would go to Pazel, our village healer. He would wear his spirit mask and know which roots to mix to draw the venom out. Mother would pound fresh seeds from the yellow flowering plants that grow in the flat rocky lowlands. She would mix that with her own saliva to make a poultice. Grandfather would lay his hands on my head and invoke the power of God to heal me.

If I was in Elam . . . but I am in a land as foreign to me as any place I have ever been.

With eyes still fixed on me I move to a stone bench made for resting. The feeling of snakes still warm and crawling on me is real. I have to tell myself I am free. For the rest of my life I will know that sensation. How long will that be?

All I can think of is to grab my heel, filthy and poisonous as it is, and put it in my mouth. I suck as hard as I can and taste bitterness and heat, as though I've bitten into a scorching pepper. I spit and spit again, but it's been so long since I've had anything to drink my tongue is dry and spongy.

For a time I do not move. A quiet, familiar plea repeats itself over and over: *Be still and know that I am God.* Eyes through the darkness close in around me. These people would kill me, return me to the pit, but now they seem afraid of me. I'm not sure why. I wonder how long until I cannot move, until the blood in my veins stops and my muscles turn to mush. There will be no time to return to Elam. I will die in a strange land, unburied, devoured by wild beasts, picked at by vultures. My bones will bake in the sun, and my mother will mourn for me.

If these are truly to be the final moments of my life, what am I to do? I remember the words of Grandfather: "When faced with a trial, know that the first words out of your mouth will set the course."

I lift my head to the sky. My shoulders go back, and my barren voice is as melodious as Mother's. "Hear, people everywhere: The Lord is our God; the Lord is One. I praise Him. I thank Him. I honor Him. He who heals all flesh can heal me now."

The road is lined with wondering people, most of them terrified that snakes might still cling to me. Their eyes search my body for the bites that surely have to be there. They look upon me like I am the walking dead. The moon still seems small, but I can see around me, make out details that a moment before were dark. The light gives me strength to imagine I am a different kind of warrior, a warrior for a higher captain. "The Messiah is Jesus Christ. He will come. He will come to redeem and save."

The words slip off my tongue differently. I have not drunk a drop of water in hours, my throat is parched, my mind is wild with what I've been subjected to, and yet I feel whole and stronger than I ever have.

People lurk, staring at me in wonder.

"The Messiah will come to you if you will come to Him."

I walk, limping but moving toward the water's edge. I can see a faint glimmer of blue-black in front of me, and the thought of immersing myself in water motivates me to keep plodding. Night stingers are thick in the air, and I slap at my neck; I hear them buzz in my ears. A few people along the path have torches, and I see their faces most clearly. Some are twisted in hatred. Others are horrified. A few recognize what I now know: They are witnessing a miracle.

I am that miracle.

My heel feels like I have stepped on white-hot coals. I'm not sure how much longer I can keep walking. My head throbs and my heart won't stop racing. I can feel it pound in my throat. Has the venom already made its way that far?

"I testify to you that the Messiah is a God of mercy and a God of justice."

What else can I say? If Nephi were here he could go on without stopping. I have to stop because as fast as my energy burst, it has waned.

Someone throws something hard and wet at me, and it slaps the side of my head. It's dark and I can't tell what has hit me. A dead fish? A piece of rotten fruit?

"Boy!"

A voice comes out of the darkness and I know it. Why do I know it? My eyes blink, and still I cannot focus. The heat in my heel, even the pain, is changing. I sit on the ground and rub the spot around my wound. Strange—I'm pressing hard, but I can't feel my own foot. I've got to get to the shore, so I stand, feeling unbalanced.

"Boy!"

That voice again.

"Who's there?"

The road is made of sandy dirt. Palm trees line both sides. The tangle is thick around the base of the trees. Two men step out from the shadows. They are holding a bed made of limbs and leaves; on it is a man's writhing body.

"Who are you?"

Someone else brings a torch, a flame that casts a sallow light on strange faces.

"Kerem."

"The prophet?" This man does not look like Kerem, the man who hours before stood strong and proud. This man is curled like a worm, quaking and sweating. One arm is normal; one arm is the size of an army club.

I try to walk past; the man's good arm reaches out and swats at me. Are they going to throw me back into the vipers' pit? Are they going to kill me? Don't they know that I am already dying?

"Your Messiah," Kerem says, his voice the croak of a dying bullfrog. "He redeems sinners?"

I shake my head—not to answer him but to try to clear my mind. My thoughts are swirling like leaves in a storm. "Yes."

"Can He redeem me?"

"You—the man without sin?"

"I am a sinner. Tell me of your Messiah and His power to redeem."

"But you prophesied that there is no Messiah and never will be."

Something dark is draining from the man's mouth, and his words are difficult to understand. "I am a dying fool."

"You . . . " one of the other men says, pointing to me, "you were saved from the vipers."

I am not saved—but I *feel* saved.

"You are unharmed."

I am dying. Can't they see that? My leg has no feeling and drags behind me like a broken limb. My eyes do not see clearly. It is difficult to draw a full breath.

"What is the light around you?"

Is the man a fool? It's his own torch.

Gently, the men set Kerem's bed on the ground. "Redeem me," he says in a beggar's tone.

I try to walk past, but Kerem thrusts himself off the pallet and rolls onto the hard dirt road. He looks like an animal gone mad. Pink froth is foaming from his mouth, and his eyes are glassy. I wonder if mine are glassy too. *You murdered me*, I want to say, and yet this man is now begging me to save him, to do for him what only the Messiah can do.

"My sins are vile," Kerem says. "Forgive them, Nephite boy. Redeem me!"

He's weeping like a punished child.

"I've seen a real prophet," Kerem goes on, sputtering words from his frothy mouth. "Lay your hands on my head; use your power to heal me."

"Only God can heal," I tell him. I try to walk past him, but Kerem's guards block me.

"Take pity on Kerem," one man says, holding out his hand. "These are yours."

I realize he is offering me back my blade and sling. He must have taken them from me before they threw me in the vipers' den.

"Forgive me," the man says, bowing his head. "You are more than a believer; you are an angel."

I have a sudden urge to laugh. The world around me is spinning, and I feel ready to vomit. "I am no angel."

"You were sent here from God, like the other prophets before you."

"I am no angel. I am no prophet. I am a believer, and I came to your city out of curiosity. I wanted to see the sea."

The men tip their heads in doubt. The one who handed me back my things says, "The light around you, it glows like that of an angel."

What light? The moon? The torches?

Kerem makes a choking noise to get my attention. "You are a believer. You have the power to heal. Heal me, I beg you; heal me!"

I do not have the power. I am not a son of the commandment; the priesthood has not been conferred upon me. I have no authority to heal this man. Only now, in that mass of snakes, did I become a true believer. I know now what I had only hoped to know before.

Kerem claws at me with his healthy hand. "I beg God, *your* God, to forgive me."

His voice changes; in my head I hear not Kerem, but Hem. Has Hem begged God for forgiveness? I should be the one begging. I have my burdens, my secrets, my sins.

"Leave me alone, let me go," I manage to say, though even to me my words are the slur of a drunk. "I have nothing to offer."

"You! You can heal me."

"I cannot. I forgive you, but I cannot heal you. It's God's forgiveness you should beg." I pause to lace my sheath around my thigh, the pouch that holds my sling and blade.

There are more people gathered near; a sunken-cheeked man with a pocked face nods and steps aside to let me pass. A tall man with no covering for his bald head holds the torch. He too steps back, allowing me to walk on. I move beyond them, dragging a leg I can no longer feel.

Kerem cries. He screams. He threatens. He begs.

His voice fills the entire night and is still ringing in my head when I finally reach the coast. The water is cool and deep and comes at me in waves. At first I stand and lift my face to a half-smiling moon. It seems to be grinning at a boy who once thought himself a grown warrior. What is he now?

The thought laps around and around, like the waves that keep coming in and going out, licking at my feet. I hope they can wash away the feeling of snakes crawling across my skin. I wade in, and as the water gets deeper, so does the darkness. "Be my light in the dark, oh, Lord," I open my mouth and force the words out past a dry, swollen tongue. "In Your great mercy You have delivered me from a pit of vipers. You are with me now; I can feel it. Do not leave me. Do not let me die alone."

A wave crashes against my chest and rocks me backward in the swell of water. Arms that I cannot see reach out to catch me as I collapse and fall face-first into the sea.

Twenty-Nine

I am a piece of driftwood on the shore—twisted, sunbaked, and alone. But I am far from dead. My heart still beats—actually throbs in my head. My lips are cracked and covered in dry, black blood. My leg is swollen and painful, but I can feel it. All this I discover as I lay in the primal wash of morning sunshine. Sand is gritty everywhere, catching between my toes and in the webs of my fingers.

As far as I can see in one direction, turquoise water scallops white sand. As far as I can see the opposite way, turquoise water scallops white sand. I think that this is what the Old World looked like when Lehi and his family camped along the shores of the sea. Is it any wonder they did not want to leave?

Painfully, I straighten myself and brush sand from my heel. The puncture marks are clear. The foot is an angry red and very tender. With great effort I manage to stand and find that I can bear the weight.

Immediately, I drag back into the water. It's too salty to drink, and it stings where my flesh is open, but I love the water, the feel of sand beneath my toes; I stay there for a very long time, savoring the sensation. It is the perfect place to pray my prayer of gratitude. "I give thanks before You, living and eternal King, merciful God who has kept me alive. How abundant is Your compassion. How faithful is your faithfulness!"

Slowly, I remember the previous day. I remember the excitement of being in a strange place. I remember the taste of fire-roasted fish and hard-ground bread. I remember Kerem preaching that there would be no Messiah. I surprised myself when I contradicted him. I close my eyes and remember angry faces. I hear the shouting and I feel the pain. I remember the snakes—hot snakes, coiling and writhing and ready to kill me. More than I can count, as many shades and sizes as nature itself.

"God Almighty! I am delivered." The weight of that reality slides off me and leaves me unable to move for a time. Even when I can move I don't want to leave the soothing waves of the water, but as the pink sun climbs higher I return to shore and find myself not alone at all. I'm still the object of spectators that watch me from a distance.

I open my mouth to call out, but I can make no sound—only a growl that frightens even me.

Children are the first to approach me.

"What are you doing here?" asks a little boy with curly dark hair and eyes that remind me of obsidian.

I indicate that I cannot speak—that I need a drink of water.

He runs, spraying sand with his bare feet. When he comes back he is carrying a small waterskin with enough fresh water in it to drench my mouth and ease the burn of my throat. I accept it gratefully and relish the water; more than that, I relish the child's kindness to me.

"How are you called?" I manage to ask.

"Abina," the boy says, his eyes darting around for his friends who are a few steps back, uncertain of my presence. Beyond them a line of adults—mostly women—wait expectantly.

"Abina, thank you." I hand back the empty skin. "I am called Kiah."

"Are you an angel?" he asks me, his little shoulders hunching, his voice going shy.

"No. I am no angel."

"My mother says that you are an angel sent from God." He points to the women; one of them nods.

I think how fast rumors race, reaching everyone in Shimnilom like a fever. "What else does the story say?" I ask.

The boy looks down. "That you killed Kerem, our prophet."

"He's dead?"

"He's dead. I saw his body as they carried it to the square to be burned for all to watch. I am going with my friends to watch Kerem burn. Do you wish to come with us?"

"No. But I did not kill Kerem. A snake bit him."

"You made the snake bite him. *You* told the death snake to bite him. You told the snakes *not* to bite you."

I lift my ankle. "Look. A snake bit me too."

Abina and some of his braver friends close in around my exposed heel. They nod when they realize that I am not an angel but an overgrown boy with a painful snakebite. They seem relieved.

"Do you want more water?"

"Yes."

Fast feet run to fetch more water and a round of bread.

I eat and drink and talk to the children of what it is like to live in a land of high hills and wild animals. They tell me what it is like to live in a land where there is water and wind, always. Where the smell of fish never leaves the air. They show me how to braid rope from thin, dried vines.

We are there by the shore for a long time before the adults finally venture close enough to call for their children.

Abina's mother is a narrow woman with trusting dark eyes. The woman next to her has a flat nose and a toothless mouth. She eyes me with suspicion and mutters something that I don't understand.

Abina jumps between us. "Kiah is just a big Nephite boy. He's no angel."

The woman sucks her lips in. Her hand darts out and she grabs hold of Abina's ear, yanks it hard, and says something else.

The boy jerks away. "Do not send someone to harm Kiah! He is like a brother."

"He cursed Kerem."

I shake my head and point to my swollen, throbbing ankle. I want her to see that I too was bitten.

She frowns and casts her dark eyes in every direction. Then she lifts her chin at me, warning me to be on my way.

"Thank you again," I tell the children, smiling broadly at Abina, who looks sad at my departure.

The heel is sore, but I can balance on the leg and I set off for the same worn road that brought me to the water's edge.

"No," Abina's mother tells me. "Go there!" Her finger points off through the high grass that scallops around the water's edge. The green leaves are sharp, waist-high, speckled black. "Follow the trail until you are safely out of Shimnilom."

I nod and feel sadness at leaving the children, but I know I must go. I turn and start off.

When I look back Abina has his arms folded across his chest in the same proud manner as Kerem when he prophesied that there never has been and never will be a Messiah.

I wave and smile.

Abina waves. I am almost out of earshot when I hear him call to me. "Walk carefully, Kiah. You never know where a viper might be hiding, just waiting to strike."

Thirty

I awake during the night to quaking earth all around me. It starts slow and builds, like a rumble in my empty stomach. The trees shake and birds in the high trees call out frantic warnings. I'm no longer on flat ground, but in an area where the land dips and rises repeatedly. It is a land of huge gray boulders and green growing ferns. The rumble sends rocks sliding and rolling all around me. Trees sway and my heart races the way it does every time the earth convulses. I know to duck behind the largest boulder, one as big as a house. There I wait for the earth to calm.

When it does I lay back down and look up at a sky that does not seem the least bit disturbed that earth has trembled and rearranged herself, if only slightly. I cannot go back to sleep for the many thoughts that chase themselves around in my head. I'm still tortured by the memory of the vipers' pit. If a leaf brushes me just so, I shudder.

"Help me, Father, to be grateful, to be useful with the life that Thou hast spared. Deliver me now from my own memories and fears."

I am a living miracle. Out of all the snakes that could have sunk their venom into me—all the snakes that *should* have sunk their venom into me—the one that bit me was not deadly.

Yes, my God is a God of miracles. Until He reached down to rescue me from a pit so vile, the Messiah was someone else's testimony, a distant idea, a hope. Now He is my personal Savior.

The trek away from Shimnilom is arduous. I'm not in a hurry to return to Elam. I feel as though I'm returning as a different person. At first my heel pains me every time I step, but as I keep moving the pain eases. Two days later there is no pain at all.

Thinking of Enos, nephew to the first prophet Nephi, I find a quiet place in the wilderness, a place where I am sure I am alone. There I kneel to thank God for saving both my body and my spirit. The sun is barely melted behind the mountain when I kneel, and I do not rise until it peeks over the opposite mountain the next morning.

I hear no voice. I do not see the light I had seen before. There is only darkness, pierced by the twinkling stars far, far above me on the blanket of a black sky. I cannot see the moon at all. But I do not feel enveloped in darkness—only light and love. When I take to my feet again, I feel stronger in both body and spirit.

The next day I discover a flock of low-flying birds, mountain gobblers, rarely seen around Elam. The law distinguishes them as clean, so the idea of taking one of them back home makes me smile. I'm fascinated by how they look and sound and forage. The males are larger, and when the sun hits their feathers I see all the colors Mother loves best: red, green, copper, bronze, and gold. The females are slight, and their feathers are the shades of dirt.

I find the right stone and take down a male bird with my sling. That night I eat its innards after I pluck feathers that I know Mother will put to good use.

I have to hurry so the meat does not spoil, but there is no pain in my heel now—only the small marks where the snake pierced me with its fangs.

Grandfather is at the synagogue when I arrive home to find Mother alone, drying ears of corn in the sunshine of our small courtyard.

"Kiah!" The wrinkles in her brow disappear when she looks at me. "I was so worried. You've been gone so long."

"Is everything well at home?" I ask, holding up the dressed bird, ready for her pot.

"It is now," she says, letting out a long-held sigh.

Thirty-One

I can't wait to leave again. Just as Calev changed, Elam is changing. Everyone in Elam is talking about Hem's ball court and what it will mean to the village and to our neighboring villages. Hem is stronger now and obsessed with the task of restoring the court—and with it, the economy that suffered so during the famine.

"The idea is favorable, but the reality is not," Mother tells me one morning while we are out in our courtyard. She is scraping the pelt of a rabbit I killed. "It's tragic, how Hem works the slaves. He starves them, drives them until they collapse, and teaches them that they are not the children of God."

"We are all children of God," I say as I adjust Grandfather's hammock so it is even.

"Kiah, your journey changed you. You left here a boy but returned a man. My heart is torn to see you leave again, but I do believe you must take advantage of every opportunity to learn."

"You know that I didn't want to go, but you're right. I'm changed."

"Hello!"

We turn to see Oshra and her shadowing sisters at the gate. "We've heard that Kiah is leaving you and we've come to weep with you, Anat."

"Thank you, but I'm not weeping," Mother says.

"Not weeping? You're a woman of sorrow. First, your husband abandons you, your eldest son returns from the war—how can I say . . . different—and now Kiah is leaving you alone. How can you not cry your eyes out?"

I want to take the rabbit pelt and throw it at Oshra, stuff it in her mouth to keep her from saying such hurtful things to Mother. But Mother's arm forms a straight gate that holds me back.

"Not to disappoint you, but my son is leaving at my request. He is going to gain an advanced education."

"That's not what we heard." Oshra looks to her friends for their nods.

Mother's attention goes back to the rabbit pelt.

Oshra's nose, pointed as an arrowhead, aims at Mother. She edges her way through the gate into the courtyard. Her voice sends the birds from the trees, and she speaks of me as if I'm not standing right in front of her. "Why not study in *our* village synagogue? He could gain his education here, even though the rest of the young men his age have already graduated. It *is* possible."

Mother lets out a long breath. "For Kiah, there is a greater opportunity in Zarahemla."

"Is it true he will be staying with the prophet Nephi's family?"

"It is true. You are aware, I'm certain, that they are our kinsmen." Mother sets the pelt down and picks up a broom; she pretends to sweep although our dirt is already swept and evened out for the day.

Oshra doesn't budge. It's like her mind is stirring up thoughts to turn into conversation. "Have you seen all the work that is being done to restore the ball court?"

"I have."

"It's very impressive. Hem has great plans for Elam."

Mother and I return to our tasks, hinting for Oshra to leave, but she only shakes her head. "It's a pity your sons are not players, Anat. Speaking of sons, Calev is seldom seen in the village."

Mother makes no reply.

"He is well into marrying age."

I stare at Oshra. Mother yawns.

"I hear that since Calev has returned he spends a great deal of time across the border—among Lamanites."

"They too are our kinsmen," Mother says.

I am amazed at the confidence that Mother is showing.

Oshra shudders. "They can get baptized, they can claim they are saved, but Lamanites will always be our enemies."

"I'm sorry you feel that way, Oshra. Many of our Lamanite brothers and sisters who have accepted the gospel are more righteous than we are."

The women gasp in unison. I could come to Mother's defense, but I'm enjoying watching her fend off this clutch of hens.

"What of Abner?" one of the other women asks.

"What of him?" Mother replies, suddenly risking her composure.

Oshra reaches out to put her hand on Mother's broomstick. She jerks it just a little bit. "Abner, a single man, has been around you for seasons, yet he has not proposed to you. Do you understand his intentions?"

Mother holds her tongue, but I can feel her emotions rise and I see from the way her shoulder blades jerk back that this is a subject she will not discuss. She tugs her broom handle free of Oshra's grip.

"Ever since Abner's wife and child died he has mourned. It is not lawful for a man to continue to mourn like Abner. When he finally stopped we all knew that his intentions were directed at Chasida." Oshra points her hawk's nose at her friend, who ducks her head. I have lived in Elam all my life, and I never knew the woman's name was Chasida. It means "stork" in the tongue of our fathers. It fits.

Is what Oshra says true? Before Mother won his affection, had Abner pursued another woman? I step forward. I clear my thoughts, and Oshra feigns that she's just now noticed my presence.

"We were just discussing the possibility of Abner becoming the father you never had," she says.

I look at Mother and wait to see what she does. She gnaws her lip.

When Oshra gets no response from Mother, I see the woman's face flush red and blotchy with frustration. "A boy like you who has never had a father will surely accept whatever offer comes."

Mother tenses. She's a wild cat ready to pounce.

Oshra isn't finished; she faces Mother and shakes her head with pity. "And a woman like you, divorced . . . no—correct my error—*sent away,* like Father Abraham sent poor Hagar . . . "

The temper I've worked so hard to contain flares like kindling on a fire. "Mother has no bill of divorcement and you know it. She was not sent away; she was *abandoned.* You know all of this. It's been fodder for your morning breakfast for years."

Oshra opens her mouth in a circle like someone just stuck an egg in it. "How dare you speak to us in such a tone!"

"Oh, I dare! Your own husband sleeps in the storage area of the synagogue so he won't have to come home to you. Abner prefers the beauty of my mother to your stork-legged friend."

I know I've gone way too far, but I relish the stunned look on Oshra's face and I want to continue.

Mother takes my elbow and pulls me back. "Stop, son."

The women are shocked and back away from me. They should. I'm furious.

Mother seems caught between moods. She's delighted that Oshra is finally choking on her own medicine, but I can see that she's hurt at my disrespect.

I make no apology. I'm weary of apologizing when it is not sincere or needed. We wait for them to leave before we both let out sighs of relief.

"You defended my honor; that had to be very difficult for you, son."

"It's not difficult at all. Those women have no right to speak and act as they do. They are shrews."

"They're just gossips."

"Mother, what *are* Abner's intentions?"

"He has not made them clear."

"I think he has. I think he intends to marry you, but can't."

Mother frowns but looks genuinely concerned. "Why can't I accept his proposal if and when he makes it?"

"Because you're not divorced. You're still married to—"

"Gidd."

Every time I hear his name my stomach tightens.

Mother looks like the name still brings her pain too.

"Do you want to marry Abner?"

Tears brim in her eyes and threaten to spill, so I stop the conversation.

That night I seek out Grandfather and walk home with him from the synagogue. I'd like Calev to be with us, but he is on an excursion to hunt ore and no one can predict when he will return.

"This is one time I wish I knew the law better," I confess. "What is proper where Mother and Abner are concerned?"

Grandfather's arm is still weak, but his legs are strong. I have to move my feet to keep up with him. He takes a trail that leads to the hills behind our house, and we walk together for a long time until he eases himself down, sure that we can talk in complete privacy.

"Your mother is neither divorced nor put out."

"My father abandoned her."

"Yes, and the only answer I have for that comes from the writings of Isaiah: 'Thou shalt no more be termed Forsaken; neither shall thy land any more be termed Desolate: but thou shalt be called Hephzibah, and thy land Beulah: for the LORD delighteth in thee, and thy land shall be married.'"

"What does that mean?"

"It means that the Lord does not blame or punish your mother for sins she did not commit."

"Has Abner spoken with you about mother?"

"Abner has said much to me. To Calev also."

"Has he asked for Mother's hand in marriage?"

"Yes."

The news surprises me, though I don't know why.

"Does Mother know?"

"Not yet, but I do not think she will be caught off guard."

"Has it been decided by the judges that Abner and Mother are allowed to marry?"

"Abner brought it before the court. Their union has been approved."

I am far from a child. I survived a vipers' pit, but I still feel like a young bird being pushed out of the nest. "Is that why she wants me to go away, so that she can start a new life with a new husband—without me underfoot?"

A squawking red *t'uul* hops from branch to branch above our heads. Grandfather watches it for a time before he replies. "Perhaps that has something to do with it, but I know your mother. Her heart is pure. She loves you and only wishes for your best."

"What will become of you?"

"I will be provided for, but I am not incapable of providing for myself."

"Come with me. Come with me to Zarahemla!"

"I have work to do here that keeps me in Elam."

"What about Calev? How does he feel about Mother marrying Abner?"

Grandfather's eyes go moist. "Calev? How does he feel about the marriage? I'm not sure Calev feels anything anymore. War has changed him—forever, I fear."

Thirty-Two

When Calev gets upset, the scar on his face turns purple. It turns purple at the news of our Mother's betrothal, even though Abner respects Calev by asking not only Grandfather's blessing, but my brother's, too.

What Grandfather said is true. Calev's muscles are stronger than ever, but his mind seems shut off. He shows no enthusiasm for anything. He works for Abner, but Calev seldom talks—just grunts.

"Calev, you're of marrying age. You're a man with an income. Isn't there a girl in all of Elam that captures your attention?"

He lifts his eyes to meet mine. The last time we hunted together he confessed to me that he was in love. He does not look like a man in love. He looks sad, and I wonder if the girl he loves is forbidden. Maybe she is already married. Such a blunder would not only be a sin, but a punishable sin. Adultery could cost them both their lives.

I want to talk to Calev. I want to tell him about the vipers' pit; I want to tell him how a newfound testimony rolled from my tongue, how my prayers were answered. When I approach him he tightens his lips and scowls.

"I'm leaving for Zarahemla soon," I say. "Let's go on a hunt before I leave. Grandfather is well enough to go with us if we help him."

"No."

"I want to talk to you, Calev. I miss talking to you."

"Talk," he says but turns away from me to let me know he is not interested in anything I have to say.

A few mornings later Calev is on the roof with me threading new banana leaves to keep the rain out. Mother brings up the subject of marriage again—not hers to Abner, but Calev's.

"You have many skills, Calev. You will make a fine husband."

"Do you say this to me because of Oshra and her gossips?"

"No. I say this to you because I love you, Calev. I want to see you happy—and since you've been back from the war you are not happy."

"And you think a wife would make me happy?"

I have never heard Calev speak in such a tone to Mother.

He reaches for a tool and I jerk it away. "What's wrong with you?"

"Everything!" Calev slides down and lands on the ground with a sullen thud. "Everything is wrong with me." He kicks at the stack of leaves and then, without an apology, storms off.

We don't see him again for days—long days during which Mother weeps and prays. I volunteer to go after him. I'm curious to discover how he finds comfort. Is there really a secret woman who has won my brother's heart? Who could she be?

"Let him alone," Grandfather says while we're eating our evening bread in the courtyard. "Like you, Calev will have to decide for himself the course of his own life."

"Let's focus on getting you ready to leave for Zarahemla," Mother calls out to me.

"Kiah is not going to Zarahemla. He is going to become a player on Elam's trickball team."

We all turn to see a sight that startles us. Hem is standing at the entrance to our yard. Eliana is not with him, but he is not alone; surrounding him are Elam's chief judge, Marpe; the brothers Mathoni and Mathonihah; Buki, the chief priest; and leaders from some of the other villages.

Mother becomes a startled animal, unmoving and fearful.

I tell myself I misunderstood Hem's announcement.

Grandfather's smile is forced, but he steps forward, opens his arms, and welcomes the intruders like they were kin.

"We are here to announce Elam's new trickball team," Buki tells Grandfather, ignoring Mother and me completely.

"Yes. I've been given power to choose the team players," Hem says.

"By what authority?" Grandfather asks.

Marpe steps forward and says in a weak voice, "Lachoneus himself has granted Hem proper authority. People as far away as the land of Manti are impressed with Hem and his ability to get hard tasks accomplished."

I flinch and my hand, as always, reaches for my blade.

Hem's right eye still droops from the days of his palsy. That does not keep him from looking smug and vengeful. His look is directed right at me.

"Kiah is no ball player," Grandfather says in a tone as hard as stone. "He is preparing to leave for Zarahemla where he will study in the synagogue there. Arrangements have already been made."

"No," Hem says. "No."

The judge looks apologetic, as though he is on a forced errand. His fat fingers shake as he says, sounding like he's rehearsed a speech, "Hem, as instigator of the project, is adamant that Kiah play on the new team we are assembling. We have made arrangements with our neighboring villages to engage in some games of competition. It will be very good for commerce. It will be very good for Elam. All boys Kiah's age are required to train and play with the team."

Boys? The twin brothers smile at me encouragingly. It makes sense why they are on the team but not me. Even when I was a child I did not play ball. I hunted. I trained to be a warrior, not a ballplayer. "Trickball is for entertainment," I say, glaring at Hem. "I do not entertain."

Hem chuckles. "Maybe we will make you dance with the girls, the ones who entertain before the judges."

Marpe bows his head.

"Kiah has no athletic ability," Grandfather says, his eyes narrowing on Hem. "The training he's received from Uriel and Calev is military."

I see Mother biting her lip, wringing her hands.

Be still and know . . . be still, Kiah. Be still. My feet step forward. I know what this is really all about. This is Hem's way of seeking revenge on me. I look at him, but he won't look at me, not until he feels victorious.

"I will train," I say. "I will give my best for Elam."

Mother's face washes pale. Grandfather shakes his head. Hem lifts his hand to wipe spittle from his chin.

Mathoni, Mathonihah, and some of the other boys are quick to slap my back and welcome me. They speak words of encouragement, telling me they will teach me all I don't know. Marpe seems relieved.

Hem's eyes lift to meet mine.

Be still . . . oh, Kiah, don't do it. Don't say it. Be still. It's all I can do to hold myself back, to keep my tongue in check.

I lift my hand. In it is my treasured blade. A rare and precious steel blade, the handle curved, inlaid with shards of jade. It is a unique design, and when the sun hits it just right, a blinding ray of reflected light strikes Hem in the face. He turns to look at me, and that is when he gives himself away. He recognizes the blade. I see it in his shocked expression, the way his face twitches.

No one else sees what I see, but it's all that I need to assure me that what I've known all along is true: Hem is a robber, an unrepentant man whose goal is to destroy me for what I know of him.

Thirty-Three

Uriel pulls me aside when he hears the news. We've been doing army training all morning, matching club for club. It's hard work to lift a heavy club over and over. My shoulders ache. "How did this happen?" my army commander demands.

"I volunteered." There are few people in Elam I respect more than Uriel. He trained and fought alongside Calev. He's been patient in helping me with my military skills, and now I see the disappointment in his face; I'm sorry to be the cause of it. "Really, once Hem made up his mind that I would be a player for the team, I had no choice."

Uriel coughs and then spits into the bush. "I was planning on advancing you in my army."

My head pops up. "But we are at peace. There is no war."

"Since Satan was unleashed on this earth there has been war. Until he is bound there will always be war. The robbers continue to swear their secret oaths. The menace they bring—sneaking down from their hiding places, robbing, kidnapping, demanding ransoms, and infiltrating our governments —is worse than outright war."

"But you lead one of the armies that helped to battle back the robbers. Calev fought with you."

"Gadianton's band might be in hiding, but that only gives them opportunity to regroup." He spits again. "Trust me, Kiah, it's an impossible task to defeat your enemy when you cannot identify your enemy."

"I understand," I say, realizing that Uriel knows the frustration I feel every time I see Hem—knowing that I cannot prove his true identity.

Uriel suddenly lunges toward me, lifts his club, and almost strikes me. Almost. I block him barely in time.

"Your feet are slow," he tells me, "but your hands are fast. I think you make a much better soldier than a ballplayer."

"It's fallen to me to do both. Hem is determined that Elam will have a team ready to compete by the season's change."

Uriel looks grim. "Hem is treated like a king in this village."

I notice how he lowers his voice when mentioning Hem. Like me, Uriel is unsure of his own army; any one of them could be a spy for Hem. "The people elect him. They continue to elevate his status, and now he wields an unspoken power far more reaching than that of the chief judge."

"Is it true that before Hem was stricken with palsy he had his sights on the chief judge's seat?"

"It is true."

I think it's strange that Uriel speaks with me like one man speaks to another. He shows me the same respect he shows Calev, and that makes me eager to battle for his army.

"Hem's position might be even more powerful than the judge's," Uriel says.

"How?"

"Think about it. He interacts with traders from every direction. He knows the latest news. He's in a position to be an emissary, an ambassador for Elam, and a spy if he wished."

Is Uriel trying to read my thoughts? His eyes are fixed on me, and I wonder if he knows of the accusations I bought against Hem. I nod in agreement, but I'm careful with my words. What if Uriel himself is a spy for Hem? No. I reprimand myself; that is impossible. I'm being overly fearful.

The only trust I cannot question is the trust I put in the power of the coming Messiah. I pray for Him to guide my life, to direct my words, and to protect my family. More and more I believe there is a purpose in my life. I want that purpose to be to testify of Christ, the Messiah. How I'll do that, I do not know, but I trust He knows and will guide me through the journey.

"If you are going to play for Elam's team, then give your all to the game. Work as hard training with the ball as you do training with the sword."

His advice is still sounding in my head when I report on the ball court.

My captain is the larger of the twin brothers. Mathoni is kind but also capable. He expects perfection from us, but the best I can offer is imperfection. His feet are fast and mine are sluggish. His knees bend high; when they impact the ball it goes straight into the air. When my knees impact the ball, it veers to the side.

The rubber ball is heavy and impossible for me to keep in the air for more than a hit or two. As a child I played the game, but never seriously. Then it was supposed to be fun. It is not fun now. Even the small children practicing on the far end of the field are more adept at keeping the ball in the air than I am. I wish that I'd practiced all of my life, but my hours were spent hunting and tracking. Of course Hem is going to challenge me where I'm weakest.

Halfway through our first practice Mathoni passes out sticks, carved evenly with handles that are made for gripping. "Try trickball."

I'm much better at trickball, partly because I'm used to a weapon in my hand and partly because the rubber ball is much smaller and lighter.

"Hem says that Lachoneus will be at the first game. We must be prepared, no matter the sacrifice."

Others try to encourage me. Some scorn me. I give my best, but it is far from sufficient.

By the end of the day I drag home feeling mostly dead. My head aches; my knees and elbows are bloody. The nails on my large toes are already turning purple.

Abner sees me hobbling home and walks alongside me. "You look like you've enjoyed your day."

I smile at his joke and share his waterskin.

"Where is Calev now?" I ask. "We haven't seen him in days."

"He's bringing ore from the southland. I have never worked with a man I trusted more than I trust Calev. He never disappoints me."

"You do not know my brother," I tell him. "The Calev who works for you is sullen. The brother I grew up with was full of life and adventure. Did you know that he has a gift for art?"

"Yes. He's very skilled."

"He used to love to craft weapons."

"Calev has seen the death and suffering those weapons are capable of inflicting. Your brother has suffered much."

For a moment I am taken with jealousy. Abner knows so much about Calev. The two of them obviously talk. Why doesn't Calev talk to me?

Abner seems to sense my feelings; he changes the subject and talks of ore and how he is working with Raz to make sheets of metal so thin they are easier to engrave.

"Raz says you tell quite a story through your depictions."

Raz gave me a piece of leather and a special instrument with a fine point so that I could draw my escape from the vipers' pit. Mother and Grandfather praised my work and my desire to record God's mercy to me.

"I'd like to see your depiction," he says.

I nod, not sure I want to show Abner something so personal, but flattered that he is interested enough to want to see it.

"How do you like trickball?" he asks.

I show him my battered elbows.

"Be careful, Kiah. Hem is plotting something."

"I know."

"You know what it is?" he asks.

"No. But I know he seeks revenge against me for the accusations that I brought against him."

"Perhaps he wants to humiliate you in front of all of Elam."

"I hope it's that simple."

"Listen, Kiah, God is your true team captain. He will watch over and protect you as you are obedient to His laws. I know that He has blessed me that way."

He's referring to my mother. It makes me happy to see that Abner's faith is growing stronger. Mother deserves a man of faith and obedience.

"Kiah, stay strong. You are a good man. Believe in what you know to be true. It's only a matter of time until Hem's deceit is revealed."

We walk for a time in silence. Abner referred to me as a "good man." Not a boy. And he believes the same thing I do about Hem.

We walk to the crossroads and bid an easy parting.

Thirty-Four

Frustrated and uneasy, I take both my military training and my trickball training seriously. My prayers take more time, and I find myself listening far more than speaking. Each word of my mandatory prayers takes on new meaning: *Lord, God, merciful, Almighty, faithful, Deliverer, powerful, Redeemer.* The name *Messiah* means "to be anointed," and I think deeply about that. The sermons Grandfather preaches no longer fall on deaf ears. I listen and I hear.

I offer my friendship to my brother but find it rejected. Calev is not interested in my friendship. When he is home he sleeps late and speaks little. Abner remains consistently cordial to me, showing interest in my obsidian and asking if I want to hunt rocks with him.

I don't. There is no time.

Grandfather spends much of his time studying and making comparisons between prophecies. Every morning sun brings him hope that we are one day closer to the coming of the Messiah.

Prophets come through Elam—some as true as Nephi, others as false as Kerem.

It is a scorching day when the official marriage covenant is finally made, when a price for my mother is negotiated. Though I am a male of age, I am left out of the discussion, excluded with Mother. Only Abner, Calev, and Grandfather set the price. I think it cannot be as high as it would be if Mother were a pure young maiden. It's not fair, I decide, thinking that a woman with seasoning, experience, and a proven ability that she can care for herself and others should fetch a high tag—but I am not consulted.

Mother seems as anxious and left out as I feel. "Let's walk," she says, casting her eyes to our small hut where the men are inside, deciding her future.

I raise my eyebrows in surprise. "Where would you like to walk?"

"I don't care. I just don't want to be here, so close, while the men discuss what I am worth."

It dawns on me that my mother has been through this process before. I look at her and see not just my mother but a woman, thin, her hair braided and wound at the nape of her neck. Her skin crinkles around her eyes but is smooth on her cheeks and forehead. Her hands are the hands of a girl, her fingers long and slender—not bulged at the knuckles like those of many women.

I think of the dreams my mother must have had when she was a girl Eliana's age. I think of the disappointment and sorrow she's known. I think of how she has raised Calev and me, never faltering in her faith. I want to reach over and embrace her, and I do. She seems surprised by my sudden affection—then I see tears in her eyes, and her warm palm touches my cheek.

A little boy runs between us. He's chasing after a lizard, and his mother is chasing after him. The road we walk is made of packed earth, smooth beneath our feet. It leads to the chief marketplace, and there are vendors along the roadside that try to sell us boiled eggs and dried fish.

I wait until we are alone, and I try to be gentle with my curiosity. "How old were you when you were married before?"

"I had fifteen years."

"Did your father negotiate your purchase price?"

"Yes.

"Did you . . . did you *love* my . . . " My tongue refuses to call him *father*.

"I did not know Gidd when he first approached my father seeking a marriage covenant."

I have to think for a time to allow her words time to make sense. My father was from Elam, but Mother came from another village outside of Bountiful. It strikes me for the first time that, although I know her parents were taken into slavery and later killed when the city was overtaken, she might still have blood relatives there. If she does, she faces shame from them for what my father did to our family. There is no question why she has no contact with them.

"What was he like?" I ask.

Mother doesn't answer right away because now that we are at the main gate, the market is crowded with people selling their wares—birds and meat and fruit and a variety of smoked meats. Tools for farming, footwear, woven cloth, and jewelry can be purchased.

"Is there something you would like, Mother?"

I think of my treasure and how I might sell it to buy her whatever she wants.

"I want nothing but for you and your brother to be happy and faithful."

We step back to let a band of Lamanite women pass us. Their bright clothes and dyed feathers, their sunbaked skin, reminds me of Shimnilom. I cringe at the memory. There are nights when I still wake up, screaming and flailing, trying to awake from the memory of how the vipers' pit felt, sounded, even smelled.

Lamanites tend to stay in groups apart from our people. Maybe they don't trust us any more than we trust them. An entire Lamanite family passes by us. They do not look at us but walk in silence with their faces turned away. A girl not much younger than I am is among them; at first I don't notice her, but when they have passed I look back and see her. She is beautiful, and she is smiling at me.

How long before something happens and they are once again our enemies? How does that happen, that a brother becomes an enemy or an enemy becomes a brother?

"You wish to know my memories of your father?" Mother asks, guiding me off the road and beneath the shade of a fat, low palm.

I nod. "It's time."

"Gidd was—he *is*—a physically strong man. A smart man with the skills of a scribe. He was once in training to become a timekeeper."

"Raz told me."

"But Gidd's heart was not in keeping time. He wanted to be a warrior just as you want to be a warrior."

"Really? I know so little of him."

She hesitates and chews the corner of her lip the way she does when she's uneasy. "I suppose it will always be painful to think back on your father and the choices that he ultimately made." She takes a deep breath and smiles at me. "I will forever be grateful to him for blessing me with you and Calev. You are my world."

"I know." I've never had reason to doubt my mother's love, yet hearing her say aloud what Calev and I mean to her makes my eyes sting and my nose run.

She is quick to change the subject. "When you are freed from your foolish responsibilities with Hem's trickball team, you will move to Zarahemla and life will become much larger than you ever imagined."

"What did you imagine your life would be when you were my age?"

Mother quickly looks away. "I imagined something very different. I suppose every girl has dreams of a kind husband and a secure home."

I feel a pang of pity for Mother. No matter what my father was like, she had no choice, because her betrothal was negotiated between her father and my father.

"We were betrothed during a very turbulent time among our people. Nephi had given up the judgment seat to Cezoram. I was called to sing for the chief judge, and that is where your father first took notice of me."

"You sang for Cezoram?"

"Yes—for all of the judges, in their court. It was a long time ago."

"So much has changed. The Gadianton robbers murdered him and when they did the history of our people changed. There was secret slaughter everywhere. Mourning cries and death filled the air. Oh, Kiah, you do not understand what it is to live in a season of war.

"I remember how confused I was. Some Lamanites that had been converted to the gospel of the Messiah were more righteous than our priests. But our government seemed to always be at risk. Brother fought brother. Father fought son. War left widows and orphans, and no man had the luxury that you do—to *choose* his path, to educate himself. There was no time for anything except war."

"It sounds like an exciting time."

"How can you say that, Kiah? Right now we are in a season of peace. Peace and prosperity. Lamanites and Nephites are once again family, not enemies. The robbers have been hunted and scourged. Look around. See the smiles on the faces of the women, the laughter coming from the men. See the children run and play without fear. This is what happens when we honor the word of the Lord. Death and destruction is what results when we do not."

"I'm a warrior, Mother. Maybe it's just in my blood."

"You do not understand what you say, Kiah. Your father was a man who relished violence and thought faith in the Messiah meant weakness. Gidd studied the teachings of Korihor, a man who preached that there could be no Atonement made for the sins of men. He believed every man fared in this life as a result of his own strength and genius. Gidd came to believe that whatever a man did was no crime."

I can't help remembering those were the same teachings of Kerem.

"You are a warrior, Kiah. A warrior for God. I've seen you grow from a boy into a man these past seasons. You amaze me with your strength and your faith." Her hands press on my shoulders, and she quietly sings a verse from the book of Psalms. "The LORD trieth the righteous: but the wicked and him that loveth violence his soul hateth."

It's as if she's slapped me, and I recoil from her. "Mother, Captain Moroni was a warrior. King David was a warrior. Joshua was a warrior who annihilated an entire city."

"Son, I know that you are not a violent soul. I've seen you tend to birds with broken wings."

"I kill those same birds for food, Mother."

"For *food*, Kiah—not for *pleasure*. You do not have the heart of your father."

"There are times when we're forced to use violence to protect ourselves and our families. Captain Moroni taught that."

"I understand, Kiah, but know this: When our first parents partook of the fruit, we all became separated from the presence of God. In that first garden there was no violence. Lion and lamb were friends. It was paradise. Brother turned against brother only *after* we were estranged from the presence of God. Do you understand what I'm saying?"

We pause to allow more people to pass, and I notice how another group of Lamanites sends Mother back into the shadows as if she is afraid of them. While we wait I think how the fall of mankind is an ongoing subject of discussion at synagogue; it's something teachers debate all the time. "I know Alma taught that after the Fall man became carnal, sensual, and devilish."

"Exactly! Don't you think it is devilish to seek war?"

"Yes, but I also think you want me to change who I am. I *am* changed. Can't you see that since I almost died in a snake pit, I am a different person?"

"Yes. I just told you as much. I know that you know the power of God delivered you. That knowledge cannot help but change you."

"But you want me to put away my weapons, bury them like the Anti-Nephi-Lehis, and sit in a synagogue to memorize the law. I'll study and learn, but I don't want to be a calendar-keeper or a scribe or a teacher. I want to be a warrior. The law does not always make sense to me, Mother. There are scriptures against violence, but what of Exodus? It states that the Lord is a man of war."

"Jesus Christ *is* a warrior, the greatest of all warriors, for truth and justice and for His Father's cause." She reaches to touch my cheek with her palm. The softness of her gesture catches me off guard, and I feel like a little boy at her skirts again. A desire, a hunger to protect her and never venture far from her, overpowers me. I can't stop the tear that leaks from the corner of my eye, a tear she catches with the side of her thumb.

"You are a warrior, Kiah, and I am so proud of your skills. Promise me that you will always fight on the side of Jesus Christ; let Him and Him alone be your captain and commander."

"I swear to you I will. But can you please tell me one more thing?"

She inhales and waits for my request.

"Tell me the true reasons he left our family?"

"Has your grandfather never told you?"

"He says my father was a coward, a shameful coward and a man of weak faith."

"That is true and sufficient to know."

"But I want to know what happened. I deserve to know."

"Your father made a good wage working for the judges. His aspirations were to gain a judgment seat himself, and he would have. He was well liked and friendly. He was smart and capable."

I can't help but think what my life might have been like if my father had been a judge instead of a man who slunk away in the night, abandoning us.

"What happened?"

"Your father always felt that the laws of Moses were too demanding—unfair—and that the traditions passed down from Nephi favored the faithful. He had a passion for challenging the teachings."

"It was more than that, though, wasn't it?"

"Yes. A report came to your grandfather that Gidd had been stealing money. The report made other accusations also, accusing him of a relationship with one of the judges' daughters, a woman who was betrothed."

My head hurts from so much information. "So they would have stoned him?"

"Perhaps, but he simply left. He joined other dissenters and left for another village. Gossip rumors say he has another wife and family."

"I've heard that also. Tell me, please, where is this village?"

Horror shapes her face. "No. You cannot go there. No, Kiah. You must stay away."

"Why? Why can't I see my own father?"

"It's not that, son. It's that your father has joined himself not just with another village—it's a Lamanite village. Gidd not only abandoned his family; he left his faith and dissented from his own people."

Thirty-Five

The flesh is white and tender. I've driven my ax into the trunk so many times I have to move on to the next tree and the next. There is something healing for me in throwing my ax, pulling it free, and letting it cut deep into fresh flesh again.

Every time I throw it I imagine Hem.

Oh, how my life would be different if I had killed him that day. Now he is strong again. Eliana is his slave. I saw her sister, Tamar, and she told me that Eliana has turned into an old woman, beaten and broken by her father's incessant demands. I feel pity for Eliana—indentured by her father, rejected by Calev.

Hem is not the high priest nor the chief judge, but no one in Elam has more power than he does. Though our government is a government of judges, Uriel is right: Hem acts like he is king, ordering the restoration of our ball court, expanding the marketplace, promoting himself higher and higher.

Calev walks toward me. He wears a man's sandals and they crush the tiny plants of the jungle floor as he comes toward me. Today is the day of our mother's marriage covenant to Abner. There will be a simple ceremony.

"How do you suppose Hem acquired so much power in Elam?"

Calev looks at me with dull eyes. "You're still obsessed with Hem?"

"Hem is ruining my life. If it weren't for him I would have gone to Zarahemla. I'd be with Jonas, learning in synagogue school. Or I could be a leader in Uriel's army. Instead I'm stuck here, training every day for a game that I have no skill at playing."

"After tomorrow you will be free."

Tomorrow is Elam's premier game. People are already streaming into our village, feeding the marketplace with commerce. We are competing against the village of Calno. Both villages belong to the land of Zarahemla. We should be friendly, but there has always been a competitive spirit between

Elam and Calno, and now Hem has escalated that by challenging Calno in trickball.

"I still can't keep the ball in the air."

"I've seen you practice, Kiah. You're better than you realize."

"Thank you. Coming from you, brother, my confidence is lifted."

"Use a broader stick," Calev tells me.

"Hem won't allow it."

Calev yawns. He yanks my ax out of the tree and turns his back to walk away. "Hurry. You cannot be late for the ceremony."

I watch him go, feeling that I'm looking at the back of a stranger. How I miss the Calev I used to know—the one who would challenge me on everything, the one who couldn't wait to show his latest weapon to Grandfather, the one who could join Mother in a song.

That afternoon I stand next to Calev at the marriage covenant ceremony. His face looks as if he is at a funeral.

"There is no single word in scripture for *marriage*," Buki says, "just as there is no single word for *religion*."

As he talks I look across the small crowd and notice Tamar. She has sprouted tall. Next to her is someone I hardly know: Eliana. I am used to seeing her with Hem, but she's not with him now. Her hair is braided in two ropes down her back; her eyes are wide and sad, like Calev's. She is looking at him. She smiles. He doesn't seem to notice she is there. She smiles wider and moves in front of Tamar. Doesn't she recall how Calev humiliated her? Has she forgiven *him*? Why can't she forgive *me*?

Buki is still talking, but I don't hear what he says. An old mix of anger and jealousy rises inside me. My face burns, and my feet shuffle back and forth as Mother and Abner drink wine from the same symbolic cup while the priest pronounces the betrothal benediction.

Calev's feet shift. I see him look toward Eliana. I see their eyes lock. He rewards her with a smile. I want to shove my brother.

When the priest pronounces the ceremony's end, Abner quietly slips back to his own home to begin the legally prescribed period of separation before the wedding.

I turn to Calev. "You can't mock Eliana's feelings. Her heart is too tender—too sincere."

Calev lowers his eyelids. "You mean *your* heart is too tender. You are in love with the girl."

I shove my brother so hard he stumbles backward, but does not lose his balance. "I don't care about her in that way. I just care about her."

"It's Mother you should care about. Abner can't return for twelve months. She's going to be alone when you go to Zarahemla."

"You'll be around. Grandfather will be with her."

His eyelids raise, and a softness returns to his face. "Kiah, you should go and learn all you can while there is peace in the land. Once war starts again your opportunity for education will be gone."

I forget about Eliana. "War? Have you heard rumors? Has Uriel told you something? Please tell me, Calev."

His hand slaps the back of my head, catching me off guard. I bite my tongue and taste blood.

"Don't be a fool, brother. Your idea of war is not war. After you have survived your first battle, then tell me what you know of war—until then ,battle the scriptures, battle learning the law, battle yourself."

Calev turns to walk away like he always does, but this time I reach out and grab him by the shoulder. I spin him to face me. "Tell me, Calev, are there rumors of war?"

"Yes."

It's the first time I smile in days.

Thirty-Six

The afternoon sun is beating like a steady drum. I am with my teammates, but I do not feel part of a team. As always, I am the outcast—the one who does not fit in. The crowd is large and excited. There is no doubt that this will be a boon to Elam's commerce. A proud Hem is elevated on the stone steps, in the place of honor next to Lachoneus, chief judge of all the land of Nephi. Eliana is nowhere in sight. Neither is Calev. The thought that the two of them might be together is unthinkable, and yet I am thinking it.

"We need you to be strong today," Mathoni tells me. "More is at stake here than just a game."

I don't know what he is talking about, but when I see Grandfather's face I realize that I've missed something. "What is it?" I call out to him.

He says nothing, only turns his head slowly, looking from one side of the court to the other. Most people seem jovial, but not Grandfather.

In spite of my loathing toward Hem, I have to give him credit for the job he's done restoring the ball court. If I were to depict it I would draw it on a huge piece of bark, making it clear that the court length is four times its width. I would use charcoal to show that the floor of the court has been made as smooth as possible so that we don't trip. I would draw the knee-high wall that encloses the court, and I would measure each spectator step carefully, making sure the landing at the top was filled with the faces of Elam's most important men. Of course, Hem's dark face would be center, next to the governor of all the land. Rightfully, in my mind, Grandfather would be there. But he's not. Only Hem and those closest to him occupy that place.

I would draw the square of Elam's synagogue in the back, high on the rise. I would sketch the roads and the people, throngs of them now descending on Elam for the important game and the return of a tradition nearly abandoned. I would sketch the sellers, hawking mangos, pineapples, guavas, grilled corn, and tubers. I would shade in smoke rising from where the vendors grill goat and chicken and the gamey *keeh* meat.

The people of Calno have made a three-day journey to support their players. They seem much more serious. Their team wears the same heavy protective gear as we do, but they have dyed their loincloths the red hue of berries—they look trained and fierce—while we wear the shade of dirt and look to be little threat.

I can't help but notice how Hem has appointed his men to direct the people, stationing the most important ones higher, the commoners outside the boundaries where it will be impossible for them to see what happens on the ball court. Of course Hem's favored men—judges, priests, merchants, and even Gomer—get the stone benches for both comfort and the ability to see the game from courtside.

I study the court again, imagining how I would draw it. It is long and narrow; two sloping walls run parallel. Three round stone markers are inset at exact distances along the walls. I look at them and feel grateful that it is not my responsibility to pass the ball through them. That is up to the twin brothers; they are our scorers. My responsibility is to keep the heavy rubber ball from touching the ground, to try to take it away from our opponents and get it to our scorers.

I've been practicing hard, sometimes after dark when it is just me against the ball. My body is bruised and battered from the wear, and still I am not confident, not like I am with a blade in my hand.

In the crowd I notice familiar faces. Raz and his entire family seem to be a good portion of the population. Three of his sons are on the team, though none of them have the brawn to be anything but runners. They wave and smile and stand ready to cheer. Merari and his sons are here. None of them are on the team; they are too valuable in other village positions. I have not hunted with Merari for a very long time, yet I remember with gratitude how he made the scriptures come alive for me. As I look out at the gathering crowd I realize I owe a debt to so many people for helping me in one way or another.

Abner's red head stands above almost everyone else. He cannot speak to my mother, but that does not mean his eyes don't search for her. I see him talk to Hem, if only in greeting, and my suspicions rise again. Is Abner a man to be trusted? If not, it is too late for my mother.

Hem makes a show of himself and his power by climbing up and down the steps to the rise. He has built a small podium and a three-sided stone box where he can take his high station and prevent himself from falling facedown onto the field.

At least Eliana is not by his side today. I hope she is in the crowd somewhere with her mother, her sister, her friends. I hope that she can enjoy this event without being a slave to her own father.

The people cheer for Hem when he lifts a staff, acting as important as Moses. I clench my teeth and almost bite my own tongue. What do I care if Hem is granted a moment of glory? Today I will see that we win the game. Then I will move far from Elam and from Hem's kingdom.

At least I'm grateful to note that Grandfather is being given a seat among the priests. He still looks uneasy, unhappy.

I have tried not to dwell on all that is really at stake here today. Uriel advised me to prepare and approach it as a battle that I cannot lose. Hem has promised the winning team a monetary reward and the honor of victory. Grandfather has privately negotiated with Hem that he will permit me to leave Elam, to keep my honor as a son of the village, as long as I am on the winning team. If we lose, Hem has indentured our entire team to join the slaves who are building a new, larger ball court between Elam and Zarahemla. That duty could take years to complete. I know Hem is counting on me to lose. I am praying to God to win.

When the hour arrives, our team members are cloaked in our protective gear, heavier than I've seen Uriel's soldiers wear. Then come the yokes that fit tight and miserable around our waists but that are necessary for us to be able to propel the ball. Mine pinches my skin and is so tight I have difficulty drawing a full breath. The stick or bat I'm handed is newly carved, and I ask for my practice bat because it feels familiar in my grip.

"No," says one of the game's judges, a man from Minon, a village on the west bank of the river Sidon. I'm told that he is an expert at the game and will tolerate no breaking of the rules. I'm also told that he is susceptible to bribes, and I've seen Calno's chief judge talking with him; I've also seen Hem being extra friendly to the man.

Elbows. Knees. Hips.

If I touch the ball with my hands or feet I will cost our team a point. One point can win or lose a game. The best way to win is to pass the ball through the markers, but that is nearly impossible, even for skilled scorers like the twin brothers.

Once attired, our team is led behind the wall where Hem stands flanked by Gomer and others. He glares at me but does not speak. Shelomoh, our team's trainer, is a burly man with few teeth. He is an idol worshipper who wears a carved figure of his god around his neck.

Mathoni whispers to me, "I've heard rumors that in Shelomoh's village the losing team is sacrificed to the god he wears tied around his neck."

"I hear he sacrificed his own brother," I whisper back.

Shelomoh is usually brutish. Today he seems nervous and keeps looking at Hem as if for approval. It makes me realize just how mighty Hem's authority has become.

"Today you play more than a game for entertainment," Shelomoh says, spraying spit through the air. "Today you play to restore the spirit of Elam. This ball that I hold symbolizes the sun, the moon, and the stars. It is our connection to the gods who grant us rain."

Hem nods with approval.

I think that I will not play to honor a god I know is false.

Mathonihah comes to stand between his brother and me. "Your rage shows on your faces. Look away. Pray in your hearts, brothers. Today we will play for the only true and living god . . . the Messiah."

Hem leers at us but does nothing to stop us. Shelomoh is oblivious to anything but his own shouting. With a cheer, our team ignites.

In the final moments before the game is announced we are permitted a visit with family. Mother is not allowed and Calev is nowhere to be seen, but Grandfather barrels toward me and tries to embrace me. It's futile, since I'm already clad in protective gear.

He is agitated. Angry. "Come with me where we can find privacy."

I follow him to a far corner of the area. It's not private, but he lowers his voice, grips my shoulder, and whispers into my ear. "Is it true that you threatened to kill Hem?"

I groan. "Where did you hear that?"

"Just tell me! Is it true that you were about to run a blade through his heart?"

There is no reason to lie to Grandfather. "It is true—but I didn't do it."

Grandfather's eyes bulge, his cheeks swell and redden until I can see little broken veins through his skin. He struggles for breath, and when he manages to get words out, I am in shock. "God forgive me. I wish you had killed him."

Thirty-Seven

Timekeepers are in place to let us know when the sun is directly above us in the sky—the point at which the game can commence. My back is already slick with sweat, and the boy assigned to bring me water has a steady job.

I wonder about the wager that Hem has made on this game. What weight has he pledged in gold? Why would Grandfather ever demonstrate such feelings toward Hem? Before now he's always been an advocate of the robber, even though I know Grandfather believes me.

There is no time to think. The drums start. The costumed dancers, Tamar among them, make their way through the crowd. Other musicians play. I take in the music and shouting and the smell of grilling meat and onions.

Mathoni gives a speech that makes even me believe we can win. I step back and watch while my teammates lift each other.

We cleanse ourselves with water.

The priests pray. Grandfather is the main voice, and he begs God to touch all hearts, to protect and watch over and guide all to the Messiah.

The very mention of the word *Messiah* shifts the energy from excitement to division. There are those, including our trainer, who recoil at the mention of Jesus Christ.

As soon as our team steps out onto the playing field there is a clamor to get our attention. People cheer and shout. Drums beat faster. I see the dancers now, up close. Tamar and the others are costumed in bright, flowing colors. They dance like brilliant flowers, and when the signal is given, they retreat like withering petals.

I have to squint into the sun, but after a moment I see the line of Elam's priests seated together. Grandfather is at the far end. I nod, but he is not looking at me. His head is bowed, and his hands are covering his eyes.

What could be so wrong that he refuses to look?

That's when the realization dawns on me. I understand what Hem has done. Systematically, one spectator at a time, he has divided the crowd—not

Elam from Calno but a division as severe as a severed limb. On one side are the unbelievers, the idol worshippers, the enemies of Christ. On the opposite side—Grandfather's side, with the priests—are the believers.

Now I understand why Grandfather is so distraught. We are not marked as such, but Hem has separated all of us into two very evenly matched sections. If he wants to start a war, the battle lines are clearly drawn, just as they were when we prayed during the time Elam nearly tore itself in half.

Father in Heaven, Thou art the God of gods. Jesus is Thy Holy Son, my Messiah. Let me fight and win for Your side this day.

Lachoneus, flanked by a band of men, climbs to the high platform. Even from my distance I can see that he is not pleased with what Hem has managed to do. They have words, and everyone waits in tense silence. The chief judge's arms swing into the air; his head covering nearly falls off. His voice gets louder, but I can't tell what he says. Hem holds his own hands up in mock defeat. I've seen him do it when he is confronted with accusations of tampering with the weights in the marketplace. He feigns innocence. I hope Lachoneus throws him from the platform.

He doesn't.

Lachoneus takes the ball when it is offered to him. We all assume our positions on the playing field. I'm a corner guard and have the responsibility to keep the ball in the air while the scorers get into position. I wish I were a frontline attacker. I would make a better attacker than a guard.

I have no choice.

Shelomoh stands barely off the field glaring at me. "You look scared, Kiah. Do not let the enemy see fear."

"I am not afraid."

"Then look brave!"

I lower my head and narrow my eyes. Calno's team is my enemy. They don't look like my enemies. They look like family. I think of Calev and glance around, but still don't see him—or Eliana.

Lachoneus shouts, "May this game ignite a spirit of unity and enjoyment for *all* of our people!" He turns around so that his back is to both teams. He then tosses the ball over his head so that it lands on the field.

There is an explosion of anger and competition.

The ball is allowed only one bounce—then the game, or rather the *war*, is on.

I run with the team, watching in amazement how the Calno players divide their ball time, managing it back and forth equally so that one player does not wear out. Their team captain, a flat-nosed scorer, can lift his knees almost as high as his shoulders. No one on our team can do that.

Shelomoh is a madman, running up and down the courtside, screaming at us. "Knock the ball from them."

I look over and realize that he is screaming at me.

The bat in my hand feels heavy and too long. I'm not sure what my range is, but when the player with the ball comes within striking distance I take the bat and knock it as hard as I can. I not only hit the ball; I hit the player square in the face.

All of Elam cheers. All of Calno hisses.

I barely bend low enough to hit the ball with top of my head to keep it in the air. Fortunately, one of my teammates is next to me to pick it the second time it comes down.

We play hard. We play fast. The longer we go the more serious the game becomes.

There is not a heartbeat's time to scan the crowd. I have to keep watching the ball because it comes my way more often than I wish it did.

Calno's players make the first attempt at scoring. The captain takes the ball from our player and brings it up the court, bouncing it from one knee to the other. When he's just about to the marker another player runs beside him and bats the ball toward the ring.

The ball hits the wall and bounces back, knocking the player to the ground. No one stops; we all run over him, some of us stepping on him just to keep the ball in the air.

This goes on and on until I feel dizzy. My eyes sting with sweat.

We keep playing.

When a player falls and fails to rise, a small team rushes onto the court to drag the fallen player off. Another player rushes in without delay.

Shelomoh determines when one of us is worn to the point of exhaustion. He then sends another player running onto the court to make a rapid exchange that does not interrupt play. My first break comes when I can no longer lift the bat.

"Play harder!"

I'm allowed a single drink and then sent back in with my old bat.

The day seems to grow hotter and hotter. Spectators cover their heads and wear simple skirts or loincloths. We are draped in heavy gear, and the yoke that pinched me earlier has worn a blistering ring around my stomach and back. My sweat beads down and stings like torture.

I play on.

Someone knocks into me and I drop my bat. Immediately I feel pain in my neck and realize I've been struck by another bat.

There are four assigned watchers, men who are supposed to call penalties when the play becomes unfair or too rough. So far the watchers have called nothing.

We play on.

Three players—two from Calno and a guard from Elam—are pulled off the field when they fall and cannot get back up. One of Calno's players is covered in blood, which ignites the crowd.

The day has reached its hottest point. Sweat pours off every player like we have been drenched beneath a waterfall.

We play on.

Another player falls.

Mathoni almost scores, but the ball is batted away by Calno's captain.

One of Calno's blockers takes a hit to the chest and has to be dragged off the field. A waiting player runs onto the court to take his place.

The sun sinks, and the starving night stingers come out, buzzing through the air, hungry for our sweat and our blood. Even when they swarm around my face, I cannot be distracted. The longer I play, the more I realize the prize at stake.

We play and play and only stop when, even by torchlight, we are unable to see the ball.

Thirty-Eight

That night I sleep with my teammates on one end of the ball court while Calno's team sleeps on the other end. Guards stand between us because there is bad blood now. Their team captain is still down, and two of our men have suffered crushed bones. There is talk of murder under the cloak of darkness. I hope it's only talk.

Families and trainers bring sustenance. Grandfather comes with water and bandages for the gash in my skull. Mother comes with a bowl of ground corn and a poultice for the brutal bruise on my shoulder.

I eat but feel sick. I guzzle water but feel almost too tired to swallow. I've never known such fatigue. My entire body aches. The backs of my legs are knotted and will not relax. My knees and elbows are raw as fresh meat. Mother covers me with a finely woven piece of cloth to keep the clouds of night stingers away. I want to talk to her, to tell her not to look so worried. I can't. I'm too tired for words.

It's not quite dawn when someone kicks the bottoms of my bare feet. Pain shoots through every part of me.

"Kiah!"

I open one eye and make out the form of my brother leaning over me.

"Where have you been?" I ask.

"I've been watching you. You said you couldn't play, but Kiah, our team would have lost without you."

He pulls me into a sitting position, and I look around groggily, realizing that most of the team is still sleeping.

"You've been watching me? I didn't see you." The idea makes me happy.

"I've been watching. Here, eat some fruit. You've got to have stamina. Today is a full day of play."

"Unless we score."

The fruit is ripe and tempting. Before I eat we wash and join the other believers in first prayer. Mathoni and Mathonihah pray. They are always praying.

The more I know of them, the more respect I have for the brothers. They are true believers and make no apology for their faith.

It feels good and right to have my brother there beside me.

"I'm proud of you," he says. His words sustain me more than the fruit.

Calev is proud of me! He helps me with my protective gear. He breaks open the stem of a healing plant and wipes the ooze across my back where the yoke has gouged a path into my flesh.

When I think no one can hear I ask, "Do you realize how Hem divided the crowd yesterday? He's separating the believers from the unbelievers."

"I know. He's also planting robbers on both sides."

"What?"

"Hem is as much a robber as he has ever been. I don't know what he is planning, but he has spies everywhere."

"How do you know this?"

"Shhh. I mean *everywhere*." He casts his eyes about, and I wonder if some of my teammates are more than trickball players. Do any of them belong to Gadianton's band?

"We'll talk after Elam claims victory."

All day long, beneath the scorch of the sun, under the battering of Calno's bats and a ball that seems heavier every time I have to hit it, I am sustained by my brother's words. He is proud of me! Calev wants to talk to me of Hem and his secret band. Finally, I am believed.

The day blends into a repeat of the day before. Every time the ball is headed for the marker it falls short. Early in the day one of Raz's sons takes a ball to the side of the head and has to be dragged off court. Shortly after that, his brother is pulled off with a broken leg. There are always more players to replace the lost ones.

My body seems stronger today than it did yesterday, but by the time the game is called for the night, my legs are rubber. My eyes cannot focus. I see Grandfather's face, but cannot make out his features. I drink, but still my throat burns. I eat, but taste nothing.

Calev. Where is he? He said we would talk again, but the only glimpse I see of him is when I am on a timed break and I glance up to see his back. I blink because what I'm seeing cannot be true. Calev is talking to Hem! They are smiling and laughing. Eliana stands behind her father, her eyes fixed on Calev.

A horrible feeling comes over me, and for the first time I think we might lose. I might lose and face a lifetime of being nothing more than Hem's slave. The thought is worse than death.

When I wake the next morning Shelomoh, not Calev, is shaking me. The sun is already up, and it is time to put the gear and yoke on. I can barely stand. My body is one giant bleeding bruise. I've been hit by enemy bats, by the ball, by collisions with other players.

The team is brought all the food we can eat, but I'm not hungry. I just want to lie back down and close my eyes for an entire season. To motivate us, Shelomoh has a pole brought in; from it hang four human heads, shriveled and gruesome. "These are the heads of the losers from my birth village. Do you want your heads to hang on this pole?"

He expects a rising "No!" from us, but all we can manage are some groans.

"When can we quit?" one of the frontline men asks.

"When one team scores. There will be no forfeit. No retreat. Do you understand?"

We understand.

Hem—without Eliana—comes down and walks among us. He looks at me and spits. "Worthless. Tomorrow after Calno claims victory, you'll all be on the road to slavery, and it will be your fault. You put forth no effort!"

I'm too worn to argue with him. I think he is going to walk away. Instead he whirls around and hisses, "That blade I saw you with—where did you get it?"

He knows where I got it.

Hem's speech does not seem slurred at all when he leans over and says so that only I can hear, "I know what you think. You think that blade will link me to a crime. But I will accuse you, Kiah, and the judges will believe me. I will have them all believing that you are a son of Gadianton. They will put *you* to death. They will torture your believer Grandfather and rape your mother. I will stand and watch, feigning sorrow."

"No one will believe you," I say, knowing that if I had my blade I would drive it into the heart of the devil who stands before me.

When the game resumes, a renewed surge of energy comes to me. I move faster on the court while the rest of the players drag. I am fighting for more than a victory.

Hem cannot accuse me of stealing his knife if no one ever sees it again.

If we win, he must honor his commitment and allow me to leave Elam.

Mathoni runs alongside me. "If you can get the ball to me while I'm beneath the marker, I believe I can put it through, but you have to knock it to me at just the right moment."

"I will."

But we don't get the chance to try our plan.

Calno's scorer knocks the ball with an elbow, and I see it soaring straight for the marker. The crowd jumps to its feet and shouts, but just as the ball is going through the marker, a bat swings out and knocks the ball short of its goal.

The crowd goes wild.

The players ignite.

I am the one who swung the bat. I don't even realize it until I hear Mathoni call my name.

His brother is beside him. "Get the ball to me. I'll pass it to Mathonihah and we'll score. I know we can."

So we work and work to get the ball away, but Calno has it. Shelomoh is calling me to come off the field and take a break. He has another player poised and ready to send in.

I refuse—pretend that I don't hear his screaming command.

The twins are positioned. Everyone else is watching the ball, but not them—they are lining up side by side.

"Lord, let this victory be for Thee."

I wish the prayer came from *my* lips, but it is shouted by the twin brothers. Let every nonbeliever there hear. They are not ashamed or afraid. They are true believers.

I had wished that Jonas was in the crowd, watching me, but now I'm glad he's not. I go for the ball and miss completely. We have to wait for another chance. And another. And another.

This time the prayer I hear comes from my own heart. *Father, for Thee.*

When the ball comes to me I am more careful. Like the mountain *chakmool* whose patience is without measure, I wait to strike. The ball handler is unaware that I am next to him until I have knocked the ball free. I bounce it with my shoulder, then with my knee, and finally with an elbow raw and numb, I launch the ball toward Mathonihah, who immediately bounces it to Mathoni, who threads it straight through the center of the marker before the crowd even realizes what has happened.

Then the place goes wild.

People pour out onto the ball court. Players stop.

Some people cry. Some scream. Ecstasy struggles to balance agony.

My eyes immediately search for Grandfather. He is standing up, his face turned heavenward. Mother is caught in the crowd, trying to make her way onto the court. Where is Calev? If he was proud of me before, I wonder what he is thinking now.

When I see him, the smile disappears from my face. His back is turned to me. This time he is not speaking with Hem, but with Eliana.

Thirty-Nine

It is time to say good-bye. It is time for a new life to begin—my life. Days have passed, and my bruises and battered limbs have recovered sufficiently for me to make the trip. Mother's lip is sore from where she has been chewing it, nervous and sad that I am really leaving for Zarahemla.

"Grandfather, come with me," I say, "You will be more than welcome at the prophet's home."

He shakes his head. "I have work to do here, son. This is a time for you to move forward with only yourself to be concerned about."

My chest aches with the thought of not seeing him, of what might happen in Elam under Hem's rule. "Hem's angry. He wanted us to lose, didn't he?"

Grandfather sighs.

"What if he takes his anger toward me out on you?"

Grandfather chuckles. "The look on his face when he had to hand you your game winnings—I'll hold that memory and cherish it like a baby."

I can't help smiling, remembering how Hem had to stand next to Lachoneus, in front of everyone, and present me with a pouch heavy with gold. His eyes threatened me, but he had to speak the same word he spoke to Elam's other players: "Congratulations."

Calno's losing team was sentenced to a year of hard labor on the newest ball court. They didn't have time to rest before they were led off toward Zarahemla, their families following, weeping.

My prayer is silent and sincere: *Oh Lord, let me use my freedom and my gold to do good.*

Calev is leaving too to hunt for ore. We haven't spoken much since the game. The promise he made to tell me what Hem was plotting seems to be a memory he forgot. The memory of him standing in plain sight, talking with Eliana, haunts me. If he has another love, why is he so blatantly flirting with

Eliana? But if my brother really is in love with someone else, why will he not reveal her identity? Why do I even care? I tell myself I don't. Calev's business is his and no one else's. The same for Eliana.

Mother hands me a sack of bread and fruit and a tear of dried meat. "Be careful, son. Stay to the main road. Please remember what happened to you the last time you ventured off into unfamiliar territory."

"I remember, Mother."

Today Calev is in one of his happy moods; he slaps me on the back. "I'll watch out for my younger brother's well-being. I'll walk with Kiah for a length of the journey."

Mother's jaw is quivering, and I know she'll hold her tears until her sons are far enough down that we can't hear her outburst. Then she'll cry for days. I want to leave Elam behind, but I don't want to leave her.

"Don't worry about your mother," Grandfather says. "She will be in my care, and I'll see that she stays safe."

As with any good-bye in our community, we take our time parting until Grandfather finally tips his head and bids us, "Peace."

I want to weep but cannot, for Calev would surely scoff, so I claim the tear in my eye is a speck of dust and say nothing until I'm sure my voice won't choke.

"You should be happy," Calev says to me, arranging his backpack once we are out on the main road. "You're leaving Elam. Isn't that what you've wanted ever since I returned from the war?"

"I *am* happy."

"Then why the sour face?"

"*I* have a sour face? You never smile, Calev. Your moods are as uncertain as the weather."

"I'm better now," he says, walking ahead of me. "There are more days of sun and less of storms, but still, you will see how war changes you."

"War cannot come too soon. I'm ready to fight."

He glares back at me with sharp, hard eyes. "You're a fool, Kiah. One day you will see that for yourself."

We walk past the ball court. The grass all around it is trampled flat by the crowds. A few slaves and a couple of overseers are cleaning and making repairs. A small group of Elam's young children are playing trickball for sport, practicing with a very small ball. Every time wood strikes rubber, I still flinch—even after all these days. The sound makes my stomach knot.

"Kiah!" one of the boys calls to me. They stop their game and wave.

"You're a hero now to them," Calev says.

I lift a hand dappled with scabs and wave. Before the trickball game I would have been invisible to these children.

When we pass the synagogue I look for Raz. I'd like to bid him a proper good-bye, but I don't want to stop with Calev. I can tell he's anxious to make haste. His legs strut out in long strides, and though every step I take hurts I say nothing and force my body to keep pace.

When we are past the busy marketplace I turn to my brother. "Calev, you said there were robbers in the crowd. Who were they and how can you tell when a man has taken the secret oath of Gadianton?"

"It's impossible to tell sometimes. Robbers are masters of deceit. They have their secret handshakes, their codes; they know each other as secret brothers."

"And Hem?"

"He is being very kind and friendly toward me. I'm sure you noticed."

I say nothing.

"I kept a close watch on the man. Anyone who greeted him, I studied."

"There were a lot of outsiders. The way he divided the spectators made very clear who were believers and who denounced the Messiah. Why did he do that?"

"Hem has a reason for everything he does."

"Did you see Hem with a man in a blue cloak? He was a stranger to me—someone who worked hard to keep his face covered."

"I saw him."

"Was he a robber?"

"Anyone who associates with Hem is suspect."

"What about you? I saw *you* talking to Hem."

Calev makes a bitter face. "Are you saying I'm a robber?"

"No. But you say that Hem is evil, and yet you talk to him freely—and to Eliana." As soon as her name comes out of my mouth I regret saying it.

Calev stops. His tone hardens. "Here is where we part ways, brother."

"I thought you were walking with me for a length of my journey. We're barely out of Elam."

"The road divides here. You're no longer a boy, Kiah. You'll be fine."

"Of course."

"Be smart and keep your gold in your pouch, strapped to your leg. Anyone who knows about the game knows you were paid."

"Peace," I say.

"And with you."

I want to tell Calev that I'm sorry for sounding so accusing. I want to take back Eliana's name. Instead, I just stand in the road with people veering around me while I watch my brother take the road that leads south to the lowlands.

Grandfather sent word to Nephi's household that I will be arriving. I should continue straight toward Zarahemla, but I don't. I wait and then I shadow my brother, keeping far enough behind him to keep from being discovered. I have no reason to follow him other than curiosity, but that is exactly what I do.

Calev backtracks, takes another detour and makes his way to Abner's shop. It's a wide, busy road with much going on. The shop next to Abner's makes weights and measures. I watch as the craftsman makes sure each cup weighs the precise amount and nestles down into the next. There are sixteen cups in a full set of measures and a balance made to fit every set. Everything must be exact, and I'm fascinated by the care of the craftsman.

I try to overhear Calev's and Abner's conversation inside the shop, but a carpenter across the way is pounding, and the words of my brother are hammered into nothing. I step back off the road into the tangle. It reminds me of the times when I was younger and more foolish, like the time I hid to watch Eliana and Tamar gather water.

My mind and heart are bursting with emotions. I'm grateful for the chance I have to go to Zarahemla and learn, but I'm afraid of showing my weaknesses in front of Jonas, who knows the scriptures so well. I'm worried that Abner's constant kindness is only a mask, one that he will remove as soon as he and Mother live as husband and wife. I am sorrowful because I'll miss Grandfather and I wish he was coming with me to live with the household of the prophet Nephi. I'm glad to be rid of Hem but worried what he'll do next. So many fears shadow me, just as I'm shadowing my brother.

Calev steps back into the light. At first I'm sure he sees me, but he doesn't, and his feet continue down the road. I don't know why I keep following him. His business is none of mine. But the faster he moves, the faster I move. He stops to drink, and when he does, I pick fruit from a tree and wait. When he starts off again, I hesitate, but only for an instant.

He keeps a steady pace for the rest of the morning and well into the afternoon. He is friendly enough with the people along the way, cautious with some—but when it becomes clear to me where my brother is headed, I stop.

Lamanite territory.

The last time I crossed into unknown domain I ended up in a pit of writhing snakes. I believe it happened not because Kerem and his followers were Lamanites but because they were idol worshippers. I know my brother is experienced, but does Calev realize the kind of danger he is headed toward?

I hesitate while my brother splashes across a small stream and disappears into the tangle.

My feet do not move while my mind turns over ideas. Then a wild thought strikes me that lifts my feet and makes me run after him. What if Calev is venturing into Lamanite territory to meet up with our father?

Forty

The idea terrifies me to my very bones. Does Calev know *our father*? Have they been in contact? I can't think of any other reason he would move so boldly toward a land that, until the latest peace treaty, required all Nephites to be bound and brought before Lamanite kings for punishment. And *punishment* often meant torture and death.

I think of Ammon.

I'm hungry.

I'm tried.

I'm afraid.

"Calev!" I call, but my brother is too far ahead to hear me. I walk on, trying to hurry, but Calev's steps are faster and sure, like he has made this trek before. Has he? And to what end?

I would not know our father if he blocked the path I'm walking. Would Calev recognize him?

"Calev!" I call again and make my weary feet rush after him. I'm not sure why. He'll be upset that I followed him. He'll be angry that I've discovered his secret, but I haven't really discovered anything. For all I know he could be venturing into Lamanite land to do business for Abner.

Yes. That's it. That has to be the explanation.

Now I can't see Calev at all. There are too many trees and vines, and the path he took is narrow and far from well-worn. I tell myself to turn back, to go on to Zarahemla. But I don't. I'm curious and driven for a purpose I don't understand. So I follow my brother deeper and deeper into a land I do not know.

I climb a small hill and feel a sense of adventure pushing me on. I'm so tired of the same familiar faces of Elam looking at me—or past me. Here every face I meet is new to me. The terrain is not as steep as it is in our part of the land, though the gorges are fierce, and I have a difficult time scaling back up once I descend down into the belly of the porous rocks.

"Calev!"

No reply. If he knows I'm following him maybe he is rushing ahead so I'll lose his trail.

Some places are as wet as others are dry. On a slope of mossy rocks I slip and slide and wonder about my fate. Is this another foolhardy decision that will lead to danger? My body is still banged up from the trickball game. I'm not physically able to keep the fast, sure stride of Calev.

I attempt to call him again and again, but if he hears me there is no answer. Still, I move forward, following the game trail. At once point a tree screams and a hundred *tz'unu'un* flit in the air, tiny colorful birds that never seem to land. It makes a spectacular but startling sight, and I stop to watch the birds form a moving cloud of color.

I track on and on, upward and across and over and down, only to ascend again. It won't be long until the sun is down; already the shadows are long and drawn. I almost lose the trail a time or two. Then night takes over, and there is only a sliver of moon; most of the stars are hidden by clouds.

Has Calev already made camp? If he has, and if he knows that I'm tracking him, he'll be waiting for me, upset and vengeful. How I wish we were brothers like I imagine brothers should be—close always.

Finally, I camp without food and without fire. I've got my jade-handled blade and a small javelin, a gift from Abner. I've also got my sling, but I don't hunt. I eat the berries and fruit from the forest and sleep beneath a blanket of white stars. Night stingers are larger here. They seem to buzz more loudly, too. I'm so tired that after slapping a few away, I fall asleep and don't even feel when they draw my blood.

The next day I eat what I can forage. I am driven to follow Calev's trail for a reason I don't understand. The next day and the day after are blurry hours spent tracking my brother in a land that becomes stranger and more alluring. When I ventured to Shimnilom I was heading toward the great sea. Though it was the land of the Lamanites, it was filled with other *-ites* that worshipped idols capable of consuming innocent maidens—and capable of torturing me with a pit of vipers that still haunts my sleep.

Here in the hills, I've seen Lamanite villages as humble and peaceful as Elam. The people are more colorful in dress but could pass for family. They stare at me, but no one has harassed me or questioned my presence in their land.

There are long stretches when I think I've lost Calev's trail, but then I pick it up, never getting close enough to spot him. Surely, he is searching this land for ore to haul back to Abner. That is his reason for being here. I'm still uncertain about what drives me on, but on I go.

The fourth morning as the sun rises I rise too, over the top of a grassy slope. The scene that stretches before me takes my breath away. It's an endless valley, laid out in perfect precision. Roads are straight and even. There are mounds here, like the ones I once saw on the outskirts of Zarahemla—houses dug into the ground, protected by great mounds of earth, miniature hills. They appear much more durable than our huts made of timber covered by banana leaves.

The trees here have white trunks with yellowish leaves. The sky is a deeper shade of blue and the clouds are whiter. I see no snakes, but the birds and the monkeys watch me; I suspect other eyes see me too. Lamanites are excellent scouts. Even in a time of peace they will not let a young Nephite warrior go unnoticed. I'm sure they watched me while I slept. That fact should scare me; instead, it urges me deeper into a land where I am tolerated, but not welcome.

Early-morning hunters are out, and I see bands of men stalking prey. When I stop to gather berries and drink from a trickling steam I hear the squeal of a rabbit. In a moment a boy hunter comes tearing through the brush with the rabbit dangling over his back. He stops when he sees me— stares with wide, dark eyes, then moves on to meet the rest of his hunting party.

I make sure my blade is in my grip. Someone else might not be so harmless.

Lamanites fill the morning with the same tasks that occupy Nephites. Stretched below me is a large village with families waking to the day, women fetching water, children fetching wood. Men are grouped into hunting parties, either going out or coming in. Other men are moving to the fields, where corn grows in straight rows.

These do not look like the idolatrous, lazy people I have heard about. Nor do they look like bloodthirsty villains. I like their houses—huts made of animal skins or mounds that allow families to dwell beneath the earth where the heat of the day does not permeate.

I hike higher, telling myself I am safe. These are not idol worshippers. I have seen no false prophets. I have also seen eyes watching me from every direction. When did I become a target of interest?

The trail is hardly a trail at all now. I think I'm heading in the direction of my brother, but I'm not certain. A family of eagles, black dots against blue sky, circles above me. A small herd of deer breaks through the bush. One comes so close I could practically spear it in the heart—if I wanted to.

Right now, all I want to do is keep moving, to find my brother, and to turn back to familiar territory. Where is Calev?

I keep going. Eventually I believe the curious eyes that were watching me have lost interest. The tangle is so thick I have to use a blade to continue on in places. The earth is moist, the rocks mossy. I can hear the rush of water, and when I round a bend and break through a wall of vines I'm met with a scene that makes my jaw drop. A band of Lamanite maidens are beneath a small waterfall, filling their pots, splashing and laughing. They are beautiful maidens who seem carefree and happy—except for one on the end who looks nervous. Her eyes keep darting around, and I wonder if she sees me.

No.

She sees Calev.

My brother is well hidden in the tangle across the way, but I can see him. The maiden sees him too, and she makes certain she is not seen as she sneaks away from her friends into the waiting embrace of my brother.

Forty-One

I elect to keep my brother's secret. I choose to swallow it and never let it spill from my lips. If Calev is in love with a Lamanite maiden, what right do I have to interfere? I am about to choose the course of my own life; Calev should be able to choose his.

I do not make my presence known. Instead, I turn around and sneak back toward Elam—toward the road to Zarahemla.

But I find myself lost.

I've spent my life exploring, yet now that I'm higher on the hillside, I see how many trails intersect through the trees and vines. I don't know which one will lead home. I look to the sun and tell myself if I head northward I'll eventually return to Nephite territory.

I'm not afraid, but there is no calm of peace in my heart either. I pray and realize that if the Lamanites were going to capture me, they would have done it by now. I try not to think of what will happen to Calev if their warriors discover he is secretly meeting one of their maidens.

My brother thrives on a life of peril.

My body is worn and weak, and I pause to rest by a stream deep enough in places to allow a total washing. The cold temperature of the rushing water feels so good I stay immersed until my limbs are numb. Then I crawl out and lie in an open patch of warm sunlight. Sleep overtakes me. When I awake, I'm surrounded by waiting Lamanites.

Children. All of them are children—younger than I was when I first started to hunt the hills of Elam alone. I open my eyes and hear them giggle. They remind me of the children of Shimnilom. One unblinking boy could be a cousin of Abina, his face is that similar. I look behind the children. I see no wall of grown Lamanites, though I suspect they are not far away.

"What are you called?" I ask the boy.

He looks at the others and makes a small birdlike noise. They disappear back into the thick of the tangle, blending in as sure as tree trunks on the hillside.

Am I in danger? They could steal the gold that is laced to my leg; they could steal my blade. They could steal my life. But I don't feel afraid. All the time I was tracking Calev I thought of how I was taught that all Lamanites are bloodthirsty devils. I've seen with my own eyes the error of that judgment.

Yes, there are Lamanites who are bloodthirsty and demonic. There are also Nephites who are just as deadly and vile. I think of how Laman's choices affected an entire people—just as Nephi's did. The difference between us has little to do with the shade of our skin and everything to do with the covenants set before us—who keeps them and who does not.

I think of the Lamanite man who delivered me when Jonas and I were mobbed in Zarahemla. I think of the Lamanite maiden who has won my brother's heart. I think of the thousands of Lamanites I've seen on this journey. Have they given me reason to doubt that their love for their families is any different from my own? Aren't we all children of Father Lehi and Father God?

My God delivered me out of a vipers' pit. For what purpose? That same God has made my heart soft toward the Lamanites—for what purpose?

There are spotted *keeh* and other wild animals, birds on every branch, and a few climbers with their long tails swinging like ropes. They screech, and I move farther down. My foot barely touches the pathway when I hear, "Brother!"

I keep walking, hoping the man is not speaking to me. But he lopes up to me and greets me with enthusiasm.

My soft heart suddenly grows suspicious, and fear burns through me like water that is heated over flame.

"Brother?"

He is a tall, thin Lamanite man dressed in a humble cloak, carrying a well-worn spear. My fist tightens around the javelin Abner made for me.

"Your face is the face of a stranger," the man says. He is older than I am, maybe three times as old. I understand what he is saying, even though he pronounces words differently than I do. I speak slowly; his tongue is rapid and clicks between words.

I say nothing. My heart pounds. Feeling like an anxious boy again, I try to decide my next move. It's just the two of us on the pathway. I could kill the man and be gone before anyone discovered him, but he looks strong and the feat might not be as easy as I imagine.

I don't want to kill him. I don't want to, but if he tries to kill me—

"I am Miyan, son of Miyan."

I understand his words, but his tongue moves differently in his mouth, and I have to listen carefully. I expect that he will take me prisoner; he might even call for others to join him. The memory of the vipers' pit makes me shudder, and I vow to myself that I will fight to my death before I allow anyone to banish me into such torture again.

Instead Miyan holds out not a weapon, but his water pouch. He offers me a drink. "You do not understand?" he asks.

"I understand."

A slight smile tugs at his lips. "You do not trust me."

"I am a Nephite."

"Nephites don't get thirsty?" Now he smiles wide and welcoming.

I take his pouch and let the water soothe my lips and go down my throat. I have to fight the desire to gulp. We are not far from a stream, yet I did not realize how thirsty I was. Still, the water could be poisoned. His kindness could be a trick.

"Tell me, brother, are you hungry?"

He hasn't asked my reason for being here. He hasn't asked where I am headed. He only asks after my well-being. The grip around my javelin loosens.

"Come." The man motions for me to follow him.

I hesitate, thinking that I can turn and run back the way I came. Instead I move forward, placing my feet where his feet trod. We walk along the pathway to a point where it diverges onto a larger, busier road. There are people moving in both directions, yet only a few look at me with suspicion. *This,* Mother would say, is a fruit of peace.

We come to a field where the man negotiates with the farmer for fresh corn. I shake my head. I have my gold, but if I show that I will surely be the target of thieves.

"If a brother is hungry and I have food, it is my obligation to offer him that food. I require no payment from you." He splays his fingers out and slaps his chest. "I am called Miyan, son of Miyan."

I understood him the first time; I just didn't respond. Now I touch my own chest and say, "I am called Kiah, grandson of Yarden. My home is a small village in the land of Zarahemla."

He pays in beans for me to eat fresh corn and dried fish and the grilled root of a plant I do not know.

"If you are weary you may take rest where my family dwells."

"Thank you, brother," I say, sounding strange to myself, speaking to a Lamanite. "I must return to my village."

"You are a member of the church of Christ?"

"Yes. My grandfather is a priest."

"And you?"

"I am a—" How can I answer? I have no station, no calling, no position. I'm a son of the commandment by age, but not by discipline. I'm caught by time between boyhood and manhood, a span where I have been trapped far too long.

"You know of the Messiah?" he asks.

"Yes."

His dark eyes glint and his smile broadens. "I was once a slave in your land. I was set free when I vowed to accept the Messiah. Can you teach us of Him?"

I am dumbstruck. He wants *me* to teach him of Jesus Christ? This has to be a trap, a trick. All I can think about is Kerem and snakes. I try not to let him see my uncertainty. "I must return to my village without delay."

Miyan's smile drops. His shoulders fall. "You will *not* teach of the Messiah?"

"I know very little." I know His power has delivered me, has pardoned me, and has guided me. But how can I put that testimony into words?

"We know less . . . only that He has power to save us from our sins. Please, you—Kiah—teach us truth about the Messiah and how He can save us."

I finger the blade of my javelin. If the man wanted to injure me he would not have treated me like a brother. The look on his face—the desperation in his tone—is sincere. What he is asking me to do strikes a fear in me greater than if I were to face a ravenous beast.

"I will arrange for my family—my entire family—to listen to you."

The man is my elder, yet he is like a child asking for a toy. He wants me to teach him the importance of the Messiah.

"I . . . I . . . I don't know. I can send my Grandfather. He is a missionary; he will be happy to teach you."

"No!" The farmer steps forward with another offering of corn. "My brother, Miyan, wishes to learn about the Messiah. You know. *You* teach him."

I clear the phlegm from my throat. What can I teach of the Messiah? I'm trying to recall a scripture, something that would at least let me sound like Grandfather or Nephi or even Jonas. Not a single scripture comes to mind.

"I'll tell you what I know of the Messiah, but I am no missionary. I am not a good student of the scriptures."

I think Miyan might break into a foot dance of joy. He quickly leads me past the cornfield, down a row of shops where weapons are made—shields, spears, slings, and blades. I've never seen anything like it. Dozens and dozens of Lamanites are working together, forging armor and weapons. I stop and stare with wide eyes.

It occurs to me that these are being made to fight me—a Nephite. Yet the men go on about their business without giving me more than a glance.

"You are a warrior?" Miyan asks.

Here is my chance to declare what I've always aspired to be, and I don't know what to say. I am a hunter. I am a tracker. I am a brother and son and grandson. I am a student. I am a friend and a trickball player. But am I a warrior?

"I always thought that's what I wanted to be," I say, staring in wonder at the weapons being fashioned all around me. One shop makes only clubs—different-sized clubs carved from a variety of wood—some carved with razor-sharp edges, some inlaid with obsidian and flint, some made for a child's grip. A child-sized club. The idea of arming children to fight sickens me.

Miyan waits impatiently while I stare. I could stay on this street for an entire season, studying the craftsmanship.

He smiles as if he can read my thoughts. Then I follow him to the end of the row. We turn down another street and I stop again. Here are shops that make things only of feathers: the hue of blood and sunset, all types of feathers. The air stinks from the scent of so many boiling dyes.

As we walk Miyan stops people to invite them to his house so that this stranger—I, a Nephite—can teach of the Messiah.

I'm shocked at how many people are already gathered at his humble mound when we arrive. Miyan's wife is a short, stout woman with a smile that rivals his. He has children, more than I can count—most of them small, naked, and happy.

I am served water and a thick, coarse round of bread made from corn and a spice that my tongue has never tasted. I would request more, but I can see that Miyan is a poor man and may well go hungry this night because his bread was given to me. One of his daughters—a little girl with long black hair hanging in curls, a little girl who can't stop giggling—hands me a cup. I put it to my lips and taste sweet berry juice.

Now all the children are looking at me, giggling, and I realize it's because I've stained my lips red. The harder I wipe with the back of my hand, the harder they giggle.

There is an easy, happy feeling at the home of Miyan. When his children laugh, it is the same sound as Nephite children make. The people gathering from every direction are beautiful, kind people with eyes that look at me with an expectation that makes me nervous.

What if I disappoint them? Will they turn on me in anger? Are these people really capable of the horrors I know of Lamanites? I'm beginning to understand how my brother could fall in love with one of them. And though there is no formal law that would punish a union between a Nephite and a Lamanite, there are individuals who view such a union as an ultimate sin. I know if my brother is discovered he could surely face torture and even death—not only from the Lamanites, but from Nephites as well.

Miyan raises his hands—apparently a signal, for everyone falls silent. Their eyes turn to me. "Teach us, Brother Kiah—teach us so that we too may know of the Messiah."

Forty-Two

The place of honor.

I've never been in such a situation, and I think for an instant that I might feel more at ease in the vipers' pit. It's easy to see that these people expect something great from me. They sit, ready for me to teach them of Jesus Christ. Where do I begin?

Father, let Thy Holy Spirit guide me.

"Messiah." I say the word, the very word, and a power comes over me. "I'm a Nephite boy, almost a man," I begin, and I see a few smiles. "I am called Kiah. I have never known my father, but I have been raised in the care and teaching of my mother and my grandfather."

More nods.

"I wish that I had been a better student of the scriptures. I wish that I could quote to you from the holy books. I can't. But I can tell you what I know.

"Once we were all brothers and sisters in a life before this life. There we lived with the Father of our spirits. There we knew each other."

Even the children are wide-eyed and silent. My hearts pounds with every word because I don't think about what I'm saying; I *feel* it. "As His children, we wanted to become like our Father, so He made a way. That way was for us to come here." I wave my arm toward the golden flatlands, then sweep it upward toward the green peaks. "We are here to learn many lessons. We are here to become like our Father in Heaven."

My audience does not look confused. They look like I'm telling them something they already know. There are nods, smiles, tears. I can't help contrasting that to the synagogue crowds in Elam or even to the crowds at the temple in Zarahemla.

"I've heard my grandfather and the prophet Nephi say that six hundred years from the time our Father Lehi left Jerusalem, a Messiah would come into the world to teach us—to show us the way we should live and to redeem us from our sins."

As soon as I say the word *redeem* I remember Kerem's reaction, and I anticipate that these people too will resent me. Will accuse me of calling them sinners. I assume the worst.

"How?" Miyan asks, tears welling in his eyes, spilling down his cheeks. "I am a man filthy with sin. How . . . how can the Messiah redeem me?"

I've never seen such humility or such eagerness to believe. I feel my heart being pulled and twisted like bread dough, reshaped by such faith. "I'm sorry," I say honestly. "I don't know how the great plan of redemption will work. I only know that it comes through the Messiah. He will be a mighty man of miracles who can raise the dead and heal the lame. On His shoulders, my grandfather says, will rest the weight of every wrong choice we've ever made, every pain we've ever suffered. That weight He will bear out of love so that we do not have to carry such burdens."

"The Messiah—He is a god, no?"

"Yes. He is the Son of God. I remember something the prophet Nephi taught me while I was staying in his home in Zarahemla. He said that Jesus Christ, the name of the Messiah, will dwell here among us in a tabernacle of clay like ours so that He can suffer and feel all that we feel—temptations, pains, hunger, thirst, fatigue."

"What are we to do?"

I stumble for an answer. "Join as family—join Christ's church."

"How?"

"Everyone must be baptized."

"Will *you* baptize us? Will you baptize us *now*?"

I look around at the eager, anxious faces, people so willing to cling to truth that they lunge for it. I can't help them, and my heart sinks. "I cannot baptize you."

"Why?"

"I don't have the authority. Only those with the power to baptize can baptize."

"Who can baptize us if you cannot?"

I think of Grandfather and how he would cherish this opportunity. I think of Nephi's entire family—how Lehi and Timothy and Nephi the Younger, even Jonas, would all know what to do to help these people come to Christ. I'm here and helpless to do much. How I wish I was a priest and had been ordained to the office so that I could perform the ordinance.

The faces of hope fall with despair.

"What else can you teach us of the Messiah?"

I'm careful as I recount the story of Father Lehi and Mother Sariah—how Nephi chose to go one direction while Laman chose a different path. I expect anger that never comes. I tell them of my experience in the vipers' pit. The children wriggle as I describe the different shapes and sizes of the snakes. The women step back as I tell of what it felt like to be thrown into that pit because, as a foolish boy fed only by faith, I stood up to a man who said there was and never would be a Messiah. The men fold their arms and look at me with respect.

I feel the muscles in my back tighten, and I stretch to be as tall as I can possibly be. "I know that I would not be here talking with you if there was no Messiah. I know that I would be dead. But I am not dead, and there is a Messiah. If He saved me He will surely save you!"

As I'm testifying of my own experiences a feeling comes over me as sure as any fire. It is hot and powerful. The Holy Spirit is testifying to me that what I am testifying to Miyan and his family is true.

I make a promise—a sacred vow—that no matter what is required, one day either I will return or I will send missionaries to baptize this family, all of these people who are so hungry for the word of God. And I promise myself that I will never again be caught unprepared as a missionary.

The burning in my bosom does not subside. My chest drums; it feels as though someone has lit it with a flaming torch. All my life the only thing I've ever really desired was to become a warrior. But now that I'm standing in front of Miyan and his family—now that I can see how desperately they want to accept and live the teachings of Christ—a new desire is born within me. I do not want to fight these people.

I want to fight *for* these people.

I want to help them in any way I can. I want to teach them and testify to them. I want them to feel the love that I have felt both from and for the Savior.

I want to be a warrior for the Messiah's army.

Forty-Three

I journey back to Zarahemla, and the first night I sleep in the prophet Nephi's courtyard I sleep alone. Jonas and his father are out working. Nephi and Lehi are out preaching. Timothy and his family have moved into the city. I'm welcomed by the servants, the children, and the women. Jonas's mother, Devora, treats me like a long lost son. She feeds me and asks every detail of Mother's life and her marriage to Abner. I try to sound supportive, but I worry about Mother and wish that she was here.

"Grandfather is watching over her."

"He is well, then?"

"Better, thank you."

I try not to let her see that I'm disappointed that the prophet is not present—because I want nothing more than to turn around and go right back to Miyan's village. I want to bring Grandfather, Nephi, Lehi, Nephi the Younger, and Jonas with me. I want to bring the gospel of Jesus Christ to all of Miyan's family. Why not to all of the Lamanites? The power that has changed my life is strong enough to change any life.

But that night I have a disturbing dream. I dream I am back among Miyan's people. We are gathered by the house when I look up the road and see Grandfather coming toward us. One of the men in the crowd stands up; I see Grandfather drop his walking stick and rush forward, calling, "Gidd! My son, Gidd!"

I wake up trembling. A mist has settled, and my hair and clothes are soaked. I wish the image from my dream would fade. My father is a dissenter. He lives among the Lamanites. He has a new family. He has never shown interest in me, so why is he haunting my dreams now?

My thoughts should be with Calev. He is deep in Lamanite territory. The risk he is taking could cost him his life, but at least now I understand why his moods change, why he disappears from time to time. Part of me wishes I'd shown myself to Calev. If anything happens to him I will always regret it.

Timothy, uncle to Jonas, arrives to check on the women and children. The man has tremendous faith, a quick laugh, and a heart that beats with love. He invites me to share morning prayer; afterward, I hear myself ask, "Have you ever preached among the Lamanites?"

"Yes. Why?"

"I want to learn all I can of them."

"Why?"

I tell him how I found myself in Lamanite territory, how I was fearful, but how one man's family treated me like family. "All my life I've kept a distance from the Lamanites. I've feared them. I thought they were evil and dirty. I know the traditions. I know the scripture stories. But I have learned for myself that there are wonderful, faithful people among the Lamanites. I am hoping to gather a band of missionaries to teach them all that I couldn't, to baptize them and help them set up a way to worship."

Timothy scratches the top of his bald head. "You've caught the fire, haven't you?"

"The fire?"

"The spirit of missionary work. Once it gets in you it runs through your veins as sure as blood."

I nod. "They begged me to tell them of the Messiah. They wanted me to explain God's plan for our happiness. I told them what I could, but it was nothing like Grandfather would have preached—or the prophet, or you. I desire to know so much more."

Timothy laughs and helps straighten a toddling baby that has stumbled. "Come, walk with me."

We exit the courtyard gates. Even though we are now in a time of peace and plenty, guards still stand by the gate and follow behind us as we walk. Timothy takes a road that leads away from the city.

"What do you wish to know about our Lamanite brethren?"

"I want to understand the curse that is on them."

He looks at me not as a man gazing on a child but as a man looking at his friend. "What would you like to understand?"

"Why is it so wrong for a Lamanite and a Nephite to marry?"

The way his eyebrows lift I realize Timothy assumes I'm talking about myself. I allow him to think it because I don't want to betray Calev.

Timothy reminds me of his uncle, Lehi—the way they both stand so straight with their shoulders pulled back, the way their hair is grey around the temples, the way they go silent when they are thinking. We walk all the way to the synagogue, where priests and believers rush to greet Timothy with the respect due the prophet's kin.

The synagogue here is many times larger than the one in Elam. In a special room at the back, dark and rounded like a cave, there are walls where sacred scrolls are tucked into burrowed holes. Timothy seems to know the exact one to reach for. He is careful; he handles the scroll with the tenderness he might use to hold a newborn baby. He examines it by the flame of a candle that he holds at arm's length from the scroll.

"Yes, this is the right one. Come with me out into the sunlight," he says.

The courtyard is a burst of color. Someone has planted brightly hued flowers, varieties of every kind, and allowed ferns to grow tall and green around the wall. The air is sweet, and all the different shades make my eyes dance.

"I spent much of my childhood here," Timothy tells me, sitting at a table, unfurling the scroll.

"You were a student of the law?" I ask.

"I was a scroll maker. Are your hands clean?"

I flip over my palms to inspect them and decide to wash the grime from the lines in my skin. The *mikvah* is across the way, and when I return from cleansing my hands, I see Timothy hunched over, squinting, studying.

He guides my hand across the smooth surface of the sacred text. "Do you know how a scroll is crafted?"

"No. Not really."

"Only the skins of the youngest animals are used, often deer. The fresh skin has to be soaked right away so it will swell, then the hair is scraped off and the skin is stretched on frames; I'm sure you've seen your mother use them."

"She stretches skins to make our clothes."

"Yes. This courtyard, before it was walled in to make an area for study, was flat and open. The walls around it challenged the wind, so it was a perfect place to stretch and dry the skins. Then they were shaved as thin as possible," he fingers the edges, "but not too thin, because over time the scroll is unfurled and read over and over."

"How did you shave it?"

"With a large, curved blade. It was my job to take that blade back and forth again and again, trying to make the surface equal. It was a miserable and time-consuming chore. The priests got so angry with me if I made a mistake. They whipped me every time I scraped through the hide."

I nod, thinking of all the times a priest has whipped me for a mistake I've made.

"Then the shaved skin had to be soaked again, this time in a special mixture that my grandfather was expert in making."

"Your grandfather was the prophet Helaman?"

"Yes. He was a very great man who taught me in the ways of his learning. For the mixture, he used citrus from the lowlands, sea salt, crushed nuts, and a thickening powder that my wife can turn into foul-tasting bread."

He laughs and I smile.

"It sounds like a drawn-out process," I say.

"Oh, it was—it still is, though I have daughters learning the skill now."

"How do you get the surface so smooth and white?"

"After the hide was soaked for days in that vile solution, it was rinsed in clear running water. Then we stretched it out again on the frames and allowed it to dry perfectly flat."

"Then it looked like this?"

"No. For a final whitening we polished it smooth with a pumice stone."

All of Timothy's information about scrolls was interesting, but it did not address my worry about Calev and his Lamanite maiden.

"Why do you think the Lord would have us go to all of this hard work to make these scrolls?"

"So that we can record the teachings of the prophets."

"For whose blessing?"

His question makes me stop and think. I answer carefully. "I suppose the scriptures are recorded to strengthen the believers but mostly to help convince and convert the unbelievers."

Timothy smiles, showing rows of straight teeth that he has cared well for. They are intact and clean. Even the dirt beneath Timothy's fingernails is scraped away. "Tell me what the teachings say about our first brother, Laman."

"He was Lehi's eldest son. He was rebellious," I explain.

"He wanted to kill his own father—that goes beyond *rebellious*. He was constantly trying to lead others away from Lehi's teachings. Nephi *had* to take the records to protect them."

I nod. "I know the story."

Timothy turns back to his scroll, fingering the writing carefully. "Did Laman have a choice?"

"A choice in what?"

"In obeying or disobeying?"

"Yes."

"Do you have a choice?"

He catches me off guard, and I have to think about whether he might be posing a trick question. "I have a choice."

"And if you chose to obey or disobey . . . what has the Lord promised?"

"I don't know."

Timothy reads carefully from the scroll, quoting Nephi: "Inasmuch as ye shall keep my commandments, ye shall prosper . . . and inasmuch as thy brethren shall rebel against thee, they shall be cut off from the presence of the Lord."

I carefully reach out to finger the parchment. It is as smooth as the surface of a scar.

"How are we cut off from the presence of the Lord?"

My teeth bite into my bottom lip the way Mother gnaws her lip when she is nervous. "We are cut off when we disobey."

"That is the curse recorded in the scriptures. Now tell me: How did the Lord distinguish Lamanites from Nephites?"

I picture the Lamanites that I have seen and the ones I now know personally—Miyan's family. "I know he made their skin darker."

"Did he do that to punish them?" he asks, but then answers his own question. "No. He did that to *distinguish* them. The change in skin was a mark. The Lord does not punish innocent children for the sins of their fathers."

I could not imagine the Lord punishing Miyan's precious, giggling children for sins Laman and Lemuel committed. It made no sense.

"There are many opinions, Kiah; even priests cannot agree on how the Lord distinguished our Lamanite brethren from our people. But know this truth if you know no other: The Lord esteemeth all flesh in one; he that is righteous is favored of God."

"So it is not a matter of skin color but of righteousness?"

"It is a matter of covenant over color. Both Laman and Nephi made sacred covenants. Who kept those covenants?"

"Is that why the scripture says that 'cursed shall be the seed of him that mixeth with their seed; for they shall be cursed even with the same cursing'?"

I keep chewing my lip.

"The curse is not a dark skin—the curse is a darkening of the spirit, and the Lord Jesus Christ is a God of light and truth. Do you understand what I am saying?"

"I'm not certain."

"The darker skin was a *sign*, but the *curse* was the withdrawal of the Spirit of the Lord. Do you know what happens to a people when the Spirit of Jesus Christ is withdrawn from them?"

"They become wicked."

"Filthy, idle, and sinful. The Lord commanded our people not to intermarry with the Lamanites who were cursed because He wants covenant-keepers to marry other covenant-keepers. When believers marry unbelievers there is a division, and the children grow up away from the Lord. The Lord commanded the Nephites not to intermarry with the Lamanites, for if they did, they would partake of the curse."

"That was six hundred years ago," I say. "Now Grandfather says that many of the Lamanites who have the gospel are more righteous than the Nephites."

"That is true. Think of the great faith of the Ammonite queen; Ammon told her that he had never seen such great faith. The Lamanites that Ammon taught became a zealous and beloved people—highly favored of the Lord—who preferred to die rather than to sin. Show me a Nephite people *that* committed to righteousness."

"So now is it lawful for a Nephite to marry a Lamanite?"

"Are you in love with a Lamanite maiden, Kiah?"

"No." I tell him again of my love for Miyan and his family, how all they desire is to belong to the Church of Christ and to have His laws set before them so that they can be obedient.

Timothy rolls up the scroll, and we walk back into the synagogue. It's cooler in there. Darker. He seems agitated and serious. "Son, I hope I have given you a bit of truth to ponder, but this is a matter that will require discussion in the future. I too know righteous Lamanites, so humble and desirous to obey that they buried their weapons. The Lord loves them, and His gospel message will reach them."

"Can we go soon back to the land of the Lamanites so that Miyan's family can hear the word? You could baptize them. I was very careful as I left there so I can locate the family again. I know how to find their village from the high hills."

Timothy looks sad. "You want to be a missionary?"

I bite my lip so hard I taste blood. "Even more than I want to be a warrior."

He points toward a small classroom where students—boys much younger than me—are reading from the sacred texts. "Then the best place for you to start that mission is here."

Forty-Four

My time in the household of the prophet proves the happiest time of my life. I share a sleeping quarter with Jonas, who treats me like I am close kin. There are nights when we lay awake and talk of the Messiah and His goodness to us until the break of dawn. Jonas begs me to tell him over and over the story of my escape from the vipers' pit. I never tire of hearing how he and his father teach unbelievers throughout the land of Zarahemla.

I want them to accompany me to Miyan's family. Instead, the prophet and his brother Lehi return for a short time to prepare for another mission, this one to Lamanite land. They assure me that they will find and teach and baptize Miyan's family and any others desiring to join the church of God.

"How will you know where to find them?"

"You will provide the best map you can, and the Lord will lead us."

When he says that I know that my promise to have someone return to teach and baptize Miyan and his family will be kept. My worries vanish.

The prophet takes time to sit with me by the well. "Kiah, long ago you told me that your great desire was to be a warrior. Has your heart changed?"

The tears that sting my eyes embarrass me. I'm a man now. I have no right to cry, yet the prophet seems to understand. "I still long to be a great warrior, to defend my faith and my family, but now my heart wants something more."

"I hear that you wish to be a preacher."

"I do."

"Then take these final days of peace and study diligently. Listen to the Lord's Spirit when it whispers. Obey. Obedience is the key to all blessings."

He teaches me the same principles my grandfather taught me.

One day they will both stand pleased with what I accomplish.

And so I begin my education in earnest. School is much different than I imagined. I pictured myself in a small setting next to Jonas, who would always know the proper answers while I struggled. The truth is that I am *not* a gifted student, deemed deserving of an advanced education. I am here seasons beyond my thirteenth year because the prophet has made arrangements as a favor to Grandfather. The teachers know it. The priests know it. The other students know it. I feel an air of resentment, but that only makes me more determined to not disappoint those who believe in me.

The head teacher, a man named Saul, is so old his skin reminds me of the shed skin of a snake. It is easy to count his veins. But he is patient with me and tells me, "A proper education should fill your head with knowledge, your hands with skills, and your heart with an attitude to live God's will."

In Elam, school was conducted only sporadically; here it is every day as long as daylight lasts. Here the competition is fierce. Minds are keen. Fathers and mothers punish children who fail to recite perfectly.

No one punishes me.

In Elam I had only one teacher, a priest named Benjamin who had no faith in my abilities and told me so repeatedly: "You have no head for scripture. You do not understand the law. You cannot remember any lesson." He slapped his cheeks with his palms and moaned like an old woman in mourning. And I could never forget Oshra's simple-minded husband, Gomer, who tarried around the grounds and snickered every time I got lashed.

Here in Zarahemla, I am allowed to sit at the back of the learning room. No one laughs at anyone's mistakes. In fact, Saul punishes any student who demeans another's efforts.

Jonas is not my competition. He is Saul's disciple and shadows him, even when the teacher is away from the synagogue. At night Jonas helps me with my memorization, especially the Sinai commandments given to Moses: "And God spake all these words, saying, I am the LORD thy God, which have brought thee out of the land of Egypt, out of the house of bondage. Thou shalt have no other gods before me. Thou shalt not make unto thee any graven image, or any likeness of any thing that is in heaven above, or that is in the earth beneath, or that is in the water under the earth."

Every commandment now seems to have purpose—just like every student, Saul teaches. "There is no age limit to become a true son of the commandment, Kiah. Never be ashamed of trying to better yourself."

As the oldest student, I should feel foolish, but I don't. I feel grateful and eager to learn—something I've never felt, not even sitting beside Raz.

After our oral lessons, I go out into the flower garden with an apprentice teacher named Solomon. He is not that much older than Calev, and I'm amazed at how fast and accurate his tongue is, both in our language and in the language of our fathers.

I cannot lie. There are days when I fail miserably. There have already been times when I wanted to cry like the little boys who still bury their faces in their mothers' skirts. But Solomon is patient and kind and finds a way to ask me questions so that I better understand.

I learn that as a missionary I am to know the scriptures and to understand the law, but that is not all. If I am to be effective, I must teach by the Spirit and not by my own power. As a student, I am not allowed to ask questions in a formal classroom setting, so I save my queries to pose to Solomon when we are in the garden. "What does a real missionary teach?"

"First, that there is a God. He who created the seas and the mountains also created us. We are made in His image. We can communicate with God through prayer."

I learn that I already know much more than I realized. Mother and Grandfather—and, yes, even my teachers in Elam—taught me of prayer, of repentance, of faith in the coming Messiah. I wish I had felt more confidence when Miyan asked me for help.

The days blend from lesson to lesson. At night and on the days we are not required to attend school, Jonas and I hunt and explore. Zarahemla is always expanding. Inside the high, gray city walls, commerce grows; outside, buildings are spread wide. There is less timber now than the last time I was here; even our favorite tall climbing tree is gone, turned into someone's home or shop.

After a break, I return to school refreshed and determined to open my mind and heart. I study the law, the scriptures, the language, the stars, the numbers, and the history of our people.

Here, as in Elam, I am confused by points of doctrine. In Elam, the church is called Christ's Church of Elam. Here it is called the Church of the Coming Messiah. Teachers and priests are always arguing over what the one right name is. When referring to the church, Grandfather always calls it "the Church of Christ."

There is also contention over when and how a person should be baptized. Some churches are rumored to be baptizing without total immersion. Solomon says immersion is the only way to properly baptize.

Priesthood authority is another point of doctrine where no one seems definite. Timothy teaches me that priesthood progresses in a direct line, and it can only be given by one who already possesses proper authority. I can't wait to have Grandfather lay his hands on my head and pass that power of God down to me. I just want to know that I am advanced enough and worthy to receive it.

Any contentions are put to rest when Nephi and Lehi return from their long missionary journey. The first thing they do is tell me how Miyan's family received the covenants with great joy, bringing with them many others. I am overjoyed and smile so long and wide that my face aches.

I learn that each member of Miyan's family was totally immersed in water when baptized in a spring beyond their village. In total, 404 Lamanites were baptized by the time Nephi and Lehi and their party left the Lamanite lands.

"How did you manage so many converts?"

"Miyan had already taught others what you taught him," Nephi tells me. "Miyan, though not baptized, was already a missionary for the church." He laughs, and I realize it's the first time I've heard the prophet laugh in a very long time.

"There must be more work done. A church must be established in Miyan's land so that the doctrine remains true."

I imagine a time when there are no disputations on doctrine, when there is no division between brothers. I imagine a time when the Messiah rules in love.

• • •

I hardly have time to celebrate my gratitude for Miyan and his family being baptized. I have oral tests to pass before I am given writing instruments and told to practice making letters in the sand. Solomon is so astounded that he asks Saul to stand beside me. "Your letters are exact."

"Thank you. I had excellent teachers."

"Who were they?"

I tell him of Raz, our timekeeper. I tell him of Grandfather. I tell him of Mother.

"Your *mother* can write?"

"Yes, and also read. She was taught by her father."

"I have daughters," Solomon says; "they are taught by me." He looks back at Jonas, who stands with his hands behind his back, a silent shadow to the teacher. "Jonas is fond of my daughter Orli. She is gifted at reading and writing. She remembers scriptures I have forgotten. When she is fifteen, she will make a good wife."

Jonas drops his head, but I see his ears redden. Later, when I ask him about Orli, I see a look on my friend's face that I have never seen.

"What happened to your feelings for Lysa?"

"I met Orli."

I laugh, and it feels good to laugh.

"Why haven't you lost your heart to anyone special?" he asks.

We are resting in our hammocks beneath a dripping sky. The air is warm and the water feels good on my bare skin. I hope it rains all night. I love the rhythm and I love the smell of rain as it washes the air clean.

"I suppose I've had Grandfather and Mother to take care of, then Calev to worry about. I don't know; I just haven't ever given too much thought to girls. Calev torments me about Eliana, but in my mind she's a sister that needs protecting."

"So you don't care for her?"

"Only as a sister."

Jonas grins and puts his smiling face in front of mine. "Good! Then I have a challenge. *I'll* find the right girl for you. *I'll* arrange your marriage." His head goes back and he laughs so loud he competes with the thunder.

Before I can think of my own marriage, I have to attend my mother's wedding to Abner.

Forty-Five

We pass the new ball court on the way back to Elam for my mother's wedding. I stop and stare at the workers. My mind fills with the possibility that I could be the one there, slaving my life away. I recognize some of Calno's ballplayers. The curly-haired captain glances up with sweat dripping down his face; he looks like his own grandfather, he has become so worn and aged.

Father, forgive me. I hate Hem.

I do not want to hate anyone, for the prophet has taught me that when there is love in a heart there is no room for hate. All these months I've been able to study and learn at the feet of Nephi, Lehi, Nephi the Younger, and Timothy. I've been changed and blessed and spared a year of servitude to build a place that looks not impressive, but oppressive. The sight of the massive ball court makes me sad, and I hurry to catch up with the others.

The allotted time has expired for the marriage of my mother to Abner. In the months since I've been gone, Mother has had time to prepare to live as Abner's wife. Now Jonas; some of his cousins; his mother, Devora; and the prophet's wife, Bosma, have come with us to make up Mother's bridal party.

Elam seems somehow smaller. I feel like an outsider returning to stares and few friendly greetings. We wind past Abner's house. It's been enlarged over these months to prepare for his bride—my mother. The thought is strange to me, though Abner greets me with nothing but enthusiasm and kindness.

"It's good to see you, Kiah. You look well."

"I've been spoiled, I'm afraid."

"No," Jonas says, greeting Abner. "Kiah works hard for his keep. Look at his muscles. He has become an expert in every aspect of cement making."

I did not know that Abner's opinion of me mattered to me, but when he stands back and grins, I feel pleased. Is this what it feels like to have a father who is proud of his son?

"I am planning for you both to join me tonight as my groomsmen. Calev will be my best man."

"Calev is here?" I ask. I have not seen Calev since I left him in Lamanite territory. I've heard from the news Mother sends that he has kept busy and stayed well. "I'm anxious to see my brother."

The smile on Abner's face vanishes for only the briefest moment. Something is wrong.

"What is it?" I ask. "Is Calev well?"

"Calev is well enough."

When we leave I lean toward Jonas and whisper, "Abner is not being truthful. He's hiding something." I have not told even Jonas the secret that I carry about my brother. Maybe that's what it is—maybe Calev's relationship with the Lamanite maiden has been made known.

"You worry too much," Jonas tells me. "Abner is just nervous to marry your mother. I know *I* would be nervous if I was the groom. But I'm not the groom, so I'm excited. I've never been in a wedding party before."

"Neither have I."

As groomsmen to Abner, Jonas and I will be part of the torchlight procession that leads from his house to Mother's. She will be made aware that he is coming, but the bride cannot be told the exact time—it builds the excitement. Jonas and I will lead the shout to warn her that Abner is about to arrive.

Mother looks exactly as I left her: thin and worn. But when she sees me she rushes through the narrow gate to greet me. "Kiah, you've grown! Look, you've got the start of a beard."

I frown, feigning annoyance, but really I'm glad people are beginning to look upon me as a man.

The women embrace Mother, and I have to wait for their chatter to die before I have a chance to ask, "Where is Calev? Abner said he is to be the best man at the wedding."

"He is working," she says and her smile fades, almost exactly like Abner's did when Calev was mentioned. "He'll be back."

"Where's Grandfather? I can't wait to see him."

She cocks her head. "Don't you know? He's been gone for a month or more. Nephi and Lehi came through Elam with their band of missionaries, and your grandfather joined them. They've gone to preach to the Lamanites."

I smile at the possibility that Grandfather might meet Miyan and his family.

"Then Grandfather will miss your wedding."

"I had hoped he'd be back by now, but there is no reason for concern; Calev will stand in."

"What is it, Mother? What is it you're not telling me?"

She shakes her head. "Why do you think there is something wrong?"

"I felt it with Abner. I feel it with you."

"It's not for me to tell. Your brother will have to tell you himself."

So people know now that Calev is in love with a Lamanite. Has there been a punishment? I need to show him my support. "Never mind. I'll go find Calev and let him tell me himself."

"No!" She starts to hold me back, but when she sees my determination she steps back.

"No? Why are you acting so strange if nothing is wrong?"

"Please, Kiah. Let this matter be."

The women surround her. They glare at me.

Bosma grips my elbow. "Kiah, you're upsetting your mother."

"I'm sorry, Mother. Forgive me."

"Oh, son, there is nothing to forgive."

Bosma shakes her head at me and leads my mother under the low archway into our home—*her* home. I feel out of place.

Devora's tone is firm and low. "If your mother says nothing is wrong, let it be. This is her wedding day. Don't let your anxiety upset her."

"I'm sorry," I apologize again.

"You two go fetch the nectar from the marketplace. It's all that we are lacking now for the feast."

Jonas takes long strides ahead of me, the way he always does. We go past Abner's shop, but it is closed for the wedding and there is no sign of Calev. By the time we reach the marketplace I have convinced myself that my family is hiding a secret for my own protection. But what could Calev's affairs of the heart have to do with me?

The marketplace surprises me. In a time of peace it should be thriving, but it's smaller and has fewer vendors. Immediately I blame Hem. I watch a woman selling peppers to another woman. The way she measures is the standard way with the cups and the balance, but she seems nervous.

The sale is made, and the vendor keeps looking back. That's when I see him. Hem is standing back, watching from a distance, his arms folded over a swollen belly. I look to see if Eliana is near him, but I see no sign of her.

"That's Hem," I tell Jonas, pointing with my chin.

We both watch as he steps up to the vendor. His hand goes out; her hand trembles as she reaches into her pocket to produce something she places in his. He looks at the offering. Frowns. She reaches back into her pocket and keeps adding to Hem's outstretched palm until he is satisfied.

"He's taking her profit," Jonas whispers.

"He's the devil he's always been."

I step toward Hem and make my presence known. He does not recognize me at first, but when he does he looks smug and moves to greet me as though we are friends.

I am not his friend. I will never be his friend.

"Kiah, you have grown. You are now a man."

And you are still a robber.

"Look at your beard, Kiah. And your strength. I don't suppose you've been playing any more trickball." He laughs.

Jonas stands beside me, as peaceful as I am irritated.

"Have you heard the good news?"

"What good news, Hem?"

"That you are I are going to be family."

I frown. What is he talking about? My mother's marriage to Abner will in no way join our family to Hem's.

Hem laughs and his whole belly shakes. The left side of his face looks like rubber.

"We are never going to be family," I say, turning away.

"We will be," he calls after me, "now that my Eliana is betrothed to your brother."

Forty-Six

I don't see Calev until we are gathered outside Abner's courtyard to join him as his groomsmen. I feel anything but joyous. I feel angry, betrayed. Mostly confused.

Calev greets me and says quietly, "Have you heard?"

It takes every bit of restraint I have to keep my hands from choking my brother. I know it's wrong, but I whisper back, "What happened to your Lamanite maiden?"

The color drains from Calev's cheeks. He grabs my elbow and jerks me away from Abner, Jonas, and the groom's party. "What are you talking about?"

"I know about the Lamanite girl, the beautiful one with hair that falls clear down her back. The one by the waterfall who rushed into your arms."

Calev scowls. "You spied on us?"

"Only to that point. All these months, I've kept your secret. And what have you done?"

Calev's face is a picture of confusion.

"What have I done? Nothing wrong."

"You deceived everyone, Calev, with your Lamanite maiden."

"She's dead."

I am not sure I heard him right—but the pained look on his face, bitter and empty, tells me I did.

"She was killed when her father discovered her feelings for me."

"How?"

"He ran a lance through her heart. She died because of me."

"I'm sorry."

"Don't feel pity for me, brother. Only you know my secret."

"But—"

"Be happy for me, Kiah. I'm about to marry Hem's daughter."

My fingers go to my temples and I press hard.

"Listen, Kiah, you told me that you have no feelings for Eliana. You told me that, Kiah!"

"And it's the truth. But you don't *love* her. Why would you agree to marry her?"

Calev shrugs and steps away from me.

Abner, like the others gathered, is oblivious to the tension between me and Calev. Even Jonas seems nothing but festive. They are happy and ready to celebrate.

Abner and Calev talk and laugh. Twice, Abner asks me if I am all right; I snap at him, assuring him I am fine. We have to wait until Abner deems the time is right to send out the shout. Waiting is awkward and horrific.

Calev will not just be Eliana's husband he will be Hem's son-in-law.

The worst kind of fear grips me. What has Hem offered Calev? What kind of pact have the two of them made?

It's dark, and Calev thrusts a torch into my hands. "Time to go to the bridal chamber."

He means our childhood home, a place now so foreign to me.

The shout goes up, and we move in one body to join what seems like the entire village. Of course Hem is here with his wife, Sherrizah. Eliana is not here, at least not that I can see. Now that she and Calev are betrothed, they are enduring their period of separation—the same span that is about to end for Mother and Abner.

I don't know what I would do or say if Eliana appeared. Should I be happy for her, knowing that she is about to enter a life of unhappiness? But is that fair? I am no seer. I cannot pretend to predict the future.

Mother's face is veiled as she and Abner greet each other. I can't read her emotion, but I can see the joy on Abner's face, and it eases my own anxiety. At least this is a union that will give Mother the love and security she has lacked for so long.

Jonas is with his mother and grandmother, seeing to their needs. I'm glad he does not see how my jaw clenches, how I turn my face away from those who would be friendly because I cannot pretend I am jovial.

Once Abner and Mother enter the bridal chamber, the rest of us wait outside. It's the longest wait of my life, seeing Hem and Calev talk and laugh like they are in on a secret that no one else knows.

Raz welcomes me like a long lost son. He wants to know all about my learning, but I'm in no mood to talk; he goes back to his wife and children, all of them as happy and as close as ever. I watch, feeling an unexpected resentment toward them for being so joyous.

Merari invites Jonas and me to join him on a hunt in the highlands. He proudly shows me a new necklace he wears made from the teeth and claws of a mountain *chakmool.* "She was not a large beast," he boasts, "small, in fact, but she was old—you can tell from the length of her teeth—and so smart she led me up, up into the highlands. Kiah, there's a small narrow of obsidian that you will have to see to believe."

She was my *cat,* I want to scream. *My chakmool!* "What has become of the obsidian?"

"Now that all of Elam knows about it, it won't last. Already the village men have made a trail to it, packing it out in loads. It's dangerous work," he says, lowering his voice. "There are caves up there infested with Gadianton's band."

My head jerks up. "There are robbers living up there now?"

"Well, yes. The robbers are back in force. I thought you would hear the news in Zarahemla."

Jonas steps forward, friendly with everyone. "Kiah has little time for anything but school."

"Your grandfather has much to say about your progress."

"I was hoping Grandfather would be here," I say, unable to keep the emotion from my tone. "I am ready to receive the priesthood, and I was planning on him conferring it to me."

Merari rests one hand on my shoulder. "There are still seven days. If he hasn't returned by then I'll be happy to do the honors. I've always thought of you as a son."

I smile. I thank him. I go through the necessary motions, but I feel nothing except a sadness that is tied to me as sure as my shadow.

I try not to think about Abner and Mother.

I try not to think about Eliana and Calev.

I try not to think at all. I wander off into the shadows—alone.

I'm sitting on the ground with my head buried in my hands when Abner emerges to make the announcement that his marriage has been consummated.

The crowd shouts its approval.

Mother's bridal party hurries in to attend to her while Abner is greeted by Calev, Jonas, and the other groomsmen.

The festivities begin in earnest.

I think I will go crazy. All of them seem happy. They eat. They pray. They dance and sing. Men joke with Calev about his own upcoming wedding, and I learn that Hem has given them some property on which Calev is constructing a new home.

On the second day Calev approaches me. "I'm going hunting with Merari's party. Come join us, Kiah. Bring Jonas."

"How could you?" I ask.

"How could I hunt? It's my favorite thing to do, brother. And these people will need more meat soon."

"Not hunt! How could you agree to marry Eliana when your heart does not belong to her?"

He laughs, and it's Hem's laugh I hear come out of his mouth.

"Calev, why Eliana?"

"So you are still holding feelings for my future wife?"

"Not those kinds of feelings. But someone should protect her. Her father treats her like a slave, and you—"

"I what? The girl has pursued me ever since I returned from battle."

It's true; she has. "Then you love Eliana?"

"No eye would miss the fact that she is beautiful."

"You once called her plain."

"I once said a great many things I now regret."

"So you *do* love her?"

His shoulders rise and fall. "Hem has agreed to make me a wealthy man. I will be the son he never had and will take over for him one day."

"Take over *what*?"

"The marketplace, Kiah. What were you thinking?"

"You know what I'm thinking, brother."

"Go back to Zarahemla, Kiah. You've outgrown our small village."

Uriel and a group of men walk past us. When Uriel sees me he greets me with fondness but says nothing to Calev. The moment is awkward; when Uriel embraces me he asks, "Are you still a believer?"

"A believer in the Messiah? More than ever."

"Then fight with me, Kiah. Stay in Elam and prepare for the battle that will surely come."

Calev laughs, and we all turn to look at him. "Uriel, you're a smart man—smart enough to know when you are on the losing side."

"I am on God's side," Uriel says.

Calev does not wither, but stands tall. "We shall see who God favors."

Uriel steps toward my brother, lowering his head like a bull. "God favors those who believe in His Son, the Messiah, and the power of His Atonement. You've fought with me in battle, Calev. You know this for a fact."

"I know that God favors the soldiers who are fed well and whose weapons are strongest."

Forty-Seven

On the fourth day Merari, Calev, Jonas, and I return from a large hunting expedition with meat enough to provide for the final days of the wedding celebration.

"Try to be happy," Jonas tells me. "I've never seen you this miserable."

"How else can I feel?"

"I'm sorry that your brother has lost his faith."

"I'm sorry too. I'm sorry for so many things."

I'm sorry that I am now an outsider, even in my own small family. I'm sorry that I am a complete outsider in Elam, a place where I never really fit in. I'm sorry that the hills I wandered as a boy are now thick with greedy men, hungry for the obsidian I foolishly thought of as my own. It isn't that far away from Elam, and it's a miracle it wasn't discovered before now. Maybe God kept it hidden for a reason.

It doesn't take a brilliant mind to understand that Elam has been overtaken by Hem and his hunger for power. The people do nothing to stop him—and as long as they elect evil to rule them, no one can help.

"They are returned!" someone cries.

"Who?"

"Your grandfather with the prophet and his brother! The missionaries are returned!"

I have never seen Grandfather so happy. His smile radiates joy and success.

"Tell me about Miyan," I say.

He tells me how Miyan was in the cornfield when they found him. How he clasped his hands over his heart and fell to his knees when he saw them.

"Has he remained faithful to his covenants?"

"He has. And now the prophet has established a church there, teaching members true doctrine so they cannot distort or dilute it."

"I knew Miyan would remain faithful."

Grandfather grins. "Now that he has been ordained to the priesthood I expect he'll be a prophet among his own people. He has great love for you, son. You taught him of the Messiah."

"Now I know more—but then, I had little to offer him."

"What you offered was sufficient. A man can only give what he has to give, and Miyan and his family still talk about the spirit they felt when you bore testimony of how the Messiah's power raised you up out of that vipers' pit."

"I'm grateful."

Grandfather and the others tell a wonderful story of how Miyan brought forty-seven more people into the waters of baptism.

"And because we were able to ordain him," Grandfather says, "he was able to baptize those he brought."

"I wish I could have been there."

"There's a time and a place for all things. Order is God's way, son. Now is the time for you to receive your education. I hear you have learned well."

"I've learned much."

The mood is festive, and I don't wish to dampen it. I eat and drink and smile. Nephi draws a crowd, for he is esteemed by many as the land's chief prophet, but there are those who stand back and whisper their harsh judgments. It's obvious to me that Elam is just as divided as it was during those horrendous days we played trickball.

Grandfather and Calev walk side by side. Is Grandfather so blinded by love for Calev that he cannot see what has become of my brother?

"Come, walk with us, Kiah. It is good for me to have you both together."

Calev smiles at me. His expression is neither kind nor unkind. At least I am glad he has emerged from his dark days of depression.

Grandfather drapes an arm over Calev's shoulder. "Hem tells me that you are already overseeing the marketplace. Is this true?"

"Hem is occupied with the construction of the new ball court. He trusts me to oversee the marketplace while he's away."

Grandfather stops. He looks back at me, then at Calev. "Can Hem be trusted? He proved himself vicious when he oversaw the trickball game."

"Hem is a complicated man."

"I will not speak evil of your future father-in-law, but I *will* warn you to be wary, son."

Grandfather does not look at me when he mentions Hem. He doesn't need to. He knows how I feel about Hem.

Grandfather listens as Calev talks about the marketplace and his grand plans to make it thrive again.

"Measure and weigh accurately, son, and you'll earn the trust of the people. When you have that, you will become a leader far superior to any leader Elam has known."

We turn the corner back to the wedding festival and find Hem talking with Buki, the high priest. They greet Grandfather with due respect. Hem sees me and makes certain he greets Calev with the affection a father would show a son. I watch Grandfather's eyes. He looks at Hem with suspicion, but not submission—not the way everyone else in Elam seems to look upon Hem.

While they eat and talk of the new ball court and the changes in the marketplace, the prophet Nephi breaks away from the throng of needy believers and approaches me. He puts a gentle hand on my shoulder. "Kiah, what's troubling you?"

How can I tell him? Can he see through the mask that Hem wears? Of course he can.

"Hem is an evil man," I say. "He's convinced everyone again and again that he isn't, but I know that he is."

"What makes you think that?"

"You know what I witnessed years ago. You know what Hem did when he oversaw the trickball game. Why don't you stop him? Why don't you call down the powers of heaven to stop him? I know you can."

"You have great faith, son."

"My faith does no good. Hem is more powerful and popular than ever. The robbers are back in the hills. War is surely coming." My face is hot and my voice is shaking; Nephi is as calm as ever.

"Sadly, the rumors of war are true. We passed through a Lamanite village that had been attacked. People were murdered, their children kidnapped."

"Why don't you stop them? Why doesn't God stop them?"

"Our hands are God's hands . . . He uses us to accomplish His purposes. And He has commanded us to hunt the robbers and extinguish them. I'm afraid our Lamanite brothers are doing a better job than we are."

"Deceit is their greatest weapon. The robbers mingle among us as innocents. They conspire in a murderous brotherhood. Hem is one of their leaders, yet he is revered as a brilliant man of enterprise and power. You could strike him with palsy again. You could—"

"I can only do what God wills, Kiah. Hem was brought before the judgment seat years ago. He was found innocent against your accusations."

"But what I said is true. All this time he taunts me, knowing my accusations are true." I pull out my blade and show it to him. "This was Hem's blade. I found it with a cache of goods the robbers left behind at their den. Do you believe me?"

"I believe you."

His words comfort me; they give me strength.

"Does Hem know that you have this blade?" the prophet asks.

"He knows. He told me that if I present it as evidence against him he'll claim that I stole it, that *I* am the robber. His word carries more authority than mine ever will."

Nephi's face changes; he takes a deep breath and looks deep into my eyes. "I promise you, Kiah, one day you will realize the true authority you wield. You have chosen to obey God's laws. You have chosen to make the most of your life. You are a man of truth; you cannot yet see your worth, but one day you will. The warrior in you will rise, and when it does you will see what I see."

Nephi wipes a single drop of sweat that beads and drips from the tip of his nose. "God's eyes see the truth. There is no thought we can think, no deed we can do without God knowing. Do you understand the foundation of the great plan that our Father in Heaven set before us?"

"I understand parts of it—but no, I do not understand it all."

"Its foundation is freedom. It allows us to choose. I choose to follow the path of the believer. You also choose that path. Hem walks a different direction, but he is free to do so."

"But . . . "

Grandfather comes up behind me and wraps his arms around me in one of his crushing hugs. "I hear from Jonas that we have cause to celebrate more than just your mother's marriage to Abner. I hear that you are qualified to be ordained to the priesthood."

"I am ready," I say, smiling at the prophet.

That night, around a blaze, people gather to hear Nephi preach, but he tells the crowd that his words are specially directed at me. He teaches of the priesthood, how it is a power more forceful than any weapon ever forged. It is the very authority to act in God's name, to do what He would do if He were me. Nephi warns me not to abuse the power, ever—for if I do, he says, looking at Hem, God's wrath will surely fall upon my head.

Grandfather then bears testimony of the holy priesthood, how it is the power by which God operates. He tells of healing the sick, of restoring the fallen, of blessing and baptizing and performing ordinances by the power of the priesthood.

Then in a circle that includes the prophet, Lehi, Jonas, Merari, Raz, and Abner, Grandfather lays his hands on my head and ordains me to the priesthood of God.

Calev misses the ordination; he's gone with his future father-in-law to check on the new ball court.

That night I seek out a place by myself. I kneel and pour out my heart's fears and gratitude to God. I'm on my knees when I hear screams that break though the darkness. They are the screams of a woman. More screams. And more.

It's a moonless night, and I rush down the trail, tripping over rocks and stumps and getting caught in vines. I'm on the path behind Elam when I encounter village guards. They tell me our village has been attacked by Gadianton's band. They've slain at least one man—beaten him with his own club and left him to die in front of his wife and children.

I run as fast as I can down the trail toward my old home. I have to be certain that Mother is all right. And Grandfather! Where is he? In my blind panic I bump into someone else running in the opposite direction.

"Kiah! Kiah, is that you?"

A woman is holding a small torch. In the light of the flame I know her.

"Eliana!"

She falls into my arms sobbing. "It's the robbers—they've taken Tamar!"

Forty-Eight

I go as far as the site of the new ball court. That is where I say my good-byes to the prophet and his band . . . to Jonas.

"Are you certain you don't want to return to Zarahemla with us? It will be safer there."

"Thank you for making me welcome, but I must stay in Elam. I've promised Uriel that I will join his band to hunt the robbers."

"The season of peace is over," Nephi says, his voice heavy with sorrow. "Even I did not know it would end so soon. Kiah, this is the time for the warrior in you to come forth. If we do not hunt and kill the robbers, they will hunt and kill us."

"I understand."

Lehi embraces me like I was his child. "You will make a fine warrior, Kiah. Always fight for the army led by our Lord and Savior, our Messiah. A time of great division is before us. You have chosen wisely, Kiah. God will bless and protect you."

"Hurry," I tell Jonas. "It's not safe for you along this road."

"I'll miss you."

"God protect us all," Nephi says, but not in the confident voice of a prophet. His voice is the hopeful but nervous voice of a grandfather.

My own grandfather is back in Elam in the synagogue. He's meeting with the priests to determine how to protect our village from further attacks. Mothers are hiding their children; fathers are assembling their weapons. Fear twists every face. Fear stinks like dead water. It is in the air as sure as morning mist.

I'm confused: Hem seems genuinely distraught. Could it be that he really *did* leave the band and that the band took Tamar out of retaliation for his disloyalty? Calev, on the other hand, shocks us all when he makes his position absolutely clear one morning out by our home courtyard. He refuses to join Uriel in fighting the robbers.

I have never seen Grandfather so stunned or livid as when Calev makes his announcement. "The Nephites deserve whatever fate befalls them. Nephites are self-righteous hypocrites."

"You will not fight with us?" Grandfather asks, a vein in his forehead bulging, blue and swollen. "You once fought these devils. You, Calev, are my grandson. There is no way you can be one of Gadianton's."

"I'm not a robber," Calev says, "but I understand why they attack, and I'm done fighting for this people."

I fear Grandfather's vein will burst.

"If you are not for us, Calev, then you are against us. Do you understand that you are dissenting from God's chosen path?"

"I understand that I'm dissenting from traditions that bind like cords. I understand that I'm dissenting from teachings that no longer apply. I understand that I am dissenting from error."

Grandfather's eyes are hard and cold. "Calev, I once gave you a sword that is very precious to me. I want you to return it to me now."

Calev turns on his heels and heads into the house, where I know a treasure box is buried. As disgusted as I am with Calev's decision, it's no reason to separate our family—yet that is exactly what is happening.

"Grandfather, please; you love Calev. He needs your love even when he is wrong. Please don't let this tear our family apart."

Grandfather shakes. He looks past me like he can no longer see clearly.

Mother's sobs can be heard from inside the house, and I wonder what she is saying to Calev. I also wonder the real reason Calev is dissenting. Like Hem, it seems there is no way to retrieve the truth from my brother.

Grandfather accepts the sword with trembling hands. "This sword was a gift to me from the prophet Helaman. I was only a boy, younger than Kiah, when it was placed in my hands. I passed it on to you, Calev, believing you would use it to defend the cause of freedom."

"I did use it, Grandfather. I have the scars of battle to prove my valor."

"I'm not questioning your valor, son. I'm questioning your loyalty to your God, your people, and your own family. Where does your heart lie?"

Calev opens his mouth but does not speak. When he turns his back on Grandfather and storms away, he does not look back.

Forty-Nine

Uriel's band is small, but strong. I feel honored to be included.

He says to me, "You wanted a chance to be a warrior. Now you have no other choice."

Abner volunteers to go with us, but because he is a new groom and because he is needed to oversee the sudden rise in weaponry, it is determined he should stay behind. I feel relieved because he will be able to watch over Mother and Grandfather, both of whom are distraught by Calev's rebellion and disappearance. We have not seen him in days. I question if we will ever see him again.

Hem and Sherrizah have gone into seclusion, mourning the kidnapping of their youngest daughter. Oshra tells me that Eliana is despondent, refusing to eat or drink.

"Your brother abandoned her just like your father abandoned your mother."

"You do not know that Calev abandoned Eliana. For all we know Calev has gone into the hills to rescue Tamar."

"If you believe that, then you are the fool everyone always thought you to be." She laughs at me the way Gomer used to laugh at me when I made a mistake in synagogue school.

I have no energy to argue with the village gossip. For all I know, Oshra might be right in her judgment about my brother.

Uriel does not treat me like I'm a fool; he listens to me, values my advice, and asks me to guide a hand of ten men into the high hills to the spot where I first saw Hem and his robbers. In his presence I feel confident like I do in the presence of Grandfather or the prophet.

Along the way we see several camps where the robbers have made no effort to conceal their presence. They burn the trees, carve the land, and leave filth and destruction behind. I cannot bring myself to think of the torture that Tamar might be suffering at their hands. A prayer for her never leaves my heart. I pray for strength and courage and wisdom to fight a good fight.

The opportunity comes the third night when we are ambushed. Our camp lookout is stabbed in the heart and our sleeping soldiers attacked. It seems more like a nightmare than reality as I raise my arms to beat back the blow of an assailant I cannot see for the cloak of darkness. He hits me once, knocks me to the ground, but I'm up and grab his feet and pull him down next to me. My blade sinks into his leg and he cries out, cursing me. I feel a sharp pain in my back where he gouges me with a rock. We fight like that for a long time, wrestling in the dark, over the uneven ground.

I feel the damp of his blood. I smell his blood. I want to vomit. All my life I've imagined myself fighting against a real enemy. This feels nothing like I imagined.

In the end, my assailant breaks free of my grip and breaks through a tangle of vines. I hear him scream. He's still screaming when I hear a terrible thud.

He's fallen over a precipice and landed on the jagged rock below.

When morning comes we make a body count. We lost one—our young lookout guard, Daniel. I'm especially sad because he is one of Raz's sons. Including the robber who fell to his death, the enemy band lost four. Uriel's orders insisted that we retrieve the bodies and bury them—not out of respect for their lives, but out of respect for the Creator of Life.

There is no attack the next night nor the next. Uriel meets up with us on the fourth day. I am ashamed to tell him that in spite of my best efforts, we lost Daniel. He does not reprimand me but informs me that he lost two of his men the night before in a surprise attack.

When we make it to the den where I first spotted Hem, we find the whole area dug up, like someone has been harrowing for treasure. I have not checked on my own little cache in so long. The few pieces of treasure that once seemed so important to me don't seem important at all anymore.

I ask Uriel about Hem. Does he think Elam's most powerful merchant is also a robber?

"He's an ill-willed, greedy man, but I have no proof that he is one of Gadianton's own. What about your brother—do you think Calev is leading a band of robbers?"

"Calev? No."

"Neither do I. I think he is confused, but I do not believe his heart has turned."

After so many nights hunting, fighting, and barely sleeping or eating, Uriel tells me that we are dividing. "You stay in the mountains, and I'll search the lowland wilderness."

I feel grateful for his trust in my leadership.

"I'll pass through Elam and send reinforcements if I can rouse them," he tells me, giving me a look of assurance.

My band is seventeen men total. Some of them are trickballers I played with during those horrible three days against Calno. Some of the men I lead are married and already have children. Some are as old as Merari. They do not treat me like a young, inexperienced commander, though that is exactly what I am.

Every commander is different, and I choose to lead my men in prayer. It is obvious to me then that even my own army is divided, the believers from the unbelievers. It is against our government's laws to force any man to believe, so I respect those who do not join us in prayer, but I also feel we are weakened by every man who relies on his own strength instead of on the arm of the Almighty.

That night we go up against a band three times our size. I lose another man to arrows and suffer a gash in my side. It seems no one comes away unscathed. Aaron, a flat-nosed man who is old enough to be my father, has studied healing with Pazel; he makes a poultice from the tender leaves of the red flowering plant that is so abundant in the high hills. The poultice stings when applied, but it draws out infection. Aaron then drowns our wounds in aloe paste and wraps them with strips of banana leaves.

I'm grateful no man suffered broken bones. One of the robbers left for dead gains consciousness. His leg is broken, and he refuses to allow Aaron to administer healing to his bleeding head.

I warn the man that he has two choices. He can hear the message of God's word and vow to accept it—meaning he promises he will cause no further harm to us and, in fact, will aid us in the hunt of his own band—or he must die.

The man chooses death over betrayal. That is when I realize our enemies are strong in ways I did not anticipate.

My men are valiant but not used to war. We tire easily, but we learn quickly. We make night camps up against a rise so only one side is vulnerable to attack. We build our fires high and keep them burning bright throughout the night. We sleep on our weapons and remind ourselves that our cause is the cause that Captain Moroni fought for: our wives, our children, our freedom, and our faith.

I don't neglect prayer. I don't allow evil forebodings. I tell my men, "As sure as I know God lives, I know He will deliver us. The robbers will be defeated."

But we are the ones defeated. After many successful battles, even after we become more cautious than ever, we are ambushed in broad daylight. I lose two more men—one to a stab in the throat and one to a rock slide set off by a band of robbers hiding above us.

It's the hardest decision I've ever made, but I know we've got to retreat. So, with our heads hanging down and our hands wounded and bloody, we take the downward trail back toward Elam.

Fifty

"My father is a liar."

I stare at Eliana, who is standing in front of me at the sparkling spring where we used to meet so long ago. We are both different people now.

"You asked to meet me so you could tell me something I already know?"

Eliana has shriveled to a skeleton. Her eyes are red and swollen. Her chin quivers as she tells me, "Father pretends he is still weak from the palsy, but he is stronger than he lets on. He wants people to think that he struggles with his arm, that he can't stand on his leg for more than a few moments—but he can. He can talk, too, plain as anyone. You've heard him."

"Why would he lie about being whole and healthy?"

"I don't know. But I know he's a liar."

"Those are harsh words for a daughter who is so devoted."

"Kiah, I was angry with you for what happened. The accusations you made against Father so long ago—I didn't believe them. I believe them now."

"I don't blame you for your devotion to your own father."

"But you *do* blame me for my feelings toward your brother."

"My brother abandoned you. What feelings for him can you possibly have other than hatred?"

She looks down at the dust on her sandals and chooses to ignore me. "I *was* completely devoted to my father. I believed my father with all my heart. I know now that he lies."

"What do you expect me to do?"

"Please. Is there any word about Tamar?" Her voice catches, and she chokes on her pain. "I think my father knows more about her kidnapping than he is willing to admit."

"Why are you telling *me* this? You should be telling Calev—but he's gone."

"I've always loved your brother. I don't believe he has abandoned me. I believe he is searching for Tamar. I believe he'll be back."

The thought crosses my mind that she might be right. Calev left in anger. In spite of his turning away from all of us, I hope my brother is safe. "What does your father say about Calev?"

"He says he is disappointed and disgusted. He also says that Calev has joined with the dissidents, not the robbers."

"Is there a difference?"

"Father says there is."

"And you have had no contact with Calev since he and Grandfather argued?"

"I vow to you, Kiah, I have not spoken a word to your brother since we were betrothed. You were away studying in Zarahemla. No one was more surprised than I when Father told me that Calev had asked for my hand in marriage."

"All that is irrelevant, Eliana. I don't understand why you are asking me for help. Hem should be out searching for Tamar, not building a monstrosity of a ball court or cheating people in Elam's marketplace."

"I'm asking you because I don't know who else to turn to. You care about me like a sister; I know that. I've always felt it. And you know my father. Why would he make such a showing of how Tamar's kidnapping has diminished his health when it hasn't?"

"Your father is a master of deceit."

"I know. But why?"

"I don't know. I've been off fighting. My army has suffered greatly because of the robbers, and I believe your father to be a leader among them."

She cries. "You may be right."

It's impossible for me to explain how the hills are infiltrated with evil men lying in wait to rob and murder. They are like flies during the rainy season—crawling everywhere, touching everything. I shake my head. "I'm sorry. I saw no sign of Tamar while I was with my army."

"Do you think my sister is still alive?" Her sob stabs at my heart as sure as a blade. "Her disappearance has broken my heart. It has nearly killed my mother."

These past months I've seen how these evil men take the virtue of an innocent young girl as a prize to be bragged about. I try to keep my face from giving away my thoughts, my fears, but Eliana reads me and breaks into a lament so sharp it stops her breath.

There is nothing I can do to console her. So I stand there, helpless, and wait until she wipes her face with her hands and looks at me through fire-red eyes.

"I do not believe, Kiah."

"Believe in your father? In my brother? In me?"

"I do not believe in the Messiah—in His power, in His mercy. He is an invisible god who allows innocent children to suffer while He does nothing to save them!" She looks at me with so much pain I reach out to break a law that could get us both stoned. I take Eliana in my arms and hold her so tight I feel her breath warm on my shoulder and feel her heart flutter against my own pounding chest.

Fifty-One

Uriel is a man who has aged years in a matter of months.

"I'm captain of a losing army," he says, reporting that all Nephite armies, from the city of Judea to the land of Manti, are being defeated by Gadianton's bands.

"*We* fight as separate armies, often warring among ourselves. *They* fight as one evil infestation, bound by their secret combinations, with spies and robbers in the highest stations in the land."

"It's what I've been saying about Hem this entire time."

Uriel whirls on me. "Hem! Hem is nobody. Nothing. We are not fighting a man or even an army, Kiah. We are battling evil."

When he calms I ask him, "Is there any way we could locate a kidnapped girl?"

"Hem's daughter?"

"Yes. Her sister asked me—"

"Spare me the details. Children and women are kidnapped every day. If the girl is not dead by now, she has become one of them."

"One of them?"

"You remember the story of the wicked priests of King Noah. The kidnapped Lamanite maids eventually bonded with their kidnappers and wanted to remain their wives."

"I know the story," I say, finding it impossible to imagine Tamar—the shy girl who loves to laugh and dance—as the wife of a robber. "What of my brother?"

Uriel sighs. "Kiah, I know that Calev said he is not a robber, but I believe that is a lie. What is a dissenter if not an enemy to God's own?"

• • •

The war I always wanted rages on. Villages all throughout the land of Zarahemla are burned. Women are raped. Children are kidnapped. Men are murdered. I become commander of a band first of fifty men, then one hundred; now one hundred and fifty men fall under my charge because Uriel was caught in an attack that left an arrow in his back.

The hills of my childhood are ravaged. The trees are cut, the birds hunted mercilessly, the game gone. I ask permission to take my men higher into the mountains where I feel certain we can find food and refuge. We will also find the homeland of the robbers.

"I will not allow it," Uriel says from his cot. "It is foolish for us to venture there. We must fortify our strongholds in our villages and cities."

I don't agree, but I obey.

"Kiah, if Calev *does* lead a band of robbers, that band will be deadly. I know how your brother fights. He battles with his mind before he ever lifts a weapon. It would be good for you to imagine the battle beforehand also."

"You are more certain than ever that Calev is a robber."

"I am. I've received reports that Calev's rank is not low."

Uriel coughs until his nose starts to bleed, a symptom from the poison-tipped arrow shot into his back. For all I know Calev may have been the one who pierced his own captain.

Mother and Grandfather carry heavy hearts. We have all been betrayed by Calev. This should be a time for Mother and Abner to celebrate, but since their marriage festivities were cut short, they appear to be mourning more than celebrating.

I go to battle. We fight. We win. We lose. My command joins forces with other commands. I make friends with the bravest men I can imagine, only to see their lives cut short by an attack from robbers who prowl like beasts, hunting in the dark, sparing not even the babes in mothers' arms.

Uriel recovers and takes command of thousands who camp in the valley of Alma; my band joins others to camp and train in the valley of Sam, where Hem's ball court is under construction. Every day we receive word by runners of which places have come under attack and which armies have fallen. Fear grows as fast as vines during the rainy season. It rustles like the tall snake grass in the lowlands. There is no getting away from fear—not of *if*, but *when* the robbers will attack next.

The protection of Elam and her surrounding villages is my responsibility. I assign armies and trek from place to place, securing broken gates and crumbled walls. Those can be rebuilt, but what of the broken lives and crumbled testimonies?

People beg me, "When is the Messiah coming? When He comes we will be safe again, won't we? The Messiah will protect us. Please, when will He come?"

Grandfather says the time is soon, but he has been saying that since I was a child at his knee.

I am grateful to Abner, whose high wall and weaponry provide safety for Mother and Grandfather. It's curious to me that Elam has been attacked but both Abner's home and my childhood home have been left unharmed. Is Calev behind such decisions? Months drag on and we do not hear from him. Mother fears he is dead. Grandfather fears he has suffered something worse than a slit throat or an arrow through the heart.

I wish Calev were here to defend himself, but he is not.

Hem is.

Hem remains in Elam, pretending to be stricken again with palsy and pretending to be outraged and heartbroken that his young daughter is in the filthy hands of the robbers. He publicly denounces the betrothal of Eliana to Calev, calling my brother a traitor.

He is very convincing—bullying his way at the marketplace, in the ball court, with the judges, and even with Grandfather's loyal priests.

Perhaps Hem's most dramatic and convincing performance comes when the marketplace is attacked by a band of men who rampage through with spears and horror. They know right when to strike and where to strike and how to steal the gold from the market treasury.

At the moment of the attack, Hem is sitting high on his overseer pedestal, a platform smaller but similar to the one he had built at Elam's ball court. He cries and makes a show of trying to get down the steps in time to help the terrified, brutalized merchants. Gomer tries to steady Hem, and Hem's arm comes back and swipes Gomer in the face, knocking him off balance. The frail man trips and tumbles downward, landing at the bottom in a spreading pool of blood.

My mother is the first person to console Oshra. She sits with Oshra and cries. She cooks for the village gossip and even washes the woman's clothes.

I argue before the judges that there is proof enough that Hem was in on the raid: The robbers had to have inside information on how to carry out such an attack. *Only* Hem could have provided such information.

Marpe, the chief judge, decrees there is not sufficient evidence to prove anything. Once again, my word means nothing. But I am not the same confused boy who first brought accusations against Hem. I'm a man—a warrior who has seen the destruction of Hem's robbers. I will not give up until everyone knows the truth about Hem.

One night while I am on duty in Elam I lay a trap. I station myself high on Hem's own marketplace pedestal. I lay flat beneath the glow of a white moon and I wait. There are supposed to be civil guards stationed at each gate, but after a while they slouch in slumber.

A band of thieves sneaks into the market and steals corn from the storage area. I know some of them—gaunt sons of Raz—and I make no move to punish them. If they are stealing food then Raz's family must be hungry. Surely, we can spare a vessel of corn, for they spared a brother in Daniel.

A troupe of *chuwen* swing over the wall and carry away peels from old fruit. A few birds peck at the dirt. I'm almost asleep when I hear the sound of voices. I have to squint, for the people do not enter within the walls of the marketplace, but stay just outside the gate. A cloud blots out the moon, and it's impossible to identify them.

One of the guards wakes and signals the other. They both stand and move toward the pack, but they move with ease and familiarity, almost like they were expecting intruders.

Voices rise, and I'm certain I recognize Hem's deep tone.

Then the cloud slips away and the moonlight bears down and I have a clear vision of Hem, his wife, and Eliana. The three of them are talking with the guards. I cannot tell what they are saying, but I see Hem's hands rise and jerk and I can tell that he is agitated.

I'm looking at Eliana when out of the shadows an unmistakable figure appears. My brother has returned without honor. He and Eliana embrace while her parents and the guards look on.

Fifty-Two

Truth is at war.

I watch as Hem and Sherrizah bid good-bye to their daughter. My eyes blink as I watch Eliana take hold of Calev's arm and as they walk together through the back gate. I wait, partly shocked and partly curious.

I lay still as I watch a fraud put into place.

"Help!" Hem cries after he is sure Calev and Eliana are gone. "Help!" His arms go up. His wife wails. The guards make no rush to bring burning torches.

"Our only remaining daughter has been kidnapped. Help us!"

The parents pretend to be distraught. They fabricate a story of how Hem came to the marketplace to check on the well-being of the guards, how his wife woke up to check on him, how when they returned to their home their daughter had been kidnapped. They show the officials how their house is disheveled, sure proof that Eliana struggled to fight her captors.

Sherrizah pretends to faint.

Hem pretends to be the victim. He does it convincingly.

I do not go in search of my brother and Eliana. Calev had his escape well planned, and I know it would be impossible to find him. Instead, I stand before the court to testify that Hem is a liar. The judges all shake their heads in disbelief at my account.

"How do you know that Eliana went willingly?" Marpe asks.

"Hem embraced Calev. They talked and laughed and even exchanged goods."

"What goods?"

"I could not see. Probably money."

"Probably? Goods you could not see? What *did* you see clearly?"

"I saw Eliana rush into the open arms of my brother."

"You speak the words of a jealous man, Kiah—one who lost his girl to his own brother."

The two night guards are brought before the court and testify that they saw nothing, heard nothing—and certainly never met with Hem or my brother.

Hem is not even brought before the judges, for he appears too weak and distraught to defend himself. His grieving wife is on her deathbed, suffering a broken heart.

In front of Grandfather, Abner, Mother, and Uriel, Marpe reprimands me for harassing Hem, a sorrowing father who has lost *both* of his daughters to kidnappers. "Since you were a boy you have held a grudge against Hem. Let it go, Kiah. If you ever bear false witness before this court again, *you* will be the one punished. Do you understand?"

What I understand is that Marpe could be among those who have taken a secret vow to uphold his brothers in crime. What I understand is that Marpe is right—it is time for me to move on.

I am dismissed.

Uriel believes me.

Grandfather believes me and seems more relieved to learn that Calev is alive than that Hem is a fraud.

Mother asks, "How did Calev look? Was he well? Happy? Wounded in any way?"

I beg Abner and Mother to bring Grandfather and return to Zarahemla with me.

"I cannot leave our home and my business," Abner says. "Not now. Beyond what we had ever hoped, your mother is expecting a baby."

• • •

I've made this trek before. I've left Elam, only to be pulled back. But this time as I walk away, I vow to myself that I will not return. There is nothing left in Elam for me. Mother has a whole new life. Grandfather is occupied with his priestly duties. I've fulfilled my military duties to Uriel.

And so I move my feet as fast as they will carry me. The roads are not safe. No face can be trusted.

The ball court in the valley of Sam is nearly complete. Even while soldiers rest and train on the property, slaves work to make the rock walls smooth, the ground of the court even. Stone benches have been built. I wonder: Will the court ever be used for sport? Will we all die before it is finished?

All along the way back to Zarahemla I see sights I have never seen. Soothsayers who, for a price, tell a desired future. Witches out in the open, staring with eyes as hard and shiny as obsidian. Their powers are real. I can feel them as I walk past.

There are also prophets. Some, as did Kerem, preach that to believe in a messiah is foolishness. Others preach repentance: If we do not repent now, we will all be cast down to a hellish destruction when the Messiah comes.

I don't feel safe until I'm behind the prophet's courtyard walls. As always, I am welcomed into Nephi's household with warmth and love.

Nephi the Younger grants me immediate employment working in the cement trade. Jonas leads his own business venture digging cisterns to hold water—but I have the chance to work alongside him because after the cisterns are dug, we coat the holes with a cement mixture that hardens when it dries, keeping water from seeping out.

Jonas asks about the battles I've fought.

I am reluctant to talk, but I tell him, "Calev was truthful about one thing—war is not at all what I imagined it would be. War is going up against another man, trying to kill him before he kills you."

"Have you killed anyone, Kiah?"

I do not reply—only to tell him the horrors of that first attack when a man I was fighting stumbled to his death.

"How can we be commanded *not* to kill and then expected *to* kill?" he asks.

"God understands war. He doesn't like it, doesn't even condone it, but knows that sometimes there is no other choice when we need to defend freedom and family."

Jonas seems relieved that he has not been called to fight.

In the days that follow I spend my spare time studying while Jonas spends his time inventing implements to make cement work easier. One is a flat tool made of special bark that allows him to smooth out wet cement without leaving uneven layers behind.

Jonas has hopes of selling in Zarahemla's marketplace, and one morning I accompany him into the city. As we approach the walls, we can tell there is more insanity than ever. Prophets preaching, calling the people to repentance or calling the faithful foolish. Prophets arguing with each other. Prophets asking for money in exchange for favorable prophecy.

One man actually spits on Jonas when he recognizes the true prophet's grandson. I want to fight him, but Jonas just wipes his face and keeps walking. "At least they no longer want to kidnap me."

"I would have fought him," I say. "I'll *still* go back and fight him."

"No need. We're different kinds of warriors, Kiah."

He smiles, and I wish with all my heart that I could know the peace that Jonas knows. He never walks in anger, revenge, or fear. He walks with his fingers unclenched and his jaw slack, ready to smile. He forgives. He does not go back and visit an offense like I do. Just by watching my friend I learn more than I learn from any sermon.

We have to wait to go through the gate.

"What's happening? Why is there such a crowd this morning?" Jonas asks.

One of the guards points his spear upward. "Because a Lamanite, insane with zeal, has climbed up on the wall to preach of the Messiah."

Jonas frowns. "The people will surely stone him."

The guard laughs. "The sooner the better."

Fifty-Three

Before Jonas seeks a business opportunity, he wants to find Orli, the daughter of the apprentice synagogue teacher. She is the girl he hopes to marry.

We walk down the main road, pushing our way through. We then walk down smaller streets. Animals run loose. A little boy, not much higher than my knees, bumps into me. He's sobbing because he's lost his older sister.

"I let go of her hand," he cries. "Now I'm lost."

I take him in my arms and dry his tears. His knee is scraped, and I use a little water from my pouch to wash it clean.

"Tarah!" The little boy squirms out of my arms. "You found me!"

I look up to see a relieved older sister rushing to retrieve him. "Joseph!" She embraces him and kisses both of his cheeks over and over. She tousles his hair. Then she sees me and stands straight. "Thank you so much."

My mouth won't close. She is a vision of grace and beauty. Her hair is wild and wavy, the color of ripe wheat.

Jonas sees my stupor and steps in front of me. "You are a friend of Orli's, aren't you?"

The girl smiles, showing a row of straight white teeth. "Orli, the daughter of the priest Solomon, is my cousin."

"I am Jonas, son of Nephi. This man who seems to have swallowed his tongue is my kin, Kiah."

I step forward, close my mouth, and feel like a foolish boy. "You are very beautiful."

"And you are very forward, but thank you." Her laugh is the sound of music.

"Is Orli at home today—do you know?" Jonas asks.

"She is in the garden tending flowers with our grandmother. You may follow us."

As we follow behind her I can't quit staring. Jonas keeps jabbing me with his elbow, grinning at my dumbstruck state. We circle back and take a road that is thick with people staring up at the Lamanite, who is still preaching atop the wall.

"He's very brave," Tarah says.

"Or foolish," I say.

"He has been coming into the city for days," she explains. "He preaches harder things than I've ever heard preached."

We listen. The Lamanite shouts, "Repent!"

"Look at the faces around us," I say, hating the way people bump into Tarah, push her. "People are very angry with him."

"He'll be dragged out—stoned or hanged like those before him."

I glance at Jonas. We both know that his grandfather is in the same danger, for his message is the same.

"May I hold Joseph for you?" I ask, and Tarah seems grateful to pass him into my arms.

We pause. I am thinking how I might convince the Lamanite to climb down when he opens his mouth, and I am astounded at how his voice carries—how the crowd goes quiet to listen. "Behold, I, Samuel, a Lamanite, do speak the words of the Lord which He doth put into my heart; and behold He hath put it into my heart to say unto this people that a sword of justice hangeth over this people . . . and nothing can save this people save it be repentance and faith on the Lord Jesus Christ, who surely shall come into the world, and shall suffer many things and shall be slain for His people."

"How do you know such things?" Jonas calls up to him.

"An angel of the Lord hath declared it unto me, and he did bring glad tidings to my soul. Therefore, thus saith the Lord: Because of the hardness of the hearts of the people of the Nephites, except they repent I will take away my word from them, and I will withdraw my Spirit from them, and I will suffer them no longer, and I will turn the hearts of their brethren against them."

I look over at Jonas. "Is he talking about the Lamanites? Is he making a threat?"

"Have you ever seen a Lamanite prophet before?" he calls over to me.

I think back to my experience with Miyan. "No, but I know Lamanites who are more righteous than most of us."

"If ye will repent and return unto the Lord your God I will turn away mine anger, saith the Lord; yea, thus saith the Lord, blessed are they who will repent and turn unto me, but wo unto him that repenteth not. Yea, wo unto this great city of Zarahemla; for behold, it is because of those who are righteous that it is saved . . . blessed are they who will repent, for them will I spare. But behold, if it were not for the righteous who are in this great city, behold, I would cause that a fire should come down out of heaven and destroy it."

The people around me scoff. It seems impossible that a city made of so much stone could ever burn.

"Get down from there!" one of the military officers demands.

Samuel's voice bellows louder: "A curse shall come upon the land, saith the Lord of Hosts, because of the peoples' sake who are upon the land, yea, because of their wickedness and their abominations. And it shall come to pass, saith the Lord of Hosts, yea, our great and true God, that whoso shall hide up treasures in the earth shall find them again no more, because of the great curse of the land, save he be a righteous man and shall hide it up unto the Lord."

Immediately, I think of my treasure cache and wonder if it is safe.

"And the day shall come that they shall hide up their treasures, because they have set their hearts upon riches; and because they have set their hearts upon their riches . . . "

Where is my heart? What is it set upon? I look at Tarah and wonder if she is spoken for. I would give every treasure I could ever own to have her look upon me the way she's smiling and looking upon her brother. With love.

"Let's get out of here before the people riot," Jonas says.

He leads the way. I hold Joseph tight in my arms and follow behind Tarah. He's right—the temperature of the crowd is rising. The more Samuel preaches of their wickedness, the angrier they get.

When we reach the living area and find the home of Tarah's grandmother, I feel grateful to know there is safety. The street seems peaceful. Her grandmother greets us with proper respect, kisses Joseph's cheeks, and smiles at Jonas. "You have come for a glimpse of my granddaughter Orli."

"I have," Jonas says, lowering his head and looking just as big a fool as I am.

"You may walk," the grandmother says, "if you stay on this street and keep together. It will not do to have you separate. I will not have my granddaughter's name tarnished."

"Never would I do such a thing."

And so we all walk in a group that includes Orli, a girl who is short and pretty, with hair braided down her back in two long ropes. Her face lights up every time she looks at Jonas, though the two of them don't speak directly. Other cousins and an aunt and uncle walk with us.

I cannot take my eyes from Tarah. I have to know. "Is she betrothed?" I ask her uncle.

He stops and pelts me with what seems a hundred questions, beginning with, "Who are you to ask such a thing?"

He seems at ease after I answer all his queries. He tells me to my great happiness that no, Tarah is not betrothed. She has just arrived at her fifteenth year.

I see her looking at me as I speak with her uncle. I see her snatching glances, and I see her smile. That smile, I sense, will be the meaning in my life that I came to Zarahemla hoping to find.

Fifty-Four

When we leave the city, Samuel is still preaching. The crowd is angrier than before; I smile thinking how brave this man is to stand before a mob of Nephites, to call them to repentance.

"Ye do not remember the Lord your God in the things with which He hath blessed you, but ye do always remember your riches, not to thank the Lord your God for them; yea, your hearts are not drawn out unto the Lord, but they do swell with great pride, unto boasting, and unto great swelling, envyings, strifes, malice, persecutions, and murders, and all manner of iniquities."

Three men bludgeon their way through the crowd. They try to get past Jonas, but he stands in their way.

"Let us through! We are going to stone this Lamanite."

"This Lamanite speaks the truth."

"He's not a prophet! He's a crazy Lamanite!" The man hurls a stone at Samuel, but it hits the back of a woman's head instead. Shouts go up. Fists fly. Anger rips through the crowd.

Samuel only prophesies louder. "If a man shall come among you and shall say: Do this, and there is no iniquity; do that and ye shall not suffer; yea, he will say: Walk after the pride of your own hearts; yea, walk after the pride of your eyes, and do whatsoever your heart desireth—and if a man shall come among you and say this, ye will receive him, and say that he is a prophet. Yea, ye will lift him up, and ye will give unto him of your substance; ye will give unto him of your gold, and of your silver, and ye will clothe him with costly apparel; and because he speaketh flattering words unto you, and he saith that all is well, then ye will not find fault with him."

A man behind me goes for an arrow, but the warrior in me surfaces and I grab his arm.

The man jerks free. "Why are you protecting a Lamanite?"

"He speaks the truth. Have you even listened to his message?"

"He's been preaching in Zarahemla for days. Now get out of my way, or you'll suffer."

The man shoves me and my anger flares. I break his arrow and threaten to break his bow.

"Back away," his friend advises. "Look at the man's eyes! He's as crazy as the Lamanite."

They both back away and disappear into the crowd.

Samuel does not flinch as stones are hurled at him. "As the Lord liveth, if a prophet come among you and declareth unto you the word of the Lord, which testifieth of your sins and iniquities, ye are angry with him, and cast him out and seek all manner of ways to destroy him; yea, you will say that he is a false prophet, and that he is a sinner, and of the devil, because he testifieth that your deeds are evil. O ye wicked and ye perverse generation; ye hardened and ye stiffnecked people, how long will ye suppose that the Lord will suffer you? Yea, how long will ye suffer yourselves to be led by foolish and blind guides? Yea, how long will ye choose darkness rather than light?"

A rage is building all around us as sure as a rainstorm. It reminds me of the time when our village attacked a priest; it reminds me of how Grandfather was trampled; it reminds me how I might have killed a man if Eliana had not stopped me. I say a silent prayer of gratitude for the intervention of the Lord on behalf of a young, foolish boy and pray that I am no longer that zealot.

"One day you will be where Samuel is," I tell Jonas as we slip through the crowd. "You have as much faith as your father and grandfather."

"And you, Kiah, have more faith than you realize."

I think of how I stood in front of Miyan's family, how I tried to express my faith—the love I feel for my Savior—yet my words fell short. I think of the nights that I lay awake with my soldiers talking of the Messiah and His redeeming power. If Miyan asked me to tell him of Christ now, I would have much more to say—but would my words mean more than to simply tell, "I know Jesus is the Christ?"

We can't make it through the mass. The people are too many and too angry.

"Do you believe that Samuel is a prophet?"

"I do," Jonas says.

"There are so many who claim they are prophets. How can you tell which ones are true and which ones are false?"

"If they teach anything contrary to the word of God, they're false. It's that simple."

"I suppose the problem is that people don't know the word of God well enough to know whether what's being preached is accurate."

"That's why we study, Kiah. It's why we keep the law. Sometimes the only way to distinguish truth from falsehood is by the whisperings of the Spirit."

I nod. I listen. All I can hear are the shouts of an angry crowd.

Fifty-Five

War does not spare anyone. In the days that follow, Jonas and I must be careful because attacks happen every day and in every place. Jonas finds one of our workers late at night; he had been robbed and beaten, ambushed in broad daylight.

"The robbers grow bolder by the day."

"Why wouldn't they? They have brothers in the courts, in the markets, in the churches. It's hard for me to trust people because I am so suspicious."

Jonas looks at me with sad eyes. He's been working with cement all day, and his face is dusted gray. "These are perilous times. Why should I wait? I'm going to ask Solomon for permission to marry Orli."

"*You're* going to ask him?"

"I mean my father will ask him for me. Do you think Solomon approves of me?"

"How could he disapprove of you, Jonas? You are the son of the prophet."

I feel a twinge, an old enemy ripping at my heart, reminding me that I am the son of a coward. Maybe it's jealousy. Maybe not, because I am genuinely happy for my friend. The thought of Jonas getting married makes me wonder what has happened between Calev and Eliana. Are they now husband and wife?

It matters little to me. My thoughts lately have been of Tarah; just her memory turns my heart over. Could a girl as beautiful and kind as Tarah ever be taken with a man like me?

"I have no money for a dowry," I tell Jonas. "How can I ever hope to ask for a wife if I can offer nothing?"

"My father will give you what you need. He thinks of you as his son."

"I would never accept such a gift from your father, Jonas. It would make me feel uneasy."

"Well, you're a hard worker. Save your wage." He grins at me. "Are you still taken with Orli's cousin, the girl with the wavy hair?"

"Will you ask Orli what Tarah thinks of me?"

"You sound like a girl, my friend. That's a request a girl would make." He laughs and teases me and I don't care. I can't get Tarah off my mind, and it feels fresh and new and exciting. It feels right.

We study the law when our hands are not crusty with cement.

Out in the flowering courtyard of the synagogue I read law books. "Did you know that in Moses' day a man was thirty before he married?"

"Read it again, Kiah. A man *had* to be married by the time he was thirty in order to obey the law."

I run my finger across the scroll. "You are right. I misread it."

"Your mind is elsewhere, Kiah. I suspect it's on a girl in Zarahemla. Think about this: If you marry Tarah and I marry Orli, we'll be kin in two ways."

"You're more than a relative," I tell him. "You're my brother."

• • •

More villages are burned. Robbers destroy a synagogue in the land of Sidon. No place is sacred.

We have been crushing limestone all morning. The hilly terrain around us is hard and dusty, mostly white. I can't see for the dust in the air, and I can't breathe for the dust in my nostrils.

Jonas sneezes white dust. "I'm tired. Let's go into the banana grove and rest where there is shade."

I think of the spiders that thrive in the banana grove—hairy and big and deadly if they choose to sting. "I'll stay and finish the work; you go into the grove."

Jonas chuckles. "What's this? My warrior friend who is not scared of the vilest robber is scared of a spider?"

"They're hairy."

"They're spiders, Kiah. Not snakes. I know you're afraid of snakes, but spiders?"

We go to the grove with its dark-trunked trees that stretch tall and bare before they sprout huge, fanning leaves. It smells both sweet and sweaty as soon as we step into the grove. It's quieter here where both the sun and the wind are blocked by the long rows of identical trees.

We think we are alone but soon discover that we are not. The Lamanite prophet, Samuel, is here, snoring in the coolness of the shade. I look to be sure no spiders are crawling on him.

"Should we wake him?"

"No. He probably needs sleep."

"I'm awake." Samuel sits up, yawns, and motions for us to sit on the ground by him. We could be enemies, but he shows no sign of fear.

"We heard you preaching at the city gate," I tell him. "What you said was true."

"The words are God's, not mine."

I offer him bread, water, and an ear of charred corn. He eats like he hasn't had a bite of food in days.

"What makes you come to the Nephites?"

Samuel smiles. "The same Spirit that sent Ammon to our people."

I think about that and realize his risk is great.

"What makes you come here, to the banana grove?"

"They cast me out."

Jonas invites Samuel to come back with us and stay within the safety of the prophet's walls. "You could preach from my grandfather's prayer tower. He does it often."

"Your grandfather is Nephi, the great prophet?"

"You are a great prophet yourself," Jonas says. "You will be welcome in my grandfather's house."

And so we go back, the three of us—first to finish our limestone work, then on to the prophet's house. I'm delighted when I hear my grandfather's voice coming over the wall. He's been out with Nephi and Lehi again, this time preaching in the land of Angola.

"Kiah! My precious son!" He embraces me like he thought he would never see me again. He greets Jonas and Samuel, and we laugh because our hands and faces are white with limestone dust.

"When you are clean please meet me in the shade of the garden trees. There's a matter I'd like to discuss in private."

I hurry and wash, drink down as much water as I can, and spit out the chalky taste. "How are you, Grandfather? You look well."

"I am well enough." His expression falls. "We passed through Elam."

"Is it Mother? Has something happened to her?"

"Your mother is fine. Abner is a devoted husband. Their baby will be born soon."

The idea of Mother and Abner having a baby is strange, especially in their older years, but a bright spot in a dark time. "What have you heard of Calev?"

"I have seen nothing of him, nor has your mother. But Hem claims that he and Eliana are together—along with Eliana's younger sister, who has married one of Gadianton's leaders."

"Tamar? She's the wife of a robber?"

"That is the rumor. Oh, Kiah, Elam has fallen under evil rule. The judges and priests have little or no say unless Hem approves. He rules the village as sure as any king."

I've heard that analogy before.

"Everyone in Elam knows that you stood up to him while no one stood with you."

"You did, Grandfather."

"Buki, the priest, told me that Hem said Calev is well."

"So Hem admits seeing Calev?"

"Hem admits nothing. He claims he received word through rumors and some prisoners who were caught robbing in Calno. Hem's very careful not to incriminate himself."

I wait for Grandfather to say more of Calev. I'm anxious for any word about my brother. No matter what he has done, I still love him.

Jonas's nieces and nephews are playing by the fence, running and chasing each other like Jonas and I once did. Their world is completely carefree, and for a moment I am envious.

"Hem supposedly reported to the judges that Calev is a leader, a mighty captain among the robbers."

Calev, the grandson who made Grandfather so proud, now leads an army for Satan, not God. It's clear this news pains Grandfather as much as it does me.

My spine straightens. "I should go back and join Uriel. I should fight."

"Uriel is dead."

"Dead?" I can hardly get the word out.

"Most of his band gone. You do not want to return to Elam, son. Stay here. Keep learning. Stay safe."

"Uriel is dead? How?"

"His wife found him in the tangle, hanging from a tree with a rope around his neck. Hem tries to persuade everyone that the man took his own life because he failed as a military leader. I do not believe Hem."

I'm sad and say very little for the rest of the day. But I watch as Nephi and Lehi greet Samuel, the Lamanite prophet. They talk at great length about the Messiah. When they are done I sit by the fireside and approach Samuel. "Years ago Jonas and I found ourselves in a dangerous situation in the city. A Lamanite rescued me. Was it you?"

Samuel's brow creases. "Were you an angry young boy anxious to fight every grown man in sight?"

"That was me."

"Yes, it was me who held you back."

"So you have been preaching in Zarahemla for a very long time."

"I wasn't preaching then. I was only in the city to worship at the temple."

I shake my head. "Life is curious. So many lives are connected."

"We are all children of the same Father."

I thank him and lean forward, searching his eyes. Samuel is a man of muscle, but he is also gentle featured; kindness is etched on his face as sure as if I'd drawn it there. I ask, "How do you know so many things about a god you cannot see?"

"I don't know it with my eyes or my head. I know it *here*." He jabs a finger over his heart. "Tell me, Kiah, of your faith, for I sense that you are a man of mighty faith."

"I suspect my faith is only ordinary. To be honest, there are seasons when it seems strong and seasons when it weakens."

"Have you ever been delivered from the power of the destroyer?"

"There are many times my Savior has delivered me." I tell him of the vipers' pit.

He shudders. "People ask me to tell them of the Messiah, and I say that it is one thing to know *about* the Messiah and a very different thing to know *Him*."

"When will He come?"

"The signs are all around us, my brother. Follow me into the city tomorrow. I will preach again, and your question will be answered."

Fifty-Six

The next morning before dawn, I join Jonas, his father, and his uncle Timothy to help sneak Samuel into the city. We have to sneak him in because the guards are positioned at the gates, searching for his face, with orders to turn Samuel away.

Samuel wears Timothy's old cloak, and we come through with a donkey, a pack animal whose back Samuel stands on while he climbs the lowest wall. He then scales onto a higher wall and finally to the highest.

The early risers are milling about, setting up for the day. As the sun rises, so does the voice of Samuel. "O that ye had repented, and had not killed the prophets, and stoned them, and cast them out. Yea, in that day ye shall say: O that we had remembered the Lord our God in the day that he gave us our riches, and then they would not have become slippery that we should lose them; for behold, our riches are gone from us."

The guards and military officers are shocked to see him standing high, preaching strong. They demand he get down from the wall.

"O that we had repented in the day that the word of the Lord came unto us. . . . Behold, we are surrounded by demons, yea, we are encircled about by the angels of him who hath sought to destroy our souls. Behold, our iniquities are great. O Lord, canst thou not turn away thine anger from us."

I have my blade, my javelin, and my sling. I am ready to protect Samuel, no matter the cost. I know from the fire that burns within me that the words he speaks so boldly are true.

"Behold, your days of probation are past; ye have procrastinated the day of your salvation until it is everlastingly too late, and your destruction is made sure; yea, for ye have sought all the days of your lives for that which ye could not obtain; and ye have sought for happiness in doing iniquity, which thing is contrary to the nature of that righteousness which is in our great and Eternal Head. O ye people of the land, that ye would hear my words! And I pray that the anger of the Lord be turned away from you, and that ye would repent and be saved."

As the day yawns open, the crowd grows. I fear for Samuel. Already there are bands of violent men, angry because his message insults them. Through the crowd I spot the prophet Nephi, Lehi, and Grandfather. They are surrounded by a band of faithful guards who accompany Nephi wherever he goes.

I cannot imagine the courage it takes for God's men like Nephi and Samuel to cry repentance to a proud and sinful people.

"If you believe the words of this Lamanite prophet," Lehi calls across the growing crowd, "my brother will baptize you into the fold of God."

I'm surprised when many in the crowd flock to Nephi's band, anxious to follow him away from the wall and out toward the waters where Nephi often baptizes.

"Do you need help?" I ask Grandfather.

"Samuel needs you more. Protect him, son. He is a true prophet of God. Listen carefully to his Messianic message. You are a warrior for God now; be brave."

A warrior for God. I smile at the phrase I've heard before, but now it seems to fit. I stand taller and feel stronger.

Jonas nudges me and we see the masses parting, making way for four men who are hoisting some sort of long box. It looks like a coffin that is missing the side panels.

"Come down from the wall, prophet. Let us put you where you belong, and we'll see if your God can deliver you."

The men laugh. The crowd laughs.

I realize the men have built a torture box. They intend to capture Samuel and tie his hands and feet, stretching him in the box. The sides are open for two reasons: so that witnesses can watch him suffer and die and so that torturers can attack him with sticks and clubs and even blades. I've heard about this method, but I've never actually seen one of the boxes, and the sight sickens me.

"What kind of tormented mind could invent such a thing?" Jonas asks.

I see from the club tight in his hand that he feels as I do. We are both ready to die to prevent anyone from putting Samuel inside that box.

I approach the lead man, a brute of a fellow, his body draped with armor, a cimeter at his side.

"Put down the box."

He looks at me as if he misunderstood.

"As God lives, you will bring no harm to the prophet standing on the wall."

Now the man blows his foul breath into my face. His teeth are the color of a ripe mango. "Get out of the way, boy."

I pray for strength and courage, because I lack both. My feet do not move, and I see that Jonas has slipped up behind the man. He's always been a thin boy, and though he's no soldier, he's braver than anyone I've seen. The love I feel for my friend threatens to burst through my chest and crack my ribs. If Jonas can do this, I can do this.

"You will bring no harm to Samuel," I tell the would-be torturer.

He laughs. "I'll bring harm to *you*." The side of his hand shoots out and catches me in the throat. As I go down I grab the man's legs and pull him down with me. He lands next to me with a thud so hard the coffin is yanked away from the others. It crashes down and breaks into pieces.

Like a hammer, the man's fist slams toward my face. I swivel just in time, and he impales his hand on a piece of splintered wood. He bellows curses and his eyes bulge, terrifying and veiny. "I'll kill you!" He jerks his bloody hand free.

"Not before I bring you a fate worse than death." My blade presses against his inner thigh.

He looks down, and I think his eyeballs might pop out of his head.

"Leave the prophet be. He speaks for God Almighty."

His shaggy head swivels as he takes in the status of his friends. The three of them are standing dumb faced, goats waiting for guidance. Jonas seems somehow taller, ready with a club in his grip. If this is what being a warrior for God feels like, then let the battle rage.

Only it doesn't.

While Samuel's voice booms like thunder, the men before me slip away, disappear like morning mist into the throngs.

I look up at Samuel. He wears no weapons and carries nothing but a testimony of Jesus Christ—yet I swear there is a shield around him. An assurance from the Spirit whispers peace that Samuel is protected by a force much greater than any weapon crafted on earth.

He looks straight at me, smiles, and lifts both his arms and his voice as he cries, "Behold, I give unto you a sign; for five years more cometh, and behold, then cometh the Son of God to redeem all those who shall believe on his name. And behold, this will I give unto you for a sign at the time of His coming; for behold, there shall be great lights in heaven, insomuch that in the night before He cometh there shall be no darkness, insomuch that it shall appear unto man as if it was day.

"Therefore, there shall be one day and a night and a day, as if it were one day and there were no night; and this shall be unto you for a sign; for ye shall know of the rising of the sun and also of its setting; therefore they shall know of a surety that there shall be two days and a night; nevertheless the night shall not be darkened; and it shall be the night before He is born.

"And behold, there shall a new star arise, such an one as ye never have beheld; and this also shall be a sign unto you. And behold this is not all, there shall be many signs and wonders in heaven. And it shall come to pass that ye shall all be amazed, and wonder, insomuch that ye shall fall to the earth. And it shall come to pass that whosoever shall believe on the Son of God, the same shall have everlasting life."

Jonas leans toward me and says, "Look across the way toward the church's platform."

So many people are pushing and shoving that it's hard to see through the crowd, but up on the rise in front of a beautiful white church is a group of young women. There must be thirty of them, and yet I immediately pick out a single smile. Tarah. She's scanning the masses, and I hope she's looking for me.

A line of military officers armed with arrows comes through, shoving others aside. Jonas and I step back on our own.

One of the officers makes a feeble attempt to remind the people, "This preacher has the right to believe what he will."

"He's a filthy Lamanite!"

Jonas and I stand shoulder to shoulder, ready to protect Samuel.

"Let him preach until he wears himself out," the officer admonishes the people.

"He's been at it for many days. Let's force him down from the wall."

"No," the officer says, showing forth a portion of authority. "Let him preach on."

I want to make our way over to the church. Maybe Tarah will talk with me. But Jonas isn't even looking at Orli anymore. His attention has turned back to Samuel.

"And behold, thus hath the Lord commanded me, by His angel, that I should come and tell this thing unto you; yea, he hath commanded that I should prophesy these things unto you; yea, he hath said unto me: Cry unto this people, repent and prepare the way of the Lord. And now, because I am a Lamanite, and have spoken unto you the words which the Lord hath commanded me, and because it was hard against you, ye are angry with me and do seek to destroy me, and have cast me out from among you. And ye shall hear my words, for, for this intent have I come up upon the walls of this city, that ye might hear and know of the judgments of God which do await you because of your iniquities, and also that ye might know the conditions of repentance; And also that ye might know of the coming of Jesus Christ, the Son of God, the Father of heaven and of earth, the Creator of all things from the beginning; and that ye might know of the signs of His coming, to the intent that ye might believe on His name."

"We believe!" a group up close to the wall shouts. "We believe in Jesus Christ!"

In all my life I have never felt what I am feeling now. Tears are wetting my cheeks, for I know where I stand—with the believers. The Spirit fills me, testifies to me that what Samuel says not only feels true, it *is* true. He, like Nephi, is a prophet speaking for God.

"And if ye believe on His name ye will repent of all your sins, that thereby ye may have a remission of them through His merits. And behold, again, another sign I give unto you, yea, a sign of His death. For behold, He surely must die that salvation may come; yea, it behooveth Him and becometh expedient that He dieth, to bring to pass the resurrection of the dead, that thereby men may be brought into the presence of the Lord."

"Where can we be baptized?" a woman shouts. "I want to have my children baptized."

"Nephi, the prophet, is by the waters just outside the city gates. He's baptizing now!"

The interchange continues as Samuel preaches on. Even the unbelievers are listening now. Samuel is saying things I've never heard any prophet preach.

"But behold, as I said unto you concerning another sign, a sign of His death, behold, in that day that He shall suffer death the sun shall be darkened and refuse to give his light unto you; and also the moon and the stars; and there shall be no light upon the face of this land, even from the time that He shall suffer death, for the space of three days, to the time that He shall rise again from the dead.

"Yea, at the time that He shall yield up the ghost there shall be thunderings and lightnings for the space of many hours, and the earth shall shake and tremble; and the rocks which are upon the face of this earth, which are both above the earth and beneath, which ye know at this time are solid, or the more part of it is one solid mass, shall be broken up; Yea, they shall be rent in twain, and shall ever after be found in seams and in cracks, and in broken fragments upon the face of the whole earth, yea, both above the earth and beneath.

"And behold, there shall be great tempests, and there shall be many mountains laid low, like unto a valley, and there shall be many places which are now called valleys which shall become mountains, whose height is great.

"And many highways shall be broken up, and many cities shall become desolate. And many graves shall be opened, and shall yield up many of their dead; and many saints shall appear unto many. And behold, thus hath the angel spoken unto me; for he said unto me that there should be thunderings and lightnings for the space of many hours. And he said unto me that while the thunder and the lightning lasted, and the tempest, that these things should be, and that darkness should cover the face of the whole earth for the space of three days."

It is difficult to imagine such a time, yet I can see it in my mind as Samuel describes it. I believe him.

"The angel said unto me that many shall see greater things than these, to the intent that they might believe that these signs and these wonders should come to pass upon all the face of this land, to the intent that there should be no cause for unbelief among the children of men—And this to the intent that whosoever will believe might be saved, and that whosoever will not believe, a righteous judgment might come upon them; and also if they are condemned they bring upon themselves their own condemnation."

"Do you feel that?"

"The power of his words?" I ask Jonas.

"We've got to repent, Kiah. I've got to repent."

"If you have need of repentance, then I need a double portion."

It's true that Samuel's words are blunt and brutal; it's also true that they speak directly to my soul. "And now remember, remember, my brethren, that whosoever perisheth, perisheth unto himself; and whosoever doeth iniquity, doeth it unto himself; for behold, ye are free; ye are permitted to act for yourselves; for behold, God hath given unto you a knowledge and he hath made you free. He hath given unto you that ye might know good from evil, and He hath given unto you that ye might choose life or death; and ye can do good and be restored unto that which is good, or have that which is good restored unto you; or ye can do evil, and have that which is evil restored unto you."

Over and over Jonas and I push back the hands that want to harm Samuel. Jonas takes a fist to the mouth, and a man shoves me in the back—challenges me to a fight that takes all of my effort to resist. The contention in the crowd grows stronger, and Samuel's message grows harsher.

By the time Samuel finishes and climbs down from the wall, it is afternoon. Jonas and I are tired and hungry. Samuel lets himself down on the outside of the wall, but even so, people rush to be near him. Some shout angry threats, and a few people even shove him, but most of his followers believe him and want to hear more.

I am one of those followers. My ears want to hear every word he says, and I have a feeling that I should somehow write down his prophecies, but I dismiss the impression, knowing how difficult it would be to acquire parchment or writing tools.

That night after everyone is resting I sit at Samuel's feet and learn of the Messiah. The way he talks of Jesus is as though Samuel is speaking of his dearest friend.

"Will you come back into the city with me tomorrow?" he asks me.

"Of course."

Samuel yawns, but his face beams with enthusiasm for his message. "I hope that the morrow will be as successful as today was."

I can think of nothing to say. If tomorrow follows the pattern of today, it will take a miracle for any of us to survive.

Fifty-Seven

Grandfather kneels by me as we say our morning prayers. He's embarrassed when I offer him a hand to stand, and he brushes me away. "You've got more important work to do. Follow Samuel and stay with him. These mobs are bent on his destruction."

I sigh. "His words are blunt and brutal. They incite anger and resentment."

"A true prophet worries about offending no one except the Lord."

"Grandfather, you have as much faith. You see visions and receive revelations; your testimony is as strong as Nephi's or Lehi's or Samuel's. Will I ever know such a testimony for myself?"

He's managed to stand straight, and he wipes the dust from his knees. "Every time we are apart and then reunited, I see the growth in you, son. Your faith was once weak. It is now strong. You've seen miracles, and you must never forget or doubt. We live in a crushing world that would wipe away our faith—that would lead us down the path of utter destruction. You've chosen to walk the higher, harder path." He chokes on his words. I know he is thinking of Calev, missing him more than I do.

A late-morning mist falls heavy as I follow Samuel back into the city, and a voice within me whispers that Grandfather is right. Though I am far from the man I should be, I am a man of growing faith. I believe that our Messiah is the Deliverer for which we hope and wait. He is our only real hope. I know that *Messiah* translates as "the anointed one." And slowly, but with a power so great it could move the distant mountains, I realize that the Messiah is more than a man, more than a promise, more than someone on which to hang our hope. The Messiah that fills my heart is my Savior, the one who will deliver *me*—from the pain of having no father, of feeling so separated from my family, of Calev's betrayal. Jesus Christ not only forgives my sins, He atones for my sorrows.

Samuel stops. "I'd like to pray. Will you join me?"

Jonas and I look at him and bow our heads. There off the main highway outside of Zarahemla I hear a prayer unlike any prayer I've ever heard. I *feel* it. It's impossible to describe the power or the intimacy of his communication with heaven. I want to open my eyes. I want to see for myself the angels I can feel surrounding us.

When "amen" is said, Samuel puts his arms around me and embraces me as a brother. "Kiah, the Messiah knows you. He loves you. He understands your heart and the trials that cause you to stumble."

I wipe the water out of my eyes—not from tears but from the mist. It's so thick around us my hair is dripping and my clothes are soaked.

"You have a testimony that is stronger than you realize."

"But I've never had a revelation. I've never seen an angel."

"You've felt promptings in your heart. You've heard a soft voice whisper direction."

"Yes."

"Then you have received revelation, as sure as I have." He lifts a hand heavenward. "Has it rained this morning?"

"No."

"Yet you are drenched as sure as if it did."

"Yes."

"Some people receive a testimony in a downpour that leaves them just as wet as you are now. Others receive it bit by bit, like walking through the mist. Both are immersed in truth. Do you understand what I'm telling you?"

"I understand." And I do. My testimony has come to me, not in a storm but drop by drop, prayer by prayer, testimony by testimony, and experience by experience, none more powerful than the gentle kiss of a morning mist.

Some of Jonas's nephews are waiting at the wall. They warn us that the captains are armed and ready to arrest Samuel, so they lead us through a stretch of tangle to a part of the wall where stones are butted together. Samuel is a stout man, broader than both Jonas and I, yet we make a human pyramid so he can stand on our backs and hoist himself onto the wall.

When we come back around to enter the city, one of the gate guards recognizes Jonas. "Where is your Lamanite friend?"

"There!" Jonas points to the wall where Samuel is taking his position.

The guard curses and calls for reinforcements.

"Do you think Samuel will be all right?" Jonas asks me.

"Did you hear his prayer? Did you feel what I felt?"

"You're right. He'll be protected."

This day's crowd seems smaller in numbers, but their faces are fierce, and hatred burns in their eyes. I catch myself looking for the face of my own brother, expecting that this is a place where I might find Calev and his Gadianton band.

Again, I have the feeling that I should find a way to write the words of Samuel, but I don't want to leave Jonas and his nephews alone. There might be a writing shop in the city, but I don't know where to look for one, and the priests in the local synagogue are not likely to provide me with materials so that I can write the words of a man they don't believe is a prophet.

"Yea, wo unto this people who are called the people of Nephi except they shall repent, when they shall see all these signs and wonders which shall be showed unto them; for behold, they have been a chosen people of the Lord; yea, the people of Nephi hath He loved, and also hath He chastened them; yea, in the days of their iniquities hath He chastened them because He loveth them. But behold my brethren, the Lamanites hath He hated because their deeds have been evil continually, and this because of the iniquity of the tradition of their fathers. But behold, salvation hath come unto them through the preaching of the Nephites; and for this intent hath the Lord prolonged their days.

"And I would that ye should behold that the more part of them are in the path of their duty, and they do walk circumspectly before God, and they do observe to keep His commandments and His statutes and His judgments according to the law of Moses. Yea, I say unto you, that the more part of them are doing this, and they are striving with unwearied diligence that they may bring the remainder of their brethren to the knowledge of the truth; therefore there are many who do add to their numbers daily."

The numbers around us are growing. People shout insults. People hurl stones, but they either fly past Samuel or hit the wall and break in shards.

"Why should we believe you?" one of the captains shouts. "Get down from there!"

Samuel keeps preaching, not losing his purpose, no matter how many sources try to distract him. "And behold, ye do know of yourselves, for ye have witnessed it, that as many of them as are brought to the knowledge of the truth, and to know of the wicked and abominable traditions of their fathers, and are led to believe the holy scriptures, yea, the prophecies of the holy prophets, which are written, which leadeth them to faith on the Lord, and unto repentance, which faith and repentance bringeth a change of heart unto them. Therefore, as many as have come to this, ye know of yourselves are firm and steadfast in the faith, and in the thing wherewith they have been made free. And ye know also that they have buried their weapons of war, and they fear to take them up lest by any means they should sin; yea, ye can see that they fear to sin—for behold they will suffer themselves that they be trodden down and slain by their enemies, and will not lift their swords against them, and this because of their faith in Christ."

To me, it's as if Samuel is describing Miyan. I'm so grateful to know that Miyan now has an understanding of the Messiah and the love of our Father in Heaven. Someday, I vow to myself, I'll see him again.

"And now, because of their steadfastness when they do believe in that thing which they do believe, for because of their firmness when they are once enlightened, behold, the Lord shall bless them and prolong their days, notwithstanding their iniquity—Yea, even if they should dwindle in unbelief the Lord shall prolong their days, until the time shall come which hath been spoken of by our fathers, and also by the prophet Zenos, and many other prophets, concerning the restoration of our brethren, the Lamanites, again to the knowledge of the truth—Yea, I say unto you, that in the latter times the promises of the Lord have been extended to our brethren, the Lamanites; and notwithstanding the many afflictions which they shall have, and notwithstanding they shall be driven to and fro upon the face of the earth, and be hunted, and shall be smitten and scattered abroad, having no place for refuge, the Lord shall be merciful unto them. And this is according to the prophecy, that they shall again be brought to the true knowledge, which is the knowledge of their Redeemer, and their great and true shepherd, and be numbered among His sheep.

"Therefore I say unto you, it shall be better for them than for you except ye repent. For behold, had the mighty works been shown unto them which have been shown unto you, yea, unto them who have dwindled in unbelief because of the traditions of their fathers, ye can see of yourselves that they never would again have dwindled in unbelief."

An arrow flies by me and *thwaks* into the wall. Another one and another. The crowd has turned into a mob.

Oh Lord, bless Samuel.

I look to the captains who are supposed to be keeping peace, but they have clearly sided with the mob leaders. In the throng I spy the shaggy head of the man I fought the first day. It's like a thunderstorm of arrows and stones and vulgar threats raining around Samuel. I try to stand steady, but people bump me, shove me, hit me. A rock even hits my back. I look over at Jonas and smile. Neither one of us is amazed at all that not one weapon is striking our Lamanite friend.

"Therefore, saith the Lord: I will not utterly destroy them, but I will cause that in the day of my wisdom they shall return again unto me, saith the Lord. And now behold, saith the Lord, concerning the people of the Nephites: If they will not repent, and observe to do my will, I will utterly destroy them, saith the Lord, because of their unbelief notwithstanding the many mighty works which I have done among them; and as surely as the Lord liveth shall these things be, saith the Lord."

Another one of the captains screams across the crowd. "He's telling us that our fathers were wrong and that the Lamanites are God's people."

"That's not what Samuel is saying," someone else contends.

The people are parted as sure as the Red Sea. There is no safe ground to walk on as far as I can tell.

"Samuel!" I call up to him, and his eyes meet mine.

"You know him? This Lamanite is your friend?"

It's one of the captains, and he shoves me hard with the butt of his club.

"He's my friend," I say boldly.

"Take this fellow and bind him," a man tells the captain.

"He hath a devil," a woman says, gnashing her teeth. "The power of the devil in him prevents us from hitting him with our stones and our arrows; therefore, take him and bind him—and away with him."

"No! You will not touch him!" For a moment those vicious mobsters around me wheel, and I am sure there will be a fight. But Samuel turns and makes a stunning leap from the highest wall.

Jonas and I try to go after him. We get tangled in the crowd, people shoving and grabbing, unsure of the miracle they've just witnessed. There are those who chase after Samuel—because he was not harmed, they realize he has to be a man of God. Others are angry and only want to kill him. Jonas and I want to protect him. But God has gone before us: When we reach the other side of the wall, there is no sign of the Lamanite prophet Samuel.

He has gone on to preach and prophesy among his own people. I can't help feeling that I've lost another brother.

Fifty-Eight

All my life I've been told that we are waiting for the Messiah, but this time the waiting is different. This time Raz and timekeepers everywhere are tracking the time from Samuel's prophecy. Five years. It seems an eternity to me.

Mother gives birth to a baby daughter with hair as red as Abner's. The child is given the name Elka, which means "an oath to God." When they bring her to the temple to present her, I'm shocked to see how Mother has aged. She's thinner than ever, and her eyes keep changing. One moment they overflow with tears, and the next they shine with joy. As always, she brightens with the support and affection she receives from the women in this household. Bosma holds the baby while Mother naps. Devora washes the baby's wraps and makes a thick gruel flavored with spices that Mother likes.

Abner and I walk a pathway out behind the house. He seems to have much on his mind. "Life is different in Elam now," he explains. "It has become Hem's village. Have you seen the monstrosity of a ball court he's overseeing?"

"I haven't been by it in a very long time."

I feel as though I've neglected my own village, my own family, and yet there is no place for me in Elam. The only family I belong to is Grandfather, who has decided to stay near the temple in Zarahemla.

I study at the synagogue and I work with Nephi and Jonas, always trying to improve the art of cement work. I help Jonas craft the implements he sells in the city. And I take every opportunity to be with Tarah. One day I will have a sufficient offering to make to her father; it's that goal that makes me rise early and work late into the night.

Grandfather has become acquainted with her father, an artisan who specializes in the green and blue stones collected by the great winding river. He inlays the precious stones in carvings for elite buildings and in weapons for the richest leaders in the land. He made a beautiful shield that was presented to Lachoneus.

His name, Abarron, means "father of a multitude"—a fitting name since he has seven daughters. Tarah falls in the middle. His oldest child is a son, and his youngest, Joseph, is a little shadow to Tarah.

I consider how my brother and Abarron would have much in common; they both treasure rare stones and know how to find them. But Abner confirms my worst fears: Calev has become the official son-in-law and apprentice to Hem. My brother has returned to Elam with Eliana. He claims that all this time he was hunting in the hills for Tamar and did not find her—but to his astonishment, he discovered his own Eliana.

"Some think your brother a hero," Abner says. "Your mother cannot think a dark thought about Calev. He is her son."

"That I expect. Calev has learned the art of deceit from his father-in-law."

"They make no confession that they are robbers, but everyone in Elam knows they lead the Gadianton bands that grow in numbers every day."

"What do they do now that everyone knows?"

"They do nothing, as always, Kiah. Hem and Calev rule like royalty."

I want to change the subject. "Did you hear that an attack was even made on temple grounds?"

"No. I have not heard."

"Both the temple here and the temple in Bountiful were attacked. Robbers stole from the money changers. Though the attacks were in separate cities, at different temples, they were planned to occur at the same time. It caused great chaos and sent a message that the robbers work as one and in unison."

"I'm sorry to hear such news. At least with Calev back in Elam, I feel he provides some protection for your mother."

He means, of course, that Calev will order his band to leave Mother unharmed. The idea should give me comfort, but I ask, "How does Calev treat Mother?"

"He treats her with respect and generosity. Offerings are left at our gate—food from the marketplace, combs for her hair, cloth for new clothing."

Guilt punches my stomach. I think of my meager buried treasure. It amounts to nothing compared to my brother's means. "I've given Mother nothing."

Abner shakes his head. "Kiah, you have given your mother a reason to hold her head high. You have given her joy when there was none. You serve the Lord, and that is all she's ever wanted from her sons."

It's an awkward moment when his long arms reach to embrace me, but his gesture is sincere, and any doubts I harbored about Abner are gone for good. We make a vow to each other that we will not let so much time pass before we see each other again.

• • •

Nephi, Lehi, Grandfather, and Nephi the Younger spend much of their time preaching with the same fervor as Samuel, crying repentance to a people who do not want to repent. Those who do are taught carefully and then baptized. I think back on my own baptism performed by Grandfather. Calev was there. I can still see his smiling face, and the memory rips at an ever-present hole in my heart. I miss the brother that I will never have back. I miss things about Elam. But I've been given a new life, and I try to stay focused on what I want it to be.

• • •

Nephi, father of Jonas, makes an agreement with Solomon, and the marriage between Jonas and Orli is arranged. Nephi offers Jonas property on which to build his own house. It is not within the walls of the family compound but behind it, on a small hill with a stream and a clear view of the valley. Jonas is overjoyed. I'm happy for my brother-friend, but a part of me writhes with jealousy. If I had a father with power and wealth, I could offer a dowry worthy of Tarah.

By the time I earn a sufficient offering she might be married to someone else.

Nephi smiles at me. "I will do the same for you, Kiah, when your heart has found the right girl."

"Thank you," I say, feeling truly grateful—but torn, too, wondering why I still feel so prideful, wondering why I could not take such an offering from the man who has been such a father to me. If I am able, I want to provide for myself. I could always retrieve my buried treasure. I could sell it or trade it for the girl that I grow to love more each time I see her. Even on the days I have no contact at all with Tarah, she never leaves my thoughts.

Those same feelings erupt again when I am helping Jonas clear the land for his new marital home. "Have faith," he tells me, slapping me on the back. "The Lord knows your feelings for Tarah. He will provide for you."

Resentment rises in me. Jealousy burns. For an instant all the love I feel for Jonas disappears and is replaced by something ugly and hard. I look at him and think how easy his life has been—how carefree and privileged. My fist squeezes around a rock. My eyes focus on a snake, small and green, sliding down a limb of the same green color. It slithers toward Jonas's bare foot. I see it but say nothing; I watch as it gets closer and closer. I see from its flat head and red-tipped tail that it is not an innocent snake but one filled with deadly venom.

I wait. I wait until the final second before I leap and smash its head with the rock.

Jonas jumps back. "What was that all about?"

"Another test for me," I say, dropping the rock and walking away.

Fifty-Nine

By the time Jonas's house is finished I have repented of my jealous resentment.

I pray for a change of heart, and the Spirit whispers to me to cultivate gratitude. It's not a difficult task. I have much to be grateful for. Grandfather is healthy in body and especially in spirit: He has seen an angel. An angel from God appeared to Grandfather to declare the good tidings of the coming Messiah. Grandfather bears witness to us of his vision, and I believe him completely. He reveals holy things to us that he commands me not to write or to share with anyone.

We live in a time when evil grows as thick and twisted as jungle vines. Idol worship used to be hidden; now its rituals are performed where everyone can see. I think there is little difference now between Zarahemla and Shimnilom. Once when Jonas and I were working in the city of Ammonihah we came upon the remains of a ritual where innocent children—hardly bigger than babies—had been sacrificed to a god made of stone. Their bodies were stretched and pulled until their joints came apart and their flesh tore.

I didn't hear their screams of agony or see their tortured faces, but I hear their screams in my nightmares and I fall sick. For days I cannot eat. I cannot sleep. The prophet Nephi lays his hands on my head to restore me to myself.

"These are times when the worst and the best clash, but good is stronger than evil, Kiah. Never doubt that."

Gadianton's band still hides in the hills, but their leaders walk our streets, sit in our judgment seats, and serve in the synagogues. They can't be brought to justice because, like Hem and my own brother, they are surrounded by other secret band members who hold them up to be innocent. And so they corrupt our laws, cheat our vendors, and weaken our faith.

• • •

"Come with me into the city," Jonas asks one morning while we are washing before our first prayer and meal. "I've got some implements to sell, and maybe you will catch a glimpse of Tarah."

My head lifts. "It's too dangerous," I say. "She could be with Orli, and you're not allowed to be around her until the final ceremony."

"That's not far away now," Jonas says, grinning. "Come with me, Kiah. All you ever do is work."

"Because one day I want my own wife and family."

"And you can have it. You *will* have it. Father has offered you help. It's your stubbornness that refuses him."

"You understand why I must do this on my own."

"I understand that my best friend is the most stubborn man in the world. I understand that my father thinks of you as his own son. I hope you feel that love."

"I do."

"Come along, Kiah. You helped make these implements. You deserve part of the pay."

I go, but not for the pay—for the chance to see Tarah. And we do. She is in the marketplace with Orli and their grandmother. Even from afar, the sight of her steals my breath. They don't see us as they take their basket from vendor to vendor, leaning over to pick the freshest fruit, talking and joking with friends they meet.

Tarah throws her head back, and her mouth opens. The laugh she laughs makes me laugh too. I can't take my eyes from her hair—it's like a trap for the sun, light getting caught in every golden curl.

Jonas chuckles. "I haven't seen you this happy since . . . since, well, maybe I've never seen you this happy, Kiah."

"Look at her. Tarah is beautiful."

"Maybe so, but my eyes are on Orli."

We almost tumble over each other, vying for the best position from which to see our girls. We are not exactly inconspicuous. Jonas and I are standing on a corner of the main road and people are all around us—yet every time we think the girls might see us we duck and hide like foolish boys. This goes on for a good span while people have to make their way around us. It feels carefree to act so boyish for just a moment.

"Solomon must command a good wage at the synagogue," I say, watching how freely the girls spend money.

Without looking at me Jonas says, "Solomon is also a judge. He sits with his brother-in-law, Lachoneus."

"Lachoneus is Orli's uncle?"

"Yes. Haven't I told you that?"

"No. In all this time you've never mentioned it. I saw Lachoneus when he came to the trickball tournament in Elam. He's the one who granted Hem so much power."

"He's a good man, a fair man, but what chance does he stand when he's surrounded by so many deceitful others?"

I feel a hand on my shoulder and hear a familiar voice.

"I hope you two were not referring to me," Hem says.

Sixty

I hardly recognize him. His hair has gone silver, and his skin is bronzed and wrinkled. The robe he wears is a deep shade of dense green with trim reserved for only the most faithful. Except for leaning on a jewel-handled walking stick, he looks strong. The sight of him causes a bitter taste to churn up from my stomach into my mouth.

"Hem. What are you doing *here?*"

"What? I have no right to come to Zarahemla?" He laughs and looks at his wife, who is a withered old woman by his side. There are others with them, an entire group, but I don't recognize any of them. I want to know where Calev and Eliana are and if Tamar is all right, but I bite my lip and say nothing.

"Yes, I thought I recognized you, Kiah. And you, Jonas, grandson of the mighty prophet Nephi. You both look well, though you appear to be spying on someone." He leans on his cane, cocks his body, and tries to see what we have been looking at.

I step in front of him and block his view.

"Ah, Kiah," he shakes his beast of a head. "This no greeting for a relative. We are family now. Eliana is due to give birth to my first grandchild soon. You will be an uncle."

The bile in my mouth burns my tongue. I want to spit in Hem's face.

"I can see from your expression that you haven't heard this good news before." He glances at Sherrizah. "We're thrilled, aren't we, wife?"

She nods.

"We're on business," Jonas says. "We must be going."

"Aren't you even going to ask about your own brother, Kiah? Don't you want to hear of Calev's success?"

"His success? His success as a robber, as your evil apprentice?"

Hem puts a hand over his heart. "You wound me. You still persist with your false accusations, Kiah? You should ask your righteous grandfather, Yarden, to lay hands on you, to rid you of the demons that torture your mind. Calev was never a robber. When we thought he was, he was actually out *hunting* the robbers, ridding Elam of their torment. He's forgiven me for misjudging him. He's married my daughter, and he's returned Tamar to us safely."

Sherrizah makes a sniveling noise. Hem glances sharply at her until she steps behind him, taking refuge.

"Tamar is home safely?"

"Yes. No. Not exactly. Our youngest daughter is not back in Elam, but we know that she is safe and being well cared for."

I don't understand. I don't need to understand.

I want to tell him that I heard Tamar was the wife of a robber, just like Eliana. But I don't want the conversation to continue. I'm angry at the good news he brings. Everyone in Hem's household is well and prospering, even though they break the laws of God like Moses smashed the holy tablets. Yet I struggle to earn a meager living while I strive to keep every commandment.

It is not fair.

"Kiah, you seem troubled at my report. Perhaps you're jealous?"

Jonas stands beside me, offering silent support—and restraint. Jonas, the friend and brother who has been the undeserving and unknowing target of my anger and jealousy. His hand grips my arm, ready to pull me back should I lunge at Hem.

Father, forgive me. Help me.

"Kiah, feel free to return to Elam. It is a changed village under the hand of Calev. Oh, my son-in-law is a young man, but already he is a wealthy man. He owns the shop that Abner used to own; in fact, Calev owns most of the shops along that row."

I don't have to ask *how* he owns them or why Abner was too humiliated to tell me that Calev strong-armed him out of his own business.

"I'm no longer interested in my brother's success or in yours." I turn to leave.

"I hope Yarden doesn't feel the same way. Calev and Eliana are, at this very moment, paying him their respects. I was with them when they stopped by the prophet's gate." Hem clicks his tongue and shakes his head, feigning concern. "Your old grandfather looked stunned to see his Calev. In fact, Yarden didn't appear well when we left him."

Hem swivels toward Jonas. "And *your* father, the younger Nephi, is a foolish man, Jonas. While I was paying my respects to Yarden, I offered your father a generous wage; we could use his cement expertise in completing the ball court project. He declined."

I don't hear Jonas's reply. I don't take the time to say good-bye, not even to Jonas. I don't even glance toward Tarah. I turn and start running through the street, past vendors and women with water vessels balanced atop their heads. I bully my way through the line at the gate, explaining to one of the guards that my grandfather is in jeopardy and I must get to him. When I tell him I'm part of the prophet Nephi's family, he allows me to rush through.

And I rush. I run as hard and as fast as I can all the way back, but when I get there I know I haven't run fast enough. Grandfather is out by the gate, slumped to the ground, clutching his chest.

Sixty-One

"Grandfather, can you breathe?"

He nods, and I wipe the sweat out of his eyes.

"Can you talk? Can you tell me where you hurt?"

He lays a trembling hand over his chest.

Jonas comes running up behind me, and we manage to get Grandfather through the gate and onto a pile of banana leaves. Hagar, one of the household servants, cries out when she sees our efforts.

"His heart!" she wails. "I heard them fighting. I feared this would happen."

I undo the necklace around Grandfather's throat. I try to get him to sip the water that Hagar offers. It only dribbles down his chin, and his eyes roll back.

"What happened?" I demand of Hagar.

"Your brother came by."

"Did he do something to Grandfather?"

Jonas leans over me and speaks in my ear. "Let go of your grandfather's hand, Kiah. You're cutting off his blood flow. You've got to calm down so you can think clearly."

I look up and see only a blurry face. I've never been this angry or afraid. "I'll kill Calev if anything happens to Grandfather."

But Jonas's father returns home, and he and Timothy lay their hands on Grandfather's head. They pronounce a blessing of healing. I have faith that Grandfather will get up and walk right away. That doesn't happen. For days he lies still, moaning, unable to eat and barely able to drink.

The days turn to weeks. I have to fight the urge to go hunt Calev down and pummel him for whatever he did or said to make Grandfather's heart stop. But every time I mean to leave, Grandfather stirs a bit and moans for me to stay.

In time the blessing is fulfilled and Grandfather opens his mouth. "I was a fool to believe the best of him. Calev, my own flesh and blood, has followed in the footsteps of his father. I'm living the nightmare of Gidd all over again."

"I'm here for you, Grandfather. Take another sip of water."

We are in a back room of the house. It reminds me of the time I came to visit when the famine was raging and the prophet himself was near death's door. It's quiet in the room except for birdsong and the croak of frogs that come through the window. Even the sound of children playing is missing—they have gone with the women to the market.

It's hard for Grandfather to draw a full breath, and the pain in his chest beads his forehead with sweat. He mutters and fumbles at even the most basic tasks. Hagar stands ready to help him, but I prefer to help Grandfather.

I send word to Abner that Grandfather has been taken ill. An epistle comes back saying that Elka is sick with rainy season fever; Abner and Mother cannot leave her. They send their prayers and well wishes. I send mine for a sister that I do not know.

I dab a cloth to wipe Grandfather's forehead. Today I wonder if the fever hasn't taken him too because he's repeating the same information over and over.

"Calev is one of Gadianton's own. He told me as much."

"Yes, Grandfather."

"He bragged about being a leader."

"Yes, Grandfather."

"The news stopped my heart."

"I know, but you are getting well now. We pray for your strength every day."

"Calev is a good boy, Kiah, like you."

I say nothing. Somewhere in the distance a *t'uul* screeches. I want to screech.

"Kiah?"

"Yes, Grandfather?"

"Are we alone?"

"Yes. Nephi and Jonas are out working, and the prophet and Lehi have taken the children and their wives in to the city to the market."

"A family day."

"Yes."

"And Timothy, where is he?"

I'm pleased that Grandfather seems more alert than I assumed. "Timothy lives in the city near the temple."

He reaches for my hand and holds it tightly. "Kiah, the Messiah is coming."

"Yes, Grandfather."

"Soon."

"Yes."

"You have always been a faithful son. I pray that you can know your own worth. I pray that you can know what it is to have a real family of your own."

"You are my family, Grandfather."

"And that is why I must tell you something, son, something that Calev told me."

"What is it? What did my brother tell you that you haven't already mentioned?"

He coughs. He lies back. He coughs again and rolls onto his side to ease the pain in his chest. "He told me that he came to warn me."

"Warn you of what?"

"His band, the robbers, they intend to kill this family."

"What?" My own chest tightens.

"I told Nephi. He knows everything."

No wonder Grandfather's heart failed. "Why would Calev tell you such a thing?"

Grandfather squeezes my hand. "Because he is a good boy. He doesn't want to harm you or me."

"You just said he wants to kill the prophet and murder this family."

"No. Not Calev. The robbers."

"But he leads the robbers."

"Your brother is a divided snake."

"Lie back down, Grandfather. You're talking out of your head. It's the fever."

"No! I know what I'm saying. Like the ringed jungle snake, Calev cannot make up his mind. He's part good, like your precious mother. He's part greed and power, like his—like *your*—father."

I'm in shock. "Calev came here to tell you that the Gadianton robbers intend to murder the prophet and his family?"

"Yes!"

"But why?"

"I just told you. Your brother is obsessed with greed and power. Nephi is the great prophet of this land. People look to him for leadership. Calev wants to be that leader."

I'm standing now, shaking as if the ground beneath me is quaking; I'm peering out the small window, not knowing what to do. "How do they intend to do it? When? The prophet is not safe. We must find him. We must protect Nephi and his entire household."

"Only God can truly shield him."

"Then I must find Calev. He has to be stopped."

"No!" Grandfather sits up. His eyes are red and watery. "No! Calev has risked his life to warn us. Nephi is a cautious man. He hires guards. He has been warned. Your brother did that for him."

Grandfather says it like we should be grateful to Calev. Calev—a Gadianton himself. Grandfather is right: My brother is a divided snake.

I'm caught between wanting to stay here alongside Grandfather and rushing out to stand beside Jonas and his family—to protect them with my very life. They mean everything to me.

"Kiah?"

"Yes, Grandfather. I'm here."

"The Messiah is coming."

"Yes, Grandfather."

"What are you doing to prepare yourself?"

I have no quick answer because it's a question I've never asked myself. I get lost in the thought.

The *t'uul* screeches again, and when I look up I see a small river of blood trickling out of Grandfather's nostril. His chest rattles and his eyes close. "Don't leave me," he whispers. "Please don't go."

"I'm right here, Grandfather. I'm won't leave you."

His hand searches for mine. It's warm and damp and surprisingly strong.

"Don't leave me, son."

"I'm right here."

"Son, don't go!"

I think fever is taking over Grandfather's mind, but I'm wrong. It's not me he is begging to stay with him; it's not this moment he is living. His mind has taken him back in time to a night when he begged another son to stay with him. Grandfather grips my hand and pulls me close to him. "You are my only son. I need you; your wife and children need you. Don't go, Gidd."

Sixty-Two

Jonas walks back and forth, pacing like a caged cat.

"You're supposed to be nervous," I say, grinning. "But don't wear yourself out. Save some of your energy for your bridal week."

He cradles his head in his hands and moans. "When should we leave?"

"That's up to your father. It's dark enough, and you know Orli is waiting."

Jonas moans again. He presses his hands against his head and squeezes his eyes closed. "This is worse than torture. Don't do it, Kiah. Don't ever get married."

I laugh, but there's hollowness to the sound. I'd give anything to trade Jonas places, to be the one taking my wife tonight. Thoughts of Tarah fill my head and heart day and night. My fear is that some wealthy father will make arrangements for her before I'm prepared. If Grandfather were healthy he could continue to communicate with Abarron, to let him know how serious my intentions are—not that Abarron doesn't know, because I make them foolishly clear. I pick flowers that I leave wilted at her garden gate. I write notes, grateful she is a girl able to read. I trip over my own tongue every time Tarah asks me how I am doing.

She and her family are part of the bride's wedding party. I'm as excited as Jonas to get the festivities underway. It's been a long time since we've had reason to celebrate. Worry and fear over Calev's warning has cast a shadow, but tonight that shadow is gone and in its place is a torch flickering with joy. Still, there are added guards to the front and in the rear. I carry not one but two blades secured to my thigh.

"Are you sure our wedding chamber is secure?" Jonas asks.

"Yes. As your best man, I assure you that you'll have your seven days of privacy."

"I wish we could come back to the house I built. The walls are covered in cement. What are the walls of the makeshift chamber made from?"

"Prayer shawls."

Another moan sounds from the nervous groom; this time Jonas in holding his stomach. His uncle Timothy slaps him on the back and whispers something in Jonas's ear that makes Jonas blush and moan again.

Lehi puts a lit torch in my hand and gives another to Jonas. Both the prophet Nephi and his son Nephi come around to give Jonas their final words of advice and blessing. The prophet spends a long time in private conversation with Jonas. I step away so they can be alone. When they're finished I try not to let them know that I can see the tears on their cheeks.

As a big family procession, we begin the trek to Orli's home. Everyone seems in a festive mood. Hagar, the prophet's faithful servant, stays behind to tend to Grandfather. An epistle inviting Mother and Abner was sent, but we've received no reply. I hate leaving Grandfather for so many days, but it can't be helped. I am the best man.

A few people along the road shout their congratulations. Some recognize the prophet and want him to stop and bless them or one of their sick children. Word of Nephi's great faith has spread throughout the land, and since Samuel's prophecies, Nephi is sought after more than ever.

I look at every face, wondering which ones belong to Gadianton. My old feelings of fierceness, of wanting to war, come now only when someone I love is threatened. Let one of the robbers come forth; I'll cut off his ear or crush his kneecap.

But there is no confrontation as we wind our way through the city gate and down the paths that lead to Solomon's property. The bride knows that we're coming in tow with Jonas, but she doesn't know the exact time of her groom's arrival. I can picture the excitement of Orli and Tarah and the other bridesmaids, waiting, anticipating.

I give Jonas one final embrace and then raise my voice to lead the shout that tells Orli her time has come and her groom is about to arrive.

One last moan and Jonas goes alone to join his bride and her attendants. Orli is veiled so that we cannot see her face, but we all know who she is and Jonas has no problem recognizing his bride. Any hesitancy he had disappears the moment he takes her hand and looks back at us.

I wait impatiently until the attendants emerge with looks of sheer bliss and approval on their faces. Tarah's hair is braided and wound around her head, set with flower petals. I've never seen anyone so beautiful. When she looks at me our eyes lock and her lips, stained with the same pink petals, curve up into a smile.

One day soon I will be the one entering the bridal chamber to claim her for my wife. I've never wanted anything more.

The wait is long. Every chance I get I glimpse Tarah, who is giddy with the bridesmaids, solemn with her father, attentive to her grandmother.

"Kiah!" Little Joseph runs up to me and jumps into my arms. I hold him like I did on the day he had been separated from his big sister.

"What are they doing in there?" His little finger points to the bridal chamber.

I laugh and hold him tight, and I see Tarah looking over at us, smiling so broad the whole world can see that she feels the same way about me as I do about her.

I've never felt happiness so unbounded.

Father, great God of all the universe, look down on one humble son and grant his heart's desire.

People mill around, some barely whispering, others laughing loudly, as we wait for Jonas to emerge. Finally, with a sheepish grin on his face, he pulls back one of the prayer shawls to let us know that he is now a truly married man.

Cheers go up. I'm supposed to stay with the wedding party as we head back to Nephi's home for the festivities, but I'm worried about Grandfather, so I rush ahead. There is a split second when I realize that tonight would be a perfect night for an ambush from the robbers. But the guards are in place, and there has been no disturbance.

Hagar tells me that Grandfather has eaten well and even taken a walk around the courtyard. I say my thanks and sit by his bedside, listening to his rattled breathing, listening to the shouts and laugher and joy of the wedding festivities.

Tarah is so close and yet so far from me. Suddenly, heaviness comes over me and I realize that I've never felt so alone.

Sixty-Three

My entire life changes once again.

Grandfather gets stronger, though he is far from healthy.

Jonas and Orli are inseparable. The only time I have to spend with Jonas is while we are working. Within the year he announces proudly that he is going to be a father.

The prophet Nephi's wife, Bosma, does not wake up one morning. Her death leaves us all stunned and saddened beyond words. It was her song, her smile, her food, and her kind words that brightened this home.

Nephi—in a state of mourning over his wife's death but more determined than ever to cry repentance and to be a missionary—bids us all good-bye and leaves. I expect him to come back like he always does, only this time there is no return. In his place, his son Nephi becomes the reigning patriarch of the family. He is entrusted with the sacred records and all the precious things that have been kept sacred since Lehi left Jerusalem.

A trio of robbers makes its attack on a moonless night. They kill one of the two guards and make their way into the compound, demanding that Nephi turn over the sword of Laban to them. When he tells them it is not in his possession, but in the temple treasury, they hesitate, giving me the chance to make my move.

I use a sword I crafted from bone and obsidian, and I use Hem's own blade to fight back the robbers. As they flee I see the signal one of them gives to the remaining guard. That's when I realize the guard that has stood at the gate for years has taken the secret oath.

Nephi has him arrested. As the guard is being led to prison he breaks down and confesses that he was bribed and paid by Hem to betray the prophet's household.

I feel little compassion for the man, but Nephi embraces him, declares his forgiveness, and even prays for the man and his family.

Then Nephi turns to me and weeps with gratitude. "Kiah, you were like a cat defending its own." He takes me in his arms and holds me. "You are a son to me as sure as those from my own loins. Tell me, what can I do for you to express proper gratitude?"

"Nothing. You've done everything by giving us refuge and opportunity."

Jonas and Orli step out from the shadows. She is great with child, and they both look shaken. "Father, you can talk to Abarron. Approach him. Kiah wishes to marry his daughter Tarah."

Nephi's eyebrows lift. "Is this true?"

"It is true," I say. "Grandfather would make the arrangements if he were well."

"I'll be honored to talk to Abarron on your behalf, Kiah. You will make a fine husband."

"It's what I want more than anything."

"Then I will see Abarron right away."

I am waiting in the road outside the city gate when Nephi and Jonas emerge. I can tell from the look on their faces that the news is not good.

My heart falls. Who was I to think that a man with so little to offer would ever be acceptable to Abarron?

"He did not say no," Jonas is quick to tell me.

"Did he say yes?" I ask.

"The price he is asking is high."

"How high? I've worked very hard for a long time. I have a dowry to offer."

Nephi scratches his head. "Abarron is being unreasonable."

"No price is too high for Tarah. Tell me. I'll meet it."

"Abarron is asking three times the price that Solomon asked for Orli. It is fixed. Abarron won't be swayed."

Three times? I blink, trying to run the figures through my head.

"I can help you," Nephi says. "I want to help you."

"Thank you, but no. This is something I must do on my own." I realize there is only one way I will be able to meet that price. I start making secret plans of my own.

• • •

Solomon, the teacher at the synagogue, encourages me to become a lawyer. He surprises me by telling me I am one of the most dedicated students he's ever seen study at the school. How can I tell him that though the wage is much less and the prestige incomparable, I much prefer to work outside with Nephi and Jonas, making homes and buildings from cement?

I work hard. I earn fair income, but it will not grow a dowry fast enough to please Abarron. I know what I must do, but I cannot leave until Grandfather is completely well. He misses the prophet Nephi, and the prophet's absence has set Grandfather's recovery back.

I'm grateful Grandfather is not with me the day I am in the city and hear a familiar voice preaching from the same wall where Samuel taught of the Messiah.

"The time is past for Samuel's words to be fulfilled! He was nothing but a foolish Lamanite." Calev, thicker about the middle and broader in the shoulders, stands tall and arrogant. No military captain demands that he get down, and no one throws stones or arrows at my brother as he shouts to an adoring crowd, "Their prophets are fools! They may have guessed some things right among so many, but we know that these great and marvelous works cannot come to pass. We know that it is not reasonable that Christ shall come. And if He is the Son of God, the Father of heaven and of earth, why will He not show Himself unto *us*, but only to them in Jerusalem?"

His words stir the crowd.

"They say that the Messiah will show Himself in the land of Jerusalem. Have you ever seen this far-distant land?"

"No!" the crowd shouts back.

"And you never will, because it is a wicked tradition that has been handed down to us by our fathers, to cause us to believe that a great and marvelous thing should come to pass . . . not among us, but in a land which we know not. They want to keep us in ignorance."

The unrest that was here when Samuel preached led the crowd to want to murder one man. Today Calev agitates them until they are anxious to destroy every believer in the Messiah. I listen to his cunning rhetoric. He is a warrior—a warrior with words, for he twists the truth and sharpens his followers as he would sharpen a blade or an arrow. Then he aims them at the innocent. He accuses men like Grandfather and Nephi, who have devoted their lives to preaching of the goodness and mercy of the Messiah's plan and of the danger of being servants of Satan.

"By the cunning and the mysterious arts of the evil one, they work some great mystery which we cannot understand, which will keep us down to be servants to their words, and also servants unto them, for we depend upon them to teach us the word; and thus will they keep us in ignorance if we will yield ourselves unto them. But we will not yield. We will destroy them before they destroy us!"

It is not only hatred that burns in the eyes of my brother, it is power. This man has a power even greater than Hem to command, to convince, and to lead. Is it any wonder that the devil desired my brother to captain his armies?

"You will destroy your own brother because I believe?"

I shout so loud every head swivels in my direction. A few people scream threats and a man shoves me hard, but I stand firm and hold a smile on my face.

Calev motions for his followers to help hoist him down. I wait until he has received his praise and adoration. Then I walk up to him and ask, "How are you, Calev?"

He looks at me as though a filthy beggar has just soiled his cloak.

"Do you not wish to know the state of Grandfather's health?"

"If he was dead I would have heard."

"Is your heart really that cold?"

He leers at me.

"He's healing. He's healing from the last visit you paid him. What he learned that day nearly broke his heart."

"He's a foolish old man, Kiah. And you too are a fool. But the old man was fine when Eliana and I left him. He was standing by the gate waving to us."

I bite back the words I'd like to say. "Congratulations on fatherhood. I hear you have a son."

The slightest flicker of tenderness shines in Calev's dark eyes. "His name is Zem."

"I would like to meet my nephew."

"Come to Elam. Pay your respects to my wife."

Now I flinch. I want to stop the reaction, but I can't.

Calev laughs, and it's Hem's laughter that comes out of his mouth.

"Are you going to train your son to be a robber like you have become?"

I'm sure Calev will strike me or maybe even raise a blade to me.

"You may be be stronger, even smarter from your schooling, but you have not changed, Kiah. You still think I'm a robber."

"You are not only a robber, my brother, but I believe you *lead* the robbers."

Calev's followers, his guards, step toward me with malice. I think how they used to have to hide in the hills—how many still do—but how our government is so corrupt that robbers live out in the open without fear of punishment because their secret brethren are in the highest positions.

Calev wipes his hands on the sides of his robe. "Aren't you going to ask after our mother? She's just given birth to our baby brother, a boy they call Abby. He has his father's ugly red hair."

"You can change the subject, Calev, but that doesn't change the truth of who you are."

My brother twists a ring around his finger; it is made from the same precious green stone as Abarron's jewels. "It's the same lie you've told for years about Hem. You are jealous of Hem, Kiah, because he always favored me. He has proven a generous father-in-law. Aren't you going to ask after Eliana?"

"She must be a very happy woman," I say, feeling nothing for her. "She finally won the man she always loved."

"She's a miserable wife," he snorts, "always complaining, always doubting me. Does it make you happy to know that my marriage is far from content?"

"No, brother. It does not make me happy."

"Let Eliana be miserable. I am not miserable. I am in a higher position than I ever dared to imagine. Kiah, you are nothing—an apprentice to a cement man. You could join me and oversee the final construction of the ball court in the valley of Sam. It is massive—four times the size of the court in Elam."

"Your power is impressive, my brother. But I am not interested in your kind of power. You use your influence to harden the hearts of the people against all that is good. How can you preach that there will be no Messiah when we both know the time is at hand?"

"Do not tell me what I believe, Kiah. You might be my brother, but you have never known me."

"Do you still have mood changes—days when you can't stop laughing followed by days when you can hardly lift your head to the sunlight? I know you waver between the good of our mother and the evil of our father."

Calev's head jerks back; he spits at my feet. "You know nothing! I ask one final time. Leave your piteous life behind, brother. Join with me. Bring Grandfather and return with me to Elam. You will be grateful that you did."

"Why? You act once again like you have a secret you're withholding."

"The time is short," he says.

"Time for what?"

"Even as we speak Hem is meeting with Lachoneus. There will be an announcement soon enough."

I refuse to play his game. "Good-bye, brother," I say before I turn and walk away.

Sixty-Four

It's a trek I've avoided for years. I never wanted to make it again, yet here I am on the road back to Elam.

For weeks there have been strange lights in the night skies, stars exploding and shooting across the black scroll of night. Some say these are the final signs of Samuel's prophecies. Soon, very soon, timekeepers say, the Messiah will be born.

Believers believe. Unbelievers wait to mock. Lately I've been pondering the question Grandfather asked me: *What am I doing to prepare for the coming of the Messiah?*

Tonight the moon is only a blue hook hanging on a star; it provides very little light as I move down the road toward the site of Hem's infamous ball court. It's been under construction for years, yet it is still not finished. I hear from Abarron that the artisan work is detailed and expensive. Hem allocated a great sum for gems to adorn his platform; I hear it's as ornate as a king's throne. How he ever rose to such power, such prominence, is unclear to me, but even Orli's uncle, the governor, breaks bread with Hem.

An old man is selling roasted meat. Its aroma makes my mouth water—but when I see that the man is selling the flesh of a large *kan*, a jungle snake capable of devouring an entire goat, I shudder and hurry past. Not only is it unclean, but it's likely carrion, something he found already dead. I wonder how our people could separate themselves so far from the command to eat no unclean beast. Are there any laws that are still kept in the land? Sometimes it seems not.

I move faster. The darker it gets the more dangerous it becomes. Robbers think nothing of killing a man for whatever he might carry. I have only my blade, sling, and some arrows. On my return trip I will have to be more careful. I hope to be carrying the treasure I buried so long ago; I hope it is still beneath the rock. Samuel prophesied that a man's treasure would disappear. I pray that is not the case with me. I intend to use it to make up the dowry that Abarron demands. Tarah is worth all that and more.

Even in the dull light I stop to stare when I come to Hem's ball court. I can't see the details, but I can see how truly gigantic it is. It would take a thousand steps to walk from one end of the court to the other. The stone risers around it must seat thousands of spectators. I know Hem has persuaded villages and cities to unite in its construction, promising them revenue, but Hem is the one who will benefit. It will no doubt feed both his pockets and his ego.

I do not go into Elam but skirt around it and move into the hills. There are foot trails where there were no trails before. I suppose they are from the robbers, and I don't let go of my blade, not for a moment. It takes an entire day for me to find the place where I hid the items I took so long ago. That boy who thought he was a man no longer exists; he's been replaced by someone who does not want to hunt animals or fight enemies but to hunt people hungry for the truth and to fight no one. All I want to do is be married and find the peace and joy that Jonas and Orli share as they await the birth of their first child.

When I see the site I feel secure that no one has disturbed it in all these years. There's too much overgrowth, vines thick with age. I'm careful this time. No nests of just-hatched snakes. I cut carefully but fast. The task is much more daunting than I anticipated. By afternoon when gray rain clouds roll in I'm grateful for the reprieve from heat. Though I can see no one around, that does not mean someone can't see me. The hills have eyes.

By nightfall I'm still not through. I wish I had brought a curved blade. I make a bed of leaves and vines and sleep fitfully, questioning every sound I hear. Mountain *chakmools* screech, and I realize how long it's been since I used to track them just for the challenge. I've never had a desire to kill one of the mountain cats, only to be fierce and independent and sleek like they are. It was tracking one of them that led me to discover Hem and his secret, a secret that altered the entire course of my life.

During the night I feel something sting my foot. I slap at the crawling sensation and smash something both wet and crunchy. Some kind of beetle or spider. The pain starts right away, tingling and hot, and I wish it was light so I could see what has pierced me. I shake it off. I've been stung often enough, but this is different. When I try to stand I fall over, as dizzy as if I've been knocked in the head.

My waterskin is almost empty, but I drink freely anyway. I feel sick to my stomach. The only thing I vomit is water because I haven't eaten anything, not even fruit. My head hurts. The stars above me seem to be spinning. I vomit again. And then I begin to shake. I can't stop.

The morning light comes, and I ache in every part of my body. I'm weak and only half remember where I am or why. Then I look at the blood and smashed remains of the spider in my palm and realize I've been stung. I'm thirsty, but when I reach for my waterskin, it's empty. I stand up to refill it, but where is the nearest spring? I can't think. I sit down to clear my head. The trees around me seem to be stirred by a wind, but there is none.

I could cry out for help, but who would hear me and who would come?

Tarah. *Tarah.* I try to imagine her face, how it makes me think of a flower in full bloom. Her hair—how I want to touch it, ring my finger around her curls. How I want to make her my wife.

I feel dizzy and nauseated. Thoughts spin around in my head. I hear thunder in the distance and the screech of night-swooping *sootz*. I know they are filling the sky like stars. I think of Hem and Calev and Eliana. I think I hear a baby cry, and I realize I will die without ever knowing my mother's young children—my own sister and brother. I hear Grandfather call my name. I hear him preach of the Messiah. Oh, I will not live to see the face of the Messiah. I weep and shudder and then shake like I'm cold, but I'm not cold. How can I be cold? The sun is climbing high and beating down with a scorching fist.

Treasure. My fingers clench and open, clench again. I think of treasure and a box filled with jewels and art. My treasure! The sun is blotted out, and I lurch over and fall face-first into my own vomit.

Sixty-Five

"Kiah? Kiah?"

The voice is familiar, but I cannot place it.

I try to open my eyes, but it feels as though someone has put rocks on my lids. I see nothing but darkness.

"Kiah, it's Merari. What has happened to you? Have you been attacked by robbers?"

Merari? Merari the hunter? I am in Elam?

"Kiah, I found you groaning here, writhing like an animal with an arrow deep in its belly. What has happened to you, my friend, and why are you here—now?"

I try to sit up, to sip the water he holds to my lips. My leg is on fire.

"This is not a safe place nor a safe time, my friend. Why are you here? Kiah? Kiah, can you hear me? Stay with me, son. Kiah!"

Eventually I open my eyes and focus on his face. It is my mentor, Merari. "Tell the story of how Moses parted the great Red Sea. No one can make the scriptures live like you can."

"You are out of your head."

"Spider," I say, remembering. I hold up my palm to show him the smashed remains, but my palm is clean. I hold up my other one. It's bloody and smeared. Then I try to hold up my foot to show him where I was stung, but my foot feels weighed down with scorching sand and I can't lift it.

"Does your mother know you are here?"

"My mother? Am I a boy?"

"Calm down, Kiah. I'll make a frame and drag you down the mountain."

"I can walk," I say, slurring my words, falling again while his one face blurs and turns into two.

• • •

I wake up on a cot not recognizing anything but pain.

"Kiah."

I know her voice.

"Mother."

"I'm here, son."

For days I hear her voice, her songs. I hear a baby cry. I hear my mother cry. I hear Abner. He's crying too, though his voice sounds distant and thin.

"The time has passed, Anat. Even Raz says it has been longer than five years since Samuel made his prophecies."

"What does that mean?" Mother asks her husband.

"It means that we are fools for believing. Hem and Calev are right. There will be no Messiah."

"No!" I roll over and fall off the cot and onto the hard floor. "There *is* a Messiah. He *will* come."

"Kiah! Kiah! Son, you're awake."

It takes two more days for the spider venom to pass through my body. Even then I am weak and sore in every muscle. I am fearful for my treasure. I pray that it is still safe.

Mother hands me a bowl of boiled roots and milk. A poultice of leaves rests heavily over the spider bite. Abner sits beside me, turning over leaves of the poultice used to draw out the poison.

"Thank you," I say through a mouth dry as famine dirt.

"Sip your gruel," Mother says, tipping the bowl to my lips.

"If Merari hadn't happened upon you, you'd be dead," Abner says. "Did he tell you how he came upon you?"

"How?" I'm thinking of my treasure. Surely, he had to have wondered what I was after and why.

"He said you were hacking away at a wall of vines, digging in the dirt. He said that you were crazy with the poison."

"Where is Merari?"

"He's gone to Bountiful. He thinks his family will be safer there."

"Safer?"

"Oh, Kiah, I do not wish to agitate you, but Elam and every village around has been overtaken by the robbers."

"You mean by Hem and Calev."

"Everyone with a head knows Hem conspires with the robbers, but there is no proof. With Calev, is it the very same. They function in society like they are normal family men who have simply lost their faith. They denounce the robbers, but no one believes them."

My head is clearing slightly. "Did I hear you tell Mother that there will be no Messiah?"

Abner looks wounded. "I am much older than you, and yet all of my life I've heard that the Messiah is coming soon. *Soon* has come and gone. I'm afraid my own faith is dwindling."

"And Mother?"

"She's torn, Kiah. Do not add to her worries."

Mother comes in with a baby in her arms and a little girl clinging to her skirts.

"I hope you feel well enough to meet your brother and sister."

My mind is on my treasure. I have to go retrieve it before someone discovers my disturbed hiding place. It's foremost in my mind.

I never thought of Abner and Mother's children as family—until I hold them in my arms. Abby—a miracle, born to my mother long after a birth could have been expected—is a ball of love, constantly touching my face and giggling. Elka sings like our mother. With Abby on one knee and Elka on the other I soon forget my own worries and the fear of losing my treasure.

For a moment I feel like a rich man must feel.

Sixty-Six

I first hear the news from Oshra.

"Forty days!" she screeches, wailing at our gate. "Forty days to live!"

My eyes squint. "What are you saying, Oshra?" I ignore any proper greeting due her. She's alone, no sisters or friends with her. And since becoming a widow she is more hunched over and withered than ever.

"Is that you, Kiah? You are a man now! Have you returned to save your mother?"

"Save her from what?"

She points to Abby, who is in a sling on my back. "Our children! Our children are going to die."

"Whose children?" I'd forgotten that Oshra has children, but she does; they are as old as Mother. "No one is going to hurt the children," I say.

"You're wrong. They are going to kill us!"

Abner isn't home. Mother is inside with Elka. I hope my little sister can't hear what Oshra is spouting like a mad woman.

"The only way to live is to deny Him. I deny Him! I don't believe anymore."

"Deny who?"

"The Messiah. The stories of Him are only stories. He will not come to save us. He did not save my Gomer."

I want to lay my hands on her shoulders and shake her back to her senses. "Oshra, you must be quiet. Are you sick?"

She grips the top of our wall, and her long, withered fingers look like the very vines she grips. Her voice slides down and her eyes are glazed. "Kiah! You have not heard. The governor, Lachoneus, just announced in an epistle that is being read throughout the land: If the signs that the Lamanite predicted do not come to pass"—she puts the back of her hand to her forehead and wails like she's in a funeral procession—"every believer in the land will be burned!"

I reach around and pull Abby from the sling. I hold him tight against my heart. I approach the fence and tell the village gossip, "You've spread enough rumors in your lifetime to fill the world with bad news, but this is unforgivable, Oshra. You should feel shame."

She slaps both of her wrinkled cheeks with wrinkled hands. Her tongue flicks out like a snake; it is lumpy and gray. "This tongue speaks the terrible truth." Then she narrows her eyes and juts her head toward me like a lizard. "You are a believer, Kiah, and you are marked for death; so is your mother and that child in your arms. Death will surely come to prove that the traditions of our fathers are foolish."

"Foolish? You are a believer, Oshra. You've always been a believer."

"No longer. I don't wish to burn alive. No Lamanite can predict what will happen tomorrow or anytime in the future. You are a fool, and so is your family, and you will all burn."

Oshra turns to shuffle down the road, spreading the word.

The word cannot be true. My mind won't let it be true.

"What's wrong?" Mother asks when I hand Abby to her.

"I'm going to go find Abner."

"What's wrong, son? Something's happened. I can see it in your face. Are you ill again?"

"No. It was Oshra. She came by."

"I thought I heard her voice. I'm sorry," she says like the very presence of Oshra is enough to make me ill. "Go to Abner; take him some bread for his midday meal, will you?"

I take the bread and run as fast as I can through the village that no longer looks the same. Homes have been burned and left as charred reminders, like bones sticking up from a graveyard. Faces are long and frightened. Businesses are closed.

"Have you heard the news?" I ask one man who seems familiar but does not recognize me.

"News?"

I breathe relief. If a proclamation had come from Lachoneus, surely everyone would know. People wouldn't be going on about their day-to-day chores.

Abner is working in his shop. His face and hands are covered in rock dust. He looks up and tries to smile.

I set the bread down and tell him of the rumored proclamation.

Twin rivers of tears down cut through the dust on his cheeks. "I've heard rumors, but I prayed it would never come to this." His hands shake.

"Then it's true?"

"I fear it is."

"I must return to Zarahemla immediately. I've got to talk to Nephi, Jonas's father; he's the new prophet since his father left. He can stop this."

Abner looks at me with red-rimmed eyes. "Of course Nephi can stop it. He can call down God's power. Oh, Kiah, how grateful I am for your faith. I'm afraid my own has dwindled."

"Come with me. You, Mother, and the children. Come with me to Zarahemla. I know that Nephi's family will make you welcome."

"I cannot go, Kiah. My work is here."

"I heard that Calev now runs this row—your business, too."

"He permits me to earn a living. It's better than most."

It strikes me how my brother, in the shadow of Hem, has stolen his power from the weak. Soon I will deal with Calev, but right now I want to be on the road back to Zarahemla before the rumor rages throughout the land.

It's too late. A man peers through the doorway with wide, terrified eyes. "Abner, the unbelievers are setting aside a day to kill us all."

"I've heard," Abner says, "but my son is going to talk to the new prophet, Nephi—he will stop it."

"No. Even God can't stop this horror." The man moves on to the next shop, calling out the bad news.

"Kiah, do you truly believe that what the Lamanite predicted will come to pass? In your heart, do you waver at all?"

"You've seen the night skies. You know that there are miracles—infirm people healed, revelations, angels, answered prayers. You, who had no family, now have a devoted wife and two children. If that's not miracle enough to make you believe, Abner, what is?"

"The darkless night—you believe it will happen?"

"I believe. No matter the cost, I believe. Please," I say again, "come with me to the city. I know a man there, Abarron, who could help find work for you."

"Not now, Kiah. I'll lose everything I've worked for. I still have family here in Elam. I cannot leave."

"All right, but I must not waste a moment. I'll be on my way."

"Wait." Abner motions for me to follow him around the back of his shop where he has stacks of different types of rock. He looks around to be certain no one is watching, and then he uses a pole as a lever to lift a huge boulder. Beneath it is a woven bag I hardly recognize. "Merari told me to be certain to give this to you."

I thank him and bid him good-bye without opening the bag. He's already looked at it, I'm sure, but when I am alone down the road, I look. It's all there.

My treasure. The woven bag is eaten away, but the box Grandfather helped me make has survived. In front of Abner I act like he has handed me something of little significance, but when I am alone I see that there are still four small jewels, a man's ring, a carved stone calendar, a war mask, and the idol, carved in the likeness of a serpent.

It is enough to make a dowry acceptable to Abarron.

I bid good-bye to Elka and Abby, to Mother and Abner. I thank them. I wish Merari was here so I could thank him. Then on legs still wobbly from being poisoned, I take to the road I pray will lead to salvation.

Sixty-Seven

One look at the new prophet's face and my heart falls.

"He's been like this since he heard the proclamation," Jonas says. "I know he misses Grandfather, and I know he feels the weight of being prophet, but I've never seen my father so distraught."

"How's Orli?"

"Oh, I miss her. She's staying in the city with her family. We decided it's safer for her there. The baby is due any time." His head hangs like a broken stick.

I think of Tarah and her family. "Are they all together, the families?"

"Yes. They are in Lachoneus's compound. It's probably the safest place in the city, but even the governor with all of his power can't stop them."

"Who?"

"The times of famine were bad, Kiah, but now they want to kill us *all*."

"Who is behind this? Who wields so much power that every believer is in jeopardy?"

"Hem for one. My father thinks Hem is the voice for all of the Gadianton bands. He thinks that's why Lachoneus has kept him close all these years."

"Hem? Hem has power only in Elam—maybe in the surrounding villages, but Hem has no power in Zarahemla."

"But he does. And Calev. No one is sure of his exact position, but Father says Calev is very popular. His reputation is known all the way to Bountiful."

"So if Hem and Calev were dead—"

"What are you saying, Kiah? Don't think such thoughts."

I press my lips together. Jonas does not want to hear them, but that doesn't stop my thoughts.

Jonas shakes my shoulders. "Friend, if we are true believers, then we cannot allow anything but faith to rule our decisions. Do you understand?"

"I understand this proclamation must be stopped. Innocent people cannot die just because they believe in the coming Messiah."

"Abinadi."

It's all Jonas says, but it is enough.

"Is there any way the timekeepers could be wrong? Maybe it hasn't yet been the five full years since Samuel made his prophecy."

"You're a timekeeper yourself, Kiah; you know the time for the sign is past."

That night Nephi gathers his family out in the courtyard. It's a large group now, with all of his children, their husbands and wives, and grandchildren. Jonas sits alone, like a solitary tree in a forest. He doesn't look right without Orli beside him.

I sit on the ground next to Grandfather, feeling grateful and humble to still be included in such a righteous clan. I want to protect them, every one of them, at any cost. I want to protect Tarah, but I don't know what I can do. I pray she's safe and knows in her heart that my thoughts are with her.

In the flickering light of a huge fire, Nephi begins by bearing pure testimony that Jesus is the Christ and the words of Samuel will be fulfilled. A warmth, as sure as the one emanating from the fire, burns in my chest. I believe him.

He then asks Jonas to tell us about Nehor. Jonas teaches us that Nehor was once a Nephite who knew the law so well he could twist it to threaten the freedom of the people. "He taught that priests and teachers should be paid and should be esteemed above the rest of the people. Nehor also taught that salvation would come to all people, not just those who kept the commandments. And he promised the people that there was no need for repentance. It was under Nehor's influence that those who believed and belonged to the Church of God were allowed to be persecuted."

"Kiah," Nephi says, "now teach us of Zeezrom and the work of Alma and Amulek."

I rise. My tongue loosens as I look into the faces of innocent, believing children, boys and girls who have been taught of the Messiah, who have seen His commandments lived by parents and grandparents. To think that in a matter of days they will die—that my baby brother and sister will die— is almost more than I can bear. Then I see Grandfather's face; his lips are moving and I realize he is praying for me. I want to do for these children what Merari did for me: make the scriptures real and powerful.

I do my best to teach them that the teachings of Nehor did not die with him, but lived on—how a lawyer named Zeezrom argued those same evil teachings with the great prophet Alma and his missionary companion, Amulek. I try to explain to the children that their grandfather, Nephi, is doing in Zarahemla exactly what Alma was doing in Ammonihah—preaching repentance to a people who hate him for it.

"Did any believe?" asks Sariah, Nephi's youngest granddaughter.

"A few repented," I say, hating where the story leads. I try to be gentle yet truthful as I describe how Alma and Amulek were captured and bound and brought before a man who held the judgment seat years before Lachoneus. As I tell how lying people witnessed against them, I can picture in my mind how Hem was brought before the judgment seat in Elam, how he lied his way out—how people like Hem and Calev and their followers will lie about Nephi and those who believe in the words of Samuel. How I will surely one day stand to be judged and how my own brother's tongue can condemn me. It all makes horrific sense to me, and I suddenly realize why Nephi asked me to recount this incident.

"Zeezrom realized he had been deceived. He had been wicked. He repented and tried to make things right, but the people would not hear it. They accused Zeezrom of the same thing they accused Samuel of—being possessed by a devil. All who believed were cast out and stoned—and then their wives and children too." I look into the trusting, innocent faces of Nephi's family, especially the women and children, and I know the fate that awaits them. I know the wives and children of the believers were cast into a fire a hundred times larger than the one that burns to keep us warm. It burned to consume those innocent people and to destroy the records that contained the holy scriptures.

I feel the pain Amulek must have felt when he witnessed those women and children screaming and dying as they burned to death. How he begged Alma to stretch forth his hand and to use the power God had given them to save the innocents.

Nephi rises and wipes the tears off my cheeks.

He then bears witness that those innocent women and children were allowed to die so the judgment against their killers would be just—the "blood of the innocent shall stand as a witness against them."

I sit down. Nephi goes on to preach the story of how Alma and Amulek stood faithful against the persecution from the judge who was after the order of Nehor, how they went on to do great missionary work. I am lost in thoughts of my own.

No matter what I have to do, I will do all I can in the days that we have left to save these children from such a fate.

I watch a leaf burn and float, turning to ash.

As it turns out, we don't even have forty days.

After we all go to sleep, there is a terrible ruckus at the gate. Two of Nephi's guards are killed. The mob comes to bind us and take us to a place where the believers are to be burned.

"Where are you taking us?" I scream.

One of the soldiers laughs. He seems familiar, and I recognize him—he is the guard who betrayed Nephi. He's supposed to be in jail, but now he's here, writhing with vengeance. "You know Hem," he says to me.

"I know Hem."

"We are taking you to his new ball court. That is the appointed place where fools like you will meet their final death."

Sixty-Eight

Like a caged beast, I do not go quietly. When I see the soldiers lay hands on Grandfather, when I hear him wince, I lunge at them; they have to beat me back. They use their clubs to crack my ribs and pound my head until I am blinded by my own blood. They rip my clothes and rob me of the blades I keep sheathed to my thigh.

They take Hem's blade.

What does it matter now?

A foot stomps my back and kicks the air out of my lungs. I choke on dirt. My hands are bound, and I'm pushed and dragged out through the gate onto the main highway to join hordes of beaten and frightened believers. They, like us, seem to have been ambushed in the night—taken from their homes, beaten and bound. I hear children crying and women wailing. I hear some men threaten, some bribe, and others pray.

Finally, I recognize a voice I know. A body is shoved next to me; our shoulders collide in the darkness.

"Kiah?"

"Yes," I say to Nephi, "it's me."

"Do not lose faith now," he admonishes me. "Pray and expect your prayer to be answered."

"Is Grandfather all right? I don't know where he is. I haven't stopped praying for him."

"I wish I could tell you. Everything happened so fast. I don't know where anyone else is."

"Are you all right? You sound like you've taken a beating."

"As have you, Kiah. Are you injured?"

"I'll be all right. Please, you're the prophet. Make them release us."

"I have only the power God gives me."

My head throbs and my cheek stings. When I touch my teeth with my tongue I feel at least one of them has been chipped.

"Devora!" Nephi calls out as a woman screams through the darkness.

A torch is whipped so close to our faces that I feel the heat burn my cheeks. From the light I see that we are many. Besides Nephi's family, other believers have been dragged into the courtyard, adding to the bound, beaten believers.

A soldier kneels before us. "Did I hear you say that you are the prophet? You are Nephi, the son of Nephi?"

Nephi's voice is choked with emotion. His wife is still screaming. "I am who you say I am."

The soldier calls for reinforcements. Men rush forward, eager to single Nephi out, to drag him into the middle of the road, to mock him, to laugh and spit and scorn.

"Leave him be!" I shout. "Nephi is a prophet of God. Take me if someone must be punished."

Two of the soldiers turn on me. They kick and spit and mock.

"Do what you will to me, but leave the prophet alone, I beg."

"You beg? You beg *us*? You should be begging your *Messiah* for the signs of Samuel to be fulfilled."

"They will be fulfilled," Nephi shouts for all to hear. "Do not lose faith now! Hold your heads high and look to God for deliverance."

The soldiers only mock louder.

In the flicker of their roving torchlights I search the human piles for any sign of Grandfather, of Jonas, or of anyone else from Nephi's family. I recognize no one.

I smell the foul scent of human waste. I hear the pitiful cries of children, torn from the arms of their mothers; I hear the mothers being dragged away. Though I can no longer hear Devora, I hear other women scream in the darkness while the soldiers laugh.

"We have a right to a trial," Nephi tells one of the captains.

He laughs. "Oh, you will be brought before a judge. You will face your accusers." Then the captain raises his club and hits Nephi so hard I think I hear his bones cracking.

My hands are still tied, but I crawl out to the road to fight with my last bit of fervor. Then the same captain raises his club, brings it down, and the wailing in my head goes silent.

Sixty-Nine

Evil, when aware of its own power, spreads like disease, blackening and rotting, gnawing until it kills. I wake to see death all around me. A scorching sun beats down, and it hurts to breathe, to blink, to form a clear thought. My throat is so dry it feels like I've gulped a mouthful of dirt. I have a faint recollection of being jerked around by the heels and being dragged; I must have bit my tongue when they were dragging me because my tongue is swollen and sore.

I'm at Hem's prized ball court with thousands of others. None of us is a spectator, and this is no game.

I try to blink away the pain that pounds like the drums in my head. Grandfather—where is he?

"You took my grandfather. I must find him!" I tell a guard who passes by.

He ignores me.

I try to move, but they've bound my hands behind my back. I cannot feel my fingers. They've bound my feet so that I cannot stand and run away. My feet feel like swollen stumps. "Grandfather!" I shout. "Grandfather!"

"Stop, please," a man next to me, old and bald and stripped of even his cloak, begs. "If you shout they will beat us."

"They took my grandfather. I have to find him. He's not well."

"Please, stay still. They've probably put a blade through his heart already."

My own heart is pierced. "Don't say such things."

"They're true. I've seen them break necks, stab people, beat the aged like me. While you were unconscious a gang of those demons stole the virtue from a girl who could not have been even marrying age. They are all Hem's devils."

"Hem? You know Hem?"

"Yes," he tells me, "I know Hem. This is his doing. All of it."

"He's just a merchant from Elam. He has no power."

"You are wrong. He has power. He's not the ultimate authority, but he is the puppet the real cowards use. Hem's is the voice that brought about this tragedy, telling the judges that we believers must be stopped because our beliefs cause contention and threaten the peace of the land."

"So the decision came before the courts?"

"Yes. But who are the judges now? Robbers and murderers."

The man is only thin bones and leathered skin. He sits on his hip, adjusts himself to conceal his nakedness.

"I am Kiah, grandson of Yarden."

"I am Zoram, son of Zoram. I come from the mountain lands of Nephi. I have family in Calno and I know this area. Yarden, the priest of Elam—is he the grandfather you seek?" He waves his hands in the air, and I realize that he is so weak the guards did not bother binding him.

"Yes. Please, when no eyes are upon us, can you help loosen my bands so I might go find my grandfather?"

"I will help you."

The man wriggles, a little at a time, until he is behind me and able to work to unknot the bands that bind my hands. All the time I feel like I am in hell. The screams. The torture. The fear that we are all going to die. In the hours that pass while Zoram is trying to untie me, I see one man kicked in the head until he lies still, all because he begged water from a guard so that he might wet the mouth of his daughter. I hear people all around me denounce the Messiah, claim they are not believers—and when they do, the guards are obliged to release them. They run only to be tracked down and beaten.

It's a sport for these demons.

Zoram is weak and very frightened. The favor he is doing for me could well cost him his life.

When I acknowledge such, he sighs, "What does it matter? We are all going to die soon anyway."

His fingers are stiff and twisted. It takes much effort for him to get the bands around my wrists loose. He finally falls asleep from the effort. While he sleeps I finish wriggling my hands free. Zoram has keeled over and is snoring when I take my leave, making certain that the guards do not see me, begging with my eyes to implore other prisoners not to report my escape.

By the time the sun comes up I am searching among the captives, avoiding the guards, desperate to find Grandfather. I move carefully, falling to the ground and pretending to be securely bound whenever a guard walks past, then getting up and moving a bit at a time.

Only once does someone try to give me away in exchange for favor.

The guard clubs the man in the head.

The entire day passes. That night we are spared a little water, a precious little—only enough to wet my tongue. I drink with my hands behind my back, pretending they are still tied. I bow my head in gratitude, and the guard moves on.

During the night I hear a man begin to wail. I recognize his cry.

"Jonas?" I whisper through the dark. My voice is dry and craggy, but I manage again. "Jonas?" There are torches set up along the way so that no captive can escape without being seen. In that faint light I see my brother, my closest friend, rocking on his haunches, weeping like his heart has been ripped out.

"Jonas. It's me, Kiah. What is wrong?"

He casts his face upward, and I can see that he's been beaten. His face is a swollen mass, bruised beyond recognition. His hand is crushed and he cannot move his leg. He smells of urine and blood.

"Jonas, it's me. I'm here." I try to take him in my arms, but he only rocks back and forth, back and forth, weeping. Sometimes he screams like he is being stabbed.

"Jonas? It's me, Kiah. I'm here for you, brother."

The man seated on the ground across from him says, "They killed his wife. Ran a sword through her belly."

My hand goes over my own stomach. "No! She was about to have a baby."

Jonas wails and rocks faster like he is trying to move away from the pain.

I've never witnessed such suffering. I've never imagined anything so horrible.

"How do you know this?" I ask, begging God that the man is mistaken.

"I heard the soldiers tell your brother. They killed his wife because her father was an important scribe, a teacher in the city synagogue. He rebelled ,and they killed his entire family."

My knees give way. My already broken body breaks again as I hit the hard ground. All I can think about is Tarah.

What they don't realize is they have murdered the sister of Lachoneus and her family. What they don't realize is that they have murdered the innocent, believing children of God.

On the third day—or is it the fourth?—we are fed mashed corn and given water.

I have not left Jonas, not even resumed my search for Grandfather. I fear Jonas will die of his broken heart. I think he wants to die.

"Denounce your faith. Join the unbelievers and I will set you free," a guard tells Jonas.

I look up and see a burly man with a necklace I've seen before.

"Shelomoh? Is that you?"

"I am Shelomoh. Who are you?"

"I am Kiah. I was on the trickball team in Elam. You were our trainer."

He squats down and I can smell his foul odor. He's so close that I can see the hair on his legs. "Kiah. Yes, I recall you. Tell your brother I will release you both if you will give up your foolish pride and deny your Messiah."

"No."

We both look over at Jonas. He's too weak and broken to sit up but not too weak and broken to defend Christ. "Kill us all, but I will never deny what I know is true."

"What is true is that you are both fools."

Shelomoh walks on.

I take Jonas in my arms and let him cry until he falls asleep. There are no words to comfort him. No words to ease my fears about Tarah.

And still we wait, not knowing if we will see the Messiah in this life or in the next.

The next morning—or is it the next day?—Shelomoh brings us a small amount of food. Jonas refuses to eat, but the food gives me enough energy to stand and walk around. I can't convince Jonas to join me.

"I must look for Grandfather and the rest of your family."

He stares at me with eyes that do not blink.

A voice sounds, magnified by a large seashell. It carries across the ball court. All eyes look up toward the platform.

Hem is standing on the platform, high above the bleachers. Standing beside him is my brother, robed in red and carrying a sword I recognize. How did he get it back from Grandfather?

Our eyes meet and hold. I hate him. No. I cannot hate. The power is no longer in me. I pity my brother, for he looks weak and sorry. Can he see from his pedestal the innocent people he is about to put to death? From the ground I cannot see Grandfather or Mother or Abner or their children, but I suppose Calev can.

Hem talks on, but I only hear what he says: "This is Raz, Elam's timekeeper. He has an important announcement to make."

Hands push what is left of the man who taught me how to record time, how to draw, and how to read the scriptures.

His voice is that of a child, fearful and apologetic, as he speaks into the shell so everyone can hear. "As timekeeper of Elam, I announce this day that the appointed time has passed. The words of the Lamanite Samuel have not been fulfilled."

He steps back, and Calev has to catch him to keep the little man from collapsing.

The air thickens with sorrow and suffering and sours with the scent of fear.

I cannot help but hear the voices that cry out, "Free me. I no longer believe in Jesus Christ. Set my family free!"

Other voices—fewer, softer—cry, "He will come. The Messiah will come."

I cannot take my eyes off Calev. We are a sea of believers; there must be tens of thousands of us spread over the ball court and the lands around it. We are bound and beaten and terrified by guards given permission to freely kill. Is Calev willing to see us all die for believing something I know that he too believes, even if that faith has smoldered for so long in the darkest corners of his heart?

Soldiers strut around. I recognize some from the days when I helped train fighters for Uriel's army. This was our training ground. This was Hem's great design. Now it will be our burial place.

No. The Messiah will come to deliver us.

But when? Before we die? After we're dead? Does it matter? He will come!

I move from pack to pack, still hoping to locate Grandfather. I see the twin brothers, Mathoni and Mathonihah, still together—still faithful, for even at death's door, they preach in tandem. I assume the women and children that surround them are their wives and children and I am sorry for their suffering. I stop to listen to the brothers promise that the Jesus Christ is the Son of God and we are all family. He will surely come in the appointed hour.

One of the guards clubs Mathonihah in the back.

Mathoni keeps preaching.

I look for any sign of those I love. I expect to see Abner's tall red head, but I do not. What fate has he met? And what of Mother? Is Calev really so hard-hearted that he will let her burn to death while clutching her two babies?

I make my way toward the platform. Because I spent so much time here I know there is a secret set of stairs beneath the bleachers that lead to the platform where my brother still stands overlooking his domain. I am almost caught, but every time a guard eyes me with suspicion, something happens to distract him and I move on.

If I can reach Calev, if I can talk to him away from Hem, maybe I can touch his heart. No, maybe the Spirit through me can touch his heart. I can do nothing to reach my brother, but God can—and maybe Calev can persuade Hem that what he is about to do amounts to the mass murder of innocent believers.

I almost make it.

"Where are you going?" a guard demands, holding a blade to my throat.

"Hem's son-in-law, Calev, is my brother. I am going to speak with him."

"You are with Hem?"

"He is with *me*."

The guard removes the blade, and I turn to see Eliana. Her eyes are wide with terror, and a young boy is clutching her hand. Zem has his father's curly hair and square chin.

He looks almost as afraid as his mother.

"It's all right," Eliana assures the guard loudly enough so the other guards and soldiers hear. "This man is my brother-in-law."

Seventy

There is no private place to talk. But so much chaos is going on around us, no one pays particular attention to us.

"Have you seen Grandfather? My mother?"

"I have not seen your grandfather," she says, "but your mother and the children are safe."

My brow furrows.

"What about Nephi's family? Where are they?"

"I don't know."

"Where is Mother?"

"Safe." Her eyes tell me to ask no more.

Has this much time gone by? Her son, Zem, looks at me with trust and weariness. His eyelids droop like his father's do, but he has the brilliance of his mother's eyes. He's only as tall as my waist, but he looks confident and strong for a child so young. "We're not supposed to be here. Father told Mother not to come, but she said we had to come."

I kneel down so that I'm eye to eye with Zem. "Are you afraid?"

"Everyone is angry. People are crying. Mother cries a lot."

The little boy moves away from Eliana and slips his hand into mine. I feel an immediate love for him the way I did when I first held Abby and Elka. Knowing they are safe allows my heart to beat again.

I still have to find Grandfather, and I have to know that Tarah is safe. Every time I think of her my throat closes.

"Calev is not evil. No matter what you think, Kiah, your brother never wanted this."

I have to bite my tongue to keep from snapping at her. Eliana looks old and tired; fear has darkened her eyes and lined her face. Zem tugs at my hand.

"Hold me."

I lift him into my arms, and the boy rests his head on my shoulder. "You look like my father," he whispers.

"I am your uncle," I say.

"Will you take us to Father? He is up high with *Sawa*." Zem uses the term our first fathers used for "grandfather."

"I have to talk to Calev, Eliana."

"You can't stop what is going to happen. Calev has no real power."

"I thought he was in command."

"He's not."

"Is your father?"

She makes a pained face. "I can't say."

"Please, send word to my brother. Allow me to speak to him."

It's too late.

Hem himself takes the shell and steps up to the platform. Next to him, his wrists bound, stands the prophet Nephi. Indescribable sorrow washes over his face. Does he know about Orli and the baby?

Hem clears his throat; the entire ball court goes quiet—even the babies stop crying. "I am Hem, appointed leader of this ball court. I stand before you to ask you: What can this man, Nephi—who claims to speak for God—say now that the time has passed and the Lamanite's prophecy has gone unfulfilled?"

The unbelievers scoff and mock.

The believers weep. I see tears fall from Eliana's cheeks and drip down onto her shaking shoulders.

"Speak, prophet! Add to the foolish traditions of your fathers. Confess your sins before us—how you have misled this people into believing that a Messiah will come to deliver them. That the very Son of God will come in a tabernacle of flesh. What a boldfaced lie!"

Nephi says nothing.

"Deny your god, and I will grant this people freedom. Continue to claim faith in the Messiah, and with your claim you will order every believer in the land executed! I will spare no woman. No child. Do you understand?"

Still not a word escapes Nephi's lips. Not a single word. He bows his head. Hem taunts him, saying that Nephi bows his head because he is shamed. I know better. Nephi is praying.

Hem is outraged.

Zem is heavy in my arms. The boy has fallen asleep with his little arms tight around my neck.

Calev leads Nephi down from the platform, out onto the flat field where people part to make room for him. Nephi completely ignores the praise that some shout at him just as he ignores the insults. In the center of the crowd he bows himself down and begins to pray.

"It is too late," Eliana sobs. "It is too late. Even if the Messiah came this very moment it would be too late for Orli and her baby."

"You know about Orli?"

She sobs.

"Pray all you want, prophet!" Hem shouts from his platform. "You are all going to die. At the going down of this day's sun you will all die unless you deny your foolish faith in a Messiah that is nothing more than an evil tradition passed down from our fathers to deceive us, to take away our freedoms by binding us with commandments that are tighter than chains."

Unbelievers cheer their support. They are four times our number. They are well fed, they have plenty of water, they have an assurance that they are right. And they are vicious, like wild beasts ready to tear their prey apart. Men are hauling forth great loads of timber, piling the wood high in stacks below the platform so that Hem might have an undisturbed view of the torture. I think of Abinadi. I think of Alma and Amulon and all of the innocent people God has allowed to die so that justice might be served and mercy might be plentiful for those who suffer.

Nephi keeps praying.

A man comes toward us, and I think I know him.

"Uncle Timothy?"

"Kiah! Are you all right?"

"Why aren't you bound?" I ask.

"I've been in Moriantum. I only now arrived here. No one has asked if I am a believer."

"It's because you look healthy and clean. They assume you are one of them." He looks sad but confident. "You know we're all going to die."

"Oh, Kiah. We *are* all going to die sometime, but not this night. Look at my brother. See his face?"

Timothy parts the crowd so that Eliana and I can see Nephi more clearly. He is still kneeling on the ground, but his face is turned upward; it shines like the sun is pointed directly at him.

"The Lord has answered!" Nephi shouts. The crowd goes still. Hem stops his murmuring.

Nephi does not need the shell to be heard. The Spirit amplifies his message. "The voice of the Lord has come to me saying, Lift up your head and be of good cheer; for behold, the time is at hand, and on this night shall the sign be given, and on the morrow come I into the world, to show unto the world that I will fulfill all that which I have caused to be spoken by the mouth of my holy prophets. Behold, I come unto my own, to fulfill all things which I have made known unto the children of men from the foundation of the world. . . . behold, the time is at hand, and *this* night shall the sign be given."

Eliana stands beside me, her son in my arms. I can't tell if the tears she is shedding are of fear or faith.

This night, I think, trying to make the prophet's message real.

Hem looks down from his platform and scoffs. He lifts the shell and shouts across the great crowd. "This night you fools will all burn—first here and then in hell!"

Seventy-One

We wait.

Nephi's family members are rounded up and brought to join him. I am not included, so I remain with Eliana and Zem. The little boy wakes up, looks at me, calls me uncle, kisses my cheek, and falls back asleep.

Calev remains on the platform with Hem. If my brother has seen me below him with his wife and son, he's made no show of opposition.

I cannot hear the words spoken between Jonas and his father, but when they see each other they fall into an embrace. I feel their love and sorrow clear across the court.

We wait.

People pray.

People sing.

I wonder what Tarah is doing. Is she safe? Is she mourning the loss of her cousins and aunt and uncle? Is Lachoneus himself safe? I do not want to die. No part of me wants to give up my life, but I am willing to, for I will never deny what I know. Jesus Christ lives. He will be born into this life and will be clad with a tabernacle of clay just like ours.

"Are you still my uncle?" Zem's little voice asks.

I shift his weight from one arm to the other. "Yes, I will always be your uncle." He nestles back down and sleeps.

I feel that eyes are watching me, and when I look around I see Marpe, Elam's chief judge, standing by the bleachers, watching me and Eliana. He ascends the stairs to the platform, and it's not long before Calev comes down.

Eliana shrinks at the sight of Calev.

He says nothing but takes Zem from me, and the little boy wakes up.

"Father! You told us not to come, but Mother said we must."

Calev kisses Zem's cheek and presses his son's head onto his shoulder. He glares at Eliana, who steps further back. Then he faces me. "What do you want?"

"I want you to stop all of this. It's cold-blooded murder."

"I have no power to stop this. The order came from the court."

"Is Lachoneus here?"

He does not answer. My brother looks nervous, sorry—even weak.

"Do you know where Grandfather is? I have not seen him since the night we were ambushed."

"Grandfather is alive."

I spin and face Calev. Anger rages in me, and I am grateful I do not have a blade in my hand. "Where is he? I have the right to see him before we all die."

"Look out, Uncle!" Zem shouts.

I feel a sharp pain in my neck.

"Kiah. Look how fate has returned us to this point." Hem jabs the point of his sword into my flesh until I feel the warmth and wetness of blood, though I do not feel any more pain.

"Father!" Eliana cries, rushing to him. "No! Kiah spared your life! Spare his, *please.*"

Hem's free hand shoots out and slaps her so hard she falls to the ground.

Zem screams, and Calev presses the little boy firmly against his shoulder.

"Kneel!" Hem commands me.

I look over at Zem and try to smile. I wish Calev would take him away so Zem will not have to live with the memory of what is about to happen.

I kneel and feel the hard ground pierce the flesh on my knees.

"How does it feel, Kiah, to be the one helpless on the ground?"

"I am not helpless, Hem."

His laugh echoes through the afternoon. "Beg for your life," Hem orders me.

"Yes, beg," Marpe says, mimicking his boss. There are others around, a great number of people, but all I can see now is the face of my nephew.

"Calev, take Zem away. Please."

Calev stands like he is unable to move, like his mind is far distant.

"*Sawa,* don't hurt Uncle," Zem says, reaching for Hem.

Hem ignores his grandson and jabs the blade deeper into my neck, bringing another rush of blood. "Get up!"

I manage to stand only because Calev reaches out to help me.

Hem wants to humiliate me. He wants to boast in his own power.

I don't care. Grandfather's voice speaks to me in my memory; it calms me. Above everything else, I hear, *Be still and know that I am God.*

Hem fumes. "On the morrow you will die. Why aren't you trembling?"

"Like you were when you thought that death had come for you?"

His eyes bulge. I'm sure he's going to slit my throat, but he only yells, "Why would I fear you, Kiah? You are nothing. As a boy you thought you were a warrior, but you were not. As a soldier you failed miserably. As a scholar you fell short. And as an artisan you again failed. You are hardly worth killing, Kiah. Yet, you are special to me, and as the chosen one you will be the first to die for a Messiah who has abandoned you just as your own father did."

Seventy-Two

I am led up the stairs to the platform.

Thankfully, Eliana has taken Zem and left.

Hem stands right behind me with his sword in hand. It takes me a while, but I realize the sword he's holding once belonged to Calev; it was our grandfather's, given to him by the great prophet Helaman. It's the sword Grandfather demanded back from Calev. They must have taken it from Mother's house.

Hem should not even be touching it.

What has happened to make Calev so weak? In Hem's presence he barely speaks, can hardly look at me. I want him to look. I want him to see that in my heart there is no malice toward him. I forgive my brother, for I do not know the life he has lived, the fears he has faced, the demons that are his alone to battle. I can't imagine the battle he's fighting right now—the battle within.

When we get to the platform Hem has me kneel again—he orders me down on my hands and knees like an animal. I feel something warm drip onto the back of my hand; I look down to see my own blood splattering.

Be still and know.

I know that Nephi and Jonas and others in their family are looking up at me, feeling fear and pity. I do not look down at them, for I feel strong now.

I feel ready.

We wait.

I think of Tarah. If we were not meant to be joined in this life, then I pray we will find each other in the next life.

I hear singing. Mournful singing.

I hear weeping.

I believe Nephi is a prophet. I believe that he has power to stop the sun from setting, yet the sun is melting down the sky.

This evening is no different from any other evening.

More wood is piled for the fires.

Lines are formed for the martyrs. In his compassion, Hem has allowed families to be burned together—husbands clinging to wives, wives clutching children.

I pray that Grandfather is far away, safe with Mother and Abner and the children.

We wait.

The answer to my prayer is a horrifying *no.*

"Look down!" Hem orders me, poking me again with the sword.

I look down and see what I prayed I would not see. Mother, Abner, Grandfather, Elka, and Abby are bound together, standing first in the line before the fire that has already started to smoke.

"God in heaven, Father of us all, have mercy. Make my faith strong."

"Deny your God now, Kiah, and you can spare your family."

"No. I will never deny the God I worship."

Calev grimaces. I can see that he'd hoped I would do as he has done. But I cannot.

Neither can I look. I have to shut my eyes to focus my faith.

Hem laughs and does not stop laughing.

When I open my eyes I see that the shadows of the day are long and growing longer. I smell smoke. I feel the heat of the flames as smoke rises and turns in the air.

I hear the terror and the sorrow and the prayers of the people.

As the temperature changes, torches are lit and raised.

"Fools!" Hem cries out. He's not alone. He has his disciples—among them my brother, his right-hand coward.

I feel sorry for Calev but not so sorry that I can bring myself to pray for him.

A song starts, and even through the sobs and the sorrow, I recognize the voice of my mother singing to me.

"Have faith, son!" Grandfather calls up to me. "You are a warrior for God."

"Yes!" Nephi shouts, "The hour is at hand. Show forth your courage."

"Kiah!" Jonas's voice lifts my head.

The sun is sinking, but my spirit is soaring.

A single drum begins to beat as the sun sinks below the horizon. The air is smoky and pink with the final rays of daylight.

Hem has torchbearers brought to the platform so that when he takes my head no one will miss the show.

Calev holds the shell that Hem shouts through. "Let this fool from Elam, a boy who has brought much grief to my own family with his lies and evil, be the first to die!"

I hear cheers, very much like I heard during the trickball tournament.

Be still and know that I am God.

I drop my head and wait to die.

But I do not die.

I don't understand what is happening around me. All I know is that the kind of darkness we believers have lived in for days and nights is now gone.

The looks of horror shift from the faces of the believers to the face of Hem. He looks confused, as if some mysterious trick has been played on him.

Calev falls on his knees next to me and begs. "Forgive me, brother; forgive me, people; forgive me, God Almighty."

The sword falls from Hem's grip and clatters onto the platform.

I look up and see that the sun has indeed set—yet there is light, a light that grows brighter with every heartbeat of every believer.

The sign is given, and the light we believed would come—the Light of the Messiah—bathes us in warmth and hope and a love so real that it stops the very darkness.

Seventy-Three

A leaf flutters from a high tree, twirls in the air, and lands gently on the surface of the great river behind the temple in Zarahemla. It floats, turning happy circles—like a child who has never known war—then gets caught in the current and is carried down the river.

That is life, I think: to fall, to flutter, to twirl, and to float away.

My life, everyone's life, changed on the night that refused to be dark.

The Messiah, the Son of God, has been born, and the sign of His birth has been given to us. No one can question it now, for they are witnesses—everyone in the land, believers and those dark with doubt. That night the sun dipped below the horizon, but the night was as bright as midday. When the sun did rise again, we knew it was the day of birth for the Savior of mankind, the Messiah, the Christ. No prophecy was wasted. Even a new star was set in the sky, a guiding star to remind us of the miracle that we had been given.

The memory of that experience is something I dream about in clear detail. The first image I see is Hem's face. He'd been looking down, mocking me, waiting to run the edge of his blade over my throat—to spill my blood, giving his bloodthirsty soldiers permission to do the same to thousands of others. The fire was stoked; the martyrs were ready to die. I was ready to die.

Death did not come.

The Messiah did.

Calev fell to his knees next to me, picked up his sword, and silently challenged anyone intent on harming me—especially Hem. Hem stood there dumbstruck as Calev helped me off the platform and down the steps into the waiting arms of Grandfather.

Calev said nothing. I suspect words would have only choked him. I saw what he wanted to say etched across his face. He was sorry. Sorry for it all. And he was scared like so many others—beyond astonished that Samuel's prophecy and Nephi's promise were being fulfilled.

"Kiah!"

Grandfather, so battered from the horror of the whole experience, took me in his arms. I will forever hold the vision of his face; it was radiant. The clouds that had covered his eyes were burned away like morning mist. He stood, legs as strong as those of a young man, and raised his face to the sunless white sky.

"The Messiah!" Tears washed down his cheeks and, like rain off leaves, dripped from his chin. "Praise God Almighty. Hear the angels sing! The sign of the Messiah has been given!"

Mother and Abner held their babies and each other.

I saw them all, the faces of the people that I loved. Nephi was a picture of relief. He wore no shock, like most faces wore, only relief that the miracle he had been promised had arrived. Jonas was at his side, the best place in the world for him to be. Yes, the sign was given, but not in time to save his wife and unborn child.

When I looked back Hem was still perched on his platform. He looked dazed, like a man who had taken a hard blow to the head. He did not speak, and for a time I thought his palsy had returned. In my mind, it would have been fitting had God so dealt with the man who would have burned and tortured and murdered those who believed in His Son. But the look I mistook for suffering was a really a face twisting in rage. Hem was furious that God had answered our prayers.

I can still see Mother's face, radiant and happy—the way she must have looked before my father's betrayal. Mother was one of the first to break into song, praising God and rejoicing that the Messiah was born. I saw how she consoled Abner, who leaned down and sobbed on Mother's shoulder, a man sorry that his faith had been so weak.

Elka ran to me first, which made Mother look up and scramble through the people to embrace me. Mother saw Calev standing behind me, his head bowed in sorrow, his arm around Grandfather's shoulder.

She went limp in my arms, the strength drained from her body—her joy full, greater than it had ever been.

"My sons!"

Seeing the smile on her face was like seeing a rainbow arc over Elam after a great storm ended.

Our joy as believers, as children spared from slaughter, was—and still is—indescribable. But the real miracle for me was not the night that remained day; it was the darkness that went out of my brother. Calev repented. He fell to his knees in front of everyone and begged forgiveness.

Everyone was not so willing to forgive. There were some who spit on him, others who kicked him, still others who made threats and called him vile names. A few threw stones at my brother, and I let them.

I looked through the throngs for Eliana and Zem but did not see them. I did see Jonas, pale and trembling with grief as he made his way toward Calev, a man who was in a very real sense responsible for Jonas's broken heart and shattered life.

My brother was down on his knees, weeping. A woman flung a fistful of pebbles in Calev's face. "We should burn you and Hem!" she shouted. "You would have allowed my family to be murdered. You would have stood by and done nothing. You are a coward!" She spit in his face.

One man kicked Calev in the ribs. Another man, a guard who was still under Calev's rule, lifted a club and brought it down so hard against Calev's back that I thought his spine was broken.

"Stop!" Jonas yelled. "Stop! This man is penitent."

Jonas, who I thought would hate my brother, was the first to put his arms around Calev—to kiss his cheeks and to forgive him. Jonas, who had lost his wife and child, held Calev while he wept. They wept together. I stood back and watched for a long time, my own soul repenting.

The miracle did not end there. The next day when the sun rose we celebrated. We prayed. We sang. We feasted on food shared by some of those who would have killed us but who now feared and trembled for their lives because they knew that no prophecy, no matter how small, had remained unfulfilled.

We were free.

I was free to find Tarah but did not know where to begin. All I knew is that her family had joined Solomon's family, and now Solomon's family was slaughtered.

Lachoneus was safe. He'd been protected. Why, then, could he not protect his own kin?

"Our chief judge is a good and righteous man," Grandfather said, trying to preserve my patience. "The man has lost his sister, brother-in-law, and nieces and nephews. He is in a confused state of mourning, as is Jonas."

I understand what Grandfather means. In all of the slaughter and all of the horror, the bodies of Orli and her family were not buried properly. Unbelievers tossed them into the great river behind the temple.

I don't want to think about such a scene. To those of us who believe that life is sacred and the body is a temple for our spirits, such treatment—depriving us of taking care of our loved ones' bodies, of preparing them for burial, of bidding them a final good-bye—is another layer of grief.

So while this is a time of great rejoicing, there are those who also have great cause to mourn.

My intent is to rush back to Zarahemla and tear every house and building apart until I find Tarah, but I am presented with an obligation that cannot be delayed.

"Sit with me," Jonas begs.

I cannot fathom the pain that Jonas is suffering, and he binds me when he requests that I sit with him for the seven required days. All around us are wrenching reminders that what was here is gone—the humble home surrounded by the flowers Orli planted. Her two cooking pots, hanging from a rack Jonas crafted. The bed they shared. The shawl Orli wove in which to wrap their baby.

"The laws of mourning," Nephi tells us on the first day, "are to focus inwardly on our own spirituality. We have just been witness to one of the greatest miracles this earth will ever know—the birth of its Savior. As we mourn, let us never forget that the spirit is eternal."

He talks of life and death and resurrection while his only son rocks back and forth, tears splashing onto the smooth cement floor that Orli had swept last. There are tears in Nephi's eyes too. And in mine.

Jonas's mother lights a servant candle and uses its flame to ignite all of ours. "Orli was like this flame, burning upward toward heaven," Devora tells her sobbing son. "It lights the candles of others without diminishing its own light."

One of Jonas's brothers-in-law brings in chairs with shortened legs so we might be reminded of our physical discomfort—a pain that heightens our mourning. One special chair stays in front of Jonas so that those who pay him respect can sit before him. Those of us who do not have chairs sit on the ground.

By law, during the first seven days of mourning Jonas is not permitted to bathe, to trim his nails, or to cut his hair; he must wear the same cloak and cannot shave. But everyone who enters the house must wash his or her hands because any contact with death requires special cleansing.

During those seven days, I note that water is a sign of life. I try to console my friend by talking about a time when he will be resurrected and rejoin Orli, but such talk brings little comfort to Jonas and only makes me anxious to go in search of Tarah.

Bread, the substance of life, takes on new meaning because for days, most of us were starved by our captors. But even warm bread brought in by neighbors is no temptation for Jonas's empty belly.

Eventually, I fall silent, knowing that there are no words to ease the pain that my best friend is suffering. My thoughts are centered on Tarah, but I also realize something about myself. My faith is no stronger because I witnessed the great miracle; my faith was strongest in those telling moments when Hem held the sword to my throat. That was my time of testing.

I knew as much then as I know now—that we are all children of a God who is our Father. In the long, quiet hours of sorrow, I think back on my life and think forward, making decisions on the course I want my future to take. Everything I plan depends on one fact: that Tarah is alive and still wants to marry me.

I pray that she is safe, for if anything has happened to her I don't know how I would live. I watch Jonas, suffering without complaint or even question, and I realize that while my faith is as strong as cement, his is as solid as granite.

Prayer service is brought to the home by a priest named Jacob. He comes the required three times each day and brings with him wisdom from the scriptures. Some messages seem to ease Jonas's pain while others leave us both hollow and hurting.

As each day passes I can sense that Jonas feels his mourning deepen, though never once does he turn to me or ask why.

"Mourning is good," Grandfather says. "This is the purpose for sitting here for seven days—to experience the memories, the pain, the loss, the suffering, and the need to go on."

At night we separate for sleep, always on the ground and always uncomfortable so we can be reminded that life is hard and love is hard. Who needs such a reminder?

On the morning of the seventh day Jacob tells all of us, including Jonas, "Arise."

We walk out into the sunlight and feel the pain in our heads as we blink back the light. We straighten our legs and feel the ache in our limbs. We breathe and fill our lungs with air not already breathed. We walk around the courtyard at first, Jonas beside me, and when we come to a hedge by the side of what was once his grandfather's side entrance, Jonas darts away from me, falls to his knees, and scrambles through the tangle and out onto the highway.

Has he gone mad?

It takes me a while to catch up with him, but when I do, I run behind him for a very long time. We run through the territory we explored as boys. We run until my already weak legs give out. Jonas keeps running, stops, looks back, and then gazes up at the sky. I hear him howl loud and unrestrained.

Back in his house, his sorrow was seeped deep into his sinews. Here, in the sunlight and fresh air, he releases that sorrow, sets the pain free.

Seventy-Four

I cannot locate Tarah.

Her father's house is wrecked and abandoned. His shop is closed.

Lachoneus has returned to court, but his guards refuse me entrance. I draft an official epistle, explaining my desires and asking that he reveal Tarah's whereabouts. I declare my love for her and make my intentions official.

Grandfather would do it for me if he could. Nephi would do it, but he has left Zarahemla again with Timothy to do missionary work in the northlands. Jonas, back in seclusion, has to complete his thirty days of mourning.

I go alone to the chambers and wait my answer.

The city is much as it was before. The people mix as one. It's impossible to tell the believers from the unbelievers; it's impossible to imagine that only days earlier one neighbor was ready and willing to murder another. Now everything has changed, but everything appears the same. Lawyers come and go. Priests walk with their heads held high, their fine linens on display. Vendors bring their wares to market. Children run and play; the rich go to school, the poor go to work. The temple smells of incense, dung, and burnt offerings.

Women scold children and calm babies. They trade or barter food. A man with a bleating lamb wrapped around his neck stops to ask me directions to the temple. He tells me that he was an unbeliever, but now he's bringing his best lamb to be sacrificed because he wants to belong to the Church of God.

I'm happy for him—happy that so many people have experienced a change of heart because the sign was given. I'm grateful for the change that occurred in my heart *before* the sign was given. It's a feeling I do not share, not even with Jonas, but keep sacred.

I walk the man to the temple gate; all the while the lamb is bleating and kicking to be free. All the while I want to get back to the court to see if Lachoneus has news about Tarah. She's all I think about. She is my future.

No news, not this day or the next. I write another epistle to be certain that Lachoneus understands that I am willing to pay the full dowry price Abarron asked. I don't know if Abarron is even still alive. The possibility that Tarah might have been injured—or worse—is unbearable, and I refuse to consider it.

Eleven days later I receive word that Tarah is still in hiding and I will not be allowed to see her. My heart rejoices that she is alive, but I'm confused as to why I'm being refused.

"Grant me an audience with Abarron then," I beg the guard. "Please, tell Lachoneus that I must talk to Abarron."

It takes days and endless begging before I'm led to a home on the river side of the city in an area where slaves work to clear the jungle. They make streets flat by rolling the ground with a stone so huge that twelve men are needed to roll it. The streets in this part of the city are flatter and wider; the walkways are made of stone, and the house I'm led to is surrounded by a high wall with an unfriendly guard at the gate. I assume such security exists because Abarron is a man in possession of so many treasured stones.

When Abarron emerges to meet me at the gate, he appears with a face I do not recognize. He is an old man with colorless hair and gray eyes. His hands tremble, and there is a deep, fresh scar across his chin. I can only imagine what he has been through, and every part of my body fears for what Tarah has suffered.

He tells me, "It is inappropriate for you to approach me about my daughter."

"I realize that, but I have no one to come in my place. I love Tarah, sir, and have made ready the entire dowry that you require for her."

"I can no longer accept it." His head hangs, and he turns back toward the open gate.

"Wait! I will pay more. I will pay anything for Tarah."

"No."

"Please, sir."

The gate guard steps in front of me. He's a Zoramite, armed and shielded. It dawns on me then that during the seven days of mourning, not one member of Orli's extended family came to sit with him. "Oh, please—please, Abarron, tell me that Tarah is alive and well."

He stops and lifts sorrowful eyes to mine. "She lives."

"I mourn with you for the loss of so many of your family members. It is a horrific ordeal we have suffered for our faith. I sat the required seven days with Jonas. After that I waited many days to be able to talk with you. Please, at least look at the offering I've brought." My fingers struggle to remove the tie on the sack that holds my dowry.

"No. It is unnecessary. I will not accept your offering."

"Why?"

Abarron dismisses the guide that led me here and nods to the Zoramite. We walk a few steps down the road so we are alone. Abarron lowers his voice to such a whisper that I have to lean toward him to hear. "There is no longer an asking price for Tarah."

I have to fight an urge to put my hands on Abarron and shake the truth from him. "She has not been betrothed to another, has she?"

"No. I can no longer ask a price for my daughter."

"What more do you want? Like Father Jacob of old, I will work for you for years; I will pay any price you ask."

"You will do nothing—for Tarah is no longer available."

The hope and life drain from me as surely as if Hem had pulled his blade across my throat. Abarron struts away and leaves me standing in the road, confused and heartbroken.

• • •

After an agonizing thirty days for both of us—after Jonas's second stage of mourning has concluded—he insists on being the one to approach Abarron. As a member of Abarron's family by marriage, he is granted a fast audience with the man who was Orli's uncle.

I am waiting in the synagogue gardens—pacing, praying, thanking God that Jonas is my mediator. In the midst of his greatest sorrow, he is reaching through his pain to help me.

"Kiah?"

When I see my friend's face I see that the news is the worst.

"He cannot accept your dowry offer."

"I don't understand."

"Sit, my friend, my brother."

"I can't sit."

"Then walk with me. There are ears too close to hear what I must tell you."

"Tell me?"

It's hard to wait until we are sure there is no one around to hear what Jonas has to say.

Jonas widens his eyes and stares right at me. "Abarron would like nothing more than for you to marry Tarah."

"I want nothing more! Where is she? What are you not telling me?"

Jonas runs his hands through his hair, tugging at it like he is agony.

"I'm sorry. I'm sorry I've put you in this position, Jonas. You're suffering, I know. But who else do I have to help me?"

"I want to help you, Kiah. But listen to me. Look into my eyes when I say what I have to say so you will not misunderstand. When the mobs of unbelievers came, when the robbers tore out of the hills and attacked the believers, they robbed Abarron of something far more precious than his metals or his money."

"I know. They murdered Orli and her parents. They—"

"Stop, Kiah! Think about what I am trying to tell you because I cannot bring myself to say it. Think about what they took that cannot be repaid to Abarron. Think about why he can no longer ask a price for Tarah."

I'm more confused than ever until I realize the terrible truth of what Jonas is saying.

"Oh, no! No. No. No. No. No!"

• • •

The next morning I am at Abarron's worksite, where he is inlaying turquoise at a new church. There are no guards around, but Abarron refuses to talk with me.

I wait. I wait all day. I come back the next morning and the next.

Finally, he stands in front of me, wordless, but willing to hear what I have to say.

"It does not matter to me," I tell him. "I still love Tarah. What happened to her brings no shame in my eyes. Please, accept my dowry offering and grant me permission to marry your daughter."

Seventy-Five

I made Tarah my wife in AD 2—according to the calendars of the Nephites, set by the year the sign was given.

It was a simple, quiet betrothal ceremony with only those closest to us present. It did not matter to me that her virtue had been robbed from her or that another's child grew within her. All that mattered was that I could not imagine a life without her by my side.

In all the years since then I have witnessed life fall and flutter, swim and drown, float away—but my devotion to my wife has only grown. She was hesitant at first to marry me. Even though I had permission from Abarron, Tarah's heart was broken; she'd lost her laugh and the confidence that I so loved about her.

For twelve endless months I honored our separation agreement—in part. I stayed far enough away from her so that I did not lay eyes on my wife-to-be, but each night I sang my love to her. For an entire year, rain or shine, I stood at the end of her street and sang until my throat was raw. I sang the scripture songs Mother sang to me. I sang songs I made up—songs about her hair and her laugh. Even when an eager young lawyer came by and threatened to have me put in jail, I kept singing.

On the night of our consummation, I sent the shout up with a song.

One of her older sisters met our grooms' party on the way to the house.

"Tarah will go through with the marriage agreement as long as you make one promise."

I was caught off guard and not sure how serious her words were. "What is the agreement?"

"You take singing lessons from your mother."

Jonas, Nephi, Calev, and my other groomsmen broke into laughter that still rings in my head.

• • •

It's hard to imagine a time when all I wanted to be was a warrior who hunted and fought. Now I want nothing more than what I have. I will fight to defend it, but violence is no longer a first option for me.

I've become a devoted missionary, a husband, and a father. Life is richer than I ever knew it could be. I live with Tarah, our two sons, and our infant daughter. Our home is humble and just a few steps up the hill from where Jonas lives with his new wife and their three identical baby boys—God's favor on a man who has proven himself. I have known great men but none greater than Jonas.

I too have felt the favor of God. He has granted me the security and the family I longed for. He has allowed me to become the father I never had.

Though Joab, my eldest, is not my son from my loins, he is my son from my heart. Never once have I looked upon him and thought he was less because of the way he was conceived. But he reminds me more of Calev than of me. The only teacher he listens to is experience. If I tell Joab the fire is hot, he feels the need to burn himself.

His younger brother by only a season, Zadok, is as obedient as Jonas. He loves to hunt the hills and prefers to be alone, much the way I did when I was a boy his age. Once he brought an orphaned baby *chuwen* home to raise. The creature sometimes still rides on Zadok's shoulder, its long tail twitching down my son's back.

Our daughter, Rinnah, was only recently presented at the temple. Time will tell which parent she resembles. I hope it is not me.

I seldom crave the solo time I used to relish. Now I cherish every moment I can spend with my wife and children.

Grandfather, who lives with us, cherishes the time he spends with Joab and Zadok. He is old now, older than most people ever live to be. His faith has never faltered, though his feet often do. The tenderness with which Tarah cares for him makes me love her more than I thought one heart could love.

Today we have returned to Elam in honor of my youngest brother's entrance into manhood. Abby is thirteen and has just finished his scripture reading beneath a thatched canopy of leaves.

I remember when I turned thirteen and became a son of the commandment by age but not by devotion. All I wanted to do was hunt in the hills and serve as a soldier. I did not know the scriptures or the songs. I had convinced myself that I could not recite the histories of our forefathers. I could not craft letters and numbers. Today I earn a living for my family crafting stories into stone. I write on buildings and walls and on synagogues. My work has even been commissioned on the temple walls. Tarah calls me an artisan. I feel proud and happy, grateful for the richness of my life.

Unlike me, my brother Abby is prepared. His recitation is flawless.

Grandfather asks, "Tell us, son, what it means to you to become a son of the commandment."

Abby is tall and lanky like his father, but like our shared mother, he is quiet and has a solid singing voice. He stands in front of Grandfather and says, "I now have the right to take part in our services. I can be one of the numbers needed to perform priesthood ordinances. I can form a binding contract. I can testify before the court. And I can marry."

We all laugh, thinking of Abby as a thirteen-year-old husband.

"But," he adds quickly, "the law does not *require* me to marry until I am thirty."

More laugher. One laugh sounds above the others, and we turn to see that Hem has appeared among the synagogue family that has gathered.

There was and is no law to punish him for what he did, for he was acting under the rulings of corrupt courts. For a time after the new star appeared, things were different; now they are shifting again. Evil lurks wherever it is allowed to enter.

I have not seen Hem in all this time. I feel my own body has reshaped itself, but as with an old tree, it is difficult to detect change in old Hem. He is still the same brute he was before, only now his hair is reduced to thin long strands of silver and his facial features seem a bit fallen. He's not alone today at the synagogue; there are other men with him. None of them is familiar to me. At Hem's side is a different wife—younger. There is something about her that is familiar, but I can't place what.

Hem's first wife, Sherrizah—Eliana's mother—was faithful to the end. Even after the sign was given and Hem was proven wrong, was humiliated and ostracized for so long, she remained silent and supportive. Then one day her aged body was found beaten and abandoned along the roadside to the shimmering springs. Oshra hurried through the village spreading the story of how Hem had hired his own robbers to murder his wife so he could marry again.

"That's Oshra's oldest daughter, Phoebe," Mother whispers to me when she sees me staring at Hem's new wife.

"Hem married Oshra's daughter? Wasn't she married before?"

"Yes. It's all very complicated and unpleasant."

"I'm sure."

Hem's very presence spoils the joy of Abby's celebration. This is a public ceremony, so he has the right to be here, but we all know that he's come to cause some sort of trouble. Calev looks over at me and frowns. Eliana does not even look in the direction of her father; I don't suppose she has since Hem publicly disowned both of them.

Zem, now taller than his father, rushes to his grandfather's side. The two of them have remained close in spite of everything.

I can see the pain that such a reunion causes my brother.

My brother.

As great as the miracle of the night without darkness was, I witnessed an even greater miracle. I witnessed the rebirth of Calev. He has proven his repentance by confessing and forsaking his sins. He has denounced Hem and even testified before the courts, but without results—the courts are still filled with members of Hem's secret society. I've given up believing that justice will come to Hem in this life.

Calev now makes his living in the city near where Abarron works. My father-in-law and my brother have become close friends. They share long treks to the winding river where the rare, beautiful turquoise is found.

Sometimes Calev even comes with me as I follow behind Nephi, preaching and teaching and baptizing everyone who repents and desires to come into the fold of Christ.

There is no joy like the joy of missionary work, even though everyone doesn't welcome us or pardon Calev for his duplicity. Twice while he's been sleeping, unknown assailants have tried to murder him. Once he was also beaten and left for dead like his mother-in-law. We know who was behind the attacks, but Hem always manages to appear innocent.

Eliana, like her mother, stands steady next to her husband. She is a woman who seldom smiles—unlike my Tarah, who seldom frowns. Eliana carries the burden of a mother whose womb could only bear one child. She's delivered other babies, but only one living. I'm truly sorry for her sorrow. I'm truly grateful that my Tarah has seen fit to befriend Eliana, who now holds our daughter, Rinnah. It tugs a smile from my wife to see the joy our baby brings Eliana.

My nephew, Zem, is the center of his parents' world. He is adept with a weapon, but he claims he wants to become a lawyer, a judge, even a chief judge one day. The priest is going on about the signs of the times and how we were saved by a miracle that so many have already diminished.

"It was no miracle, my brethren," Hem says, turning all the attention to himself. "That night what we saw was no prophecy fulfilled, but an act of Satan to deceive our very eyes."

"It *was* a miracle," Calev says, standing tall. "You can deny it all you want, but I testify of God's goodness and mercy and the birth of His Son, our Messiah."

A man standing behind Hem laughs. He wears a blue cloak, an unusual cloak that seems vaguely familiar. "Your Messiah?" The man laughs, and the sound echoes around Elam's synagogue garden, off the stone floors and rock walls where I used to get so frustrated trying to learn the letters and numbers of the scriptures.

Grandfather makes a strangled sound as he sits taller on his mat. I see Mother bury her face in the crook of Abner's arm; she's obviously upset that Hem and his cohorts are disturbing a happy family gathering.

The man in the blue cloak who steps out from the shadow of Hem is a stranger, yet his voice is as familiar as it is commanding.

Where have I seen him before? That blue cloak. My mind winds back . . . back—back to a time I've tried so hard to forget. A man with a cloak just as blue once stood in the crowd with Hem as he condemned every believer to death.

The man's voice booms like a drum as he upstages Abby. "This Messiah of which you testify—where is He? Have you seen Him? Have you heard His voice or witnessed His power? No, you have not, and this is because you are fools who still cling to the traditions that bind you as sure as chains. I know those traditions, for I was also taught them, here in this very synagogue. I, like all of you, am a son of Elam."

Grandfather' hand reaches up, bats at mine. I glance down to see that the color has drained from his face, and I fear that his heart is stopping. His mouth is open and he's gasping for breath. Eliana and I both kneel beside him as the man continues ranting.

My own sons flank me, worrying over Grandfather, a man they dearly love.

"What is the matter?" I ask. "Are you in pain? What do you need?"

Like a fish on the bank, Grandfather's mouth goes open and closed. He's trying to tell me something, and I turn my ear toward him. I feel a hand press on my shoulder and turn to see that the stranger has joined us and is lowering himself down on his haunches so he is eye to eye with Grandfather. There is a priggish smile on his face that I don't understand.

Grandfather gasps, and his hands slide up to press against his wrinkled cheeks. He cannot speak, but the man can. He leans forward and says loud enough for everyone to hear, "Greetings, Father. It has been far too long."

Seventy-Six

Every muscle in my body tightens. My stomach turns over. There is thunder in my head. "Stay back," I warn the man who wears more than an expensive blue cloak—he wears my brother's broad nose and my wide eyes. "You will not harm Grandfather."

The man throws his head back and laughs then lets his head snap back. He hisses at me. "Harm him? I'm not here to harm anyone, my youngest son. What do they call you—Kiah?"

I feel Tarah clutch my arm, feel her fingernails bite into my skin. "Your grandfather—focus on *him*."

I turn back and know without anyone telling me that Grandfather is dying.

"Joab!" I yell. "Run and bring Pazel." Elderly Pazel is still the village healer.

Already there is a group gathered around Grandfather. Mother is there on her knees. Gidd does not take his eyes from her, but she refuses to give her attention to anyone but Grandfather. Tarah, too, is by Grandfather's side.

"Leave," I tell Gidd, wanting him to back down, but he holds his ground.

"Yarden is *my* father. If he is dying, I have the right to attend him."

"You have no rights here."

Hem's form looms above us. His arms are crossed over his chest. Next to him stands Zem, looking both frightened and captivated. "Gidd has every right to be here," Hem says. "He is a man of authority."

My entire body, every sinew, aches to beat these two men who are clearly conspirators. I feel something I have not felt in all the years since Tarah became my wife; I feel the craving for violence. I strain, reaching for my blade. I want desperately to sink it through Hem's heart—to pull it free and sink it into the heart of the man who is my father.

Instead, I search the crowd with desperate eyes. When I see Calev I feel an unbearable load lift from my back. My eyes beg him for help.

"Move!" Calev orders Gidd. He does not look stunned like I am. "Get back and stay out of the way." When Calev speaks he is not speaking to a stranger. He *knows* this man.

We take our grandfather in our arms and cradle him to the shade of the synagogue canopy. His body is limp, and it's hard for him to keep his eyes open.

"My sons," he whispers. "My sons."

"We're here, Grandfather. Calev and I are both here. What do you need?"

"I need to bear witness," he says in a voice too strong to be that of a dying man. "I need you to know that the Messiah has been born. He lives as I die. It is only through Him that redemption can come. Stay strong, my sons. Keep the commandments. All of them. Fools will tell you that the law is fulfilled because they no longer want to keep the law of Moses, but it will not be fulfilled until the Messiah comes here—until He walks and talks among you."

Tears boil in my eyes as I realize that after all the times I have nearly lost Grandfather, this time he will not be saved. The man responsible for his death stands across the way—not far, next to Hem, looking on with no expression of guilt. He says nothing, but there is smugness in the way his lips turn upward.

He is our *father*? No. I have no father.

Mother and Tarah are weeping, kissing Grandfather's cheeks and squeezing his hand. Eliana stands back, Rinnah still safe in her arms. Zadok weeps. He clings to my side, as terrified as I am.

Zem steps forward and offers Grandfather water from his own waterskin, but Grandfather cannot swallow.

"I'm sorry," Zem says, fighting back tears.

Grandfather reaches to embrace him, but his arms lack the strength. "Keep the commandments, Zem. You are my great-grandson, and you are a loved boy."

Calev's arm slips over Zem's quivering shoulder.

"What more can we do for you?" I ask Grandfather.

"Listen to a dying man's declaration. Keep the commandments and prosper. Break the commandments and suffer." Every breath is a struggle. I desperately look for Pazel; he will know how to ease the suffering, but he has not arrived.

Gidd flares out the excess material of his cloak, as if boasting of his wealth. He scoffs and mutters something I cannot hear. I feel feelings I have not battled in years. I want to reach for my blade now and do unimaginable harm to the intruder.

I am astonished and angry, shocked and sad beyond words. Tarah's eyes give me strength and control. My eyes warn the man to keep his mouth shut.

"Calev, you know the miracle of the Atonement of Jesus Christ."

My brother nods. "Yes, Grandfather. I know the power; it has restored my life."

"Kiah, you do not know your own worth. God has shown you favor for a reason. I beg you, forgive."

Grandfather lifts a trembling finger and points it toward the stranger. "Gidd."

Gidd. The man I have always been desperate to know. The man who comes forward as Mother backs into the waiting arms of Abner, like she is backing away from a striking snake. I understand the hatred in her eyes; it burns in my heart.

Calev stands and makes his body a shield between Grandfather and Gidd. "You do anything to injure Grandfather and I will murder you with my bare hands." My brother means to whisper, but we all hear his quaking threat.

Gidd jeers. "You are no threat to me—to anyone. You've proven yourself a coward, a man who does not honor his oath. Now step back, Calev, so I can attend my father."

"Son," Grandfather says, his voice faltering.

"Father." He stands above Grandfather, looking down. His feet are clad with hand-stitched leather. On his center finger is a ring that very much resembles the ring I found so long ago at the robbers' camp—a ring I gave to Abarron as part of a dowry he did not demand of me.

My eyes take in every detail about the man: the gray at his temples, the scar on his chin, the cold dark eyes that look upon his dying father with no emotion. Though Grandfather's hand struggles to reach for Gidd, he does not reach for Grandfather. His hands fold in front of him, and I notice they are soft like a child's—they do not bear the scars of a warrior or a working man.

Grandfather tries to clear his throat. "My prayers are answered, my son. You have returned to your family to make amends."

Gidd's chuckle explodes into a mocking laugh. "Father, no. Your prayers are *not* answered. I have returned to demand that the people of Elam give back what they have stolen from *my* people."

Grandfather's voice tightens. He grimaces like he's been struck with a sword. "We have stolen nothing from you, Gidd. *You* are the one who stole the money from the treasury. You are the thief—the one who could not face your own sins, so you ran and hid."

"You are mistaken, Father. I am not a thief. I am a man of power and influence. You ought to be proud of me."

I feel the drum of Grandfather's heart beneath my touch. It's unsteady but fast. He has to blink away the sweat from his eyes. His finger shakes, though he cannot keep his hand in the air. "You are a thief, Gidd."

"And you, my aged father, are still a fool."

I turn into an animal, ready to lunge for the life vein in his throat, but Grandfather's hand tries to tug me away. His head turns from side to side, and his watery eyes beg me to check myself.

Gidd goes on, attacking Grandfather with words as sharp as arrows. "You still show faith to a faithless god who does not show Himself to you. Where is this Christ you claim? In some faraway land called Jerusalem? You have no proof that such a place exists. You have wasted your life following foolish traditions. Those traditions have stolen what is rightfully ours."

"Yours?"

"I am here to warn all of Elam that if they do not turn over their weapons and their wealth, my band and I will take them by force."

"You are a leader of the robbers?"

"I am the chief of all of Gadianton's band. Are you not finally proud of me, Father?"

Grandfather gasps, shock registering on his paling face. My own heart leaps in my pinched chest. Grandfather struggles to prop himself up on his elbow. I cradle him in my arms.

"I forgive you, Giddianhi."

The man forfeits all composure. His hands fly high into the air. "Forgive *me*? I have done nothing that requires your forgiveness."

"May our merciful Messiah forgive you as you repent and come to Him."

Gidd glares at me and laughs. I swear that I can feel Grandfather's heart split down the center.

Calev barrels through and wraps his arms tight around Gidd. There's a shuffle and accusations that make no sense to me—words like *coward* and *traitor* are batted around. My attention is on the fight when I realize that the beating beneath my palm has gone still.

"Grandfather!"

His eyes are open and stare heavenward, but there is no life left behind them.

Mother weeps. So do the other women. I pull Grandfather tighter to me and let his head fall against my chest. His hand falls limp and sways so that his fingers brush against my knee. I know he is gone, for I imagine that I feel the brush of his spirit on my cheek as it departs his body.

I hear Grandfather's voice admonishing my faith to stay steady. *Be still.* I hear his voice as clear as a morning cock, and yet he is not speaking, for he is dead—murdered by his own son, my father, as sure as if Giddianhi had driven a blade through Grandfather's heart.

Seventy-Seven

I'm told Calev had to hold me back from killing our father. I'm told I lunged at Giddianhi and did my best to strangle him. As it was, I ripped a piece of his expensive blue cloak off and shoved it down his throat. I'm told it was Calev and Zem who restrained me. I'm told it was Hem who raised his strong hand to hit me with his walking stick. I'm told my blade—once Hem's blade—fell from the sheath around my thigh, and that Hem picked it up and departed with it tight in his grip. I'm told I fought like a *chakmool* until Giddianhi's elbow managed to strike me at the base of my neck.

I woke up in the rank and vile cell of Elam's dungeon, my head bruised, my memories foggy and painful.

Three days later, I am now brought before Elam's judgment seat. Giddianhi is gone, back into one of his hiding holes, but Hem is there in the chamber made of timber and gray cement. His face bruised and his arm in a sling, he is the picture of a victim.

Pazel is also there. The village healer has been called to testify because by the time Joab brought him back to the synagogue, Grandfather was dead—but Hem was in need of care. Pazel is a small, strange man who shaves all but a tail at the nape of his neck, who wears a cloak with many pockets that hold his healing herbs. The left side of his face twitches, like the tail of Zadok's *chuwen*.

"I testify before the court," Pazel says in his high, thin voice, "that what has befallen Kiah and his family is a tragedy. All of Elam has lost a great man in Yarden. His injury was not intentional, but a misfortune brought on by . . . as I understand it, the reappearance of Giddianhi, Yarden's negligent son. The shock of seeing him, of learning that the man now leads the Gadianton robbers, was enough to kill Yarden's heart."

Hem drops his chin and shakes his head as if he had nothing to do with my father's sudden appearance in Elam.

Marpe scratches his head, trying to appear serious. He looks to Hem. "The court will hear from you, for you are the injured party."

I remember Eliana once telling me how her father is capable of feigning a much more serious injury than the one he actually has. I catch a glimpse of Tarah standing at the back of the room and I hope I will be free to console her. She loved Grandfather almost as much as I did. It's his murder that should be brought before the court. Hem and Giddianhi should be charged with the highest crime. They caused Grandfather's death by conspiring to bring Giddianhi here.

Hem insists on standing and having all the attention. "I have mercy in my heart toward Kiah. He has spent much of his life wrongfully accusing me of crimes he imagines. He is a man troubled by a life without the guidance of his real father, a father who returned to set matters right. Unfortunately, Giddianhi was not received in the same spirit in which he returned to Elam." He winces like he's in pain.

Hem looks right at me and lifts his voice. "Your presence here in Elam, even if temporary to witness your young brother's entrance into manhood—a ceremony you missed in your own life—has been disruptive to the peace of our village. You come with your misdirected anger and accusations. Return to Zarahemla, Kiah, and leave matters here alone," Hem warns me, making a show of his mercy and generosity. "Out of respect for Yarden, we release you on the condition that you leave Elam and do not return with your trouble and trail of lies. Since you were a boy wandering the hills your tongue has told nothing but lies."

Tarah makes a little gasp; her eyes beg me to restrain myself. I search the faces of the elders of Elam. It's still impossible to tell which ones have taken the secret oaths that bind them to Hem and his sins. Maybe they are all brothers bound by conspiracy.

"I will leave Elam," I agree, "after the proper time to mourn Grandfather has passed."

Marpe nods as if that is agreeable, but Hem's face puffs red.

"My daughter, grandson, and son-in-law are sitting in mourning as we speak. You will not join them, but leave Elam *now*."

And so I leave.

In spite of my pleas to Abner, he refuses to leave Elam, so I bid good-bye to Mother, Elka, and Abby. Elka is almost a woman, and Abby is now a son of the commandment. Life moves swiftly, a river swollen by the rainy season.

Tarah, Joab, Zadok, and Rinnah walk with me mostly in silence, knowing how broken my heart is. Grandfather is dead. We have all lost someone we loved deeply.

When tears fall down my cheeks, Tarah stands on her toes so she can kiss them dry. When I tremble, she wraps her arms around me and whispers, "The Messiah will soon pave the way so that Grandfather and all of us will be resurrected."

We make a fire along the roadside, off into the tangle, and rest. We talk about the Messiah and the Atonement that He is about to make for all mankind.

Joab asks, "His own people will kill Him?"

"Yes, according to the prophets, they will crucify Him."

Zadok grimaces. "He's supposed to be a god. Why doesn't He stop them?"

"Because Christ has to be a willing sacrifice, just like Isaac on the altar Abraham built."

"But Isaac was a baby."

"No, he wasn't. Isaac was grown, older than you. His father bound him with cords. God the Father binds Christ through commandments and obedience to those commandments. Isaac knew what was going to happen to him, and he was willing. In the same way, the Messiah trusts His Father completely."

"But Isaac didn't die," Joab says. "Christ will."

I nod, grateful that I can talk about such things with my family. "Yes, the Messiah will be lifted on a cross. He will die. He will be buried and mourned, and on the third day He will rise from the dead so that we might all be resurrected."

Zadok jumps to his feet. "This is the third day Grandfather has been buried! Maybe he will rise and live again. We should go back to his grave at Elam."

I smile at my son's faith but explain to him that until Christ paves the way, the road to resurrection is not passable for anyone—even a man as faithful as Grandfather.

"When will that be, Father? When will the Messiah come?"

"That is a question I must have asked Grandfather a hundred times."

• • •

Back in Zarahemla I mourn Grandfather's death properly. Our house lies not far from Jonas's; our property was a gift to us from Nephi. It is a timber house, coated in gray cement, square in structure, with four rooms inside and a ladder and flat roof above where the children sleep, where I go to meditate and pray much like Jonas's grandfather, Nephi, used to go up to his tower to pray.

The house is darkened, the mud walls cool. We all wedge in to sit in sorrow. We mourn like the law says we must mourn, yet in my head I still hear his voice. In my saddest moments I feel his arms go around me. And in my heart I know we will once again be together.

Tarah does not leave my side, and in our solemn moments I confess to her something I've never told anyone.

"I know men who have talked with angels. I know men who receive revelation. None of those things has happened to me, and yet I know, Tarah—I *know* that Jesus is the Christ. His arm of mercy is strong. It has lifted me when I've fallen; it has held me back from sinning. His love has held me tight in times like this when my heart is heavy with sorrow. Grandfather taught me many things, but the two things that stand out to me are that pride is the root of decline and that to know God, *really* know Him, we must be still."

And so we sit still. In the silence I hear things so sacred, even now I cannot whisper them.

When Grandfather has been properly mourned I emerge to a world at war.

"It's everywhere," Jonas tells me. "Can't you feel the danger in the air? All anyone talks about is how the robbers are destroying whole villages, murdering and plundering. It's only a matter of time until they attack Zarahemla."

The robbers are led by my father. I know that Giddianhi is capable of great destruction, but can he destroy our land and our people the same way he destroyed our family?

I venture into the city at Abarron's shop where Jonas works in back designing a secret weapon to help fight the robbers. He proudly shows off a catapult that fires small balls of hard cement. It is my idea to inlay them with shards of obsidian and other sharp stones. It's a vicious contraption, one the gentle warrior in me hopes we'll never have to use.

"Calev should be working here," I tell Jonas. "My brother used to love to imagine and design weapons." My brother knew our father—once conspired with him. Maybe Calev didn't want me to know because it was one more thing to drive a wedge between us, but I've forgiven my brother. I don't know that he will ever be able to forgive himself.

Jonas tells me, "The armies are in full training—not just in the cities but in every village in the land. The women huddle together, terrified. Gidgiddoni is calling for every able man to fight; he says that even the children will be armed. My boys are too young, but yours are both adept with a blade and a slingshot."

A lump rises in my throat. "Joab will face the challenge fine. He's the warrior I always wanted to be. But Zadok doesn't have the heart. The other day his mother caught him crying over a slaughtered lamb."

"Then the days ahead will be his greatest challenge."

I think back to when I was a boy who yearned for war in times of peace. Grandfather warned me that I would regret it. He was so right.

Seventy-Eight

Time passes and the rumors rumble louder. We hear accounts of entire villages being plundered and burned. We hear that Nephite prisoners are being sacrificed to hungry gods who cry for the blood of the innocents. I try to hold my family close and safe, but my sons are growing into men and I know I cannot stop time.

One night I am awakened by a gate guard to tell me that my brother has come. I have grown to love Calev as a brother should love a brother, but I am still angry with him for not telling me of our father. He knew that Gidd was the Gadianton leader, yet he said nothing to warn us. Would it have made a difference to Grandfather? What would I have done with such information?

"What is it?" I ask when I see Calev's pale face in the moonlight.

"It's Zem. He's dissented. He's joined Giddianhi."

My back slides down the wall. I sit on the hard earth and listen as my brother sobs out the story of how Zem made such a decision—how our vile father sent a band to persuade the young people of Elam to join with him, promising them wealth and freedom and how Zem was enticed with added temptations. "The men actually paraded slave girls before our young warriors, making promises that sent Eliana to her sickbed."

"I can imagine."

Calev weeps like a baby. A strand of his long black hair has come out of his headband and falls over his eyes. "Zem means everything to us. But what other options did his life hold for him? I have not set the example I should have. With Hem and Giddianhi as his grandfathers . . . Oh, Kiah, I blame myself."

There is a part of me that remembers what our mother suffered when she learned that Calev had joined the robbers. Maybe he is suffering what he deserves. But another part of me reaches out to embrace my brother. "Zem is a grown boy—almost a man. He knows you love him."

"Love from a father stands no chance of winning against the enticement of a woman. It was a sinful sight to see those slave girls, to hear the promises being made to our young men. And the wealth the robbers promised—not to mention the power and the freedom. I know the strength of their enticements all too well."

"You know much that I don't know. Tell me now: How do you know our father so well when he is still a stranger to me?"

"Count yourself fortunate. When I was working for Hem I was introduced to Giddianhi. I knew he was my father without anyone telling me. I could see myself and you in his face and the way he holds his shoulders back and walks with long strides—the way you walk, Kiah. I heard us in his voice. I *knew*. And so did he. He had long conditioned Hem to entice me."

"Why you?" I can't help wondering—if he knew about Calev, did he know about me? Why didn't he try to entice me too? I should be glad he didn't, but part of me feels rejected.

"Perhaps because I am his eldest son. It does not matter. He is cruel and vicious and smooth as rain over rocks. Nothing he says can be trusted."

"I blame him for Grandfather's death."

"And you should."

"Doesn't Giddianhi have another family and other sons?"

"Yes. But a man like him is driven by greed. He always wants what he doesn't have. I think the man still has feelings for Mother. I think that is why he used Hem to get to me and me to get to Mother."

"But Mother hates him."

"And that is what intrigues Giddianhi. Do you know he is now married to Tamar?"

"What?"

"Tamar, the younger sister of Eliana."

"I know who she is, but I thought Tamar—I don't know what I thought about Tamar. The truth is, I haven't thought of her in years."

"She was kidnapped and brought to Giddianhi as a virgin bride."

"By Hem?"

"Yes, or at least by men who were accountable to him."

The reality sinks slowly into my brain. "Does Eliana know?"

"She does."

"So Hem has always been—"

"For a very long time Hem has been Giddianhi's puppet. The man is careful that there is never any evidence against him. No connection between the two could be proven in court. You were the only one in all of Elam to ever dare challenge him."

"My word meant nothing to the judges."

"That is because the majority of those who sit in judgment are secret robbers."

"And there is no way to prove this?"

"No. One brother takes a blood oath to protect the other."

"How did you get out alive?"

"I live only because I am our father's eldest son. I can think of no other reason. Please, Kiah, you have to help me find a way to help my son now that he is in the clutches of this evil. I fear Eliana will never recover."

The question forms in my heart long before it escapes my lips. "Do you love Eliana?"

He hesitates. "Not the way a husband should love a wife. She deserved a better life. I only used her as Hem used me."

I feel like a sling, pulled back and ready to fire. It takes all my restraint not to judge my brother for the pain he has brought others. "You know the workings of the robbers. You know what Zem is being taught."

"I fear he will never come back."

"You once took their oath, and now you are returned to us. God will provide a way for Zem to return if he wishes to return."

"It is not as easy as you make it sound, Kiah. You are a man who has kept himself free of the stains and scars of sin. You might not see them, but I wear them still, and they are a heavy burden to carry. Heavier than you can fathom."

I face my brother and wait until he has lifted his chin to look at me. "What is repentance for if not to wash you clean and lift the guilt from your shoulders? That is the purpose of the Messiah. He is not just a god; Jesus Christ is *the* God and Savior of this world. He loves you, Calev. Even when you were counted among the robbers, Christ loved you. He loves Zem, and if Zem wants a way back, the path is marked."

"Do you really think there is hope for my son?"

"I know there is a way out. I've been in a different pit of snakes, and I was rescued. You were rescued. Bow your head with me now. Let us pray for my nephew and your son, Zemnarihah."

Seventy-Nine

History repeats and repeats. Good tells truth; evil tells lies. I watch my children learn and grow and wonder if they will ever know a time of true peace. War is everywhere—even in the churches—because it reigns in the heart of the people.

Calev and Eliana move close to us so that Eliana can find solace in Rinnah. My brother and I are in my small garden talking about his failed efforts to return Zem to his home and to his mother. My brother is bleaker than he was when he first returned from war during what seemed to be an endless famine.

Eliana is inside our home with Tarah. Eliana too seems lifeless now that her only son is gone. She sits quietly, day after day, playing with Rinnah; she serves my brother as a dutiful wife, but there is no hint of pleasure in anything Eliana does.

Torch-carrying soldiers come up the road and stop to inform us that Calev, I, and all other mature males in the household are to present themselves before the chief judge of all the land, a man called Gidgiddoni.

"You are to report without delay," the lead soldier tells us.

I know Gidgiddoni as a good man, a prophet and great leader who has done missionary work with Nephi. Now he has been appointed head of all the chief captains. I have served in the military, but it's been a long while since I was active. Lately Joab has been in training, and I fear he'll be called to active duty. I fear for Zadok too, who is too tender to do all that is required of a soldier during war.

Calev volunteers for full-time duty; he's willing to fight the robbers hand-to-hand. I know why. I am assigned a part-time duty training new soldiers on the same ball court in the valley of Sam where we believers were led to be slaughtered. It's like stepping backwards in my own life, and I despise the idea, though it feels good, even right, to be back in military training.

Even as I teach men how to fight to take a life, I also teach them about the Giver of all life. I am not the shy, unprepared missionary I was standing before Miyan all those years ago. Now my chest burns with truth as I testify that the day is coming when all people in our land, Nephites and Lamanites alike, will see the Savior of mankind walk among us, talk with us, teach us, and restore us.

Tarah tells me that my first missionary duty is within our own family. My little daughter, Rinnah, sits on my knee and cocks her head attentively as I tell stories Mother told me. As I share all I know of Jesus Christ, Joab turns a deaf ear. He would rather wander the tangle, exploring and hunting. My blood might not run through his veins, but he is my son.

"Pray while you are in the tangle," I tell him. "Pray like Enos. God hears all sincere prayers."

He only looks at me.

Zadok has the tender heart of Tarah. He does the chores required but prefers to tend our little flock of mountain sheep. I wish my sons were closer, better friends, but then I think of Calev and me and realize that closeness will come—in time. I love my family and rejoice in watching my wife press her lips to the forehead of our fourth child, a young babe we call Jonathan.

• • •

As war rages on I learn just how destructive my father is. His bands lay waste to village after village, not sparing the women or the children. It's hard to picture Zem capable of the kind of mayhem that is reported to us. Young men his age—cloaked in blood-soaked animal skins, their hair dyed red—attack and murder innocents. Villagers who fight against them are tortured, their bodies hanged from trees, pieces cut and left in synagogue courtyards. Giddianhi kills the children he cannot recruit.

I fear Giddianhi will target my sons—his grandsons—and I fear most for Joab.

One evening after synagogue prayers I walk home with my hand on Joab's shoulder. We are both in our military cloaks. He's taller than I, and his muscles bulge. But it's not only his physical strength I admire; Joab is a son of the commandment by age and honor. He reads without pause and writes the letters without flaw. When he was younger he wanted to draw like I do. I spent endless hours trying to teach him, but he finally gave up in frustration. I admire, but also fear, the strength of his independence, his fierce will.

Tonight we have armed ourselves, ready for an ambush if robbers should appear from the tangle or any dark, shadowy place.

"I love you, son."

They are words I never heard—never *will* hear—from my own father, but I say them easily and often to my own sons. "I am grateful for your service to our people, but I am also aware of the temptations that the devil places in your path. They are the same enticings that led your cousin Zem to join the robbers."

Joab only narrows his eyes and looks at me. "Father, I am no boy. I make my own choices, and I promise you, joining Giddianhi will never be one of them."

Robbers kidnap and mothers mourn, not knowing the fate of their missing children. I think of Tamar and the path that had to have led to her becoming Giddianhi's wife—my stepmother. As much as I loathe Hem's evil, it's difficult to imagine that he orchestrated his own daughter's kidnapping. I remember the genuine suffering he put Eliana though, not to mention her mother—Hem's own wife! It makes me hold my own daughter more tightly against my breast. Joab joins me in military training, but we have no problem convincing Zadok to stay near home, watching out for the safety of his mother, sister, and baby brother.

Jonas also keeps his children close, though they are too young to be called into service. His second wife, Zara, reminds me of his dead grandmother, Bosma. She is short and quick and loves to prepare meals. Zara admires Tarah, and I'm grateful the women are friends. Behind the high walls of Nephi's courtyard, I still feel as protected as I did as a boy.

I'm told that Hem continues to reside in Elam—claiming, as always, that he is nothing more than a powerful merchant, Elam's great leader, wrongfully accused of an alliance with Gadianton's own. "Of course I have to do business with them!" he explains. "Gadianton's own wield the power and the wealth."

After all these years, no punishment is yet doled out to Hem.

Eighty

A hundred of us are assembled on a flat grassy parchment of land, dressed in matching uniforms made from the soft fiber plants of the lowlands, spun into fabric by our diligent women. On our legs and arms is protective armor made from tree bark that has been soaked and molded to fit us, to help stave off the blows we receive in battle. We are captains in Gidgiddoni's army, lined up in ten straight rows as he marches in front of us, lecturing.

"Did you see the wonders in the skies last night?" Gidgiddoni asks. "They are signs of what is happening in Jerusalem with our mortal Messiah."

I have not given adequate thought to what Jesus Christ is doing at this very moment. He is a man young enough to be my son—a man who has kept every commandment, who has the power to heal the lame and raise the dead. When people see such miracles wrought by His hands, how will they be able to lift Him on a cross and crucify their very God? Yet that is the end His mortal life is approaching.

Calev stands beside me. He has a new scar on his cheek next to the one he received during his first tour of duty so many years ago; this one is so fresh it has not completely scabbed over. I will make a poultice to draw out the infection later when we are alone.

"We saw the brightness of the newest star," a soldier reports. "We saw the wonders glowing in the heavens."

"Did any of you witness the death and resurrection of one of my soldiers?"

Gidgiddoni refers to a battle the day before. One of his front men was taken out during an ambush. I helped carry his lifeless body back to camp. Gidgiddoni laid hands on him to restore the spirit of life into his body.

There were many witnesses to the miracle.

Gidgiddoni's face goes thin and tight with anger. "These are times of great miracles, yet where is the astonishment? It's not on your faces. You report a miracle as though you were reporting the weather. We have hardened our hearts, blinded our minds. For this we will pay. Do you not think it a miracle how our once-enemy brother has united with us against the robbers?"

He points to Calev.

Will my brother ever live separately from his past mistakes?

"In our camp we have both Lamanites and Nephites, eating, sleeping, fighting together against the robbers. Is this not a miracle?"

We all agree, and I think how he is right. How many signs and wonders have I seen, yet where is my astonishment? Where is my gratitude? Where is my record of all things sacred? I tell myself that when there is more time I will acquire plates and engrave the miracles and even the teachings of Samuel, the Lamanite prophet, so that my children and grandchildren might know the goodness of God.

• • •

One night I am called away and led by guards to the heavily protected court where Lachoneus presides. He meets me in the courtyard beneath the shadow of the great temple pyramid. It's dark, and his face flickers in the torchlight. "I have received an epistle from your father. I want you to read it before I have it read among our people."

"*My* father?"

A soldier holds a candle, and I read by flickering light. I read, unable to comprehend the audacity of the man Giddianhi.

Lachoneus, most noble and chief governor of the land, behold, I write this epistle unto you, and do give unto you exceedingly great praise because of your firmness, and also the firmness of your people, in maintaining that which ye suppose to be your right and liberty; yea, ye do stand well, as if ye were supported by the hand of a god, in the defense of your liberty, and your property, and your country, or that which ye do call so. And it seemeth a pity unto me, most noble Lachoneus, that ye should be so foolish and vain as to suppose that ye can stand against so many brave men who are at my command, who do now at this time stand in their arms, and do await with great anxiety for the word—Go down upon the Nephites and destroy them.

As I read I picture my nephew, Zem, as one of Giddianhi's brave men.

And I, knowing of their unconquerable spirit, having proved them in the field of battle, and knowing of their everlasting hatred towards you because of the many wrongs which ye have done unto them, therefore if they should come down against you they would visit you with utter destruction. Therefore I have written this epistle, sealing it with mine own hand, feeling for your welfare, because of your firmness in that which ye believe to be right, and your noble spirit in the field of battle.

Therefore I write unto you, desiring that ye would yield up unto this my people, your cities, your lands, and your possessions, rather than that they should visit you with the sword and that destruction should come upon you.

Or in other words, yield yourselves up unto us, and unite with us and become acquainted with our secret works, and become our brethren that ye may be like unto us—not our slaves, but our brethren and partners of all our substance. And behold, I swear unto you, if ye will do this, with an oath, ye shall not be destroyed; but if ye will not do this, I swear unto you with an oath, that on the morrow month I will command that my armies shall come down against you, and they shall not stay their hand and shall spare not, but shall slay you, and shall let fall the sword upon you even until ye shall become extinct. And behold, I am Giddianhi; and I am the governor of this the secret society of Gadianton; which society and the works thereof I know to be good; and they are of ancient date and they have been handed down unto us.

And I write this epistle unto you, Lachoneus, and I hope that ye will deliver up your lands and your possessions, without the shedding of blood, that this my people may recover their rights and government, who have dissented away from you because of your wickedness in retaining from them their rights of government, and except ye do this, I will avenge their wrongs. I am Giddianhi.

I am so shocked by the boldness of the declaration that the torch has to be replaced before I can form words. "What are you going to do?" I finally ask.

Lachoneus sighs. "I am astounded by the boldness of your father."

"I do not know this man—have never known him—as my father."

"There is only one way to combat evil—I will have our people cry unto the Lord."

Eighty-One

I watch my youngest son, still a toddler, chasing little chicks around our courtyard. He goes one way; they divide and go every way.

"Hurry. Gather them up and we'll take them with us," I tell Jonathan.

"Why do we have to move away?" he asks in his innocent, little-boy voice.

"Just gather the chicks."

He tries. The whole family tries. But only when the mother hen spreads out her wings do the little chicks scramble together beneath the safety of her shelter.

"What if we don't move? What if we just stay here behind Nephi's wall? We'll be safe." Joab scoots the hen forward with the edge of his foot, fighting her fluttering wings, trying to ease her into the crate he's made from timber.

"We'll die if we stay here." Zadok helps his brother and chases one of the chicks that has gotten away.

"No, we won't!" Joab counters. "I'll fight them off—by myself if I have to."

I smile at my sons, so grown. "We've got to obey. The robbers are laying waste to even the most secure homes. They've made a covenant with each other to destroy God's purposes—family and freedom."

"They want to destroy our liberty," Zadok says, "by putting a king over us instead of relying on the judgment seat."

"With the corruption in the courts, what difference would a king make?" Joab asks.

I listen to them debate while we finish packing the last of our family belongings. When Lachoneus realized the stubbornness of my father, he sent a proclamation throughout the land to gather all of the people into one body and one place. It's drastic, but it's necessary.

The Gadianton robbers, under the vicious power of my father, have taken hold like never before. They take their covenant to destroy God's people and God's teachings so seriously they are willing to die—but more willing to kill.

They rob, they murder, they torture, and no one is safe. As long as our people are spread out and divided, it's easy for the robbers to take one family, one village at a time. This way, they will have to come against us in our united strength.

At first I was with the people who wanted to gather all the Nephite armies into one and go into the high hills to fight the robbers face-to-face. But Lachoneus showed forth great patience and wisdom. "We will not go against them," he said, "but we will wait until they shall come against us. As the Lord liveth, if we do He will deliver them into our hands."

The people, for the most part, support Lachoneus. The land he's chosen to assemble us in is expansive. It covers the great stretch from the land of Zarahemla all the way to the land of Bountiful and from there to the border of the land of Desolation. It's rich with game and offers valleys, hills, streams, and established villages. Can so many people—tens, perhaps hundreds of thousands—be able to get along living in such close proximity? Time will tell.

Since Giddianhi's oath to kill us all, I have been working with Jonas and my sons, helping to build fortifications around the selected land so that when the robbers do come forth they cannot break into our stronghold.

I'm pleased to see the content man that Jonas has become. He lost years in sorrow while he mourned Orli and their baby. He never grew bitter, only worked all of the time perfecting his cement craft and learning every aspect of construction. His skills are now demanded and respected.

I'm especially grateful Jonas has an influence on my sons. They have both grown into independent young men. Zadok finds peace in obedience and seldom questions why a law exists. Joab is a bull of a boy, more sullen and fast to question why a law exists or why his mother makes him do a certain chore. He was always strong willed, but these past few months he has grown hard and eager to fight. His temper flashes like my own used to.

Oh, how I miss Grandfather. He had a way of making all of us want to hear what he had to say. His lessons on pride and faith resound with me still.

I know of no other time there has been a call to assemble all the people in one body; it makes me think of Moses gathering the children of Israel, leading them around and around the same mountain. If they had been obedient and made the trek straight into the Promised Land, their journey would have taken only eleven days. That's what Grandfather taught me—how an eleven-day journey turned into forty years, all because of disobedience. I pray that we can stay unified and obedient and defeat the robbers soon so that our journey away from home might be shortened. But the hard truth is that Lachoneus has had us gather enough food and supplies to last for a seven-year siege.

It's painful to watch Tarah try her best to be brave. She cleans our house, packs the few things we have into packs for our backs, sweeps the dirt floor of our home the way Mother used to, and cries.

"The robbers will destroy it, won't they?"

Tarah is looking at her little garden out back where she grows vegetables and herbs—flowers too, red, yellow, and purple. The sun is shining in her hair, turning it to curls of gold. I move up behind her, put my arms around her, and hold her until her shoulders stop shaking and her tears are spent. All I can think to say is, "If anything happens to our home I'll build you a new one, I swear."

She spins around and takes my face in her hands. "It's not this house, not the garden; it's you, Kiah. If anything happens to you or to one of our children, I'll die. You are my world, and every day that we survive the robbers is a miracle to me."

• • •

It's the very last day we are permitted to gather. After today the great gates will be closed, the government guards will join their own families behind the protected compound, and anyone left outside in the cities or the villages will be on their own against the robbers.

I expected Mother and Abner to abandon Elam and join us by now. It's been weeks since I sent an epistle to Elam, telling them that we would wait for them until the final day. Now the last day of the exodus is upon us. I hope Abner is not being stubborn about leaving Elam. If he delays, they will be easy prey for the robbers who are watching from the hills, just waiting to attack stragglers and abandoned strongholds.

My stomach knots thinking of the danger they will be in if they are left to themselves. Abner is no longer a young man. Mother walks slowly, her spine curved by the years. My sister Elka has grown into a young woman legally ready to wed, but I am grateful to hear that she has no prospects. Mother has taught her to read and write, and Elka teaches other girls the same. Abby is a proven student with aspirations of becoming a lawyer. I'm anxious to see them and have them join with our family.

The day wears down. Jonathan sits atop my shoulders. Rinnah and Tarah both have baskets filled and ready to put atop their heads. I have a cart to push, and I wish Joab and Zadok were here, but they've gone ahead—Joab with his army of guards, and Zadok to serve as a guide at the camp entrance, leading people to know where their assigned portion of the land is. Imagine a million families uprooted, designated to live in a square plot of land in row after exact row with others just as displaced. It would take days to walk from one end of the camp to the next, so there is room enough for the people to organize themselves. I just don't know if there is room sufficient to exist over a long period of time.

"At least Father, Mother, and my sisters will be near us," Tarah says. "There's some solace in knowing that. We can be each other's comfort."

"I think Gidgiddoni is wise in organizing families to stay close to each other."

"I wish Joab and Zadok were with us."

"Be proud of them for fulfilling their responsibilities," I tell Tarah. "We'll soon be together too often and in such tight surroundings that you'll tire of having everyone underfoot."

"As long as we're safe," she says, putting her hands to her mouth. I can't help noticing that her fingernails are chewed to the quick, something she does when she is nervous.

The highway that leads through the city and out through the back gate toward the camp is thick with people, mostly clustered into extended families with parents, grandparents, uncles, aunts, and cousins. None of them looks any happier than I feel.

Jonathan gets down and wants to play with an *aak* that lives by the stream that runs behind our house. It's a small creature with a hard, round shell and a head that only sticks out when it feels safe. It's head is tucked tight away now because Jonathan is after it, lifting it, carrying it, dropping it.

"How long will we be gone?" Rinnah asks. She has my wide eyes and her mother's dimpled cheeks. Right now her fists are dug into her hips and her head leans to one side.

I touch Rinnah's soft cheek and tell her what I told her mother—"It doesn't matter how long it takes as long as we are together."

"You're a captain, aren't you?" someone calls as I stand by the gate hoping to catch a sign of Abner's tall head—or Abby's, for he is a match for his father.

"Yes," I say. "I'm an army captain."

"Will we be safe, gathered together as one people?"

"Gidgiddoni has an organized plan. It's not perfect, but it assures we'll be safer than we are now."

I am honored that Gidgiddoni, chief over all the chief captains, has appointed me a chief captain over a band of ten thousand, some of them Lamanites. I hope to eventually find Miyan and his family during the isolation. But for now I'm hoping to find Mother.

"I realize you're worried about your mother, but we can't wait much longer," Tarah says. "The gates will close if we don't hurry." Tarah kisses my lips.

And so we gather, pray, and take our refuge.

"Is Grandmother coming?" Rinnah asks me. "Is that why you keep looking back?"

"I hope she comes. I hope she's hurrying."

The exodus for our family is short; we only have to enter one side of Zarahemla and come out the other where a mighty gate stands open to allow entrance into the designated camping area. Thankfully, the guards there know me, and they allow our family to enter without delayed inspection.

I've been working for a very long time trying to prepare this camp, yet now that it is packed with people and their belongings, the once-massive expanse of land seems smaller. We are a human sea, dipping and rolling.

Zadok spots us and comes with his spear to point the direction in which we are to camp. "Mother, your side of the family is already in place. Grandfather is not happy, not happy at all. He's worried the robbers will steal the precious stones he's hidden in his shop."

I think Abarron has cause to worry, but I don't say so. I'm hoping the guards assigned to the inner part of Zarahemla will be able to keep the robbers at bay.

As we navigate through the maze I am impressed at Gidgiddoni's organizational skills. The roads are wide enough to accommodate huge crowds. There are small markets and an enormous chief market. Seeing that market—comprised of vendors from the north to the south and the east to the west—I wonder what Hem would think. He hardly ever crosses my mind, but now it dawns on me that he will be here too, living among us. He's probably already arrived, and I find myself scanning the rows of fruits and vegetables, the rows of baskets and meats, the rows of tents and weapons. The colorful linens of the market are woven from different plants, dyed by different berries and leaves, some decorated with brilliant feathers, beads, and other ornamentations.

It takes me back to the time when I wandered through Lamanite territory with Miyan. I can still hear the *clink* of craftsmen as they made swords and blades and weapons of every kind. Where are those weapons now—in the hands of our people, or in the fists of the robbers?

We are led to the plot allotted my family. It is part of a larger space with Abarron's family on one side and Nephi's family to the other. Right away the women and children come to greet Tarah and the baby. Rinnah runs to play with her cousins.

"Where's your father?" I ask Jonas.

"As prophet, he is making rounds to preach and teach." He sets off and I follow him; all three of his sons, looking as alike as three growing chicks, tag along.

"I've never imagined this many people," I tell him.

"And there will be more before this ends. Lachoneus has invited everyone who believes in Christ to enter through the gates and take refuge."

"What of those who only *claim* to believe? How do we know for certain that we are not allowing disguised robbers in to live among us?"

Jonas shakes his head. "They've been living among us all of our lives, brother."

We walk up and down, but the same sight is repeated again and again. People are afraid. People are angry. People are clinging to each other, praying for the safety of their warrior loved ones.

"Where's Calev?" Jonas asks me.

"He is with Gidgiddoni, being instructed in how to make weapons. He used to be very good at it. I'm thinking that Abarron will join them later, once he gets his family settled."

"You look worried, Kiah."

"There is no sign of Mother."

"I thought she was coming in your caravan."

"I thought so too, but they never showed up."

The afternoon wears on. We pitch our tents while the women prepare food. Children are everywhere, making new friends, exploring new boundaries. The noise is incredible, a million people or more talking, laughing, crying. People dot the land like trees dot the distant hillside.

Once my family is as settled as possible with our tent opening set to face the temple, I leave for my military responsibilities. I make the rounds to check on my band of people. I soon learn how great our needs are. There are families without food and proper shelter. There are people who are injured and sick. There are women who are ready to give birth, and children who are terrified.

We are all thinking the same thing: The robbers are out there, sallying down from the hills, already overtaking everything that was left behind. The thought of them going through my own home, destroying Tarah's flowers and sleeping in the courtyard where Joab and Zadok slept is something I can't dwell on. I'll go crazy.

By the time the sun sinks low, ready to touch the horizon, I feel ill. The thought of Mother and Abner being alone, unprotected with the children on the road somewhere, steals any appetite I might have had. The possibilities of what could happen to them are endless and terrifying. I would go out myself, but it is too dangerous, so I can't expect anyone else to go in search of them either.

The moon is a round white shadow against a blue-black sky.

"Under your watchful eye, Almighty Father, let my mother and her family be safe."

A trumpet sounds to signal that the gate is being drawn shut. After tonight, those wishing to enter will have a difficult time proving why they did not adhere to the appointed day Lachoneus set. If they are turned away, it will surely mean death at the merciless hands of the robbers.

I make my way to the entrance and speak with the guards, making certain that if my mother comes she will be given instructions where to meet up with us.

The guard assures me, "I am from Elam. I know your mother, Captain Kiah. If she and her family enters, I will lead them to you."

Torches burn and flutter blue and orange. People are finding their way around as they settle in for the first night of rest as a closed camp. A few disputes arise, but for the most part, people are peaceful.

As the main gate—three times the height of a man—is drawn closed, my heart is drawn. I am a little boy again, frightened and alone without my mother.

"Stop!" the guard calls, and the men pulling the ropes stop.

A final band of refugees is spotting coming in from the south. A man's voice cries out, "Wait! We are here!"

I know the voice. "Abner!" I cry, pushing past the guards and out onto the road to meet the rest of my family.

Eighty-Two

We think we are safe. We think living like this is better. But we are human beings meant to live free, not confined and thrown together like animals in a cage with predators on the other side of our bars, always there, always hungry and ready to kill us.

It's not that we don't have food—we do. It's not that we don't have structure. There are marketplaces and schools and every captain sees that his band's basic needs are met. But we don't have freedom and we can't live unafraid.

• • •

Seasons pass. Children are born. Children grow. People die. Life goes on, but it is not the same.

Jonas's great-uncle Lehi is preaching when he keels over dead. The last word from his lips was the same last word my own grandfather spoke: *Jesus.*

One morning a distraught Tarah stands before me, wringing her hands. "Eliana won't eat. She refuses. Oh, Kiah, she's already so thin; I fear this will kill her."

"Why won't she eat?" I ask, occupied with my own worries. One of my best guards hung himself last night. I had to tell his wife and children.

Tarah touches my face, twists a strand of hair behind my ear. I look up into the face that always looks like an angel.

"Why won't Eliana eat?" I ask.

"Because Zem is out there starving."

Out there means he is on the other side of our refuge. The robbers have destroyed the lands we left desolate. They've eaten everything, and they have no time to replant crops—when they tarry, our men kill them. They must stay on the move, and now even the game in the wilderness is gone. The robbers are without food.

"He's a robber, Tarah. Zem *should* be starving."

"Zem is your nephew, Kiah. Don't you have compassion for him?"

"Not much. He chose to follow his grandfathers."

"But Hem is not with Giddianhi; he's with us."

"A wolf among the sheep, Tarah. We both know it."

Hem and his new wife are stationed in a tent at the end of our row. He had no other family to care for him. Tamar is "out there" with her husband, Giddianhi. I know they have children—children that are brothers and sisters to me—yet I feel no attachment or desire to know them. I avoid Hem, but have no desire to harm him, for he is old now and spends most of his time walking through the marketplace, talking to anyone who will talk to him.

Tarah is determined. "I can do nothing about Zem, but I *will* make Eliana eat."

"What do you want me to do about Eliana not eating?"

"Will you talk to Calev—tell him?"

"I'll talk to him."

"He barely acknowledges his own wife. It makes my heart heavy to see a married couple who acts like they hardly know each other."

I wrap Tarah in my arms and hold her to me. Her hair smells of wood smoke, and her skin is still as soft as it was on the day we were married. I whisper in her ear until she blushes and laughs like the girl I first fell in love with.

I find my brother right where I expect to find him: working. He and Abarron labor all of the time to fashion weapons that are strong and deadly enough to withstand the weapons of our enemies. Calev's specialty is a cimeter fashioned after similar weapons the Lamanites first used in the days of our forefathers.

The hilt is like the hilt of a sword, but the blade is curved—made for cutting, not stabbing. He usually shapes it from hard wood; on rare occasions, he uses bone. It can take days to craft a single cimeter, to make the edge both strong and sharp enough to sever a man's forearm.

Every day we lose men to the robbers. They lay in wait. When our men venture out of the fortifications to tend crops or hunt, they are the ones hunted and murdered.

Gadianton's men are more animal than human.

Jonas has also made contributions to weapon designs with his catapult, but his cement skills are called upon more. He stays busy fortifying our gates and strongholds, making watchtowers, and repairing the buildings that already existed on this land.

I find Calev bent over his bench, carving a blade. Since Zem left to live with Giddianhi, my brother has been a man alive, but not living. He's sunk into his deepest depression yet—grunting, unable to look anyone in the eyes, muttering to himself.

"Tarah is worried because Eliana won't eat."

His shoulders shrug and his hammer lifts.

"Calev, Eliana is worried about Zem."

At the mention of his son's name, Calev lifts his head. "I'm making a sword that might well end of the life of my son."

"You're doing your job, brother." I am helpless to console Calev.

"Do you think my son is starving?"

"I know Giddionhi's men want for food."

"They're starving." Calev winces. "I would give my life if I could go back and change the choices I've made."

"I know you would."

"Kiah, you understand the word of God. Tell me, what good does my repentance do when my actions have led to the destruction of my son's soul?"

What answer can I offer? Calev's choices exposed Zem to the life he is living now. If his father had made different choices, would Zem be here with us, safe in his father's care? Who can say?

"Would you like to pray?" I ask.

Calev shakes his head. "You pray, Kiah. Your prayers are heard."

• • •

While we have grain and barley, meat and fruit, the robbers' situation grows more grave. Gidgiddoni says that the robbers are desperate. They will soon have no other choice than to come against us, try to scale our walls and attack our strongholds. That will be a battle I do not wish to fight.

One day while Joab is accompanying me on my military rounds, he tells me, "I can't wait for the robbers to come against us. I've spent my life preparing for war."

I sigh, wishing I could spare my son what is about to happen. But I have no power to stop what will not be stopped. We have no choice. We either fight or die. Gidgiddoni announces the day appointed for an all-out war.

The robbers ready themselves. We ready ourselves.

Gidgiddoni believes our first line of defense is faith. We pray. Nephi preaches, and his faith and valor remind me of his father. We have seen nothing of Jonas's grandfather, Nephi, in such a long time, and the believing people talk among themselves, saying that he was taken in spirit to live with the God of all gods.

When Nephi isn't preaching, his brother Timothy is. Timothy has mighty faith and I've seen him work miracles, once blessing a crippled child to stand and walk, another time talking a man out of suicide. If I didn't know better, I could be fooled into thinking that Nephi and Timothy are the same man; they are that much alike outwardly and inwardly.

Jonas grows in faith too. Though he doesn't do a lot of preaching, he works to make sure the fortifications of our camp are secure. Abner spends a lot of his efforts working with Jonas, Calev, and Abarron. Abner favors swords that are dipped in a metal coating, but the supplies of ore are scant, so most of our weapons are made from timber and bone. My design to inlay obsidian is replicated until every fighter has a blade that's not just capable of cutting but of shredding an enemy.

Why did I ever relish war?

The women and children are made as secure as possible in a special set of fortresses built toward the center of our camp. I can see the fear in my little son Jonathan's eyes. Rinnah clings to me, asking, "What is a Gadianton robber?"

"Someone who makes a covenant to destroy the things of God."

It's the best answer I can give her, though it's so much more complicated than that.

Rinnah's eyes search mine. "Why, Father, would anyone want to destroy the things of God?"

I have no answer.

Gidgiddoni calls all priests to meet on the north side of the temple. I am honored when I receive the bid to be there among company like Nephi, Timothy, Jonas, and the twin brothers Mathoni and Mathonihah. There are many others—some I know, others I do not.

Nephi prays for us, and Timothy is then is asked to speak to us.

He looks upon me and smiles; I feel an added strength surge through my entire body. "We are a united people," he begins, "because we are compelled to unite against the power and destruction of Gadianton's band. But we are not a united people in spirit or heart. There are those among us who believe that the great pyramid has four sides: the north side is for us, the priests; the south side for the people; the east for the rain god; and the west for the sun god."

The sun hits Lehi's face and my heart catches. He seems illuminated.

"But I testify to you, my brethren, my fellow priests, that the sun god and the rain god are one god. There is but ONE god we worship—our Almghty Creator, the Father of our spirits, the Father of our coming Messiah!"

His testimony stirs us all and makes us realize that it is for the Messiah and His Atonement, for our families and our freedom to live and worship, that we go to battle. It is not to destroy but to defend ourselves from those who would destroy us.

Nephi then stands before us. Our great prophet is a powerful preacher, and like Benjamin, he refuses to live off the work of the people. His muscles are large and strong because he works for his own living, repairing the walls with Jonas, building and working cement. He also knows how to wield a sword. Today his weapon hangs by his side, ready to fight if necessary.

"The robbers are about to come upon us," he warns; his voice carries across the wave of priests and far beyond so that everyone can hear what our prophet has to tell us. It's not a miracle that his voice carries as it does—it's because the pyramid was constructed by our ancestors so that when a speaker stands in a certain place, his voice carries as if he's shouting through a giant seashell. Though we number in the thousands, we hear Nephi clearly. "Do not fear the robbers. Fear God. Supplicate Him for your protection. Fear God. Not man."

When he is finished we wait.

And wait.

I know from experience that we are like a bride, knowing the groom will come but anxious, not knowing when he will arrive.

It's my own son Joab who breaks the tension when he appears with the other young soldiers and is called to take his place at the bottom step of the rising pyramid. He claps his hand; the sound echoes right back as the cry of the singing bird with the green feathered head and rich red breast: the *Quetzal,* a symbol of creation and the willingness of the Great Creator to move in our lives.

Joab steps down with the sound of the *Quetzal* still crying in our ears.

We return to waiting.

At the peak of the sun up from its slumber, the battle cry is given and the enemy attacks. We fight. We fight for our lives, our families, our freedom, and our faith. We fight like animals with swords and clubs and blades. We fight to kill. I hate it.

Joab and Zadok fight under another command. They are placed far inside the compound where they should be safer; still I worry.

"Kiah!"

I turn to see that my young brother, Abby, fights beside me. Abner has made him the strongest possible sword, the hilt inlaid with turquoise. There is fear in his eyes, and that frightens me.

I've been in many battles, but this one determines our future. If we win we will be allowed to return to our homes, to restore what was lost, and to await the coming of the Messiah among us. If the robbers win, we lose our lives, our freedom. I could be separated from Tarah and the children, made a slave. I could end my days alone and miserable.

I fight with the fervor of my youth but not the desire for violence.

When the robbers attack, the very sight terrifies me. They have shorn their heads to the scalp; around their waists they wear lambskins dyed in blood. They have breastplates and head plates and scream with murder as they fall upon us.

We are as great as the east sea.

They are as great as the west sea.

The first robber who charges me is a short, stout man. He is as old as Abner; taking him with my sword requires only one sidestep and a swing.

I'm sickened by the sound and the feel of my blade slicing through flesh then hitting bone.

Abby screams every time he raises his blade. I suppose it gives him power.

We fight.

We fight and we kill. Every enemy that falls makes me think of Joab and Zadok. Are they safe? I try to focus my mind on my sons and not on the horror that envelopes me. Joab and Zadok have reached the point in their lives when their minds are on girls. Tarah's cousin has a daughter who has caught Joab's eye, a young girl who likes to giggle at everything Joab says. Zadok favors a girl who came from Shimnilom with Miyan's cousins. I was heartbroken to learn that Miyan was killed by robbers while helping his brother in the cornfields.

The thought makes me battle harder.

I take a hard hit to the shoulder and fall down. My attacker lifts a club to bash my head, but I whirl and knock him off his feet. We wrestle and finally the man runs off.

A horn sounds, and the battle ends for the night.

This goes on for days. Hundreds of our men die. Hundreds of their men die.

At night the bodies of our soldiers are dragged toward the center of camp where the women search for their husbands and sons. The dead of the robbers are dragged away, but we hear no wailing from their women and children.

This is war. Death and suffering.

Days pass and bleed together.

Hundreds of dead turn into thousands, and I wonder if we will stop before we are all dead. The ground is wet and red with blood. The air is thick with the scent of death and the sound of the dying. My own body is sliced and bruised, and I want nothing more than to be back in the arms of my wife, safe, with our children around us. I want peace.

Nephi comes again and preaches to us, trying to lift our spirits.

I don't remember his words, but the feeling I get when he speaks restores me as sure as a solid night's sleep.

The next day our tender soldiers are sent out to fight with the seasoned ones. My sons go forth, but I do not know where they fight. I have not seen Abby in days and fear that he has died.

"Kiah!" Calev finds me and battles beside me.

"Look!" he yells.

I look and see that the robbers—so terrifying in their blood-dyed skins and shorn heads and high head plates—are attacking in a ferocious line and I see our young soldiers fall to their knees, one by one.

Then I see him—a warrior in a horrendously familiar blue cloak and a feathered headplate. Giddianhi—our father. Where is *his* line of defense? Surely, the leader of the robbers has defensemen. But he is alone.

I see from the pinched look on Calev's face that he has seen him too.

"Fall!" Calev screams at me. "Fall to your knees!"

"Why?"

"Fall, brother. Trust me. Fall!"

My knees bend and I go down. Calev kneels beside me. He begins praying, aloud and with mighty faith. Louder and louder.

Our position is a lure, and it brings him to us. Giddianhi comes over and stands ready to take our lives—though with our heads bowed, our bodies clad in armor, he has no idea we are his sons.

"You are cowards!" he shouts. "You fear your God, but He will not save you. It's me you should fear!"

But we are not afraid. In unison, Calev and I jump to our feet and give our father the surprise of his miserable life.

Eighty-Three

Calev takes him from the back, has his sword laid flat against the shoulders of our father. I come at Giddianhi from the front and lay my blade across his throat.

Giddianhi stands still. His eyes go wide, and there is a flicker of horror on his face. Then Calev speaks. "You deserve to die."

Giddianhi smirks. "Is that you, Calev, hiding behind me? How typical! Still the coward you've always been." He laughs just as he did as he watched Grandfather breathe his last breath.

"My brother is no coward," I say, feeling my jaw clench, my fingers tighten. "You're a snake," I tell him, "and you deserve to lose your head."

He laughs again. "My foolish son, you know that the serpent's head is a powerful symbol. A snake like me glides through life, moving side to side just as creation moves from day to night. I am no coward. I am as God is."

Our weapons tighten.

"Look at me, Kiah!" Giddianhi commands. "You're trembling like a coward. Go ahead, slit my throat."

I want to. All I have to do is slide my blade, and the man who broke my mother's heart, who stopped Grandfather's heart from beating, who blinded my brother, who stole my nephew, who made my life hell—the man who brought death and fear upon all of our people will be gone.

"Tell me where Zem is," Calev demands. "I want my son back!"

Of course, this is why Calev came to fight with my band. He wanted to find Giddianhi so he could find his missing son.

"Zem! My grandson. He's a brilliant warrior. He honors his oath—unlike you, Calev. He makes me proud."

There are soldiers fighting all around us. We've got to kill Giddianhi now or one of his robbers will surely see him and come to fight us.

Calev's voice is hoarse and desperate. "Where is my son?"

"Are you weeping, Calev? Is that weakness I hear in your voice?"

I press my blade against the man's throat the same way Hem pressed his against mine. I have a scar to remind me of that every time I see my reflection or touch my neck.

"My sons. I think how different you would have turned out if I had raised you instead of your mother."

He winces as a trickle of blood oozes around my blade.

"Please," Calev says, "return my son to me. Zem is a good boy, more like his mother instead of me."

His lips turn upward. I glance at Calev, and in that instant Giddianhi bends his knees, dips to the ground and frees himself.

My brother falls to the ground and I fear he's been wounded, but the wound did not come from our father's sword, and my brother quickly rises. But we do not pursue the man. He gets away. We move on to the next attacker and the next.

There are screams and cries and the moan of the dying, but drowning out all of that is the sound of Giddianhi's laughter thundering in my head.

In all the land there has never been such slaughter. For days and days the battle continues to rage. The women leave the children to come and drag the dead off to the perimeters so that we can continue to fight. My thoughts never leave Tarah and the children. I fight for them.

The robbers threaten to slaughter us and they have, but with God's name on our lips, we manage to fight them back. I cannot describe the horror, the gruesome carnage of fighting hand-to-hand. Gidgiddoni has prepared us well with armor—breastplates, thick clothing—but the heat takes a toll, and now men are dropping from fatigue.

Death howls like a wind that will not stop.

"Go after them as far as the far border of the wilderness," Gidgiddoni commands us. "If they fall into your hands, slay them. Spare none!"

I have no word from my sons, and I worry for them as sure as Calev worries for Zem. There is still no news of Abby, and I have not seen Calev in days, not since we nearly killed Giddianhi. But now he is back, handing out armor to those who need it. Most of the shields and plates are drenched in blood, taken from the heads and chests and limbs of fallen soldiers.

Gidgiddoni has me order my dwindled band to march on the frontl ines.

I go, and Calev marches with me. I can tell from the anguish in his eyes that he has had no word about Zem.

We leave the flatlands and go toward the rising hills because that is the direction in which the robbers retreat. We are exhausted and fearful for our sons, but we are warriors, and we march. I do all I can to encourage and fortify my own men. It feels good and right to have my brother beside me, but it does not feel right to chase men, even robbers, when they are in full retreat. Both Nephites and Lamanites always battle in a position of defense. Even when we attack first, we do it to defend our freedom. This death march feels different.

The strategy is to force the robbers back into their hiding places while they are limited in numbers, weak and broken. They will die from their wounds; they will starve—and we will be able to return to our lives.

"Kiah!"

Calev calls me over to inspect the body of a fallen soldier.

Right away, I recognize his signature blue cloak and his feathered headplate.

Once again, we are face-to-face with our father.

"Giddianhi," Calev says, "it seems we are meant to slay you."

I see no wound, but the man is down, drained from fatigue and stricken by the unblinking sun.

Calev picks up Giddianhi's sword and hands it to me.

"Where is Zem?"

Giddianhi's lips are baked and bleed fresh when he moves them to answer. "Zem is safe."

"How do you know?"

"He will replace me when you lift your blade to kill me."

"Why not one of your own sons?"

He tries to laugh. "Look at your own reflection, Calev. Look at Kiah. All my sons, it seems, are unworthy. Not Zemnarihah. He makes me proud."

Calev groans.

"Go ahead," Giddianhi taunts, "kill me."

"I will not kill you, but take you prisoner."

I know that taking anyone, even Gadianton's leader, is against our orders, but I know what my brother is thinking. An exchange can be made: Giddianhi for Zem.

The man looks ready to die, and it takes both Calev and me to lift him to his feet.

He hisses at Calev. "You took an oath and you broke it."

"I want my son back."

"You are my son, and you vowed you would join with me and stay with me."

"And you made an oath to our mother," I say, feeling all of the hatred leave my body like sweat from pores. All of my life I've hated this man, and now that he is limp and weak and dying before me, I no longer hate him. I pity him. The day is at hand when he will be faced with all the pain he has caused, all of the destruction. He will discover then that he has pledged his loyalty to the wrong leader.

My arm goes around his waist as Calev lifts him from the opposite side.

Giddianhi's face swivels toward me. I breathe in his foul breath. "Kiah, surely you have more courage to stand and fight for what is right than your elder brother. Join with me, son."

Son. All my life I wanted to hear my father—not my grandfather, not my stepfather, but my father—call me *son.*

Now it means nothing coming from Giddianhi. Nothing.

"No."

"So you still wait and watch for a Messiah that will not come?"

"He will come."

"If He does appear in this land, He will not show Himself to you, Kiah. For you are a coward. Come, join me and I will make of you a true man, a warrior."

"I will die first."

"Then you will die!"

I feel a sudden sharp pain in my abdomen, and I realize that Giddianhi, the snake that he is, has struck. He's pressed a blade against my stomach. But before I can cry out, Calev has thrown the man back down onto the ground.

My hands reach up beneath my breastplate and touch my bare stomach. It is warm and wet with my own blood.

Giddianhi hisses, "Cowards! You are both cowards, not fit for the covenant of Gadianton."

Calev looks at me, then down at our father.

"Tell me where my son is."

"Your son is a robber now, and he will die a robber."

Giddianhi slithers and tries to escape, but it is no effort for Calev to catch up with him. The man shows no fear, only hatred, as he curses us, curses our mother, and curses Zemnarihah. I watch as my brother's knee bends, as his leg lifts high, and in one powerful thrust his heel comes down on Giddianhi's throat.

Then Calev comes to aid me. The two of us hobble off the battlefield, together, leaving our father to strangle on the venomous words he's still hissing out against us.

Eighty-Four

"Father, when can we go home?"

I look into the face of my daughter, Rinnah. Her features have softened in all the time we've been refugees. Jonathan runs to chase the *chuwen* that used to be Zadok's constant companion. War changes everyone.

"As soon as it is safe," I tell Rinnah, wondering when that will be. I thought the war would end when Giddianhi died, but the robbers live by their oath. They lay in wait to murder us. Any time we venture out of our secure places, they attack.

Their loss was greater than ours, yet we do not hear them mourn for their dead. The cries in our camp continue for an entire year. We bury our dead and tend to our wounded.

Tarah tends to me until all I have left is a fierce scar across my belly. I look down at it and see the form of a snake. A fitting reminder.

Abby was wounded in the leg. He heals, though he will always walk with a limp. His father—our father—takes an interest in medicine, and he and Mother grow herbs and learn from Pazel and others how to best care for our wounded.

Calev shows a sudden favor to Joab. My son takes to his uncle, and the two of them spend much time together, crafting weapons and armor.

Eliana proves she has a gift for weaving river reeds into breastplates that can withstand a heavy blade blow. She knows just how to twist and twine the reeds, and when Gidgiddoni comes by on a relatively peaceful afternoon it is Calev who is proud to boast of his wife's design.

Gidgiddoni not only praises Eliana, but tries on one of the reed breastplates. He lifts his arms and swings them in circles. He looks pleased.

"Lift up your sword and strike me," our chief captain orders Zadok.

My son looks confused.

Our chief captain smiles. "I want to test this armor. I want to see for myself what it can withstand."

Zadok does not move from the entrance of our tent. "I cannot strike you. You're my commander."

"*I* can strike you!" Rinnah has a sword in her clutch and comes rushing at Gidgiddoni.

He tries to sidestep to keep from taking a blow, but he's not quick enough. When he turns, Rinnah brings the blade down hard on his shoulder.

He flinches. Everyone rushes to take the sword from my daughter and to see that our chief captain is all right.

"I'm unharmed," he says, sounding both pleased and embarrassed.

• • •

In the days that follow, Gidgiddoni works with Eliana to further improve what Gidgiddoni sees as an inspired design. In the end they craft a breastplate made from heavy cotton clothing, layers of bark, and braided reeds.

"This will save many lives," he tells everyone in a reenactment where he implores Rinnah to attack him again.

There is much laughter, and for a time we almost forget that our lives revolve around war and its endless horrors. Life in the camp consists of constant military training. Even the women and the children are taught how to use weapons. Some men are appointed to grow grain and are given military guards to protect their ventures out into the growing fields closer to the hill country.

In his wisdom, Gidgiddoni creates training camps within our camp. Every person must have an area where he becomes expert. Mine is in military training. Calev's in is weaponry. In addition to our expertise, we must all learn the fundamentals of every craft. Our commander expects every member of the camp to make a contribution.

At first the men protest violently. They do not want to have to learn the chores that have always belonged to women. But Gidgiddoni is wise and patient and commanding. Every man takes a course in how to fetch and carry water, how to gut and skin a deer, how to grind corn and prepare meals. Every woman learns how to make a weapon from any material available, be it wood, horn, or bone. The women also get educated in the craft of creating armor.

Priests are assigned the task of teaching our children reading and writing. Even girls who are of age are permitted to sit in on afternoon sessions once their morning chores are completed.

Everyone, even children, must learn from the healers how to make poultices and which herbs to blend to attend to basic wounds. Mother and Abner, along with Elka, lead these training camps.

Engineers teach us means of eliminating waste.

Carpenters teach us construction. Jonas and his family teach the art of cement making, mixing, and application.

Nephi and Timothy preach the teachings of God. Nephi also contributes a special design for a headplate that is coated in a thin layer of cement. Gidgiddoni deems the idea good, but not practical because of the weight.

Lachoneus instructs great classes on the workings of a free government. Even my little son Jonathan learns why a judgment seat is better for the people than a kingship.

The most important instruction comes from the prophets when they teach us of the coming Messiah. Nephi is chief prophet, but there are others who preach and prophesy with great power. Gidgiddoni is one voice that makes it very clear that we should all look to the coming Messiah to deliver us.

Now that we are camped as refugees, the idea of a deliverer becomes very real to me. I preach within my own family, trying to teach my children what I know in my heart to be true. The time will come, in their very lifetimes, when they will see the Messiah. But will I? Grandfather, with all of his faith and obedience, did not live to see the face he so worshiped. If I am alive when the Messiah shows himself to our people, will I be worthy to see Him myself? Or will He turn away from me because I am a man so flawed? Does it even matter?

Years ago I wondered what was happening in the land of our forefathers. I wonder still. Is Christ healing the blind? Raising the dead? With whom does He associate? What are the men like He has called to serve with Him? What's the Messiah's mortal family like? Does His mother sing to Him as mine sang to me? In my wondering, the Messiah becomes real to me.

More time drags by. We have been enclosed in this camp for five years now, but we are still not safe to return to the places we call home. Of course there are disputatioms and outbreaks of violence among our own people, but for the most part, we dwell in peace within.

Without is only violence. The robbers are now laying siege, trying to close us in on all sides, preying on anyone who ventures outside of our fortifications.

One night I am awakened by a woman's cry outside our tent door. She looks familiar, but I do not know her.

"I am the daughter of Oshra, from Elam. Hem is my husband," she whispers in a voice hoarse but not tearful. "He is dying and has requested that you come and lay hands on him."

I have spent the past years avoiding Hem whenever possible. We have said little to each other. There is no reason he would request me at such a time.

"You must be mistaken," I tell the woman. "Your husband and I are not friends, not kin. He has no regard for me."

"That is not so. He has great regard for you."

Tarah has awoken and gone to fetch Eliana. We go together to the humble tent of Hem. He is on a mat on the ground, his mouth open, his face the wrinkled face of a man I do not know.

"Lay your hands on my head," he says when he sees my shadow at the entrance. "Kiah, bless me."

I kneel beside him. I wish Joab or Zadok was with me, but they are with their armies in their own camps. I am alone to do this.

His wife lights a lamp, and in the flicker of the thin flame I see a small table set in the corner. On it are Hem's most treasured items: a man's ring, a necklace, and a blade, the handle set in jade. I blink, and then I notice the table itself. It is made from a piece of carved wood I know. It is a piece of the reading table from Elam's synagogue, the artwork done by one of my ancestors. So Hem disassembled the synagogue before the robbers swarmed. He was and still is a robber as far as I'm concerned.

"Hem, why me?"

"You are a man of God."

A hard place in my heart softens, breaks loose, and lodges in my throat.

"You have always been a warrior for God, Kiah. I am a sorry man, a man who begs God's forgiveness. Lay your hands on my head and tell me now that God has forgiven my sins."

I turn and motion for Eliana to come forward. She does and kneels on the other side of her father.

"Beg the forgiveness of your daughter, Hem. You have done much harm to Eliana."

"Eliana?" The old man's eyes are clouded, and the odor about him is foul.

"I forgive you, Father."

Hem gurgles. "I do not ask your forgiveness, Eliana. You are a woman, easily led and easily fooled. It is God's forgiveness, not yours, that I seek."

The lump in my throat dislodges. All I feel now is pity. "And you, Hem, are a man who does not know God's grace when it looks him in the face."

He turns toward me. I rest my hands on his head and pray silently to know the things I should say, the proper words—not what *I* will, but what *God* wills. Hem breathes a rattled breath and before any words come to me, he does not breathe again.

That morning Lachoneus receives another epistle, this one confirming Calev's worst fears. "The robbers have appointed a new leader—Zemnarihah."

Calev begs, "Let me go out and speak with him. He is my son."

Lachoneus agrees. Eliana cries, fearing one or both of her most-loved men will die. She begs to go out to meet her son alongside Calev, but Gidgiddoni refuses her.

My own feelings are mixed. It could be a trap, and my brother could die by the hand of his own son.

A time and place is appointed.

I say, "It is not safe to go forth at night. The darkness is a cloak."

"I must see Zem, no matter the cost."

"I understand."

The sun goes down. We wait. I am positioned high on one of the lookouts, and I see nothing except the band of expected soldiers marching forth.

Calev goes forward in good faith to meet his own son, refusing to wear any armor or carry any weapon. He is barely outside the gate when an army of robbers, disguised as Nephites, attacks and attempts to break through the gate and enter our fortress.

It is a savage, unwarranted, unjust battle. Two arrows go into Calev—one in his chest and one in his back. He falls and is dragged back through the gate by authentic Nephite guards.

The rest of the robbers are defeated, either killed or driven back.

The wound in my brother's chest is not deep, but it takes both me and Abner to pull the arrow free from Calev's back. He loses much blood and cannot keep his eyes open.

Over the next month I bless my brother, pray for him, and expect him to die.

Eliana does not leave her husband's side. Mother and Abner use their newfound knowledge in healing to do all they can for Calev.

I do not have the will to reveal what I know—that both arrows pulled from Calev were marked with the sign of Gadianton's chief leader—his son, Zemnarihah.

Nephi preaches to us, encouraging us and promising just as he did years before that the sign is coming and the Savior will appear to us. We will see with our own eyes and hear with our own ears the love God has for us.

I believe what he says is true. I believe it so much I ask Nephi if I can make rounds with him around the camp to teach and testify and uplift downtrodden spirits.

I ask my sons to go with me, but Joab stays close to Calev, showing him the latest weapons and armor. Zadok goes with me but hardly speaks. When he does he seems bitter and doubtful. I try to open his heart and open his mouth, but war has changed him as war has changed us all.

Every night our soldiers go out and fall upon the armies of the robbers. The more success we have, the more destruction the robbers suffer. Every battle we celebrate causes my brother and his wife pain. Our victory could be their son's final defeat.

I just want this way of life to be over. In the beginning I was worried about caging Joab, the son I thought would go insane so confined, but it is me who cannot sleep at night, can't taste my meals, and can't remember what laughter sounds like.

After a series of brutal battles that leave thousands of robbers to be buried, Zemnarihah gives the command that they withdraw from the siege.

Gidgiddoni announces, "Zemnarihah has given command to his people to march northward."

Calev refuses to stay behind when Gidgiddoni sends for my army to join two other bands. We are commanded to cut off the robbers' retreat. He knows the way of their retreat; he has us leave during the night so that in the morning we are in place when the robbers attempt their escape. With three armies, we are able to surround them.

The robbers who meet us are not the same robbers who first came against us years ago. They are worn, starved, and beaten.

Thousands surrender without a fight, believing slavery under Gidgiddoni is better than freedom under the rule of Zemnarihah. Those who refuse to surrender are slain with the sword. I am grateful I am not required to serve on the execution line, though that is where Zadok is required to serve.

The battle rages sore. I try to keep an eye out for Calev, sure his weakened body cannot stand up, but he is driven to find his lost son.

The cry of victory goes up after many days of fighting.

"Zemnarihah has been captured!" someone reports.

I have to run to keep up with Calev.

But it's too late.

By the time we arrive at the place of capture, my nephew, now a man that I cannot recognize, is hanging high from a tree, the life already gone out of him.

Our armies break into rejoicing while soldiers fell the tree, a final sign of victory and vengeance.

I hold my brother upright as he watches the violent fate of a son who might have chosen differently had his father, long before, chosen another direction. But Calev goes limp and eases himself down on the ground.

"When the others leave him, will you help me bury my son?" Calev sobs.

"Of course I will."

And the soldiers, realizing that the war has finally ended, break into singing and praising God for the great thing He has done for them in preserving them from falling into the hands of their enemies.

"Hosanna to the Most High God! Blessed be the name of the Lord God Almighty, the Most High God!"

One of my soldiers approaches me with glee. "It is because of our repentance and humility that we've been delivered from everlasting destruction."

I can think of nothing to say. The burden of relief and regret is too heavy.

"Everyone is rejoicing!" the soldier cries.

"Not everyone," I manage, and turn from the festivities to lift my fallen brother.

Eighty-Five

The woman's hands and feet are tied, wrapped tight with thin vines. Her body is starved, reduced in size to that of a child. She is one of thousands of Gadianton's prisoners. It has befallen Calev to help oversee the influx of prisoners, but I have no reason to think he has sent this woman to stand before me.

I wipe the sweat out of my eyes and set down my etching tool. Lachoneus has commissioned me to depict the recent battle our people won against the robbers. He's given me a wall on the main courthouse to tell the story in pictures.

The officer tells me, "The woman requested to be brought before you."

I frown. Most of the robbers taken prisoner have either been killed or have agreed to enter into a covenant to keep the peace. "Who is she?"

The man clears his throat. "She says she's a member of your family."

"*My* family?" I bend down so that I can see her bowed face. It is old and haggard, scarred. I do not know her.

"Should we take her back to the prison?"

"No. Not yet."

The woman lifts her head and searches my eyes. Still, I do not know her.

"What are you called?" I ask.

"Once, I was called Tamar."

I never thought much about the fact that Gadianton's band was made of families, just as we are. The men who robbed and murdered also had wives and children. Tamar is the mother of five—three sons and two daughters, all of them grown, the sons dead, the daughters missing. I can't help feeling torn, realizing that Tamar's children are brothers and sisters to me, for we shared the same father. There are others out there also, brothers and sisters of mine that I do not know . . . will never know.

Eliana is elated to be reunited, and tends to her sister just as she did when they were young girls. If they make mention of Hem, I do not hear it.

Life resumes and we restore. Villages are cleaned and fields replanted. Cities are rebuilt and roads cleared. Within the ensuing years civilization thrives.

Jonathan goes to school and teaches Rinnah all that he learns; both take to reading and writing with an enthusiasm that eluded me. Zadok studies all of the time; he wanted to become a lawyer, but he is also interested in becoming a priest. He's still usually quiet, but not when his *chuwen* is found dead at the top of the prayer tower in Nephi's garden. Zadok weeps and says that God is a merciless God.

I try to console him. He's seen men die, but it is the death of a tree crawler that finally breaks the heart of my son.

Joab works with Calev, allotting land to the slaves who entered into the covenant of peace. He matures fast and is thoughtful, bringing flowers to his mother that she braids into her hair.

Finally, my family knows a time of peace, for the people now listen with open hearts to the teachings of Nephi and Gidgiddoni. We repent. We forsake our sins and vow to never return to them.

Abner sets up shop with Abarron, and they employ Abby along with Elka's new husband, Dan. Mother amazes me with her strength; she appears as weak as a newly hatched chick, but she weathers every storm, singing and smiling in the presence of her children and grandchildren.

Abby is next to marry. He is tall, and his hair is fiery red like his father's once was. His wife is the daughter of one of Tarah's cousins. They live in a house by the great river; Abby will make a fair and honest lawyer one day. Elka and her husband live close enough for Mother to help with my sister's two small daughters that arrive in the first years of her marriage.

All in all, we are a large and content family. At night I fall asleep in the arms of my wife as she talks on about how blessed we are.

• • •

And so the days go, and I know of no one in the land who does not accept the words of Nephi as prophecy. If they do not believe, they keep their doubt to themselves.

This night we have gathered, as we often do, in Nephi's courtyard, beneath the shade of the prayer tower, in front of a roaring blaze that fights away the night stingers.

"What are the signs of the coming of the Messiah?"

Nephi smiles at Joab's question. "There will be a storm unlike any we have known. It will be so strong the very earth will be torn apart. As there was light at His birth, there will be darkness at His death."

"Someone once asked me what I am doing to prepare," I say aloud. "What should we be doing?"

Nephi smiles at me. "You should be living as you are, my son. Providing for your family, serving your fellowman, repenting of your own sins, and helping others repent of theirs."

Hearing Nephi refer to me as his *son* means more to me than I can tell him. I'm a grown man, old enough to be a grandfather, and Nephi is already a great-grandfather. We have shared so much together, and I will forever be grateful to be included in his family.

I think of the Messiah every day I live.

I know He lives. But sometimes, in the back corners of my mind where I hide my past—my sins and my insecurities—I mull over my doubts, and I wonder if the Messiah even knows that I exist.

Eighty-Six

Years pass away in continuing peace. Rainy seasons, dry seasons, thunderstorms and sunshine. As a covenant-keeping people we prosper and wax great. Churches and synagogues brim full. The temple becomes the place of worship it was intended to be.

My family grows and prospers.

Joab marries the daughter of a priest from Bountiful, and we rejoice when Chava enters our family. We learn from her that she is named after our first forefather Nephi's wife. Her name means "life." While my son proves to be a husband able to provide, he is not a husband who is patient with his wife or attentive to her needs. I fear his mind is elsewhere, for I hear rumors that he has been enticed by the harlots who prey on our returned soldiers.

Zadok has changed too; he is more distant and determined. He becomes a priest. I try to convince him to spend more time with the family, but he is attentive to his duties and spends both days and nights at the synagogue and in the temple.

Rinnah marries a merchant named Tad when she is barely of age and gives birth to twin sons: Yarden and Calev. The birth is hard on her; she falls into a state of despair, and while she recovers Tarah, Eliana, and Tamar take turns caring for the twin boys.

Jonathan studies hard with Abby. He wants to one day sit on the judgment seat.

Jonas moves to Bountiful to work there helping repair the damage that was done to the temple. I miss him more than I can say.

One morning Rinnah comes into the yard weeping, calling Tarah's name. She's come to tell us that Mother was singing to Tarah's baby daughter and then went silent.

"Her eyes didn't even close; the life just went out of her while she was singing."

We bury her next to Abner, who died the year before.

• • •

As sure as the sun rises and sets, I can prophesy the days ahead.

We rise in prosperity and stumble in pride.

I enjoy my work and strive to better my depictions, but I relish the time I spend at the temple courtyard teaching young boys who struggle to read and write and recite.

From my service I see how the people are now being distinguished by ranks. Those who have riches have opportunities; their children are educated. Those who have money are esteemed and esteem themselves above those who don't.

I make my teaching open to all children and am told at the temple that only the rich can learn. So I take my lessons to the street, and the poor children come in droves.

One young fatherless boy wins my heart. He has a booming voice and enthusiasm for the scriptures. He is called Sam, after Lehi's son. Sam is small and rib thin, his scalp is infested with pests, and his feet are ringed with the disease that infects most of the city's waste-gatherers. His mother gleans the fields, and they live in an old abandoned tent, pieces left over from the years of siege when the robbers drove us into refuge.

Tarah takes pity and brings the mother clothes and food.

I witness pure gratitude when Sam's mother kisses my hand for teaching her son lessons that will allow him to rise out of poverty.

"When I was your age," I tell Sam, "I spent my time in the high hills behind Elam, hunting and exploring."

"Why aren't you a warrior?" Sam asks.

"I'm what my grandfather would call a different type of warrior."

I think back and remember when all I wanted to do was raise my blade to defend my cause, whatever it was. When I became a man and received the priesthood, my greatest joy was being a missionary, teaching people of Christ. Now that I am more advanced in life, my greatest joy is helping those who cannot help me in return.

Sam's mother weeps with gratitude and brings Tarah flowers for her hair. And I thank God for the feeling of worth that service brings me. That's why the next morning I'm confused and heartsick when I see Sam. His chin is bleeding, his knees scraped, and his eyes swollen from crying.

"What happened to you?"

He swipes the back of his hand under his runny nose. "While I was hauling out the garbage through the dung gate of the city, a group of men came out and mocked me."

"Men?"

He sniffles. "Grown men."

I help him clean up. "Would you know them if you saw them again?" I ask.

Sam nods and shows me a chipped-tooth smile. "I would know the one who put his foot in my back and knocked me forward into the cart."

I have not felt such rage in years. Sam is a child, still years away from the age of a son of the commandment. I hold his hand and let him lead me to where the grown men persecuted a child.

What kind of men would do this to Sam—to any child?

We wait, and just as my patience has reached its thinnest point, Sam points to a group of three priests walking toward us.

"He is the one on the right."

I look and my heart turns over. "Are you sure that is the man who kicked you?"

The boy nods. "And he called me names I cannot repeat."

The three men who walk toward me are priests, with their high turbans, blue seamless robes, and ornate breastplates. The priest on the right recognizes me and kisses my cheek. "Greetings, Father," he says.

"Hello, Zadok."

Eighty-Seven

My reflection is that of a man I hardly know. The scar on my neck reminds me of my past foolishness, but my face is unusually smooth for the face of a warrior except for the wrinkles of time. I still stand straight, and there is light in my eyes.

How can this be? I'm a man of struggle. I have seen death and suffering all around me. I live with fierce disappointment. Yet I pray that through the Messiah's Atonement my burdens may be made light, just as He eased the burdens of the people of Alma.

When I came to the water's edge I expected to see the image of a man beaten by life. Instead I see a man I do not know . . . he's strong and able, younger in appearance than I imagined possible.

No matter how much longer I must wait, I will hold out faithful until the coming of the Messiah. I saw Raz was at the temple, there to present his great-grandson; he told me that according to Samuel's prophecies, the time must be soon. *Soon.* It is a word I've heard all of my life.

I think of Zadok and how he and his fellow priests mistreated an innocent poor child. I remember with pain in my heart how my own son tried to justify his cruelty by saying that the boy got in the way of the priests and that no one should stand in the way of holy men. *This* coming from a boy who cried and cried when his pet *chuwen* died.

It was the first time in a very long time that the violence in my nature rose. I *wanted* to beat my own son—to kick him, to chip his teeth and humiliate him in front of his fellow priests. I did not. I waited and tried to talk to him later in private, but Zadok has no interest in what I have to say.

A small fish darts around, flips up out of the water, and splashes back in. The ground beneath my feet does not feel secure, and I step back to watch as the rushing water eats away at the bank of the stream. It takes only little bites from the soil, but soon enough the bank will erode and collapse. And so it is that the power of those who have taken secret oaths comes back into our lives, taking little bites out of our foundation of faith, little nibbles that will eventually crumble our foundation, and here we are—falling apart again.

Zadok. My own once-shy son is now among those priests who most boldly persecute the poor. How can that be? His mother taught him by example to love and serve the poor. I have taught him to love and serve God by loving and serving others. Now Zadok loves and serves only himself.

Joab, the son that concerned me most, has proven to have a kind heart, tender to hear the word of God and to accept it. He still works with his Uncle Calev.

Rinnah has added a third child to her family, a baby boy who was born unable to see or hear. It is a tragedy to my daughter, but Tarah, as grandmother, holds the child for hours, rocking him, comforting him, and calling him Michael, a name that means "angel."

Jonathan studies the law with Abby, who is now a renowned lawyer in Zarahemla. I hope he can make a difference for good for our judgment seat is in jeopardy. The judges are as corrupt as they were in Elam when I was Jonathan's age. It is impossible to tell which are joined in conspiracy with those who would destroy our freedom.

"It's time," Tarah tells me, resting a soft hand on my shoulder.

I turn around and try to smile at her. She takes my hand, and we walk away from the water's edge back toward the temple, where the people have gathered to mourn the death of Lachoneus.

My own heart weeps at the loss of our great leader, but his son, also called Lachoneus, stands ready to take his father's place and power. I pray for him. At the close of the funeral, Tarah goes with her aged mother and some of her sisters back to their childhood home to visit while I walk through the city, gathering my thoughts.

"Kiah!"

I whip around at the sound of the familiar voice. "Jonas!"

We embrace each other as lost family found again.

"I am here in the city with my Uncle Timothy. We've been preaching."

There is much to learn of Jonas's life, now in Bountiful, but first we stop to listen as Timothy stands outside the temple gates to preach. He too is old, but he is strong and his voice carries far. The message is always the same, but Timothy, like Nephi, delivers it with grace and power. "The Messiah will soon appear among us. He will teach us and heal us and deliver us. Repent now and prepare for that day."

There are those who listen and those who immediately mock.

A man approaches us and asks if we are interested in trading money for the pleasures of the flesh. He points to two young girls standing at the door of an inn.

We are next to holy ground! I want to put a fist in the man's face, but like he has done so many times before, Jonas stops me from my own violence.

Someone yells at Timothy and a stone is thrown. Then another. The third one hits Timothy's forehead and lays open a bloody gash.

Jonas and I are quick to get him down. We take a few rocks as well in our effort.

"Let me preach the truth," a finely robed man says, reaching to help Timothy down.

Jonas pulls away from him. "I know you. You're Jacob, the would-be king."

He laughs. "I *will* be king, preacher. One day you will bow before me and I will not be so ready to lift a hand to aid you."

We leave, but as we do I hear Jacob preaching his message: "The judgment seat must be replaced by a leader that can unite the people as one."

"He's an anti-Christ, Kiah. He preaches against every principle that supports freedom."

"This thinking is very popular in the smaller villages," Timothy says. "For a time I believe our lawyers and priests and judges were honest, but corruption has crept back in. I know of at least two men of God who were put to death for doing exactly what I just did."

I hold a cloth to Timothy's head to stop the bleeding.

"But no one, not even a judge, can have a man executed without the governor signing the order."

"These men, the anti-Christs, do it in secret, never bringing the matter before the governor."

I think what a hard and dangerous job the younger Lachoneus has just taken on. As the new governor, how can he stop men like Jacob?

• • •

Evil and horror are everywhere. I gather my children and grandchildren, even Zadok, and offer priesthood blessings and prayer and fasting. No matter what the rest of our people do, my family will honor God's word.

Nephi and his fellow preachers stay around Zarahemla preaching with great power and authority. Since Timothy's near-stoning it is necessary to take defenders, armed and prepared to die to protect the prophet.

Timothy and Jonas make a powerful duo that preach in and around the land of Bountiful. The message is to remind the people what they have forgotten. They are warned of the great day of destruction that is coming if they do not repent.

Every day I need to repent of my doubts, my fears, my quick temper, and every other vice that so easily besets me. A day does not go by when I do not kneel and beg God to forgive and prepare me, to guide me as I try to protect and guide my family.

In my very sinews I feel that the Messiah is coming soon to teach us from His own mouth. My heart grows heavy thinking of the prophecies that have foretold how He will be mocked and ultimately betrayed. The King of Kings, the Son of God, rejected and crucified. Resurrected and glorified.

• • •

Tarah has been with Devora at the market when I see the women come hurrying back.

"Open the gate!" Tarah cries. Her face is red and drenched in tears. Devora's hand is over her mouth to quell her sobs.

"What is it?"

"It's Timothy. They've stoned him to death!"

Jonas comes through the gate with his uncle's battered, bloody body over his shoulder.

The women weep. I weep too and am not ashamed of my tears.

"I didn't even know you and Timothy were back in Zarahemla," I say to Jonas, who is also weeping.

"We were coming to see my father. Timothy had a dream that he was supposed to see my father."

"Where is your father?"

"I sent my nephews in search of him. He'll come."

"He'll be so sorrowful. They were as close as two brothers can be."

"Like us," Jonas says, wiping his tears.

Tarah brings a blanket, and we lay Timothy's body out with respect and tenderness. His face has only a few bruises, but his chest and back are battered. How could this have happened again? What kind of demons lurk all around us?

I lay my ear to his chest and hear nothing. I feel his wrist for a beat; there is not so much as a flutter. I rest a flat shiny piece of obsidian beneath his nostrils and see sign no of breath. The prophet is dead.

"This is my fault," Jonas sobs. "He sent me to get bread. I did not know that he would start to preach without me there to protect him."

"This is *not* your fault, Jonas. This is the fault of those devils who are so filled with hatred they would stone a prophet."

The weather has been mild, but this day the sun is pounding and I know we must hurry to bury Timothy's body within the law's allotted twenty-four hours.

"Where is Timothy's wife?"

"She is back in Bountiful. When we left she prayed for his safety, making my uncle promise to be careful where he preached."

Jonas and I wash the body as the family members that are close by begin their mourning. Neighbors join in. Then strangers come to see the prophet's brother, a prophet himself, laid out as the martyr that Timothy has become.

We anoint the body with various oils and spices, fragrant enough to perfume the air with the reminders that a death has occurred.

We face a dilemma. By law, Timothy must be buried within twenty-four hours after death, and he must be buried outside the village where he lived. There is no way we can travel to Bountiful within the given time.

A priest is called to help us decide what is the most lawful thing to do.

"Zarahemla was once Timothy's place of residence. Bury him outside the village in the tomb where the other members of your family are buried."

Zadok helps prepare the epistle that is sent to Timothy's wife to inform her of the tragedy. I'm grateful to have my children gathered around me. By the time the nephews bring Nephi through the gate, Timothy's body has been wrapped in burial linen and set on a stone slab so that we might carry him to the tomb.

Nephi is somber but not tearful. He says nothing to us, just kneels beside his brother's body and prays silently.

A crowd is gathering, and no one stops people from entering through the gate. I look around, always protective and now suspicious. Are the men who stoned Timothy here, ready to mock—or worse, ready to bring further death to this family?

I motion for Tarah to take the women and go inside the house, but she shakes her head no.

"I've seen angels and had them minister to me," Nephi says, rising to his feet.

We all go silent, even those who have come to mock.

"I've cast out devils. I've cast out unclean spirits. I can cast out death."

And there, before our eyes, we witness a miracle so great none among us can match it.

Nephi, the prophet of all the land, lays his hands on his brother's lifeless head and commands that life return to him.

I hold my breath and dare not look away.

Then I feel a hand on my shoulder. Zadok has slipped up beside me.

"Nephi is insane with grief," he whispers in my ear. "You'd better clear this crowd before word gets out that he has no such power. You don't want the man who claims to be a prophet of God making a fool of himself in front of so many witnesses."

I try not to flinch.

My prayer is silent but spills out of my heart. The petition I put before God is not only to restore life to Timothy—it is to restore faith to my doubting son.

Timothy blinks, then opens his eyes.

The crowd stumbles back, gasping as the dead preacher comes back to life.

The burial linens fall from his face as Timothy sits up.

"Brother!" Nephi embraces him, and I turn to look at each one of my children's faces. Joab's mouth is agape. Jonathan's eyes are wide. Rinnah's head is buried in her mother's shoulder. Zadok's expression is blank.

How, I question, how can any of my children ever again doubt the power and love of God?

Eighty-Eight

Her name is Rachel, and when she laughs I forget that our land and our people are eroding toward utter destruction. Her mother, Chava, is the wife that Joab betrayed. She came to us one night with the little girl and announced that she wanted to remarry, but her prospective new husband would not accept Rachel.

Tarah's arms were already open, cradling our granddaughter, telling Chava that with us the girl would always have a home. She also assured Chava that if the time ever came that she wanted Rachel back, there would be no disputation.

Chava never returned, and Joab has shown no interest in being the child's father.

"Sawa! Sawa!" She is calling me *grandfather* as she chases a bulging grasshopper, as green as the blades of snake grass it hops onto. My fearless granddaughter hops right along with it, squealing all the while.

"Be careful in the tangle," I tell Rachel. "There are snakes in the tangle."

She goes stiff in midair and thuds hard onto the ground. Then she rushes back to me and scrambles up on my lap. "Oh, *Sawa*, I'm afraid of snakes."

I lean down and whisper in her ear, "Let me tell you a secret. I'm afraid of snakes too."

I hold Rachel as I hold my other grandchildren. Each one is precious beyond measure. Each one is unique from the others. Each is a creation of God—a child, a work of the Master.

I can feel the love He has for them even if I sometimes struggle to feel the love He has for me. It's not that I'm not blessed. It's not that my prayers haven't been answered. It's just that I tremble before the idea of the Messiah, not knowing if I'll live to see Him. If I do, will I be worthy to look upon Him?

As each day draws to a close I feel we are one day nearer to the signs that have been promised. My life becomes dedicated to preaching what I believe.

Let them stone me if they will—I cannot stop my tongue from testifying of the coming Messiah.

I am not a smooth, powerful speaker like Nephi. I cannot tell a story like Jonas. Even Calev is so blunt people listen to him. My message is the same as theirs, but my delivery is lacking.

Yesterday when I was preaching outside the city wall a woman threw hot oil at me. Today my leg is still red and burning. It hurts when Rachel's bare feet accidentally kick against it.

I thought people would feel differently after what Nephi did; after all, word of the miracle spread rapidly. But even my own son Zadok is angry with Nephi for raising Timothy from the dead because it has stirred up a division among the people. Unbelievers are turning into believers, and believers are losing their faith, saying that what Nephi did was done by the power of the devil.

And now the chief judge has been murdered.

Once again our people are being divided, only this time we are not separated into Nephites and Lamanites. This time we have been separated into tribes, large families grouped together not by faith or location, but by blood.

My wife and children join with me, as do our in-laws and their families. In turn, I join our family to that of Nephi, grateful to be included in their family. My inclusion is possible because a man who doesn't have a family of his own is permitted to join with a friend's family.

The government is a skeleton of what it should be, a body without the muscle to command authority. The government we have known all my life is overthrown, and the man Jonas and I met the day Timothy was first stoned by the temple—the man Jacob—leads a tribe who have covenanted through the secret combinations of old to make him king.

Even after everything I've witnessed in my life, I'm still shocked that this Jacob—one of the loudest in raising his voice against Nephi, Timothy, Gidgiddoni, and the other prophets who testify of Jesus—has gained power so quickly.

We might be divided into different tribes, we might dispute with each other, but we are united against those who have entered into a covenant to destroy the government and the freedom of the people. It's not far different than when we all united to fight the robbers, only this time we are divided into hundreds of families, some with greater numbers, strength, and wealth than others.

Nephi's tribe is one of the largest, organized with Nephi at the head, established with our individual laws, separate from the other tribes. I thank God when Nephi makes Calev, Eliana, and Tamar welcome.

We divide into bands so we might go among our own kin to preach repentance. Nephi is always ready to baptize those willing to enter the waters and covenant with God to join His church and keep His laws.

I begin to know the heartache that Calev felt when Zem chose to join the robbers, for my own Zadok refuses to align himself with his blood relatives. Instead, he becomes part of King Jacob's tribe, doing all he can to dissuade people from believing in the coming Messiah.

"My father is a fool!" I hear him shout. "He has been deceived all the days of his life. If only he'd listened to his father, my grandfather, whose vision it was to break away from the lies we were told since Nephi stole the records of our forefathers and polluted the truths."

I stand in front of him, but he refuses to meet my eyes. He goes on, "It is time to break the curse and rid our people of the foolish traditions and laws that bind us from freedom and happiness."

That night Jonas walks with me beneath a wink of a moon; wispy clouds keep blowing across it, giving me an ominous feeling of things to come. In my mind I go over something Samuel taught us: There are two deaths, one of the body and one of the spirit. Spiritual death is to be cut off from the presence of God. Only Christ, through His Resurrection, can redeem us from the first—and only Christ, through His Atonement, can redeem us from the second.

"I have failed my God," I say.

"How?" Jonas asks.

"I have not been the father that I so desperately wanted to be."

"You think this because of Zadok?"

"Yes. I lose my temper with him; I say things I should never say. If I had been a better father, Zadok would not have chosen to turn away from the laws of God. Joab would have stayed within the boundaries God set."

"Kiah, if what you say is true—that you failed your God—then my God failed me."

I stop and look at Jonas, confused and shocked to hear him say such a thing.

He is quick to continue. "But my God did not fail me when He allowed Orli and my unborn son to be murdered. And you did not fail God when you allowed Zadok to make his own choices."

I try to understand his comparison. It comes down to agency, our gift from a loving Father who allows us to choose for ourselves. We live in a world that is unfair and unjust, but we know that in God's time and through the Atonement of His Son, all that is wrong will be set right. I wish I had the words to say all that my heart is feeling.

Jonas's tone is firm. "Kiah, I watched you raise your children. I admired the time you spent with them, the way you made opportunities to teach them and to give them chances for learning. Even Rinnah knows how to read and write."

"But—"

"I want you to remember that the Atonement of Jesus Christ not only atones for our sins, it atones for our sufferings. You're in pain. Lay that pain on the altar before the Lord and see the miracle that will happen."

"At least Joab is coming around. I heard him tell Calev that he wants to confess his sins to Nephi and to enter back into the fold."

But the coming days bring news that Joab has been enticed by harlots, led away to another tribe to live in sin.

Tarah takes to her sickbed and refuses to rise. She won't even hold the grandchildren—not even Michael, whom she loves to hold and comfort.

Eliana and Tamar come to stay with her.

Just when I think our circumstances can't get worse, we receive word that another prophet has been killed—this one tortured to death, torn asunder in one of the open-framed boxes unbelievers wanted to use to kill Samuel the Lamanite. I am sorrowful, but doubly so when I learn that the prophet tortured and killed was Gidgiddoni.

I fall into a depression as dark as my wife's. Even Calev and Jonas cannot drag me out of my despair.

Only when Jonathan enters our courtyard and finds me lying in my hammock do I realize what I am doing.

"What about me, Father?" my youngest son asks.

I stare at him blankly.

"I hear you mourn the loss of your wayward sons. Well, what of me? I believe in the Messiah and all that His word teaches. I keep the covenants I've made. I work hard. I will one day become a righteous lawyer. Do I not count as one of your sons?"

My head snaps up. My heart breaks open, and the days of my pitiful mourning come to an abrupt end.

Eighty-Nine

Nephi and Timothy return to preaching. Timothy draws a crowd simply because people are curious to see the man who was raised from the dead.

Nephi announces that his family clan is moving closer to Bountiful. He assures me that there is work for me to do on the palace of the chief judge and plenty of opportunities to do missionary work. Tarah brightens at the prospect of change.

"This land is not the land I know," she says. "Maybe a great change is exactly what our family needs."

Abarron requires two walking sticks to make the trek, but we caravan slowly and steadily, inviting every member of our family to join us. I'm grateful that most of Tarah's family comes along; it makes for a grand exodus out from Zarahemla.

Calev and Jonathan lead the way. It breaks my heart not to have Joab or Zadok with us, but Jonathan is right—he is a good son and one I will no longer neglect.

Jonas and I bring up the rear. The women and children occupy the middle where they are most protected.

It is a time of heightened soothsayers and witches, false prophets and anti-Christs. Any vice or pleasure of the flesh can be purchased for money. I want to shield my grandchildren from the lust and sinful sights, but there is no shielding them. The only armor is to testify and teach them to obey.

If I were young and walking the trek alone, I could make it from Zarahemla to Bountiful in just more than a day. People did it in that length of time when this stretch of land was part of our great camp during the siege with the robbers. But it takes us days; we are laden and slowed by the small, tired feet of children and old men. One afternoon the wind blows dirt in our faces; it gets between our teeth and even in our ears. The scorners are loud and ready to spit on us, and the children murmur. It is then I hear a voice in my head: *Be still and know God. Know that He will not be mocked.*

Grandfather is buried back in Elam, but his voice still fills my head, testifying to me.

I lift my voice and, in spite of the dust, I sing. Others soon lift their voices to join mine. Before we have gone much farther, the entire tribe of Nephi is singing praises to the God whose appearance we so desperately await.

• • •

The land of Bountiful is lush and watery. The rainfall here is heavier and more frequent than in Zarahemla. The dirt is more brown than red, and the homes and buildings are whitewashed with a thin cement like Jonas is adept at making.

We see the pyramid of the temple courtyard far off in the distance; its point gleams like an arrow pointing heavenward. The temple is made of lighter stone, almost white in some parts, and it shimmers in the sunlight.

The roads are narrow in some places and barbed with agitated guards that demand Nephi show them papers that prove who we are—who he is. The papers came from the officials in Zarahemla, a set issued to the head of each tribe. Ours grant permission for Nephi's clan to move to Bountiful, give us license to preach there, and allow his family work opportunities.

I feel like a stranger here. Even though the land is so close, it feels different. The layout of Bountiful is much like the layout of Zarahemla. Some homes are humble mounds or tents; others are structures made of wood or stone. The nicer homes sit at the top of the slope, while the huts like the one I grew up in line the blocks closer to the shore.

I promise my grandchildren that we will go to the ocean and splash— that we will eat fresh fish and we will all run in the sand. But once we enter through the main gates, the sights and sounds and smells of the city turn my stomach. It's as though sin has congregated here. Harlots are at every corner, making offers that turn Tarah's face bright red. Leering men look at our children in ways no man should ever look upon a child.

Nephi urges us to march without delay. He wants to worship at the temple. But the temple is not used to worship the God of all creation. It is used to worship the creature man has made of himself through sin. Priests trade the favors of the flesh for the remittance of sin and guilt. Some priests hint that for a price, human sacrifices can be made to gods I do not know.

Here on ground that is supposed to be holy, sin thrives as sure as moss. Fermented nectar to make a man drunk is as plentiful here as water. Women try to entice men to follow them into back rooms and forbidden places. Men abuse women and children openly, and no punishment befalls them. Vendors sell a plant with the promise that by chewing the leaves, the mind will imagine visions and whisperings that are not of this world. The message that rings all around us is that Christ is a foolish tradition made to bind the children of men and to keep them from enjoying the life that God meant for them to enjoy.

Prophets are punished for preaching anything that mentions the Messiah. I fear for Nephi's life. I fear for the safety of my family. For all of us.

We leave the temple courtyard and exit out the far gate that leads toward the sea. At least the sight of the ocean is as beautiful as ever. It shimmers and glistens blue and white and silver. I can't walk fast enough, but the children and the women are bone weary.

A curly-headed man with a goat draped over his shoulders greets Nephi. The goat drops to the ground, runs off bleating, and the two men embrace. Nephi has found his cousin, and our tribe is led down another winding road to camp with his family. The man's name is Nathan, and he is a man of God. His camp is neither large nor small—five or six hundred people who are camped together, mostly in tents. Our family joins with his, and we are greeted with warmth and kinship.

Despite the order and cleanliness in Nathan's camp, it does not feel like home. My children and grandchildren feel it.

Men talk in angry tones of how the government has displaced us so it can control us. Even the children are confused.

"I wanted a complete change," Tarah says, "but not this. This is worse than when we were forced to camp all those years while the robbers ravaged the land."

"We've brought this on by sin," I say, remembering the promise that comes with the land. It seems unfair to me that our family would suffer so— that Nephi's family would suffer. Haven't we done our best to be obedient? Yet we are without land and without homes.

After days of adjusting, Tarah makes a routine of going down to the seashore with Michael. This morning is no different; she holds our little grandson's hand and helps him feel the things he cannot see or hear. She places a bit of wet seaweed in his palm so he can feel its slippery coolness; she puts a hollow shell over his ear so he can sense the hum of the ocean. I gaze at her from across the way, watching how the light dances on her face and makes the silver in her hair shine much the same way the sun once made her hair appear golden.

One morning after first prayer Jonathan tells me that some men have come to talk with me. I recognize all four of them as mirror images of their father.

"Raz's sons! Welcome. Tell me, how is your father?"

Their faces tell me that he is dead.

"He was put to death, tortured by burning faggots."

I sit on a bench and hold my head in my hands. I cannot bear the thought of Raz suffering such a death. "What crime did your father commit that warranted such an end?"

"He was brought before the priests and judges in Zarahemla and told to report his time records. He told them that according to his calculations, nearly thirty-three years have passed since the signs of Christ's birth. Father told the priests that the time is now at hand for the other sign to be given."

"The three days of darkness?"

"Yes. When Christ is crucified in the old world, here in the new world the sun, the moon, and the stars will be darkened for the space of three days."

"And during those three days?"

"Christ will ascend home to the Father who granted Him life. We will suffer the most horrific destruction we will ever know."

"And the courts put your father to death for speaking the truth?"

"They did."

Raz's son, Micah, speaks with the power of a prophet. His goodness makes me think of Daniel, his brother who died in my first army command.

As Micah talks I think of a place I've only heard about—a land of sand and white stone, a land of the great temple and the growing ground of our first fathers. Somewhere across the seas, the Savior of mankind is facing His own torture and rejection; He is suffering for the sins of all mankind. *My* sins.

The days that follow are filled with great effort. People are trying to get along, but now there is no unity, only tolerance.

Tarah tries to plant flowers by our tent. Within moments they are trampled—not by young children or animals, but by other women who mock her for her effort.

She cries in my arms like a sad little girl.

I want to go after the women who remind me somehow of Oshra, but Calev happens by just then with Eliana by his side. "Let's hunt," he says to me.

"We have sufficient meat and more than enough fish," I tell him.

"It's not hunting for meat I want to do. Join me, brother. Let us hunt to save the souls of men."

Eliana smiles at me. "Please, Kiah, go with Calev. My husband wants nothing more than to preach with zeal."

Calev reaches out to squeeze her fingers. A look passes between them, and I realize there is a binding love between them.

"Bountiful is a dangerous place to preach," I say.

"Since when have you been afraid of danger? Besides, we are new, and the people in the land of Bountiful may be more receptive to different voices."

Tarah smiles for the first time in weeks.

I find it heartwarming that Calev wants me to be his missionary companion, so we take to the city to preach. Calev is right: Every face is foreign and every place is unfamiliar—dangerous and exciting.

Calev lifts his voice high. "Repent, for your days are dwindling! The Messiah cometh soon!"

We don't even make it to the gates before we are ambushed from behind. Calev is knocked unconscious by a group of men who then throw some type of fishing net over me and bind me so tight that I can't reach for my blade. Their feet kick me and their clubs pummel me.

"Calev!" I scream. "Calev!"

He is lying in the road, blood puddling around his head. I can't tell if my brother is alive or dead.

The men drag me down the road and prop me up by a gate for passersby to see.

"Preach to us, prophet. Tell us that we are sinners, damned to burn. Tell us about your Messiah who will darken our sun and set fire to our cities. Tell us all about Jesus."

They laugh. They spit in my face. One man drenches me with his urine.

Father, bless Calev. Bless me.

A crowd gathers. A man in the fine robes of a priest approaches me. "What message do you preach?"

"Jesus is the Christ, the Son of the living God."

"This Jesus, He is your Messiah?"

"Yes."

"Where is this Messiah now?"

"He is in the land of our fathers, atoning for the very sins you are committing."

The man recoils, then comes at me with a fist to the side of my head. Swinging from his neck is an idol in the form of a snake.

"So you have never seen Him?" the man demands.

"No."

"Never?"

"No."

The people laugh.

"How do you know that He exists?"

"I know through the testimonies of the prophets before me. I know through the written word of scriptures. I know from the testimony that burns within my own heart."

"Did you say *burns?*"

More laughter, then someone hands the priest a torch.

So I will die the death of Raz and Abinadi and so many other faithful Saints. I will die before the Messiah appears.

So be it.

Children run to fetch wood and dried leaves, which are piled all around me.

Another man steps forward. "What is going on here?"

The priest smirks. "This man, a stranger to our land, is a preacher sent by God."

"Whose god?" the man asks.

"*His* God—the mighty Messiah that no man has seen or spoken to."

"The Messiah. As a lawyer, I've heard of Him. He will come to destroy us because we are sinners. Is that the God of which you preach?" he asks me.

"Yes," I say; I flinch because the children are now poking me with the sticks they'll use to fuel the fire that will consume me.

"Unfortunately, King Jacob and his tribe have now fled the city. They have gone to Jacobugath." His head dips, his shoulders raise, and he shakes his head like a beast before charging. "Our king was driven out by self-righteous people like *you*, thinking your God is more powerful than ours."

My thoughts shift to Zadok. He is with the wicked king in Jacobugath, a city I know is ripe with sin.

Like a worm, the vein in the lawyer's forehead swells and twists. He grins. "We are law-abiding people and you, a stranger to our land, have been accused of a crime." He holds his chin in his hands and pretends to think. "Hmmm. What is your crime?"

"Blasphemy!" someone calls out. Another yells, "Treason!"

"Treason? Such a serious crime." He spins in a circle to be sure all eyes are fixed on him. "Should we put this stranger on trial for crimes against our government and our way of life?"

The people cheer.

And so, with Calev bleeding to death, I am tried in the street, bound tight in a fishing net, and poked by sticks while others fetch sufficient wood to burn me alive.

Each time I open my mouth to ask after my brother or to speak in my own defense, pointed sticks are shoved into my flesh or someone lands a foot in my face. As I lose consciousness I hear laughter and mockery. Then I hear a voice familiar and soothing.

"Permit me to speak, please."

I open one eye to see Calev standing in the road, the people mobbing around him. His head is bloody and his hand is pressed over one eye. "The man you try is my brother. He has a wife and a family who need him. I know him to be a just and merciful man, a faithful and great warrior."

I choke on the lump that closes my throat.

"My brother, Kiah, is needed. My only son was killed in war and now I am a lone man, except for a wife who is in the good care of her family. I beg of you all, execute me in place of my brother."

"No!" I scream, "no!" as a club cracks down on my head and my whole world goes black.

Ninety

Little Rachel brings me broth and holds the cup to my lips. "Father in Heaven, bless my *sawa* to get better."

I wince at the pain that surges through my battered head.

We are in the final day of mourning my brother's martyrdom. I have not been able to speak a word since Calev's death. My heart is too full of both sorrow and love.

For seven days Eliana has hardly moved from her spot on the hard ground of the small tent she shared with Calev. Tamar attends her, but the grieving widow refuses even the barest comforts.

Tarah has hardly left my side since Jonas found me lying on the roadside and returned me to my family. I am beaten and bruised, stung by dozens of small wounds from being jabbed with pointed sticks. My arm is broken and my fingers crushed. But I am alive.

My brother is not.

Our final night of mourning seems endless. There is no position in which I can manage to find rest. It is miserable, as it should be.

Jonathan brings the priest in the morning to announce the end of our seven days.

My son reminds me that according to Raz's record, preserved by his sons, today is the thirty and fourth year, in the first month, on the fourth day of the month.

"How much longer, Father, must we wait for the Messiah?"

I only stare at Jonathan, thinking that Christ is now suffering—being beaten and abused, being martyred.

"Is it already morning?" Tarah asks. "It's so dark outside."

"A storm is coming," the priest says, opening the tent flap so that we blink against the filtered light of a gray sky and a whirling wind.

I crawl to the front of the tent on my hands and knees and study the sky.

"The sign is being given," I say. "The Son of God dies for our sins."

"What are we to do?"

"There is no place the wrath of God cannot reach."

Tarah kneels before me. "You're frightening us, Kiah. What should we do to be safe?"

"Repent."

I sit upright with my back to the tent door. I look across the way at Eliana, who is sitting cross-legged, rocking like a terrified child.

The wind picks up, and I think that we should move to a place where the wind will not whip so fiercely. But where? Seawater sprays through the air. Dirt comes at us in clouds.

"Father," Jonathan says. "Father! Come to your senses. Already trees are being blown over. Jonas sends word that we are all to meet in the valley of the boulders."

Rachel throws her little arms around my neck. "Save us, *Sawa*. The wind is scaring me."

I blink, and my dark world is flooded with sudden light.

"Gather everyone! Leave no one behind."

By the time my family is assembled, even Joab—who came when he heard of Calev's death—has joined us. We all know this is no ordinary tempest.

"The sign!" Jonas screams, trying to be heard over the raging wind. "The sign!"

His three sons are all there, huddling with their families. Devora is with the grandchildren, but I don't see Nephi.

"Where is your father?" I shout. My head feels like it will burst from my injuries and from the roaring sound of the storm.

Jonas shakes his head.

The thought of Nephi out in this storm alone is terrifying. Then I realize he is not alone. God will hold him safe.

A mist unlike any I have ever seen smothers the land. Black clouds as large as villages touch their swollen bellies to the ground. The wind howls; people cry. Branches bow down and roots break out of the ground, toppling mighty trees, crushing anyone in the way.

Tarah tries to stay beside me, but she has Michael in her arms, and he is kicking and pounding his fists in fear. All of the children are crying. Rachel runs to the safety of her father's arms; the golden curls of her hair fly in the wind.

Most people seek refuge beneath the strength of the mighty pyramid, but they do not know which side offers protection—the wind seems to be coming from all directions at once. Families I recognize and families I don't recognize are hunkering down to wait out the fury. I pray for them but push my family onward to a place that keeps entering my mind—a spot I've seen when I've gone walking with Tarah.

A ferocious gust bellows across the field in front of us, and I see men and women and children lifted off the ground, blown high into the air and carried away, easy as leaves. Birds stand no chance in the tempest, but even *chuwens* and four-legged beasts are blown about like feathers. I feel pity. I feel sorrow. I feel nothing compared to the pain that Almighty God is suffering at the torture and crucifixion of His Only Begotten.

The ground beneath us rumbles and shakes. This is how it must feel to be in a boat caught on a raging sea. It gets darker, and the rumbling sound threatens to burst my eardrums.

"Tarah!"

I can't see her. The air around me is growing darker.

"Rachel!"

I can't see anyone.

Smoke and ash coat my nostrils. My eyes burn. I flail my arms, reaching desperately to grab those I love, to hold them tight. But there is no holding and there is no security except in knowing that what is happening is a promise being fulfilled by God.

I feel something slap my face. I reach for it—feel and know the hand. "Tarah!" I pull her to me and wrap my arms around her body. We fall to the ground, pressing ourselves and our family onward.

The divot in the earth is like a long, jagged wound. Around us are smooth gray boulders that people are trying to use for shelter, but I tell my family to crawl right down into the broken earth—to crawl as deep as they can and to hold to each other. I don't know if they can hear me, but when I show them by lowering Tarah first and then others, everyone follows. People wedge together, standing on each other, threatening to smother or trample one other.

The world around us tears apart. Sheets of rain slam into us, carrying boulders and trees and more people away. The mountains crack, the ground breaks open, the seas slosh until we are drenched and choking. I fear this refuge might turn into our grave. The earth is cracking again. The sound is deafening. But I know this is the place I was led to bring my family. The Spirit guided me here, so I pray, knowing that God is mindful of us.

The earth cracks and splits again and again, but the refuge we have sought proves safe. It grows wider, allowing more people to seek shelter with us. I know they are here, but I see nothing with my eyes; the darkness all around me is so thick even flame cannot breathe. I know the prophecies of Samuel, that entire cities will be burned or swallowed. That mountains will break apart and roads will be ripped up.

I hold my wife in my arms and we cry together, afraid of what is happening to those we love.

"Lord, God Almighty. Be with my family. Be with Nephi and his family."

The tempest rages. Bolts of lighting tear through an endless black sky. I smell fire, but I see no orange flames. I feel heat, but it is washed away by another wall of water.

The pyramids shake. The ground quakes. It's impossible to scream over the roar of the storm.

Be still and know that I am God.

Be still.

Know God.

Messiah. All my life I have lived for this prophesy to be fulfilled. Whenever I heard that the Messiah was coming soon, I would question the concept of *soon*. Soon is now.

The Messiah has died. As I cling to Tarah and pray, is Christ's mortal body still bleeding? Is it yet upon the cross, or is it being washed and dressed for burial? Is the Redeemer's spirit back home in the arms of His Father?

No matter. Let the Spirit of God fill me with strength to endure what I must.

For hours I hear a voice whisper, *Be still.*

Even as the earth is rent, my garments are rent in mourning of my dead brother. Even as we hear mighty walls and buildings break into pieces, our ears break at the sharpness of the thunder.

Then the storm dies and the darkness is so thick it cannot be permeated.

People scream and cry and weep and wail. They are wounded. They mourn for those they have lost and those they cannot find. My own Tarah cries in my arms.

"It is Kiah," my voice cries through the sudden quiet. "Who is out there in the darkness?"

"God be praised!" Jonas cries. "My wife and sons are safe."

There are tears and wailing until our family manages to find each other and huddle together in the darkness. No candle will light. No torch will give flame.

We are injured. We are terrified. We are soaked and choked and lost in darkness.

Even after the great battle during the siege with the robbers, even after we lost thousands and thousands of our soldiers, that wailing and mourning was a bird's chirp compared to the suffering all around us.

I hear a voice that sounds near. "O that we had repented before this great and terrible day, and had not killed and stoned the prophets, and cast them out; then would our mothers and our fair daughters, and our children have been spared!"

The air is sweltering. Our lungs clog with the vapor of darkness and the ash and the suffering. We call out to each other through the vapor. We cling to those we can find and hold. We shiver when the temperature plummets from sweltering to cold.

We do not eat.

We do not drink.

We suffer as Samuel warned we would suffer.

Those of us with strength to crawl up out of the broken earth lay on the flat surface and quiver. When sleep comes it brings nightmares.

It is impossible to tell daylight from darkness, for all is darkness.

I do my best to console my family, to remind them that while others are gone, we are together. That is not completely true. Joab and Zadok are not with us. No one can find Tamar or Eliana. And Rinnah is wild with worry because the winds tore Michael from her husband's grip; Tad has wandered off though the black mist in search of their son.

Abby prays.

Jonathan recites scriptures.

Nothing can stop the wailing.

After what seems to me three days there is a shift in the air. The darkness does not go away, but the feeling changes. Even through the vapor of blackness comes a voice that stills even the most pitiful moan.

"Wo, wo, wo unto this people; wo unto the inhabitants of the whole earth except they shall repent; for the devil laugheth, and his angels rejoice, because of the slain of the fair sons and daughters of my people; and it is because of their iniquity and abominations that they are fallen!"

It comes from the sea; it comes from the tops of the mountains, over the vast valleys and down from the skies. It speaks up from the earth to my heart. This voice, unlike any voice I've ever heard, speaks so even the deaf can hear.

It tells of the destruction that has occurred. The great city Zarahemla, a place I doubted could be burned, has been burned. The great city Moroni has sunk into the sea, the inhabitants drowned. Moronihah, a city where prophets and Saints were murdered for preaching of the Messiah, has been covered with earth to hide the iniquities and abominations. Gilgal has sunken into the earth.

No place and no people have escaped.

And then the warm blood in my veins runs cold. For the voice announces the fate of my Zadok—"That great city Jacobugath, which was inhabited by the people of king Jacob, have I caused to be burned with fire because of their sins and their wickedness, which was above all the wickedness of the whole earth, because of their secret murders and combinations; for it was they that did destroy the peace of my people and the government of the land; therefore I did cause them to be burned, to destroy them from before my face, that the blood of the prophets and the saints should not come up unto me any more against them."

The voice goes on. I hear it, but I cannot tell what it speaks, for Tarah sobs in my arms. The breaking of my own heart is as loud in my head as was the sound of mountains breaking.

" . . . many great destructions have I caused to come upon this land, and upon this people, because of their wickedness and their abominations. O all ye that are spared because ye were more righteous than they, will ye not now return unto me, and repent of your sins, and be converted, that I may heal you?"

Tarah stops sobbing and pulls away from me. I can tell she is listening, aching for any shred of hope.

The earth continues to rumble, and the sound of rocks breaking forth, of the earth heaving, of the land around us changing, is real.

"Yea, verily I say unto you, if ye will come unto me ye shall have eternal life. Behold, mine arm of mercy is extended towards you, and whosoever will come, him will I receive; and blessed are those who come unto me."

I don't pretend to know what Tarah is feeling. I have not counted the loss in my own family. All I know is that a love dwells in my heart that I cannot contain. I slide down to my knees and beg, "Father, let me come. Let me come and feel the arm of mercy wrap around me."

Tarah slips to her knees and is beside me, crying on my neck.

And that's when the voice says what I've lived all my life to hear.

"Behold, I am Jesus Christ, the Son of God."

Ninety-One

Our astonishment is so great that we all cease lamenting and howling for the loss of our kindred. We listen as the Messiah delivers His message.

"I created the heavens and the earth, and all things that in them are. I was with the Father from the beginning. I am in the Father, and the Father in me; and in me hath the Father glorified his name. I came unto my own, and my own received me not. And the scriptures concerning my coming are fulfilled.

"And as many as have received me, to them have I given to become the sons of God; and even so will I to as many as shall believe on my name, for behold, by me redemption cometh, and in me is the law of Moses fulfilled."

I hear Jonathan sigh, and I feel a weight lifted from my own shoulders: The hundreds of laws that have bound us like chains are now severed. The Maker of all laws speaks to us.

"I am the light and the life of the world. I am Alpha and Omega, the beginning and the end. And ye shall offer up unto me no more the shedding of blood; yea, your sacrifices and your burnt offerings shall be done away, for I will accept none of your sacrifices and your burnt offerings."

Rachel finds her way to my lap and snuggles down. Her hair smells of smoke, and her little hands are warm around my neck. "Listen to the voice, *Sawa*. It's Jesus."

"And ye shall offer for a sacrifice unto me a broken heart and a contrite spirit. And whoso cometh unto me with a broken heart and a contrite spirit, him will I baptize with fire and with the Holy Ghost, even as the Lamanites, because of their faith in me at the time of their conversion, were baptized with fire and with the Holy Ghost, and they knew it not. Behold, I have come unto the world to bring redemption unto the world, to save the world from sin. Therefore, whoso repenteth and cometh unto me as a little child, him will I receive, for of such is the kingdom of God. Behold, for such I have laid down my life, and have taken it up again; therefore repent, and come unto me ye ends of the earth, and be saved."

When the voice ceases we cannot find our own voices.

We all heard it. We are all witnesses that the signs promised have been fulfilled.

For hours we remain in utter silence, contemplating what this means in our own lives. I pray. Through the might of the priesthood given me by my grandfather, I silently call down the powers of heaven to heal the hearts and open the ears of my family—to heal my own heart.

Hours pass, and in the stillness, I know what I've known for so long . . . that God is God.

Then the voice speaks again, penetrating the darkness.

"O ye people of these great cities which have fallen, who are descendants of Jacob, yea, who are of the house of Israel, how oft have I gathered you as a hen gathereth her chickens under her wings, and have nourished you."

Immediately, memories flood my mind of chasing little chicks, trying to gather them—the impossibility of that task. I recall the times my children and grandchildren undertook the same chore.

Now Jesus paints an image with words that I can understand.

"And again, how oft would I have gathered you as a hen gathereth her chickens under her wings, yea, O ye people of the house of Israel, who have fallen; yea, O ye people of the house of Israel, ye that dwell at Jerusalem, as ye that have fallen; yea, how oft would I have gathered you as a hen gathereth her chickens, and ye would not."

When the voice ceases Rinnah begins to howl. "Mother! Father! Help!"

Michael is still missing. We call for him until our already raspy voices become even more hoarse. Tad is still out searching. We are not the only ones weeping and wailing. Everyone cries, for everyone has lost loved ones.

The blackness remains.

People are coughing from the smoke and ash. People are crying out in pain from the injuries they suffer. If the sorrow of a million funerals could be heard, that is the sound that fills my ears.

"Come close," I tell my family. We gather as one, crawling up from the cracked earth, from behind boulders, from the shelter of the great pyramid.

Jonas prays, and his prayer is unexpected: "Father, God Almighty, we thank Thee for the darkness, for we know that it is prophecy fulfilled. We thank Thee for the destruction, for we know that it is the end of the evil that has plagued our land. We thank Thee that our lives are spared and pray for Thy mercy to attend those who have died."

More weeping. More quakes. More rumblings. More destruction.

God Almighty is weeping and rejoicing with us.

• • •

Three days of absolute darkness.

Was not the Messiah's body laid in a dark tomb for three days?

When morning finally comes, the darkness is shattered by the light.

The sun is allowed to shine through. We blink away the darkness and let our eyes adjust to the massive changes all around us.

We actually see and hear the broken earth come together again. There is so much ash in the air that when the pinks and oranges of the morning sun backlight the floating particles, it looks like heaven has been brought down from the skies and set on earth that we might walk and talk like angels.

The light restores our hope.

Cries of joy and thanksgiving echo across the reformed land.

And those of us who have been spared lift our voices and sing. We pray. We praise the Lord Jesus Christ, our Redeemer. And we go in search of our missing loved ones.

Ninety-Two

There is little I can do to console Tarah when she realizes that Joab and Zadok are both gone. Her faith is strong, but her sorrow is also strong. Thankfully, we find Michael—all alone and terrified but safe, wandering not far from where our tent was pitched. We cannot find his father, Tad, and my daughter is inconsolable. Eliana and Tamar are still missing, too.

In spite of our anguish we remain in awe. There has never been a time like this and never will be again. Our lives are forever changed. We marvel at the great change that has come upon our land and ourselves. Nothing is as it was. Nothing can approach the joy of knowing that Jesus Christ knows us.

The tents we had pitched have blown away with the wind. When I am not out searching for Tad, I am with Rinnah or her children. The twins are old enough to understand that their father might be dead; I bless them and pray with them. When I lay my hands on Michael's head he pushes them away. Michael has no way to tell us what he feels, but at night when he wakes up shaking I go to him. He allows me to hold him, and I can feel his fear.

I pray for every member of my family, my friends, myself. I never cease praying, for how can I stop thanking Him for allowing me to hear the voice of the Messiah?

There is no doubt that God is loving, but He is also capable of great justice. Our land and our people suffer while we marvel. Nephi calls on us to restore what we can, to take care of those who need to be attended to. There are many broken arms and legs. The particles that flew through the air caused some to be blinded, others to be wounded. Those wounds now require poultices and herbs.

The lamenting does not stop, for while we are in awe of what has occurred, we are also in agony over what has occurred. Yet as we bury our dead and mourn the loss of our loved ones, there is only support and love from one another. There is a spirit among us now that did not exist before—a spirit of faith unlike any I've known. We fast. We pray. We hope and go about in wonder.

When Jonas appears with a familiar leather armband in his hand, I recognize it and know that Tad is dead.

"I buried him myself," Jonas says, tears in his eyes. "Tad and seven other men, two women, and a child."

We immediately mourn. I think I have never known such sorrow because the pain is not for me—it is for my daughter and her fatherless sons. Yet I know that through the Messiah, this little family will one day be with their father again.

"I know it, too," Rinnah says through her tears. "But it hurts *now*."

I don't know how to console her. I hear her weeping in the night when her boys are sleeping. I see the sorrow in Tarah's eyes whenever anyone mentions Joab or Zadok. When I look in Rachel's eyes I see the light that used to be in Joab's eyes, and a pain catches in my heart. Is that pain a sign that I lack faith? How can I lack faith after I've heard the Son of God?

Sometime in the night I awake to realize that little Rachel has crawled into bed with Tarah and me to be cradled in her grandmother's arms. Tarah talks to her of angels who watch over all of us.

I feel a tug at my side and look over to see Michael. His eyes can't see and his ears can't hear, yet he is familiar enough with our surroundings to search me out. I take him in my arms and hold him to my chest. I kiss the top of his head and feel his breath soft against my cheek. If I could give my eyes and ears to give him sight and sound, I would.

"What's an angel?" Rachel asks her grandmother.

Tarah scoots over to make more room for Michael and me. "An angel is a person sent from God to help others."

"Are you an angel?" Rachel asks.

Tarah chuckles, but I lean over and whisper, "Yes, Rachel, I think your grandmother is an angel."

When everyone else is sound asleep I walk by myself down along the shore. The moon glows blue, and the stars glitter silver. The sound of the waves are gentle, waxing and waning. The wet sand soothes the ache of my feet. I weep great tears of gratitude and grief. I pray without words, for there are no words adequate to express all that I'm feeling.

"Kiah."

I look up to see a man walking toward me. He is wearing white, and his person glows brighter than the moon.

I know him.

"Grandfather!"

He talks to me. He ministers to me. He is as real and alive as he was during the days we walked the hills behind Elam. I pour my heart out to him. I apologize. I testify to him of what has happened in our family.

He testifies to me of a Messiah who has been resurrected and of a glorious Heavenly Father. Because of that Resurrection, he is able to be with me. Grandfather holds me as we talk of Calev and Joab and Zadok.

When the sun rises Grandfather is gone, and I return to my grieving wife and daughter with a heart mended.

The mortal needs of life make their demands. We remain human, even though we've had such a spiritual manifestation. Nephi shows concern for each family, for our wounds and our losses and our welfare. Great efforts are made to find shelter for the people. We are given a place within the city to dwell. There is no home until Jonathan and I build one, but there is a patch for a garden, and it takes Tarah no time to start planting.

She takes me by both hands and looks into my eyes. "My sons are not coming back, but I have hope that Eliana and Tamar will be found."

• • •

They are not found.

There are many who are not found, and we as a people mourn together for the loss of those we love. We mourn for the destruction around us. We mourn because we all know that we should have been more obedient—that obedience could have saved so many.

I hunt for food and am able to supply sufficient meat for our family and others. A neighbor brings fresh fish by to share with all of us. We can't seem to stop talking, recounting the destruction, reporting what others have seen and experienced. Our tongues will not be still when it comes to praising the Messiah whose voice our ears have heard.

Life goes on and time passes, but we are a changed people, changed from the inside out.

• • •

Nephi sends word that we are all to gather at the great temple in Bountiful. People flock, no longer belonging to one tribe or another, but belonging to the fold of God.

Everywhere I look the face of the land has changed. Many great buildings and palaces were destroyed, while a few simple timber homes were left untouched. How is that possible? I now know anything is possible with God.

My fingers are woven between Tarah's as we make our way to the temple site. The temple is back; gone are the soothsayers and harlots and false prophets.

An entire multitude has gathered.

"Look at the court. It has crumbled to powder," Jonathan says.

I look across the courtyard to see that the once mighty and ornate judges' chamber is little more than dust.

Jonas is anxious to talk about the Messiah, His voice and His message. We have talked of little else since those days. Even Jonas doesn't understand everything we heard.

While people are talking, another voice sounds. This voice distinctly comes from above us.

We all cast our eyes toward the sky.

I cannot understand what the voice is saying. But I can feel my heart catch fire at the sound of it. It's neither harsh nor loud, but in its smallness it pierces me to the very center of my being. My legs go weak; my body quakes as sure as the ground quaked.

I look to Tarah and see that her face is streaked with tears.

Again, the voice sounds, but no one seems to understand it. I cast a prayer heavenward from my heart. *Father, help us to hear with open ears and open hearts.*

The third time we look heavenward and hear the voice, we understand. The truth makes my knees bend, and I fall to the ground in a posture of worship.

"Behold my Beloved Son, in whom I am well pleased, in whom I have glorified my name—hear ye him."

A brilliant ray of light breaks through the misty air. A man clothed in a white robe is descending from heaven.

I try to bow but realize I am already on my knees. There is not an eye in the entire multitude that is not focused on this figure, for we have never seen or even imagined what we are witnessing.

A heavenly being stands in the midst of us, and every eye is turned on Him.

"Behold, I am Jesus Christ, whom the prophets testified shall come into the world.

"And behold, I am the light and the life of the world; and I have drunk out of that bitter cup which the Father hath given me, and have glorified the Father in taking upon me the sins of the world, in the which I have suffered the will of the Father in all things from the beginning."

The sight I did not know if I would ever see stands before me.

No word can describe the look on the Messiah's face except *love*.

"Arise," He tells us, "come forth unto me, that ye may thrust your hands into my side, and also that ye may feel the prints of the nails in my hands and in my feet, that ye may know that I am the God of Israel, and the God of the whole earth, and have been slain for the sins of the world."

Tarah and the children go forward. Jonathan looks back at me, but I nod for my son to stay with his mother and sister. I stand back, unable to move—hardly able to breathe. My eyes look upon Jesus, and even from where I stand I can see the rise of brutal pink scars in His hands and wrists. The ones in His feet make me wince. The sight rips my heart in pieces.

What has the world done to the Savior of the World?

One by one, the men and women silently go forth to feel for themselves that He is real—that He suffered for their sins. He smiles at Tarah, and her tears fall down on His scarred feet.

The God of this world who formed the mountains and filled the seas, who painted my cherished black *chakmool's* coat with rosettes that glisten in the sunlight, who designed every flower that Tarah treasures—*this* is the God whose mercy pulled me from a pit of vipers. Who spared me on the battlefield. Who heard the pleadings of a fatherless boy lost in the high hills beyond Elam. Who consoled me when my only brother died in my place.

This is the God I worship.

This is the God I have always worshipped.

I know Him.

But does the Messiah know me? The question is as sharp as edged obsidian.

I wait. Jesus is so patient with every person who comes forth. He rushes no one, and in His presence the spirit of selfishness and greed that has plagued this people vanishes. I feel only patience and love.

The Messiah allows each person to touch Him, to look into His eyes, to know what I already know without approaching Him.

Two thousand five hundred people wait to touch the Son of God.

I wait.

I see Jonas and his family fall before the feet of Jesus and worship.

I see Nephi kiss those feet.

I wait.

And when the final man rises, a shout goes up and echoes off the temple walls. "Hosanna! Blessed be the name of the Most High God!"

In unison, the crowd falls as I have already fallen, and from our knees we worship Jesus, the Messiah.

I bow my head and let my tears fall in a tempest of gratitude.

Father, God Almighty, thank Thee for Thy Son and for His sacrifice for me, a sinner.

The crowd goes quiet, and I feel a hand on my shoulder. When I look up, I look into the eyes of Jesus Christ. *He* has come to *me*.

He smiles and holds out His hand.

Once again, my Savior lifts me from where I have fallen.

Ninety-Three

Christ stands on the rise of the great temple. Sunlight halos His hair and rims His white robes with a glow that almost seems alive. We look upon Him and barely dare to breathe. No one wants to disturb the perfect vision. As promised for so long and by so many, the Messiah has come to show Himself among our people.

I think of Grandfather and smile, knowing things I cannot speak. I think of Calev and my chin quivers. I think of Raz, who counted down the days and still did not live to see this prophecy fulfilled. If she were here, Mother would sing her praises to Jesus the Christ. And my missing sons—what more could I have done to persuade them to believe in Jesus Christ?

Jonathan stands holding his nephews, Calev and Yarden, by the hands. He is here to witness the miracle of miracles. I give God thanks for the faith of my youngest son. Rinnah stands next to me, a peaceful Michael in her clutch. I would give anything to take her pain away. Tarah slips her arm around my waist, and Rachel slips her tiny fingers between mine. I am a man blessed beyond measure.

Jesus calls forth His prophet.

We back away, allowing Nephi to make his way out of the crowd to the rise so we all can see as he bows before the Messiah and kisses the Master's feet again. I look to see Nephi's wife, Devora, along with Jonas and the rest of the family. Their eyes are riveted.

"Arise," the Lord says, His voice resounding so all can hear.

Nephi stands before Christ while we all watch and listen, not wanting to miss a single word uttered from His holy lips. "I give unto you power that ye shall baptize this people when I am again ascended into heaven."

Then Jesus looks upon the crowd and calls others forth, one by one.

Timothy.

The prophet's brother, who once was dead but who now lives, rushes forward like a young man instead of the old man he is to stand before the Messiah—who was also once dead and yet now lives.

Jonas.

My heart breaks wide with joy for the look on my friend's face as he approaches the Savior—not only as a worshipper, but also as a disciple whose very name Jesus knows.

Kumen.

Mathoni.

I squint to be certain that the man who steps forward is the man I think he is: one of the twin brothers who long ago played trickball with me in Elam—one who testified with boldness thirty-four years ago when we were about to be burned alive for believing.

I'm not surprised to next hear his twin brother's name called.

Mathonihah.

Shemnon.

Kumenonhi.

This man wears the robes of a priest, and I am grateful to see a man who clearly lived worthy of the sacred office.

Jeremiah.

Isaiah.

Isaiah has been wounded. He walks with a limp. Jonas is the first to hurry forward to help him up to the rise.

Eleven in all. All men who have lived lives worthy to be called forth by the Messiah Himself, to be mentioned by name and entrusted to carry forth His holy work in His holy name.

One more name is called.

Zedekiah.

I look around the crowd. No man steps forward.

Jesus waits.

Both Jonas and Nephi look down at me with smiles on their faces.

Still, no one emerges to answer the Messiah's beckon.

Then Tarah's arm tightens around my waist. "The Messiah is calling you."

Zedekiah—my given name. No one has called me that since I was a baby.

I think my very bones will melt and my legs will give way, but I manage to step forward into the arms of the Messiah. I then stand in line along with eleven others the Lord has chosen.

He gives us power to baptize.

"On this wise shall ye baptize; and there shall be no disputations among you."

How many arguments have I witnessed between priests who disputed the proper way to baptize and the authority necessary for the ordinance to take effect?

Christ leaves no question how it must be done.

"Verily I say unto you, that whoso repenteth of his sins through your words, and desireth to be baptized in my name, on this wise shall ye baptize them—Behold, ye shall go down and stand in the water, and in my name shall ye baptize them. And now behold, these are the words which ye shall say, calling them by name, saying: Having authority given me of Jesus Christ, I baptize you in the name of the Father, and of the Son, and of the Holy Ghost. Amen.

"And then shall ye immerse them in the water, and come forth again out of the water. And after this manner shall ye baptize in my name; for behold, verily I say unto you, that the Father, and the Son, and the Holy Ghost are one; and I am in the Father, and the Father in me, and the Father and I are one."

We stand behind Him, and He turns to face the people. His arms go wide, and He speaks to us as a loving father might speak to his children.

" . . . verily I say unto you, he that hath the spirit of contention is not of me, but is of the devil, who is the father of contention, and he stirreth up the hearts of men to contend with anger, one with another. Behold, this is not my doctrine, to stir up the hearts of men with anger, one against another; but this is my doctrine, that such things should be done away.

"And this is my doctrine, and it is the doctrine which the Father hath given unto me; and I bear record of the Father, and the Father beareth record of me, and the Holy Ghost beareth record of the Father and me; and I bear record that the Father commandeth all men, everywhere, to repent and believe in me. And whoso believeth in me, and is baptized, the same shall be saved; and they are they who shall inherit the kingdom of God."

While Jesus teaches us I see the faces of Rachel and even Michael, who can't see at all, yet he turns his face toward the Messiah as if his deaf ears have been unstopped.

The Savior gravitates to the children.

"And again I say unto you, ye must repent, and become as a little child, and be baptized in my name, or ye can in nowise receive these things."

It is as if His eyes bore into mine when He says, "Go forth unto this people, and declare the words which I have spoken, unto the ends of the earth."

I will.

Thoughts of the people in diverse places who have also survived the earth's upheaval enter my mind, and I feel a concern for all of them. How many others are out there—wounded or lost or afraid—who know nothing of the miracle we are witnessing?

Jesus stretches forth His hand unto the multitude. "Blessed are ye if ye shall give heed unto the words of these twelve whom I have chosen from among you to minister unto you, and to be your servants; and unto them I have given power that they may baptize you with water; and after that ye are baptized with water, behold, I will baptize you with fire and with the Holy Ghost; therefore blessed are ye if ye shall believe in me and be baptized, after that ye have seen me and know that I am."

My mind pauses on something He teaches: We are called to be the *servants* of the people—not to stand above them or before them but to stand behind them and among them. To serve.

Father, let me be worthy to be a servant.

As a beckoned servant, the Messiah Himself commissions me with power and authority to baptize in His name. How can I not think of Miyan and his family? How can I not want to rush out and help the whole world?

I see Tarah and I thank God that we both lived to experience this moment together. What would it be without her?

Ninety-Four

In the days that follow I learn what it is to follow the Messiah.

He ministers to the multitudes, but He cares about the individual. That is what was always missing from the sermons I preached. I cared more about the words and the way I spoke them than I cared about the people I spoke to.

When Christ preaches, "Blessed are all they that mourn," He kneels before a sobbing widow. He gathers children in His arms when he says, "Blessed are the pure in heart." And to Timothy he offers a special beatitude: "Blessed are all they who are persecuted for my name's sake, for theirs is the kingdom of heaven."

The land around us was destroyed. Homes were devastated. Entire cities and peoples are gone. In spite of Grandfather's appearance to me, in spite of my own faith, I still suffer pain when I think of my lost loved ones or when I look upon my daughter's stricken countenance or when I hear my wife weep.

Christ helps us see beyond the destruction; He gives us eyes to see that we are a people healed in four distinct ways, one for each side of the great pyramids. First, we are no longer a divided family. For six hundred years we have been Nephites and Lamanites. Now we are brothers and sisters. Second, He lets us know that we are children of a divine inheritance. We do not need to ever bemoan the fact that we are not of our first father's Jerusalem—we are allotted our own promised land, and to keep it free, we must obey the laws of the land that God establishes. Next, and most importantly, Christ heals us from our sins. I cannot understand how He atoned for the anger and hatred that used to reside in my heart, but I know that He did. It's gone, replaced with a love as powerful as the great winds that went through the land. And finally, Jesus Christ has healed us from our suffering. We endured the most terrible disaster; no one was spared losing a loved one. Yet now we are alive—being ministered to and caring for others.

When I doubt that my best efforts are enough, Jesus gives a sermon that speaks directly to me: "Your heavenly Father knoweth that ye have need of all these things. . . . Seek ye first the kingdom of God and his righteousness, and all these things shall be added unto you."

I think my prayers are more faithful and heartfelt than ever, but when Jesus sets the pattern for all prayer, I realize that my memorized prayers are only words. Christ's words have power because they come from gratitude, faith, and love. When I hear Jesus speak to His Father, it is as though He rents the heavens so God and every angel hears.

"Our Father who art in heaven, hallowed be thy name. Thy will be done on earth as it is in heaven. And forgive us our debts, as we forgive our debtors. And lead us not into temptation, but deliver us from evil. For thine is the kingdom, and the power, and the glory, forever. Amen."

The Messiah's way of serving blots out the way I've learned to serve—to be seen and credited for every kindness I show. Instead, Jesus inspires us to serve with our hearts, quietly and sincerely. "I say that I would that ye should do alms unto the poor; but take heed that ye do not your alms before men to be seen of them; otherwise ye have no reward of your Father who is in heaven."

The multitude grows as word spreads, and Jesus seems pleased. Because I flanked Nephi on so many missionary journeys, I know how to keep the crowds back, to keep people from being too aggressive in their adoration. Jesus doesn't mind the crowds pressing toward Him; in fact, He welcomes the opportunities to hold a child, to touch a cheek or listen to a story.

When a father crazed with concern for his missing son rushes at Jesus, I stand in the man's way while another disciple holds him back from approaching the Messiah. The man is loud and aggressive.

Jesus has just finished one sermon and is moving to the other side of the temple to speak again, but He stops and opens His arms to the man. He takes the time to listen to the father's fears. Then he turns away from us and speaks words of consolation that no one else can hear.

To us He warns, "Judge not, that ye be not judged. For with what judgment ye judge, ye shall be judged; and with what measure ye mete, it shall be measured to you again."

• • •

Time passes in bliss, and I wonder as I shadow the Messiah. In my weakness, my mind wanders to the concerns I have for my family. Tarah is without me while I follow my Master. I worry about her and the children. How are they cared for while I am doing what I am called to do?

Christ teaches me that my requests of God should not be broad and vague, but sincere and specific. He also paints pictures with words that I can see and relate to. When Christ speaks, the scriptures take on life and become personal to me—just as they did when Merari spoke so long ago.

"For every one that asketh, receiveth; and he that seeketh, findeth; and to him that knocketh, it shall be opened. Or what man is there of you, who, if his son ask bread, will give him a stone? Or if he ask a fish, will he give him a serpent? If ye then, being evil, know how to give good gifts unto your children, how much more shall your Father who is in heaven give good things to them that ask him?"

Every sentence He utters is a lesson in life. One that strikes me hard is when I realize that a man caught between fear and faith is a man torn apart: "No man can serve two masters; for either he will hate the one and love the other, or else he will hold to the one and despise the other. Ye cannot serve God and Mammon."

He stops when He is done speaking to the crowd and directs His words to us, His chosen twelve. "Remember the words which I have spoken. For behold, ye are they whom I have chosen to minister unto this people."

Remember.

I am grateful there are those, like Jonathan, who are writing down the teachings of the Messiah, but I want to put into practice what I've learned. When the time is right, I bow my head and speak to my Father in Heaven with an assurance that I've never felt before: "Father, I thank Thee for hearing my prayer. I ask Thee in the name of Thy Son to help me remember the words He speaks. Make my memory clear and exact, that I might be able to teach others what I am learning. Make me, Father, Thy warrior."

Ninety-Five

As we minister with Him, Christ understands that we are human—He has just come through life, dwelling in a mortal shell. He allows us time to tend to our families and our physical needs. But He is God's resurrected Son, and not a moment is wasted in idleness. He teaches, preaches, administers, listens, blesses, and heals.

As I walk through the people I hear murmuring. Some are unclear on what the Messiah meant when He announced that in Him the law of Moses was fulfilled.

"I'm not sure I understand everything the Messiah teaches," I confess to Jonas.

"Neither do I. But we will learn, line upon line."

Christ is patient with us as He says, "Marvel not that I said unto you that old things had passed away, and that all things had become new. Behold, I say unto you that the law is fulfilled that was given unto Moses.

"Behold, I am he that gave the law, and I am he who covenanted with my people Israel; therefore, the law in me is fulfilled, for I have come to fulfill the law; therefore it hath an end."

I don't see how His message could be more clear. The old laws are over. Now we are bound to live a higher law.

I begin to understand as I observe the way Jesus treats people.

It swells my heart every time He turns to us and says, "Ye are my disciples."

I am one of Christ's chosen. He makes me feel as if I can accomplish anything. He does the same for others; I can see it in their faces.

He assures us. "Ye are my disciples; and ye are a light unto this people."

I still don't understand everything He says because so much of the truths are new to me. He speaks of other sheep—Gentiles, and the gathering of Israel.

I don't know.

But I will learn.

. . .

There is no misunderstanding when Christ says, "I command you that ye shall write these sayings after I am gone, that if it so be that my people at Jerusalem, they who have seen me and been with me in my ministry, do not ask the Father in my name, that they may receive a knowledge of you by the Holy Ghost, and also of the other tribes whom they know not of, that these sayings which ye shall write shall be kept and shall be manifested unto the Gentiles, that through the fullness of the Gentiles, the remnant of their seed, who shall be scattered forth upon the face of the earth because of their unbelief, may be brought in, or may be brought to a knowledge of me, their Redeemer."

It is plain. The things we write will one day be made known to God's children who live in distant lands and times to come. They will read of the Messiah's appearance to us; they will know of His teachings just as we do.

There is a vague tug at my memory—all those times when the Holy Ghost prompted me to write down Samuel's warnings. I vow to myself that I will make records not only of Samuel, but I will record the messages of all of the prophets—the stories I've been told and the experiences God has permitted me to know. I will put my faith in writing—not now, because there is no time, but someday soon.

Jesus knows our minds and hearts. I ache for Him to stay with us always, though I know that is not possible.

He must know my thoughts because He tells us that "my time is at hand. I perceive that ye are weak, that ye cannot understand all my words which I am commanded of the Father to speak unto you at this time. Therefore, go ye unto your homes, and ponder upon the things which I have said, and ask of the Father, in my name, that ye may understand, and prepare your minds for the morrow, and I come unto you again."

I look through the crowd and find Tarah's face. She has Michael in her arms, and her eyes fill with tears at the thought of Jesus leaving, even for a moment.

He continues, "But now I go unto the Father, and also to show myself unto the lost tribes of Israel, for they are not lost unto the Father, for he knoweth whither he hath taken them."

Tarah is not the only one begging Him to stay.

"Behold, my bowels are filled with compassion towards you. Have ye any that are sick among you? Bring them hither. Have ye any that are lame, or blind, or halt, or maimed, or leprous, or that are withered, or that are deaf, or that are afflicted in any manner? Bring them hither and I will heal them, for I have compassion upon you; my bowels are filled with mercy."

The people groan their gratitude.

In days past, they might have stampeded to get to Jesus. But now people help each other. There is order. There is concern for neighbors.

Jesus does not sit on the temple pedestal; He does not even stay on the rise. He comes down among the people and touches the bleeding, the infected, the lame, the blind, and the dumb. I want to help each one, to see them helped and made whole.

My heart pounds in my chest at the miracle for which I am praying. I don't mind waiting for myself, staying at the back of the line—but when I see Michael in Jonathan's arms, and Jonathan making his way forward with Rinnah and Tarah, I want to clear the people away so Michael can be touched by Christ first.

Tarah smiles at me through her tears, hope burning brightly on her face.

When Michael is brought before the Messiah, He knows without being told that the boy belongs to my family. Jesus beckons me to come forth, and I stand with Jesus as He lays His hands on Michael's head. Michael does not squirm but pushes Himself closer to the beating heart of the Savior.

Christ bows His head and prays. When Michael blinks, the first face he ever sees belongs to the Master Healer.

Those who are healed and those who brought the afflicted forward all bow at Christ's feet in gratitude and worship. Then Christ—the mighty Messiah, the Deliverer we have all believed in and waited for—commands that all the little children be brought to Him.

He has already allowed the children to touch His scars and feel the nail prints in His hands. He has already healed the sick and wounded children. Now He asks that they be placed on the ground around Him.

He stands in the center, waiting until every single child is brought to sit before Him. Gently, He commands the rest of us to kneel on the ground.

Jesus groans. I hear it. I hear His prayer, "Father, I am troubled because of the wickedness of the people of the house of Israel."

His own knees bend, and He kneels with the rest of us.

I am close enough to hear the rest of His prayer—but so great and marvelous are the things He prays, I cannot write them. I have no words. I have no way. But I can testify that our joy overcomes us.

"Arise," Jesus commands.

"Blessed are ye because of your faith. And now behold, my joy is full."

His joy. Jesus Christ's joy is full.

Nephi is on His right. I stand to His left, next to Jonas. We both see the tears that well in the Savior's eyes and spill down his cheeks. Then Jesus calls for the children to come forth; one by one, He takes each child in His arms, blessing each and praying for each.

When my grandchildren are in His arms, I know what it is to feel joy at its fullest.

Or do I?

For Jesus weeps again, this time so all the multitude can see and bear record.

He turns to the parents, the grandparents, the elder siblings, and the caregivers of the children and commands, "Behold your little ones."

Our eyes are cast heavenward, and just as we all witnessed Christ come down from the heavens, we witness angels descending as if it were in the midst of fire. Christ beckons the angels to come down and encircle those little ones about with fire. I watch Calev and Yarden flanking Michael, whose eyes are wide as he looks up at the face of Christ. I see Rachel and watch as she looks at Jesus; then I see angels come to my little granddaughter and minister to her.

Just when I think I know love, Jesus teaches me a new lesson.

Ninety-Six

Food is difficult to find. Though we have rebuilt what we can, so many trees were uprooted that there is now little fruit. So many crops were destroyed that there is little grain to make bread. But Jesus commands us twelve to bring forth bread and wine.

When we return with bread and wine, we see that Jesus has commanded the multitude to sit on the earth.

He breaks and blesses the bread and gives it to His disciples to eat. I have not eaten a morsel in days, and the bread dissolves on my tongue. When we are filled, He commands us to administer the bread to the multitude in the same manner as He administered it to us.

He teaches by doing first.

"Behold there shall one be ordained among you, and to him will I give power that he shall break bread and bless it and give it unto the people of my church, unto all those who shall believe and be baptized in my name."

He not only teaches us what to do, but why we should do it.

"And this shall ye do in remembrance of my body, which I have shown unto you. And it shall be a testimony unto the Father that ye do always remember me. And if ye do always remember me ye shall have my Spirit to be with you."

We repeat the ordinance with the wine.

"Blessed are ye for this thing which ye have done, for this is fulfilling my commandments, and this doth witness unto the Father that ye are willing to do that which I have commanded you. And this shall ye always do to those who repent and are baptized in my name; and ye shall do it in remembrance of my blood, which I have shed for you, that ye may witness unto the Father that ye do always remember me. And if ye do always remember me ye shall have my Spirit to be with you."

What a promised gift—Christ's spirit to always be with us.

He teaches more and then turns back to the twelve. "Behold verily, verily, I say unto you, I give unto you another commandment, and then I must go unto my Father that I may fulfill other commandments which he hath given me. And now behold, this is the commandment which I give unto you, that ye shall not suffer any one knowingly to partake of my flesh and blood unworthily, when ye shall minister it; For whoso eateth and drinketh my flesh and blood unworthily eateth and drinketh damnation to his soul; therefore if ye know that a man is unworthy to eat and drink of my flesh and blood ye shall forbid him.

"Nevertheless, ye shall not cast him out from among you, but ye shall minister unto him and shall pray for him unto the Father, in my name; and if it so be that he repenteth and is baptized in my name, then shall ye receive him, and shall minister unto him of my flesh and blood."

I look at Jonas. He does not seem overwhelmed like I feel. His confidence is in Christ. That's where I need to place mine too. For if my confidence is in my own ability, I will surely fail—but if my confidence is in Christ, He will make up all that I lack, and more.

I know Jesus is a resurrected being, but He looks fatigued, worn to the core.

"And now I go unto the Father, because it is expedient that I should go unto the Father for your sakes."

It is impossible not to notice that everything the Savior does, He does for someone else's sake. But before He goes He touches each one of us. With His hand on my head and my name on His lips, he gives me the power of the Holy Ghost. I could hope for no greater gift or companion.

When we have all received the gift, a cloud descends—not on Jesus, but over the multitude so they cannot see. But I see. I see Jesus as He ascends back into heaven.

Ninety-Seven

The house where we now live is small, but Tarah has made it into a home. She's gathered stones and outlined a garden that is beginning to grow in green rows. She has planted vines and flowers and has woven mats for sleeping. We have very little, yet we have so much.

The grandchildren sleep with Jonathan on the flat of the roof. I sleep with Tarah in a room off from the main area. Rinnah takes a back room that we built from cane sticks and banana leaves just for her privacy.

I am down on the ground showing Yarden and Calev how to make an arrowhead when Michael climbs down the ladder and runs to jump on my back. The sound of his laughter makes me laugh. Rachel is busy braiding little flowers into her grandmother's hair; Tarah then braids the same kinds of blossoms into Rachel's long locks.

Rinnah comes out when her mother starts grilling dough to make fire bread. She puts on a brave face for the sake of her children, but I imagine how desperately she misses Tad.

"Come join us," I say, and my daughter eases herself on the ground next to me. She helps teach her boys what she knows about making arrows.

I am surprised and ask, "How did you learn such skills? I never taught you."

She smiles and brushes a fallen piece of hair out of my eye. "Father, I watched you. You taught me more than you realize."

In the morning I discover the multitude has swelled like a sponge. People have made great efforts to be here, expecting the Messiah's return. Nephi decides that the multitude is so great it must be divided into twelve bodies.

I am humbled to be trusted to teach my group the things that Christ taught me.

The day unfolds in ways that are difficult to describe.

We pray. We minister. We baptize, and I feel the power of the Holy Ghost.

It is the greatest of God's gifts, for it guides us, protects us, comforts us, and testifies of the truth. It's the gift I most desire for those I love.

Like the children, we are encircled about by fire, a fire that does not scorch or consume. Angels minister to us.

Jesus comes again. We pray to Him, with Him, and through Him.

Then I hear Jesus offer a prayer: "I thank thee that thou hast given the Holy Ghost unto these whom I have chosen; and it is because of their belief in me that I have chosen them out of the world. Father, I pray thee that thou wilt give the Holy Ghost unto all them that shall believe in their words."

The miracles of this day of prayer—the signs and wonders—only grow.

After we have listened and lead our own prayers, Jesus tells us, "So great faith have I never seen among all the Jews; wherefore I could not show unto them so great miracles, because of their unbelief. Verily I say unto you, there are none of them that have seen so great things as ye have seen; neither have they heard so great things as ye have heard."

A warmth fills my heart as hot as an inner flame. Peace encompasses me. Heaven, I learn, is not so hard to reach.

Ninety-Eight

The teachings continue with an intensity that astounds me. I learn so much, yet understand that I have much yet to learn. Christ is always patient and willing to repeat His message and present it in different ways so that all might understand. He talks of His next coming—a coming in power and glory when the world will not be flooded or ripped apart but will suffer and burn by flames.

It is a vivid image to me. Even after all this time, the scent of smoke is still in the air.

Jesus has empowered us to go forth and do His work. He teaches us that in the body of Christ, we are His hands and feet to get the work accomplished, the mouths to get the word preached.

He expects us to take what He has given us and to teach and edify others.

• • •

Jesus teaches us from the very scriptures Benjamin tried so diligently to teach me back in the synagogue in Elam. He quotes Isaiah with power and purpose.

"Bring forth the record which ye have kept," Christ tells Nephi.

We help Nephi gather the records from the temple, grateful they were not destroyed during the great fires and tempests. When they are all stacked before the Master, He looks at them. His brow furrows. "I commanded my servant Samuel, the Lamanite, that he should testify unto this people, that at the day that the Father should glorify his name in me that there were many saints who should arise from the dead, and should appear unto many, and should minister unto them."

I think of my walk with Grandfather along the shores of the great sea, and I know that the words were fulfilled. I smile at Jonas as I remember Samuel and his mighty prophecies; we've witnessed them being fulfilled. Why didn't I write them down all the times I was prompted to write them?

Christ looks at Nephi, then right at me. "Was it not so?"

"Yea, Lord, Samuel did prophesy according to thy words, and all his words were fulfilled," I say.

Still looking at me, the Messiah asks, "How be it that ye have not written this thing, that many saints did arise and appear unto many and did minister unto them?"

Nephi nearly weeps. The look on his face is one of total remorse.

When Jesus commands that it should be written, I am given another chance. I sit for many nights with my son Jonathan, writing the prophecies and the accounts of those like me who were ministered to by Saints who arose and came forth when Christ was resurrected. We record the teachings of Samuel; when I read them back to Jonas, he makes certain I am accurate. Nephi also goes over the record and is pleased when it is finished.

I am grateful that the Messiah did not scold or condemn, but convicted me and allowed me to do what I should have already done.

Every moment, every hour, every day the Savior ministers and teaches is a treasure. Word spreads, and our numbers grow. We face some disputations. So the twelve of us unite to fast and pray with the kind of faith that Jesus has bestowed upon us.

Jesus shows Himself to us. "What will ye that I shall give unto you?"

"Lord, Nephi speaks for us, we will that thou wouldst tell us the name whereby we shall call this church; for there are disputations among the people concerning this matter."

It is the first time Jesus has been so firm with His reply: "Why is it that the people should murmur and dispute because of this thing? Have they not read the scriptures, which say ye must take upon you the name of Christ, which is my name?"

When He presents it in such a forthright way, the answer seems simple. He is never unkind, though we are often like little children—confused but committed.

The love Christ shows to the children is consuming. He not only blesses them, but calls down angels to minister to them. He looses their tongues that even the youngest children are able to speak things so marvelous we cannot record them.

My grandson Michael follows Jesus around. At first I tried to pull the child away, but Jesus bid me to leave him be—to let Michael hang on Jesus' cloak, to let Michael tug at His beard. Michael touches the scars on the Savior's hands and cries, "Ouch!" Then Michael cranes his little neck upward to kiss Jesus on the cheek.

Ninety-Nine

The time draws to a close. Soon the Messiah will ascend and we will no longer walk and talk with Him. The reality makes me dizzy with grief but grateful for His confidence in the twelve of us.

In *me*.

This morning the air is scrubbed clean by the night's rain, and the birds are singing. My precious Tarah is teaching our children the things God has taught us. I can hardly contain my emotions.

Rinnah comes up the road with a load of firewood atop her head and Rachel alongside her, a bundle of sticks balanced on her head. I rush to help them and to get the morning cooking fire flaming.

Rinnah smiles, and I realize that day by day her grief is becoming less pronounced.

While she sings and talks of angels and the blessings of heaven, my children are laughing and playing, exploring all the changes in the land. When the men and women are returned to their daily labors, Christ calls each one of us to spend some time with Him alone.

Then again we gather around Him as a group. I gaze into His eyes. "What is it that ye desire of me, after that I am gone to the Father?"

I know what is in my heart, but I hold my tongue and wait for the others to speak their desires before me.

All but three voice the same heartfelt want. "We desire that after we have lived unto the age of man, that our ministry, wherein thou hast called us, may have an end, that we may speedily come unto thee in thy kingdom."

"Blessed are ye because ye desired this thing of me; therefore, after that ye are seventy and two years old ye shall come unto me in my kingdom; and with me ye shall find rest."

Then Christ turns to Jeremiah, Kumenonhi, and me, and asks, "What will ye that I should do unto you, when I am gone unto the Father?"

My heart aches, for I do not wish to ask for my heart's true desire. It's too great—perhaps even selfish. After all of these years, I still want to be a warrior. I want to battle for the souls of God's children.

"I know your thoughts," Jesus tells us, "and ye have desired the thing which John, my beloved, who was with me in my ministry, before that I was lifted up by the Jews, desired of me.

"Therefore, more blessed are ye, for ye shall never taste of death; but ye shall live to behold all the doings of the Father unto the children of men, even until all things shall be fulfilled according to the will of the Father, when I shall come in my glory with the powers of heaven. And ye shall never endure the pains of death; but when I shall come in my glory ye shall be changed in the twinkling of an eye from mortality to immortality; and then shall ye be blessed in the kingdom of my Father.

"And again, ye shall not have pain while ye shall dwell in the flesh, neither sorrow save it be for the sins of the world; and all this will I do because of the thing which ye have desired of me, for ye have desired that ye might bring the souls of men unto me, while the world shall stand."

My knees automatically bend, for my Savior does know my heart. There is no hidden corner, no pain, no weakness, no dream He cannot read.

"And for this cause ye shall have fullness of joy; and ye shall sit down in the kingdom of my Father; yea, your joy shall be full. . . . "

Jesus then touches the nine, including Nephi and Jonas and Simon, who look at me with smiles so broad their eyes are almost closed.

Then the heavens open, and we are caught up where we hear teachings so sacred I cannot reveal them; in those moments of pure revelation we are prepared for the mission we have requested. Whether we remain in our bodies or are removed out of them, I cannot tell, but I do know we are changed from our tabernacles of flesh into immortal states that we might behold the things of God.

• • •

It's late by the time I return to our little home where everyone is sleeping. The gate torch has gone out, and the only light I have to see by is the gentle glow from a waning moon.

"Grandfather?" A tender little voice, so confident, comes from the rooftop.

"Yes, Michael."

"Will you hold me?"

"Yes, come down the ladder. I'll help you and I'll hold you."

When Michael is tight and safe in my arms I sit with him in the courtyard hammock, swaying back and forth, looking at his perfect little face bathed with moonlight. I press his head to my chest.

"I hear your heart beat, Grandfather."

"Yes, Michael." I breathe in the scent of his damp hair and his skin that smells of sea salt. I pull him tighter, and I say a prayer that beats with the rhythm of my heart: "I thank Thee, I thank Thee, I thank Thee."

I cradle my grandson and tell him how when I was his age all I wanted was to be a warrior. I tell him how I hunted and explored and trained to be a soldier so I might go to war.

"Did you ever go to war?"

"Yes, Michael."

"Are you a warrior now?"

I sigh. "Not the kind of warrior I thought I'd be."

A gentle breeze blows, and I smell the fragrance of the blossoms that Tarah has planted and nurtured in her tiny garden. I am truly a blessed man. My heart is filled with love like the sea is filled with water.

"Grandfather?"

"Yes, Michael."

"Grandmother says angels are sent from God to help people who need help."

"That is true. That's what an angel does."

"Grandfather?"

My lips press against Michael's forehead. My weary eyes close. "Yes, son."

"Are *you* an angel?"

My eyes open. The question catches me off guard. Last night I would have laughed and answered no. Tonight, after a commission so sacred I have yet to comprehend it, I'm not sure how to reply. So for a long time I sit in the moonlight with Michael pressed tightly to my chest. I kiss his forehead over and over and look deep into his eyes—eyes that did not see but see clearly now.

"Michael?"

He giggles. "Yes, Grandfather."

"What do *you* think an angel is?"

Michael's little hand reaches up to touch my face. His pudgy finger traces the outline of my eyes, my nose, my mouth, and my ears. Then he puts his palm over my heart and presses. "*You*, Grandfather. *You're* an angel."